BOOKS BY

Lori L. Lake
=====================

The Milk of Human Kindness:
Lesbian Authors Write about Mothers & Daughters

Stepping Out: Short Stories

Different Dress

Under the Gun

Gun Shy

Ricochet in Time

## Advance praise for *Have Gun We'll Travel*

**Ellen Hart,** author of the Jane Lawless mystery series
"*Have Gun We'll Travel* is one kick-ass debut thriller. Set in the woods of Northern Minnesota, the story is riveting, the writing lean, tough and tense. I'd met Dez Reilly and Jaylynn Savage before, but in this book, author Lori L. Lake doesn't pull any punches. She puts her cop heroines in danger that doesn't let up, pushing them to the very edge of their physical and emotional limits. Lake's north wood's tale is full of passion and terror, twists and heartbreak, but in the end, the message is all about friendship. If you miss this one, you'll miss one of the year's best."

**Radclyffe,** author of the "Honor" and "Justice" series
"*Have Gun We'll Travel* has it all: action, intrigue, danger, and devotion. The newest entry in Lori L. Lake's "Gun series" (*Gun Shy, Under The Gun*) featuring police officers and lovers Dez Reilly and Jaylynn Savage starts out with a bang, and the action never lets up during the ensuing eighteen tumultuous hours. Against the backdrop of a daring prison break, underworld intrigue, and Jaylynn's kidnapping, Dez's control and skills are tested as never before as she races against time to rescue her lover. The chase careens over rocky terrain, both emotionally and physically, as both women struggle to stay alive long enough to find one another. The labyrinth path of revenge and retribution is a spellbinding journey not to be missed."

**Cheri Rosenberg,** reviewer for *The Independent Gay Writer*
"Beautiful Dez Reilly, adept at police work, is "gun shy" in matters of the heart. Her energetic partner, Jaylynn Savage, is not the only one who falls in love with Dez . . . you will too. Lake's characters came to life on the pages of *Gun Shy* and *Under The Gun*. Don't miss *Have Gun We'll Travel* for the continuing adventures of these two heroines. You'll remember Dez and Jay long after the last pages are turned."

**Jean Stewart,** author of the "Isis" series
"Jaylynn and Dez, two of the most intriguing characters in lesbian fiction, are suddenly faced with a series of desperate, life-and-death challenges. Fast-paced, utterly convincing and completely unpredictable, this story will take you on a wild run through the deep woods of Minnesota. Be warned: after the initial set-up, I could not put this novel down. This is a broad canvas, full of well-rendered, wonderful characters and nonstop action. Lori Lake is one of the best adventure-romance writers in print, and this book is a worthy and courageous number three in a very solid series. I want more — and soon!"


**Nann Dunne,** author of *The War Between the Hearts*
In *Have Gun We'll Travel*, Lori L. Lake interweaves heart-thumping tension and action with strongly drawn characterizations and love-affirming relationships. The well-structured, compact presentation of this latest novel in Lake's "Gun" series contributes even more to its worth. I enjoyed it immensely!


**Jennifer Fulton,** author of the "Moon Island" series
"Lori L. Lake writes richly detailed novels that are full of heart. Her characters are real people who seem to have stepped out of real life to share their stories with us."

# Praise for Lori L. Lake's previous novels

**Booklist**
"Lake's tale [*Different Dress*] takes its leisurely good time as this love affair runs into detours and unexpected roadblocks. This lesbian romance is full of entrancing details that make the day-to-day tour come alive as the dazzle of show business and the joy of making music serve as backdrops to the lovers' deepening relationship."

**Midwest Book Review**
"Lori Lake is one of the best novelists working in the field of lesbian fiction today."

**Lavender Magazine**
"Considered one of the best authors of modern lesbian fiction, her work — part action, part drama, and part romance — gleefully defies categorization."

**Jean Stewart,** author of *Emerald City Blues* and the *ISIS* series
"This is the best book about police officers I've ever read. Lori Lake takes us to a world where just doing your job requires putting your life on the line at a moment's notice. The brave, skilled women of *Under The Gun* are an inspiration and a revelation. And who would have thought that for tough, intimidating, super-cop Dez Reilly, opening her heart to Jaylynn Savage would be the most frightening experience of all?"

**Marianne K. Martin,** author of *Mirrors, Love in the Balance,* and *Legacy of Love*
"I am thrilled to see a writer like Lake take the risk, leave formula and genre restrictions behind, and be willing to put in the hard work necessary to put forth a truly creative product. Lake continues to grow and mature in her craft and is poised to guide the characters she has sent out into the world through the grappling necessary for their own maturity."

# *Have Gun We'll Travel*

## Lori L. Lake

Quest Books

Nederland, Texas

Copyright © 2005 by Lori L. Lake

ISBN 1-932300-33-3


First Printing 2005

9 8 7 6 5 4 3 2 1


Cover design by Donna Pawlowski


Published by:

Yellow Rose Books
PMB 210, 8691 9th Avenue
Port Arthur, Texas 77642-8025


Find us on the World Wide Web at
http://www.regalcrest.biz


Printed in the United States of America

## Acknowledgments

So many people have encouraged me to write this third "Gun" book. Thanks especially to Jan and Carrie Carr for believing in this one from the start, and to Ellen Hart for being a helpful and steady presence as I learned all about a new genre. I can hardly express how much I appreciate the editorial expertise of Jennifer Fulton, Sylverre, and Nann Dunne. Each of you helped make this book much better than I ever dreamed. Great cover once again, Donna Pawlowski! You make it look so easy. Thanks to Cathy LeNoir for continual patience when the course of this book's production didn't go at all as planned.

Law enforcement information and manhunt expertise were generously shared by Erin Linn and Patty Schramm, both of whom also read early drafts and assured me when I was off track—and when I was on. With thanks to Marilyn Orr for instructive walks in the woods, and a formal bow to the kind tellers at Vermillion State Bank for educating me about how small packages of money actually are. Love and appreciation to the Taco Tuesday group: Denise, Jules, Kristen, Mary Ann, and Sidney for cheering and encouraging me—even through the ulcer when I couldn't eat tacos.

I am indebted to a number of readers and proofers who were so generous with their time including: Pat Boehnhardt, Carrie Carr, Barb Coles, Betty Crandall, Nann Dunne, Skip Germain, Ann German, Maya Indigal, Erin Linn, Joyce McNeil, Kim Miller, Day Petersen, Patty Schramm (who read the manuscript three times!), Jean Stewart, and my judicious proofer Norma.

My thanks to the helpful staff at the Minnesota Department of Natural Resources who provided me with charts, trail maps, lake data, and information about the Crane Lake, Echo Lake, and Lake Jeanette areas. While Superior National Forest, Kabetogama State Forest, and Lake Jeanette State Forest are real places and all the lakes, streams, and creeks mentioned herein really exist, I have taken some liberties with various details. Any errors or omissions of fact are the fault of the author and not of the fine individuals who work and live up in the North Woods of Minnesota.

But most of all, I thank Diane for her love and patience during the very difficult time while this book was written and finished. I love you. Always.

Lori L. Lake
February, 2005

This one's for Pat
With love and thanks
for friendship and honesty
for music and laughs
And for cleverly hanging on to Kathy all these years...
Here's hoping we don't end up selling shoes

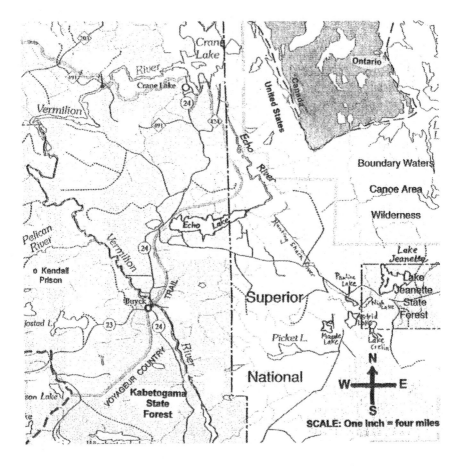

SCALE: One inch = four miles

# Chapter
# One

THE ONLY THING police officer Dez Reilly hated more than answering domestic assault calls or notifying next of kin of a death was her yearly performance evaluation. Today, instead of patrolling the mean streets of St. Paul, she was stuck in her lieutenant's office discussing her job goals. As Lt. Malcolm read glowing comments aloud, she sneaked a glance at her watch. He'd told her to block out ninety minutes from her schedule. Fifteen minutes had passed since she'd squeezed into his cubbyhole of an office, and Dez had already heard enough. She was ready to sign whatever he had written.

Lt. Malcolm finished reading the comments under the section entitled "Job Knowledge." He looked up and asked, "Is there anything I've forgotten? Something else to add?"

"No, sir." She shifted her six-foot frame in the uncomfortable visitor's chair and put her elbows on the stiff armrests. Leafing through the review pages she held, she said, "In fact, the whole thing looks great to me. I'm honored you've scored me so high. Why don't I just sign it?" She reached for the ballpoint pen in her breast pocket, but Lt. Malcolm shook his head.

"Hold your horses, Reilly. Part of the beauty of this new evaluation system is that it gives each officer the opportunity to add data or dispute different assessments. We need to go through it one section at a time and make sure all of your accomplishments are properly documented and recognized."

It was all Dez could do to stifle a groan. "Really, Lieutenant, that's not necessary. I've read it all. You've been more than thorough."

Lt. Malcolm let out a sigh and leaned back in his tattered leather chair as he pulled at his mustache and chuckled. He'd recently celebrated his fiftieth birthday, and the ceiling was still festooned with lengths of black crepe paper, a piece of which he reached up and batted away. "I recall being a patrol cop, Reilly, way back in the dark ages, of course, but I don't ever remember being as reticent about performance evaluations as you and your colleagues are."

Dez smiled. "That's why you're the lieutenant, and we're beat cops."

"No, Dez. That's not the way it should be. You've been at this, what, twelve years?"

"Something like that."

"Are you satisfied driving around every shift, doing the same thing day after day?"

"I like my job all right."

He shifted some papers to the side of the desk and slipped off his suit jacket. She watched with amusement as he rolled up his cuffs to mid-forearm, then leaned on the desk and focused gray eyes upon her. "Dez, you underestimate your abilities."

She didn't think she underestimated herself. Ever since she'd been involved in one critical incident too many, though, the brass had stopped encouraging her. She felt like she was walking around with a cloud over her head. Sure, Lt. Malcolm had always been in her corner, even when she'd suffered from the worst of post-traumatic stress, but nothing else was the same. Commander Paar avoided her. The chief ignored her. Everyone was polite, but the feeling of ease she used to have around upper management—the sense of connection—wasn't there anymore. She didn't want to get into that now. "I'm doing fine." With her free hand, Dez gestured at the evaluation she held. "This seems to indicate that."

"You used to talk about applying for SWAT."

"I have applied for SWAT."

"Not lately."

"They turned me down six times. I got the hint."

"I thought once you got your criminal justice degree you would want to move up. What about taking the sergeant's exam or applying to move to investigations?"

Dez shrugged. "Things are a-okay now, Loot. Don't worry."

She spent the next half hour going over the evaluation with him, all the while anxious to get out of the stuffy office. She tried not to let the lieutenant know that, though.

DEZ JOINED TOUR III—also known as Third Watch—at half past three. She was certain she'd ride alone for the rest of her shift, but to her surprise, they stuck her with another late start,

Brendan Schaake. At six-foot-six, Schaake was a half-foot taller than Dez, but awkward and gangly. He always reminded Dez of a dark blue-and-white praying mantis. He'd passed probation and was in his second year of policing, and she'd ridden with him often.

"You want to drive?" Dez asked. As senior officer, she had the right to make that choice, but she liked to give the young officers the opportunity. *God knows they all need lots of driving practice!* Schaake took her up on the offer, and they headed toward their assigned sector.

The afternoon was slow with only a fireworks complaint at five p.m. She and Schaake chased some youths down an alley, through a backyard, and over a fence, but when she banged her ribs going over the wooden fence, she gave up and let the kids go.

Schaake caught up, out of breath. "Lose 'em?"

"Yeah, but I don't think they'll be coming around any more today."

"Good. We've done our job then." They fell into step and headed back to the patrol car.

After sundown, Dez and Schaake were still touring around the Como Park area with no action happening. "Geez," he said. "It's boring as hell tonight. Not even a drunk or some jerk with road rage."

"Be careful what you wish for."

"You always say that."

Dez didn't answer. Her eye was on a red Grand Am with a noisy muffler. The car pulled out of the driveway of a four-plex across the street from the grass slope leading down to the lake. "Check it out, Schaake."

He dropped back, and they watched the car weave down the road, turn into another driveway two blocks away, and stop in the parking lot.

Dez pointed. "You want to go on up and turn around?"

"Sure." Schaake drove to the intersection and reversed course. He pulled off to the side of the street near the Lutheran church and doused the lights. The two cops waited as the two occupants sat in the idling car. Dez couldn't tell much about either of the people, except that they were both white. Someone came out of the four-plex and crept up to the car, and Dez went on full alert. The people in the Grand Am didn't seem to notice the intruder. With one hand on the door, Dez was ready to get out in a hurry, but as the dark figure approached the driver's side, the window went down. A hand came out of the car, and something was exchanged.

"Looks like a hot one," Schaake said.

"Seems like it."

The dark figure backed away and disappeared. The Grand Am's engine roared, and tires squealed as the vehicle backed up and blasted out of the lot.

As the car whizzed by, Schaake said, "Will you look at that? One taillight!"

Dez laughed. "Take 'em."

Schaake took off. "Isn't it 35 here?"

"Yeah."

"Well, they're going way over 35."

"You know what to do." As he approached the fleeing vehicle, Dez hit the overhead lights. Schaake pulled up behind the car and bumped the siren on, then off. The red Grand Am abruptly swerved into the lane for oncoming traffic. Dez keyed her mic to call out the pursuit as the driver drove up onto a curb and screeched to a stop. The nose of the vehicle faced down toward the lake. Both of the Grand Am's doors whipped open and two people piled out. "They're bailing!" Dez shouted as she wrenched open her door. "Call for backup."

She grabbed her flashlight and went after the two figures, one in a white t-shirt and one in pale blue, headed down the grassy slope toward Como Lake. They reached the biking path and went north. Dez followed, keeping an eye on her quarry while holding down her shoulder mic to give information to dispatch. She decided the fleeing figures were men. In the dim light, the colors of their shirts danced in front of her, in and out of the beam of the flashlight. "Stop! Police!" White Shirt glanced over his shoulder, then increased speed. As they approached the Como Park Pavilion, Blue Shirt peeled off to the right toward the street. She keyed her mic, "Schaake! I've got White Shirt. Follow the other guy."

The cruiser's lights disappeared from Dez's line of sight. The cement path turned, and she picked up her pace.

The runner slowed, perhaps tiring, and Dez gained a dozen yards on him. Dez again commanded him to stop, but he kept running. He cut through the parking lot, crossed Lexington Parkway, and plunged into the trees and foliage on the other side of the road. She'd run a good three hundred yards, and was only now feeling warmed up. It had taken a while to get into a stride, but she thought she could keep pace with him until he dropped over.

Over the sound of her own breath, she listened to the radio traffic from other units converging on the scene. She heard Schaake's voice. For the rookie's sake, Dez hoped Blue Shirt wasn't armed.

Dispatch reported that a K-9 unit was en route, and a perimeter was being set up. She made it to the other side of the parkway and scrambled up a grassy hill. The smell of pollen and dirt was strong as she moved into a stand of maple trees. White Shirt was no longer visible. She slowed to a stop. Forcing down the rasp of her breath, she listened. If he was still fleeing, she would hear noise, but all was silent. Even the crickets and night critters had fallen still. *The guy is hunkered down in the woods here. Just have to wait him out and he'll turn up.* She keyed her mic and quietly told her location to dispatch and the other units.

In less than a minute, other officers called out their perimeter locations and asked for a description. Dez didn't have much to give them. The interchange of reports went on for at least two minutes, and during that time Dez caught her breath. Then, she heard sticks cracking. Keeping low, she waited, and then it came—a steady crashing and rustling. The man bolted across her line of sight and burst out into an open glade abutting the parkway. He no longer wore the white t-shirt.

Dez gave chase at a full sprint, focusing on her footing. It wouldn't do at all for her to step in a hole or fall when so close. "Stop! Police." At full sprint, she was gaining and satisfied to know she had backup within a block. The man staggered across the parkway and back toward the lake, passing the World War II Torpedo Monument near Churchill Street. He was no longer fleet-footed.

He fell. Dez was on him before he could get up.

"Get off me!" he choked out.

"Stay down!" Dez said. "You're under arrest." She straddled his back, keeping her gun hip angled slightly away. She pressed him into the ground. He squirmed, trying to roll out from under. "I said stay down!" Dez dropped the flashlight and groped for her handcuffs.

All the fight went out of the man. She managed to cuff him just as backup arrived. She heard a growling sound and the K-9 officer, Walt Peterson, called out a command. Rocket, Peterson's German Shepherd, sat panting with his tongue lolling out. Peterson charged up. "Reilly? You okay?"

"Yup. He's cuffed." As Dez reported to dispatch, Peterson reached down and grabbed one of the suspect's arms. Dez gripped the other to pull the man up. He had scratch marks across his chest and back. When he swayed, Peterson had to steady him. The stench of alcohol and BO wafted in the air. Dez quickly searched the suspect, coming up with a switchblade, but no gun and no wallet. "What's your name, buddy?"

"Gimme a lawyer." He wheezed and coughed. "I'm bleeding. Police brutality. I want a lawyer."

Peterson spun the man around and prodded him forward. "Yeah, yeah, that's what they all say. You did this to yourself, mister. Now, identify yourself."

The man refused to speak, so they led him up to Lexington Parkway. Schaake drove up in the unit, lights flashing. He got out of the car, leaving the door open, and rushed toward them. "You okay, Reilly?" His voice was edgy, worried.

"All clear here, Schaake."

"Glad you called in reports, Reilly. I got worried when you didn't come out of the woods right away."

"Thanks." She easily recalled the apprehensive feeling when one's partner was out of sight. Patrol cops worked in pairs or relied a great deal on backup because it was too easy for unexpected disasters to occur. Even though Schaake was still a rookie cop, he had good instincts.

"Good collar," Schaake said. "Wow! It was fun to watch it all go down."

"What about Blue Shirt?" she asked.

"Another unit nailed him hiding in the backyard of one of those houses over there." He pointed off toward the northwest side of the lake, then helped her load the suspect into the cruiser.

"Good. What do we have on these guys?"

Schaake said, "Dispatch says the Grand Am was stolen in Coon Rapids earlier today. I saw drugs on the floor. Other guy was carrying a .22. Your guy have a gun or any drugs on him?"

"No," Dez answered.

Peterson said, "But we may find something yet tonight or in the morning when we search the woods."

"Yeah," Dez said, "look near his ditched t-shirt."

Lights flashing, two cop cars approached, one from the north, the other from the south. Lt. Andres, Dez's least favorite Tour III lieutenant, got out of the lead car. "What have we got here?" he barked out.

With a nod to Schaake, Dez inched back and let the rookie cop make the report. Schaake did so with some hesitation. Andres made everyone nervous.

When Schaake came to the part where he described Dez's tackle, Andres got a sour look on his face. "You weren't overly rough on the suspect, were you, Reilly? We wouldn't want a complaint now, would we?"

"No, sir."

The suspect said, "Yes, she was! Police brutality. Look at

me! I'm bleeding."

The K-9 officer said, "I saw it go down, Lieutenant, and I can assure you that it all went by the book."

"It better have," Andres said. He gave her a long, cold look, but Dez didn't dignify his comment with a response. "Take him downtown and process him."

Dez turned away while Schaake put the man in the cruiser. She stomped over to the passenger door and got in, shaking with fury. The inside of the car already reeked of booze and BO, and the man in the backseat started complaining immediately.

*Just great. It's going to be a long night now.*

# Chapter
# Two

St. Paul, Minnesota
Thursday, October 14, 11:20 p.m.

JAYLYNN SAVAGE SAT on the big couch in her living room trying to keep her mind on a TV movie. She looked at her watch, realized it was after eleven, and wondered when Dez would get home. She hoped it wouldn't be too much later since they planned to leave early in the morning. With the remote, she muted the TV, then tipped her head back against the couch and closed her eyes.

A click brought her out of the half-sleep into which she had slipped, and her heartbeat raced. The front door swung wide as Jaylynn rose and hustled across the soft carpet. Dez muscled a canvas satchel through the doorway and dropped it at Jaylynn's feet. With a smirk, she said, "Hi, honey, I'm home."

Jaylynn stepped over the bag and melted into the taller woman's arms. "I'm so glad you're home."

"Yeah, yeah, I bet you say that to *all* the girls."

Dez pulled her tight against a warm sweatshirt, and a thrill of happiness coursed through Jaylynn. Still gripping Dez's middle, she leaned back and looked up into kind, blue eyes. "Not anymore. All those girls have been supplanted."

"Supplanted, huh? You been watching the History Channel again?"

Jaylynn laughed. "Are you hungry?"

"Not really. We stopped at nine and had sandwiches." Moving to the side, Dez stepped around the duffel bag and pulled Jaylynn along with her toward the living room. They sank down onto the sofa. "It feels good to sit on something soft. I swear those cruiser seats get worse every day. And then there was the little matter of a foot pursuit."

"Oh, I know how you love that. Did you nail somebody?"

"Yup. Druggies who stole a car. But Jay, I felt a little out of shape."

"You're not."

"Felt that way. And I'm tired now. My quads feel tight. I think I might even be a little sore tomorrow. I had to go from zero to ninety in seconds with no warm-up."

"Well, let's go hit the hay then and rest up. C'mon." Jaylynn grabbed Dez's hand and rose, pulling insistently. Dez met her eyes, a puzzled look on her face. Jaylynn sank down onto the couch. "What?" She reached up and caressed the side of Dez's face. She loved to look at the high cheekbones, dark brows, and bright blue eyes. Tonight those bright eyes seemed tired.

Dez looked down into her lap. "It's nothing all that big, really, but Lt. Malcolm gave me my review today, and he made me think a lot about my career. About promotions and SWAT and the future. And then on patrol I had a run-in with Andres again. Nothing big, but he's still an asshole where I'm concerned."

Jaylynn's stomach muscles tightened, and a fist-like knot began to form somewhere in her solar plexus. She forced herself to keep her voice light. "What happened?"

Dez shook her head impatiently. "No matter what I do, it seems I can't get out from under the shadow of that damn post-traumatic stress business."

"What do you mean? You haven't had an episode for ages."

"It's just that the brass watches me. Sometimes I think the commanders don't quite trust me, and Andres still treats me like a failure."

"He treats everyone like crap."

"But it's not just him—it's—it's more than that. Makes me uncomfortable, then mad."

For the past two years Dez had concentrated on taking the final classes she needed to get her bachelor's degree in criminal justice. She'd graduated with a 4.0 grade-point average at the end of August, and since then, Dez had often seemed preoccupied. She hadn't seemed ready to talk about whatever was bothering her, and Jaylynn had learned to wait. Her sometimes taciturn partner usually needed time to work things out for herself. But Jaylynn could no longer stifle her curiosity and ventured out with the key question that worried her most. "Are you wanting to join SWAT then? Is that it?"

Dez smiled. "I wish I could say that you're totally faking me out with your nonchalance, Jay, but you're not. I can tell you don't want me on that team."

"I never said that!"

"I know, but I can read you like a book." She took a long breath, not speaking for a moment. "The thing is, as much as I wanted on SWAT when I was younger, the desire hasn't really carried over. I wish I'd had the experience as a young pup, but now it doesn't have the same draw. Don't get me wrong. I've enjoyed the basic weapons and tactics training the SWAT guys have shared, and I learned a lot in my classes, but it's not that." She let out a sigh. "I guess Malcolm made me face this. What I *do* want is to get off patrol. I'm tired of chasing down the dregs of society in the dark." She drew Jaylynn's hand into her lap and with her thumb stroked the soft skin at Jaylynn's wrist. "Trouble is, I'm concerned I couldn't get a different assignment."

Jaylynn rarely heard Dez speak with such uncertainty regarding her job. "Are you saying you'd like to take the sergeant's exam?"

Dez shook her head. "No, that doesn't interest me. I think I might like to work in investigations. Get off the street and do something slightly more cerebral."

"Really?" Jaylynn sat back. "I didn't realize that."

"I didn't either, not until today. I think I've got detectives who'll vouch for me, and after our discussion, I can tell Malcolm would be supportive, but there will be a lot of others weighing in on it."

"And it's really bugging you." It was obvious to Jaylynn, but she wanted to hear Dez's point of view.

"It is. How do I prove myself? How do I show the brass and the head of detectives and assholes like Andres that I can keep my head under pressure? That I can work independently and that my partner can depend upon me one hundred percent?"

Jaylynn didn't answer the rhetorical question, for that was what it was. Dez was going to have to find her own way with this. No matter what she heard from Jaylynn, Dez would still have her doubts even though she was well respected and trusted by others in the precinct. In a flash of understanding, Jaylynn realized that it wasn't so much the brass Dez needed to convince, but herself. Only time could do that.

Jaylynn rose once more. "I'll let you prove yourself. I'm sure I could give some glowing recommendations regarding your special skills." She gave her partner a wicked smile. "Come to bed."

Grinning, Dez gazed up at her, but didn't budge. "Not quite yet, little missy. Sit down." She patted the sofa cushion. "Before you get me into bed and have your way with me—in other words, while I still have any sense left in my head—tell me where the plans stand for tomorrow."

Jaylynn plopped down next to her. "Ha! Ever the realist. Okay, I typed up a trip manifest on the computer, and after about two thousand amendments, I think we have everything we could possibly need. Most of the stuff is miniature. Did you know they make little tubes of matches about the size of half a pack of Lifesavers?"

"Small and light. That's the goal." Smiling, Dez said, "Like you, Jay. Dainty and dinky."

Outraged, Jaylynn protested. "I'm not dainty!" She flexed her fingers and made a growling sound, then grabbed at Dez's middle, tickling her while Dez laughingly fended her off.

"Small and dainty, small and dainty."

"Take it back!"

"Hey, I've got too much padding. You're not going to send me off into hysterics." Dez frowned.

Kneeling on the couch next to her, Jaylynn paused. "What?"

"Nothing."

"No, tell me. What?"

Dez let out a sigh. "You just reminded me of all the weight I've gained."

Jaylynn snickered. "Well, believe me, it doesn't show." She settled against Dez's middle and snuggled in, her head tucked under the other woman's chin. "You don't look fat, Dez, you look powerful." She felt Dez shrug. "What? You don't believe me?"

"Cripes, this is the hugest I've ever been in my whole life."

"You know what they say about being happily married." She peeked up at Dez's face and was dismayed to see that she was truly anguished. "Dez, you look terrific. You just got spoiled with the bodybuilding when you were skin and bones and your muscles were popping out all over. That was unnatural—temporary, too. Just because your muscles are covered with a bit of insulation now isn't bad. You look like a normal person. And consider the great side benefits for me. You certainly keep me warm, and I know I'll appreciate that in our dinky tent."

Dez tightened her grip. "Okay, I'll try to believe you. I need to get more lifting workouts in, though."

Jaylynn laughed. "More?"

"All right. *Some.* I haven't had much time to lift lately, and I'd like to get more cardio, too. I feel out of shape, and tonight reminded me of it."

"Ooh, the great Dez Reilly, sucking wind on the hiking trails of northern Minnesota. What fun!"

"Don't laugh. You'll be old like me before too long."

Jaylynn rolled her eyes. Dez was a mere four years and eight months older and usually liked to use that to her advantage, but today she sounded defeated. Jaylynn worked a hand up under Dez's sweatshirt and felt the soft cotton of a t-shirt. She pulled at the shirt, and Dez let out a groan. Jaylynn froze. "Oh, no. Did I hurt you?"

"I'm a mass of bruises."

"Really? Let me see."

Dez untucked the rest of her shirt, then lifted it away from her middle. Jaylynn's mouth dropped open. Dez's porcelain-white torso was mottled pale purple. She reached out to touch an angry-looking spot on Dez's right rib. "Wow. Bruises always show up like neon on you."

"Yeah. I'm glad the guys can't tell."

"How'd these happen?"

"I slipped while scaling a six-foot wooden wall in someone's yard tonight. I banged my ribs and skinned my arm. Even the Kevlar vest didn't protect my middle from the impact."

Jaylynn dipped her head down and put a kiss on Dez's midsection, then nuzzled against her and felt a shiver go through her partner. She looked up. Dez's head bent, and their lips met. Jaylynn moved closer. Her hands pressed upward, along Dez's sides, around the muscle of her upper back, stroking and kneading.

Dez broke off the kiss. "Ow . . . I hate to be a wuss, but ouch. Let's get out of all these constricting clothes so you can see where you can and cannot touch me."

"Sounds like a good plan." She got up from the couch, holding Dez's hand, and pulled her up. "Come on, sweetie. Let's go to bed."

# Chapter
# Three

HERMAN R. KENDALL Medium-Security Correctional Facility sat nestled in the birch and poplar trees of northern Minnesota, just south of Pelican River. Privately run and financed by a contract with the State of Minnesota, the prison had been in business for less than four years. Already it was near capacity with inmates from all over the Midwest. The 200-plus convicts, housed two to a cell, could look out their small windows and see the leaves of the deciduous trees changing from green to brilliant magenta, orange, red, and gold. Most of the inmates also gazed north, wondering how far it was to Canada, if they ever had a chance to flee in that direction.

Birds flew from tree to tree, twittering in the distance. A prisoner, peering out his little porthole to the world, watched a squirrel dart one way, then another, in a search for anything edible on the ground. The man, Keith Randall, leaned his forehead against the hardened pane of glass, feeling as though he might cry. *What I wouldn't give for a hot cup of decent coffee and my freedom.*

He heard a noise behind him as his cellmate stirred in the upper bunk. The man had only recently detoxed from drugs and alcohol. Surly when awake, he spent most of his time sleeping or lying in the bunk, staring at the ceiling. Keith preferred the new guy — so far anyway — to his former cellmate.

Keith shuddered. The last man had been brutal and crude. It was a stroke of the best fortune that he had managed to keep the other convict from sexually assaulting him.

Keith moved to sit on the edge of his bunk and wait for the morning buzzer to sound. They had been in lockdown all afternoon and overnight after a major altercation on the yard.

When one or two men messed up, everyone was punished. After being shut in for the last eighteen hours, any minute they should be released to go to the mess hall, and Keith was eager to get out and stretch his legs.

He'd already used the tiny sink stacked over the metal toilet in the corner to wash his hands and face with cold water. *What an arrangement. Nothing like straddling the toilet seat every time I want to wash up. Jesus. I'm not gonna miss that.*

He was hungry. It had taken a long time for him to grow accustomed to the food in jail, but after the first month, when he had dropped nearly ten pounds, he realized he would have to eat the poor meals just to keep up his strength. Now he tried not to think about the lumpy potatoes, runny eggs, rubbery, barely buttered toast, or the weak coffee he downed in the mornings. He'd been in the slammer for almost all of his three-year sentence for burglary, and in thirty-three more days, he was out. He couldn't wait. *Thirty-three mornings left of that crappy food . . . or no. Thirty-two. I'll skip that shitty meal on the last day and take myself out for breakfast once I'm out of here.*

Rising from the bottom bunk, he rolled his shoulders, stretched his arms out to the side, and yawned. His stomach grumbled. People said prison was supposed to rehabilitate, but it didn't happen in the way the regular citizen expected. One became hardened, barbaric, and merciless . . . or became a target for the hardened, barbaric, and merciless. Two simple fates: lose one's humanity or become an animal. He didn't like either option and had spent all his time in jail playing a game of survival. Keith wasn't sure how a man who had at least *some* ethics was supposed to survive in the joint, but he had done his best. He moved toward the bars of his cell, crossed his arms, and leaned until his forehead touched the cool metal. Now if only he could make it thirty-three more days, he could walk away from this hellhole.

The morning buzzer, a loud, ear-piercing squawk, echoed from above, and Keith sprang back as the bars to his metal cage automatically unlocked and slid left. He waited for the guard's whistle indicating that he could proceed to the chow hall. When it came, he stepped away from the cell with the same relief he felt every time he was released from the small enclosure. But the relief changed, as it did every day, to edginess, because now, out in the open, there were predators with whom to contend. He shuffled along, keeping his eyes on the floor.

# Chapter
# Four

St. Paul, Minnesota
Friday, October 15, 7:00 a.m.

FRIDAY MORNING DAWNED clear and cool in St. Paul. Dez rose at seven a.m. and noted the 38-degree temperature outside. Minnesota's October weather is fickle, at times chilly with a harbinger of winter, but also full of mild days hearkening back to spring. *Excellent,* she thought. *This is perfect weather for hiking and camping. The bugs will all be dead.* She hated the gnats, no-see-ems, and mosquitoes of summer, but they sure loved her. She was glad to know that she'd get few, if any, bug bites. The forecast for the next five days was for sun and temperature highs in the 50s, dropping into the low 30s at night. It would be somewhat cooler two hundred fifty miles north, near the Canadian border. *This camping trip is already shaping up to be pleasant and memorable.*

Wearing cotton shorts and sweatshirt, she moved through the house quietly, not yet ready to awaken Jaylynn. In the kitchen, she rinsed out spoons and ice cream bowls from the previous night and put them in the dishwasher, then assembled the ingredients for an omelet. When it was time to heat it, she could toss it together in minutes.

Dez poured a tumbler full of milk, took a banana from the bunch, set both down on the table, and went to the front of the house to open the door and retrieve the newspaper. She took it to the table and sat to read it while munching on the fruit. In one of the lead news articles, she saw that the St. Paul chief of police had survived a flurry of inquiries by the city council. They had voted for her 5-1 with one abstention. Dez disliked the chief personally. She was rude, abrupt, and just as hard on herself as on everyone around her. But Dez respected that she got the job done.

Only once had she seen a tiny glimmer of vulnerability in

the chief, and that was back when Dez had taken a bullet in the vest during a convenience store holdup. The Chief had swept into the emergency room, verbally pistol-whipped the attending doctors and nurses, then shoehorned her way into the tiny bay where Dez lay in pain. For one brief flicker, Dez saw anguish and concern in the chief's face—then it was gone, replaced by the hard, analytical look she usually wore.

"Pay attention to the doctor's orders, and follow them to the letter," the chief had snapped out. "You're on approved leave until you're healed up." Then she turned and disappeared, leaving Dez to wonder if she had imagined the chief's momentary lapse.

Hearing stirring elsewhere in the house, Dez folded up the newspaper.

Jaylynn shuffled in, yawning. She wore a tattered green robe and flannel pajamas. "Good morning, sweetie. When did you get up?"

"Not long ago." Dez scooted her chair away from the table, and Jaylynn settled sideways onto her lap and leaned onto her shoulder. "Why are you up so early?"

Jaylynn yawned again. "I told Crystal I would give them a wake-up call at seven."

"That's probably a good idea since the two of them never get anywhere on time. Did you lie to them about the estimated time of departure?"

"Nah, I didn't. I said nine, but who cares if it's a little later. Last night, Crystal and I really did finish packing everything they could possibly need. They could literally fall out of bed, dress, shoulder a pack, and be ready."

Dez laughed. "I hope you left them enough time to shower!"

"Showering is optional while camping. We'll probably all smell like wild coyote women by Sunday or Monday anyway." She yawned again.

Dez nuzzled her face into Jaylynn's short, white-blond hair and inhaled her sweet scent. Closing her eyes, she relaxed, feeling the solid warmth of the woman in her arms. Lately, she'd felt so content. The panic and desperation in the year following the shooting death of her work partner, Ryan Michaelson, had gradually receded, especially with the help of counseling. The post-traumatic stress aberrations she had once experienced gradually abated, and now all that was left was a tiny scar—perhaps more like a little cave in her heart—where she harbored the memories of her friend. She still thought of Ryan often, imagined the deep tones of his voice, saw him laughing in her mind's eye. She wished he were around to see how she had changed and softened. He'd often teased her about being a tough, career-minded, single butch whom only love would reform. Periodically, he'd pointed out eligible women — women in high heels and pantyhose who *he* thought were attractive. Dez definitely did not share his tastes. She smiled ruefully into Jaylynn's hair. If Ryan were alive, she didn't think she'd even mind the ribbing he'd have given her about the way she'd slipped so easily into domesticity. And she thought — no, she *knew* — he would have loved Jaylynn like a sister.

Jaylynn let out a sigh. "How can you be so warm? I'm in this terry-cloth monstrosity, and you're in shorts." Dez didn't answer. They'd had this conversation so many times that there was nothing left to say about it. "Are you making something delectable for us to eat?"

"Yup."

"Good. I'll go get in the shower. You perform your kitchen slave duties." She unfolded herself from Dez's lap and rose, pulling the robe tighter around her.

"You want onion in your omelet?"

Jaylynn paused to consider. "I don't think so. We'll all be sitting in the car for five hours. Urping up onion doesn't sound pleasant for me or others."

Dez grinned. "That's exactly what I thought you'd say. I might also mention that I'm glad you're not starting out the trip smelling like a wild coyote woman."

Jaylynn rolled her eyes. "Oh, right. As if."

IN A REMARKABLE feat of punctuality, Shayna and Crystal wheeled into the driveway and came to a stop in front of the closed garage door only ten minutes past nine. Jaylynn stepped out onto the back porch stoop and waved, then descended the stairs. Crystal had finally ditched the antiquated Chevy Impala she had driven for years and purchased a new, cherry-red Jeep Liberty in its place. Jaylynn had already ridden in it twice, but Dez hadn't seen it yet.

The screen door whapped shut, and Jaylynn turned to see her partner descending the stairs two at a time. Dez let out a whistle. "Wow, Crys, what a nice vehicle."

Shayna got out of the car and rolled her eyes, which made Jaylynn laugh. She said, "Jay, honey, let's let them crawl around the *car*, while you and me have a nice cup of coffee."

"Good idea. I've got butter-cream coffee and some half-and-half we should use up. Let's have at it." She turned and led the way into the house.

When Jaylynn had first met Shayna, shortly after joining the police force, the African-American woman had been much heavier. Since then, Shayna had been diagnosed with Metabolic Syndrome X—a precursor to diabetes—but she didn't yet have the disease. Several members of Shayna's family had severe diabetes, so she'd made many changes in her diet and exercise patterns, dropping about forty pounds in the process. Because of her build, Shayna was never going to be "skinny," but her five-foot-seven frame no longer supported her former plumpness. She looked fit.

"Go ahead and give me that big mug, Jay, and fill 'er up. I read that a person weighing 150 pounds and carrying a backpack can burn up 1,200 calories in four hours."

"How fast do you have to be hiking?"

Shayna thought for a moment. "I think it said two miles per hour."

"Shoot, that's an easy stroll. The trails are pretty flat up there. We should be able to make better time than that. We'll both load up on the half-and-half." Sipping their hot drinks, they giggled together.

The back door opened, and Dez entered the kitchen, followed by Crystal. "In an act of supreme confidence," Dez said, "I am trusting that you three have managed to bring every single thing on the packing manifest."

"Yes, dear," Jaylynn said.

Crystal nodded. "In fact, we spent a shitload of money on extra lightweight stuff, too."

"Thankfully," Shayna said. "I still can't believe I'm going on this dumb-ass trip!"

Jaylynn looked at Shayna, then caught sight of Crystal's grim expression. *Uh oh, a little trouble in paradise.* Seeking a diversion, she set down her coffee mug, pulled away the Velcro flap on the side of her hiking pants, and reached into the pocket to grab a dark blue and silver object. "Look! I got this cool Swiss Army knife. It's got scissors, bottle opener, even tweezers and a toothpick."

Dez reached into the side pocket of her own cargo pants and came up with something silver. "Leatherman Wave Multi-Tool." She held it out in the palm of her hand. "I'll see your scissors, opener, and tweezers, and raise you two screwdrivers, a saw, pliers, and a wire cutter."

Jaylynn gazed up into twinkling blue eyes. "Mine only weighs a few ounces."

"Half a pound—eight ounces of power and grace."

Shayna let out a chuckle. "Well, we all know who to come to if a boulder rolls down and traps one of our arms."

Jaylynn shuddered. "Oh, ick. That was a terrible story! I felt so bad for that Aron Ralston guy." She pointed at the Leatherman in Dez's hand. "Is that what he used to take his arm off?"

Dez pocketed the multi-tool. "I don't know if it was this brand, but yeah. He used a multi-tool."

Crystal gave Dez a light punch on the shoulder. "I say we get this adventure started. Are we ready to rock 'n' roll?"

"I am," Jaylynn said. She glanced at Shayna and saw the resigned look on her face. After a last swig of coffee, Jaylynn set the mug in the sink and ran it full of water. "Let's go check our gear and get rolling."

Shayna handed over her mug, too. "How far is the drive?"

Crystal grinned and slipped an arm around her partner's waist. "What she's really asking is how many hours will we be stuck in the car?"

Dez looked up toward the ceiling. Jaylynn tried not to smile. She could almost see the gears whirring in her partner's head. "The 150 miles from here to Duluth are a breeze. Probably only take us a little over two hours. Traffic will be light mid-morning on a Friday. Then we have to go another 135 miles to Crane Lake, but it's only a two-lane highway most of the way, so that slows us way down. After stopping for lunch along the way, I'd say we're looking at six hours."

"ETA four bells," Crystal said. "Will that work for you, my love?"

Shayna swatted Crystal away. "Of course it will. I am almost certain that I brought enough CDs to last that long. So let's get a move on."

NORTHERN MINNESOTA HAD always been one of Dez's favorite vacation places, and she loved autumn best. Though the forests were laced with plenty of balsam fir and evergreen pine trees, the majority of the trees she saw were deciduous. The chlorophyll count had dropped, the carotene count was up, and the change of fall colors was underway. Some pale green could still be seen here and there, but the leaves of most of the poplar, birch, honey locust, maple, green ash, and oaks flamed with color. The sumac bushes blazed as though on fire, and without a cloud in the sky, the day was quite simply gorgeous.

Dez sat in the Jeep's back seat next to Crystal, half-listening to the conversation Jaylynn and Shayna were carrying on in the front. Crystal had driven until they got to Duluth, then after lunch, Jaylynn offered to take the wheel. Dez figured she would get a chance to drive the new Jeep before the weekend was over, but since she was the one who knew the area, it was better that she have the maps available so she could navigate.

As a kid, Dez and her father and brother had often camped and canoed the Boundary Waters Canoe Area and hiked all over the woods and forests, but she hadn't been to Crane Lake since about the time she joined the police force well over a decade earlier. She'd spent most of her twenties being a loner, and she didn't think it was safe to camp, hike, or portage alone. Besides, it was no fun. The one time she did go on a two-day trip by herself, the night at the campfire was unbearably lonely. She recalled wondering, at the time, why she was destined for a solitary life. It hadn't seemed fair to her, and during that hiking trip, she struggled to reconcile herself to the fact. She would never have guessed that someone like Jaylynn would come into her life.

The few other times she had camped as an adult had been with her work partner, Ryan, and his wife and kids. She didn't call an overnight visit to a nearby state park "real" camping. She smiled as she recalled Ryan's kids, Jill and Jeremy, toddling around the campsite, filthy as little hedgehogs. As they got older, they loved the outdoors, and to Dez's way of thinking, that was the most important aspect of taking kids to sleep overnight in a tent. Respecting the land, the trees, the animals— this was a value of bedrock importance and one Dez thought far too few parents taught their children nowadays. She saw youngsters in St. Paul every day who had never been outside the confines of their concrete and pavement world. She found that sad.

"Dez!"

Startled out of her thoughts, Dez looked up into the rearview mirror and met Jaylynn's eyes. "Huh?"

"I asked you what highway I'm looking for."

Dez pointed ahead to a green and white sign in the distance. "Just follow the signs to Buyck. That's Highway 23, but in Buyck, the highway changes to 24 to get to Crane Lake. I think they'll have it well marked."

Shayna peered around the front seat to meet Dez's eyes. "There sure are a lot of native names for things up here."

"Yup."

"I thought we'd be in the Superior National Forest."

Dez said, "Not too much, though the first night we'll camp on the Echo River, probably right next to it, then move on to Echo Lake. The Echo Lake area is mostly west of Superior Forest."

Jaylynn asked, "How the heck do you say that name that

starts with K?"

"Kabetogama. We're actually doing most of our hiking through Kabetogama State Forest."

Crystal laughed. "Well, that's a mouthful."

Dez smiled back at her. "Just remember, it's not Spanish, which might have the emphasis on different syllables. It's Ka-bah-*toe*-guh-ma. Altogether now, Ka-bah-*toe*-guh-ma."

Everybody giggled over that, and Jaylynn said, "If I didn't know better, I'd swear we picked up Mr. Rogers at the last stop." Dez leaned forward and gently squeezed the back of Jaylynn's neck, prompting a startled shriek. "Hey! No harassing the driver!"

Dez laughed. She let her hand slide to the right, along the side of the soft neck, and to the warm shoulder, which she squeezed before sitting back.

Crystal whapped Dez's thigh with the back of her hand. "Exactly how far do we hike today?"

"Not far." Dez unfolded one of the maps in her lap and pointed. "See here? We'll park at Crane Lake, then travel south a couple miles. Actually, I think it's about three miles. It's hard to say exactly how far from looking at the map. The trails tend to meander and weave around."

Jaylynn held up her new compass and glanced over her shoulder. "I'll get to use this. Isn't it hard to do the orienteering thing if the trails are all over the place?"

Dez shrugged. "Not really. You just have to get a mental picture of the area, and then work from that. It's good if you have a sense of direction." She looked pointedly at Shayna.

"Hey, girl! Don't you be making fun of me! I'm just along for the ride."

"Yeah, right. Today isn't too big a deal. We go a little ways, and as soon as we find a suitable place to make camp near Echo River, we can quit for the day. Tomorrow we'll walk a lot farther—maybe five or six miles until we get to Echo Lake. That's a pretty area. Lots to explore and trails to hike. Sunday we can head back toward Crane Lake in one long marathon hike. If you really love the camping, we can car-camp Sunday night, but I'm thinking by then a motel, showers, and restaurant food will sound good."

The other women chuckled, and Shayna said, "Now ya got your head screwed on straight, woman. Sounds like a plan. What happens if we get lost?"

"We won't get lost," Dez said. "I know the area, and we'll check in at the national park station and file our hiking plan. Besides," she patted her cargo pants side pocket, "I've got trail and topo maps."

Shayna asked, "Topo? What's that?"

All three cops answered. "Topography."

"Is that anything like finger-ography?" Shayna giggled, and no one dignified her comment with a response. "Okay, Dez, our lives are in your hands. We'll be facing bears, scarce food, and frozen tundra. Hope you can keep us safe."

Dez recognized Shayna's comments for what they were: teasing. But she did feel serious about their safety. "It *is* possible to run into a bear. There are thousands of them in northern Minnesota. Should we discuss what to—"

"Yeah, yeah, yeah," Jaylynn called out. "We went over that. I can recite the six rules by heart. And how to put out the fire properly. And proper trail etiquette. Not to mention proper pooping technique."

Shayna laughed hard at that. "We'll try not to embarrass you in front of Bambi and Thumper, Dez."

Crystal said, "It's the buddy system, *mi amiga*. If a bear shows up on the trail, I'll give them my buddy." She reached over and punched Dez in the upper arm. "That's you, by the way."

Dez glanced up to the front and saw Jaylynn looking in the rearview mirror, her hazel eyes squinting in the sun streaming into the Jeep. She winked and Jaylynn winked back. "Well, people," Jaylynn said, "I do believe we have reached the lovely town of Buyck."

Dez leaned forward and stretched out a long arm over Jaylynn's shoulder. "Go that way—see the sign to Crane Lake Road? Take that to Highway 24—right up ahead."

About two miles outside town, they passed a paved road to the left. A modest wood sign painted in maroon-red sat low to the ground. *HERMAN R. KENDALL CORRECTIONAL FACILITY.* In smaller letters underneath, the script read: "A Private Company Excelling for the Public Good."

Crystal pointed as they passed. "I always wondered exactly where that was. Never knew it was this close to civilization."

Shayna said, "I'll bet that place has more residents than Buyck does."

Dez nodded. "Yeah, and it's *way* off in the sticks. If I remember correctly, it's several more miles before you come to it. They put it in such a remote site on purpose to discourage guys from trying to break out."

"Good plan," Jaylynn said.

JAYLYNN AND HER companions stopped for a rest when they came to a huge tree that had fallen across the trail. With a sigh, Jaylynn let her pack slip off her shoulders, then clambered up to sit on the widest part of the tree trunk. Crystal and Shayna followed suit, while Dez backed up to lean against the tree and let the pack be supported by it. Jaylynn knew Shayna was sick of hiking but was being a good sport. Of their party, Jaylynn was certain Dez was the only one not tired and cranky.

Crystal, sitting next to and slightly above Dez, slid a leg over and nudged her tall friend. "I thought you said you haven't been working out."

"I haven't. I've run lately, but haven't had time for much lifting."

"Could've fooled me," Shayna said.

Jaylynn took a pull on her canteen, screwed the lid back on, and wiped her mouth on the sleeve of her t-shirt. "I could swear we've walked five miles."

Dez nodded. "It feels that way because you're loaded down. And this last bit has been more up and down than I remembered it."

Crystal said, "Isn't that the truth!"

Shayna wiped her face on the shoulder of Crystal's shirt. "You would've never gotten me out of the car if I'd known it would be such a long hike. I sure as hell hope we're almost there."

Dez reached into the side pocket of her cargo pants and slipped out the topo map and compass. "Let's see if I can figure out how close we are. Want me to show you how this works, you guys? You never know when you might want to do some orienteering."

"Never mind," Jaylynn said as she hopped down. "I can smell water. We're almost there."

Crystal and Shayna looked at her for a brief moment, then burst into laughter. "You smell water?" asked the laughing Latina. "What's it smell like?"

"Ice," Shayna said. They both giggled uproariously.

Hands on hips, Jaylynn gave them a mocking grin, then reached down for her pack. Bent over, she paused and gauged the tree for a moment. Instead of picking up the heavy pack, she dragged it a bit and shoved it through an open spot under a place where the tree trunk rested on a wide rock. She climbed up and over the thick trunk, jumped down, then stood looking at the three women from the other side. "Anyone want to hand me your pack? Believe me, you can *really* smell the water from this side."

NO MORE THAN five hundred yards down the trail, Dez saw that Jaylynn was correct. Echo River stretched out ahead of them, rushing merrily into the distance where it dumped into Echo Lake. Before they'd walked much farther, they came upon a clearing with a fire pit in the middle and space for as many as two or three small tents on either side. A stand of trees, dripping with gold and red leaves, encircled them like a protective wall.

Dez said, "Huh. You were right, Jay." She looked up at the tall oaks, poplars, and maples and spun slowly in a full circle. "Wow. This is pretty much just how I remembered it."

Down a slope, through a stand of trees, and perhaps only twenty yards away, the river gurgled by.

"Yeah," Shayna said, nodding. "This is sweet."

They set to work clearing brush and twigs away from the flat areas, and in no time, they'd staked and pitched their tents. While the others gathered firewood, Dez detached a lightweight hatchet from her outer pack strap, dragged over a log, and used the ax to remove small branches. "There we go," she said. "Now we have something to sit on."

Jaylynn looked up at her and smiled. "Now if only your fine chair had a back on it."

Dez rolled her eyes. "Picky, picky." With a grin, she set down the ax and rubbed her hands together. The left one was covered with sticky pitch that she didn't want to get on her pants or jacket. She strolled over to the stand of trees, slipped between two, and made her way through some brush onto a deer path that led down to the river.

The water bubbled as it flowed past. She squatted down and rinsed her hands, picked up some craggy stones, and rubbed them against her palms to wear away the pitch. When her hands felt clean, she let them drip dry, watching the blue and silver ripples of water. It was easy to get lost in the moment, and she squatted, elbows on knees with hands relaxed in front of her. Bird calls. Soft breeze. The smell of pine. She thought that this was what people meant by a "Zen moment," losing all track of anything other than a feeling of well-being. She smiled to think about how rarely this feeling of relaxation and contentment came over her, other than after making love. When Ryan had been shot to death on the job, such moments ceased completely for a very long while. But over time, that grief had lessened. Dez took a deep breath and watched the river run. *Ryan would have loved this place.* She was sorry he would never get the chance to see it, and she was glad Jaylynn and their friends were alive to experience it.

She heard another two-tone bird call, followed by a rustling noise. Footsteps. She shot to her feet and turned. A little way up the slope, Jaylynn stood, a perplexed look on her face. "I was *wondering* where you disappeared to! Didn't you hear me whistling for you?"

"Hmm? Whistling?"

Jaylynn whistled a high sound, then a lower one, which Dez recognized as the bird call that had registered in the back of her consciousness. She laughed. "Jay, honey, I don't answer to a whistle. I'm not one of the Von Trapp kids, and you're not the Captain." She took a few steps up toward her partner.

Jaylynn let out a belly laugh. "Fat chance of that! However, I'm sure my singing *could* be confused with Julie Andrews' fine voice."

Dez reached her and took her hand. "Come on. And don't go breaking into 'The Lonely Goatherd.' Now *there's* a song you can never get out of your head."

Bumping Dez with her hip, Jaylynn said, "I'll be sure to hum it right before we go to sleep, so you can dream about it all night."

"How thoughtful of you. You are such a brat!" She tightened her grip on Jaylynn's hand, and they cut back through the trees to find that Shayna and Crystal had stacked up a huge pile of fallen timber.

Crystal held the hatchet and swung down into a jagged chunk of wood. It not only split, but the two halves also shattered into smaller pieces. "Whoa . . . check this out."

Dez pointed. "That's punky shit — it's no — "

Shayna let out a high-pitched howl. "Punky shit! Punky shit! Ha ha ha. Dez, you really crack me up."

Jaylynn leaned in, and Dez put an arm across her shoulders as they stood listening to Shayna and Crystal's cackling. Dez shook her head slowly and smiled. "The only thing all that *punky shit*," she paused for effect, "is good for is kindling. It's rotted and so dry, it'll burn in record time."

Crystal whacked the hatchet blade into a chunk of wood and left it there. "I'll remember that technical term for when I take my brother's little *muchachos* camping. They're getting to be old enough now."

Jaylynn said, "So how exactly does 'punky shit' translate in Spanish?"

Shayna rolled her eyes. "I'm sure your nephews will enjoy learning that. Nothing eight-year-old boys like better than potty humor." She shaded her eyes and looked off toward the rapidly descending sun. "What the heck time does it get dark around here? All of a sudden, seems like we're losing sunlight."

"Yup," Dez said. "According to the chart I saw in the ranger station, the sun sets at 5:49." Shayna seemed surprised, so Dez went on. "Actually, the sun sets at that point, but apparent sunset occurs slightly later than *actual* sunset. After the sun crosses below the horizon, it's apparent sunset, but with air pressure and humidity, they really can't predict the exact effects of atmospheric refraction on sunset time—and this goes for sunrise, too." Shayna was looking at her like she had grown a second head. "What?" Dez asked.

Shayna swung her attention to Dez's partner. "Jaylynn, honey, I would strongly advise you to cancel her subscription to whatever the hell magazines she's been reading. *Scientific American? Popular Science?* Hello! Earth to Dez. Nobody on the planet knows shit like that."

Everybody laughed, and Dez said, "Just some interesting facts I thought you should memorize. In case you're ever out in the woods and need to know, say, what time the fireflies come out."

Shayna said, "How 'bout I'll just make sure I go to a forest where cell phones actually work, and I'll call ya!"

Dez handed her two chunks of wood. "Meanwhile, make yourself useful and haul this over to the stack."

"Yes, ma'am. Now do I call you Lewis? Or Clark?"

# Chapter
# Five

A TIGHT CIRCLE of some four dozen inmates pressed together, shouting and struggling to see two men fighting on the ground. "Kill him, King!" some of them shouted. Others rooted for McCallum, who had thrown the first punch. King, the bigger of the two combatants, grunted and swore. He connected with a blow to the side of McCallum's head, then managed to roll out from under the attack. King got to his knees, shoved the other man back, and fell upon him. With forearms against McCallum's neck, King tried to hold him down as McCallum spat and kicked and swung wildly.

Keith Randall stood between two sweating spectators. One of them jostled him, and he could no longer see the fight. But then he heard shrill whistles and rushing footsteps. The prison guards pushed their way into the huddle. The inmates stopped cheering and stepped back, none of them wanting to call attention to himself. Nobody wanted yet another lockdown any time soon.

Keith angled toward the tall chain-link fence and away from the suddenly silent crowd. He stuck his hands in the pockets of his orange jumpsuit and waited to see whether both men rose. Sometimes one of the inmates got shanked and stayed down, bleeding or even dead. The thought gave him the shivers. He'd been attacked three days earlier, thankfully with fists only. He opened his mouth and moved his jaw, which was still sore and bruised. The only good thing about fights on the yard was that few attacks lasted longer than fifteen or twenty seconds before the guards broke things up. Still, any inmate could land an amazing number of blows in that short span of time.

A tall figure loomed to his left, and he glanced up in

surprise. Wary, he stepped a quarter-turn and steeled himself for an attack. Instead, a creep named Stanley Bostwick stood smiling over him. Against sallow white skin, the man's lips were unnaturally red, as though he'd been chewing something bloody. He ran a large, hairy mitt over the top of his bald head. "Must've been quite a fight, huh? Sorry I missed it. I was meeting with my new lawyer."

Keith nodded once, as he tried to pretend that his heart didn't feel like it was beating right out of his chest. He couldn't have answered if he'd wanted to. At the moment, his mouth was too dry to offer up any witty retorts.

"Guess they'll both make it, though."

Keith glanced to the right and back at Bostwick. Both of the fighters were on their feet and being hauled off by the guards. Keith cleared his throat and choked out, "Yeah."

Eyes narrowed and with head bobbing up and down, Bostwick stood watching a few seconds longer, then abruptly turned and moved away.

Keith couldn't prevent a sigh of relief. *Oh, boy.* He swallowed, and for a moment, it was hard to make his throat work. *Shit. I did not want to be on that man's radar.* He headed for a corner of the yard within clear sight of the guard's station and waited for the whistle to blow.

# Chapter
# Six

THREE MEN ARGUED in the cramped back room of the Best Jobs Printing Company in Chicago. Sergei Gubenko sat silently at the head of the table, arms crossed over his chest. Victor Lukin, Gubenko's legal counsel, and Alexei Zhukovich, Gubenko's nephew from New York, still had energy left, although none of them had slept in thirty-six hours.

All night long, Gubenko had listened to his nephew and the lawyer brainstorm and argue. The two men, heated and looking desperate, spoke in Russian. They'd fought about tactics. Discussed the problem on the phone with other family members. Tried to call in favors. Now they were going in circles, and Gubenko was bleary-eyed and had a pounding headache. He held up his hand. "I am tired." Slumping forward, elbows on the table, he said, "All I want to know is if there is any way to save Leonid."

The two men looked at one another, then at Gubenko. The lawyer said, "We are down to the one last plan, which has already been put into motion."

For at least the fifth time, Zhukovich said, "There is absolutely *no guarantee* that this man you speak of can make his idea work."

Lukin, the lawyer, shook his head vigorously. "It matters not, Alexei. We are down to our last chance. I am the only one who has spoken to him personally, and in my judgment, there is a chance. He said it is possible, a long shot, but worth a try."

Gubenko said, "There is no other way, then." It wasn't a question.

His nephew reached over and patted Gubenko's forearm. "Everything that can be done must be done. Leonid must not go to jail."

"I agree," Lukin said, "but there is only so much we are capable of doing."

"That is no answer!" Zhukovich shouted. "My uncle has been like a father to you, a help to your family. You wouldn't be a lawyer without his generosity!"

Lukin sighed. "Do you think I am unaware of that? Alexei, get a grip on yourself! They targeted Leonid. He made some mistakes—*we* made some mistakes. There is very little we can do to bring pressure to bear. Unless someone else has an idea, then I suggest we wait and see if this man attempts his plan. If he succeeds, we have the leverage to deter the testimony, and Leonid will go free."

Gubenko sighed. "Enough. Stop fighting. You have both done the best you can. It is a difficult situation."

The Zhukovich and Gubenko families were intertwined like vines in a grape arbor. The Gubenkos had always been the brains of their business operations, while the Zhukovichs supplied the will and ability to carry out any plan. The whole clan had been located solely in New York until just eight years earlier when Sergei Gubenko was tapped by his now-deceased father to open up shop in Chicago. Ever since his brother's arrest, Gubenko had had to stay put and run the Chicago operation, and he had felt helpless to act on Leonid's behalf. Until now. Now Lukin's plan might allow Gubenko to help his brother.

In a low voice, Gubenko said, "If I understand this correctly, tonight or Sunday, perhaps Monday, maybe even Tuesday, this felon will manage a breakout." He sighed and shook his head in disbelief. "There is a meeting place to make the pickup in the woods, and you will send Grigor."

The lawyer's face reddened. "Actually, I took the initiative and have already done that."

"Without my approval."

"Yes, sir."

"I see. So some guy we have never met and who owes us nothing will bring the man to us, and then we have leverage?" The two men continued to nod. Gubenko sat back, looking disgusted. "This is the craziest plan I have ever heard. All our hopes rest upon one man, and he isn't even Russian."

Lukin looked uncomfortable at that statement. "Any man of his caliber can be bought, Russian or not. His price is fifty thousand dollars."

Gubenko closed his eyes and exhaled. "That is the easy part, my friends. And Leonid is worth that price many times over." He opened his eyes, and for the first time, Gubenko felt the slightest bit of hope. "This idea has—how do they say it?—one snowball's chance in hell, but we will hope and pray. It is good you sent Grigor."

Lukin said, "I took the liberty of having him get a vehicle from Domo's chop shop—something reliable that cannot be traced to the Gubenko name. He will track down the men at the meeting place and assist them. The man will be brought to the safe house and you will be contacted."

"Good. Very good. I will also call Vanya. He must be alerted of the need to assist, just in case anything should go wrong." Gubenko rose. "I am going in search of a decent meal. When I get back, you two better have good news for me."

# Chapter
# Seven

Kendall Correctional Facility
Outside Buyck, Minnesota
Saturday, October 16, 4:00 p.m.

IN THE PRISON yard, along the sidelines of the cement basketball court, Keith Randall leaned against the granite wall. The late afternoon sun was close to disappearing behind the trees, and in mere minutes, yard time would be over. He tucked his hands into his jumpsuit pockets, shivering in the cool light breeze. If he were playing basketball with the other men, he'd stay sufficiently warm, but last time he'd ventured on the court, he'd gotten clocked but good, and it took three days for the swelling over his eye to recede. He looked down at himself, realizing he was too slim, too short, and not fierce enough to compete. Unlike the point guard, Swiff, who was one of the smallest inmates, Keith didn't have the speed or acceleration. Or the shoes. Where had a guy like Swiff gotten the nice basketball high-tops?

He watched Swiff take a pass from Bostwick, one of the biggest, meatiest men on the court, then laughingly cut through and pass off. The small black man's face shone with sweat and glee. He looked like he lived for basketball. Upon reflection, Keith thought maybe Swiff did. He moved like a jackrabbit and was obviously a favorite of Bostwick's. The big oaf played center like a linebacker, but he was surprisingly quick on his feet.

Keith turned from the breeze until he felt it on his back. He stepped away from the cracked court. He knew the facility was still quite new, and yet already the cement in the yard was pitted and split. Keith wasn't sure if it was shabby workmanship or the rigors of the harsh Minnesota winters. All he knew for sure was that if his luck held, he would be out of the prison before the snow flew and it cracked any further. He couldn't wait.

When the buzzer sounded, he shuffled into the dank-smelling prison, his senses assaulted once more by the noise and stench of sweating men. *When I get out of here, I never want to smell shit like this again.*

Two hours remained until the meal bell rang, and it was time to report to the laundry. Keith joined the procession of men moving toward the work wing. On the outside, men of different races were expected to cooperate, to tolerate, to get along, but inside the joint it was a far different story. Other than out on the yard, black and white avoided one another, except to taunt or occasionally fight. The number of Latinos, Asians, and Native Americans had increased in the time Keith had been inside, but they were still an ignored minority. Despite the enmity of the black convicts, they weren't the inmates Keith feared the most. Those of his own race posed far more problems for him.

And today, as he pulled wet bed sheets from the giant washer, he sensed a tension in the room, an unusual quiet that raised his hackles. He half-turned, pulling the wash toward the rolling cart, and it was just the smallest of movement in the corner of his eye that alerted him. Wresting his hands from the slimy sheets, he sprang to the side. Too late. Two inmates—two big, sweating creeps over six feet tall—grabbed him by the arms.

"Sonuvabitch! Get offa me!" He elbowed one, heard an oomph, kicked the other. "I said get off!" Someone laughed a deep, choking chuckle. Keith rolled his head right, then left, looking for a guard. No one was in sight.

The putrid-smelling monster on the right grabbed hold of the back of Keith's jumpsuit. With his buddy's help, they turned their captive around and wedged him against the dryer.

Keith shouted. Swore. Kicked. He panted with fatigue, his muscles tight, as he struggled to loosen himself from their grip. To his dismay, a strangled sob came out. "No! I'll have you killed! Get off me." *Keep fighting—no matter what. Fight to the death!*

It was no use. They smashed his face against the top of a hot dryer. His arms were pinned to his sides. Rough hands beat his forehead against the hard surface, and he felt dangerously close to passing out. *God! I've only got a month in here. Please, please, God . . .*

The neck of the back of his jumpsuit suddenly tightened, jerking his head back. A muffled voice said, "What the fuck?"

And then Keith flew across the room, fell over the heap of wet sheets in the rolling basket, and slammed into the bay of washers. He slid down, his head spinning. The last thing he heard sounded strange and made no sense to him: "Hit me here. And don't miss."

A TAN FORD Explorer sat at the side of a dusty logging road two miles north of the Kendall prison. A yellow happy face flag hung from a plastic flag-holder attached to the passenger's side window. Grigor Rossel was glad he didn't have to see the stupid thing. Of all the ridiculous indicators, that one had to be the worst. He would never have picked that for a signal, but he had his orders.

Rossel slumped in the driver's seat, a cigarette in one hand. He thought he saw a flash of movement off in the woods. He reached to pick up a pair of binoculars for what seemed like the hundredth time in the last hour. After a long drag on the last of his cigarette, he crushed it out in the overflowing ashtray and brought the field glasses up. Holding his breath, he peered through the lenses, scanning the forest. There it was — another movement up ahead and to the left. Focusing intently, he watched, waited, wondered . . . then a deer in the gold and tan foliage spooked and leapt away.

The last of the cigarette smoke escaped from his nose and mouth as Rossel exhaled. He spat out a string of Russian expletives, then felt sheepish. He knew it didn't help to be either impatient or angry. He just wished he could reach Gubenko and give him an update. Each time he checked the cell phone in his shirt pocket, the display read "No Service," and he didn't dare use a land line to call. Gubenko had known that the cell might not work in the wilderness; still, Rossel felt upset about it. Being out of contact with Gubenko was not a good thing.

He tossed the binoculars on top of two birding books that rested on the center console, glad no one at the hotel had been paying the slightest bit of attention to him. The place was packed with hikers and birders and tourists admiring the fall colors. Since he was posing as a bird-watcher, nobody seemed to care that he was keeping strangely unconventional hours.

The CB scanner let out a squawk, and he turned down the volume. All had been quiet for most of the night, though he had picked up a series of faint transmissions six hours earlier. Apparently an all-night convenience store on the highway outside Buyck had been held up. For a few brief moments, Rossel had been tense and nervous with the fear that the hired kidnapper had done something stupid. But then he managed to decipher enough of the police dispatch to hear that the two robbers were teenagers. His relief had been palpable.

Truth be told, Rossel was growing more nervous by the hour. It didn't help that he was exhausted. Since Friday night when he'd driven from Chicago to northern Minnesota, his regular sleep patterns had been off. He knew the prison break had to occur under cover of darkness, so since he had arrived, he had roamed the back roads north of the prison from dusk to the next day. By early afternoon each day, he had knocked off, returned to the hotel, and tried to sleep. His thoughts and dreams were troubled with images of his boss's brother. Leonid Gubenko's health had declined. He would not fare well in federal prison, and at his age, he would likely die there long before his sentence was served. Not if Rossel could help it.

So he waited. He lit another cigarette and started the Explorer. Time to move. Time to survey the back roads again. He bit his lip and frowned in frustration as he put the car into drive. Another hour, and then he would return to the hotel for four hours of sleep.

WHEN KEITH AWOKE, lying on a stiff cot, it was all he could do to keep from throwing up. He heard the sound of a distant wake-up buzzer squawking on and on, never stopping, never wavering. As he struggled to consciousness, the sound receded, and after a moment, he realized the sound was in his head. He had a headache that wouldn't quit, and his ears rang. He turned his head from side to side, but it didn't help at all, instead hurting his neck and skull. His face was on fire, and a dull pounding beat at the base of his neck. He reached up, touched his forehead, ran his fingers over his brow. His fingers probed the bone under the skin but found no apparent cracks or dents. The back of his head was another story. He now understood why they called certain lumps goose-eggs. It felt like a thick lump of Silly Putty had oozed out.

In the distance, he heard a dull rasping. It stopped, then started again. *Scrape, scrape, scrape.*

He swung his legs over the side of the cot, sat up, and looked around the dim room. "Shit. Ow." The only light in the room came in through the windows from a sliver of the moon. Part of the window was obscured by the outline of someone – but he couldn't tell who. "Who's there?"

"Shhhh! Shut up!" The form drew nearer. "Just *shut* up."

"Who –"

A hand grabbed his shoulder, and a harsh whisper sounded in his ears: "I said, shut the hell up. You hear me?"

Keith nodded, and when the iron grip released him, he squinted up at the man, trying to figure out who he was.

In nearly three years, Keith had only been to the infirmary wing twice – once for a tetanus shot after cutting his hand open on a shard of metal in a laundry tub, and the other time to get his lungs checked when he had bronchitis. Neither time had he been

admitted; however, now that his eyes had adjusted, he decided
he must be in one of the patient rooms behind the examining
area.

The other man murmured, "You just sit tight. I'll get us out
of here."

"What?" Keith whispered. "What do you mean—out?"

"Out. As in free. Damn fools run this place. Bunch of idiots."
The man moved back toward the window, and a beam of
moonlight passed over his face so that Keith could identify him.
*Bostwick. Oh, no.* Keith stayed as far away from him and his
"friends" as possible. *Oh, my God, I'm stuck in a room with this
vicious animal!* He took a deep breath and looked toward the exit
as the quiet scraping noise resumed. He knew the door would be
shut and locked. Could he get to the door in time to beat on it,
make enough of a scene to alert someone? He doubted it. On
weekends, the infirmary ran a skeleton crew. In fact, the entire
prison was staffed with fewer guards, and many extra security
measures were in place.

Head spinning, Keith slid onto his side and pulled the
blanket up. If he had been unconscious for just a few hours, then
it was likely to be late Saturday night—perhaps Sunday
morning. If Bostwick wanted solitary confinement in the
infirmary, he couldn't have picked a better day to get in a fracas.
*Is he sick? Or did he get involved when the two lugs in the laundry
jumped me?*

"Yes!" Bostwick let out a jubilant whisper, and Keith heard a
thunking sound. A gust of cold air blew across the room, and
Keith shuddered. Bostwick whispered, "C'mon!"

Keith lay shivering on the cold cot, his eyes squeezed shut.

"I said c'mon!" Bostwick made his way around two cots and
stood over Keith. "We're outta here. Let's go."

The temptation was great, but Keith was well aware that he
had only a month left on his sentence. There was no way he
wanted to come so close and then be on the run. The authorities
added on years for escaping—made examples of escapees. He
opened his eyes. "No. You go. I can't—I—can't."

"Get the hell up, Randy," the big man growled.

"You've got me confused with someone else. I'm Keith
Rand—"

"Shut the hell up, little man. I know exactly who you are.
Get up. We're going." Keith shrank away from him, and
Bostwick's face loomed above him. "I saved your ass, Randy,
and you're coming with me."

"But...but my head..."

A big paw grabbed Keith by the front of the jumpsuit and

half-lifted him off the cot. "Get your fuckin' shoes on. We're goin'!"

Keith fell back. A wave of nausea passed over him, and he choked on two dry heaves before Bostwick dropped to his knees and searched around the floor with his hands. Next thing Keith knew, his shabby tennis shoes were being jammed on his bare feet, and Bostwick stood him up.

When Keith teetered, Bostwick lost his patience. "You damn dumbshit! I saved you for a reason. Get your goddamn ass in gear. We're going." Bostwick scurried around, plumping up pillows under blankets on their cots. He rose up to his full height and dragged the reluctant Keith over to the window.

There was hardly any light, but Keith could see how some of the window frame had been removed. The metal mesh on the outside had rusted and broken away from where it was supposed to be fastened, leaving a gap. He didn't think he could fit through it, much less Bostwick who was twice his size, but Bostwick pressed on the rusty latticework, and with a thunk-thunk-thunk sound, the entire bottom came loose and the sides detached. Keith didn't have time to consider the fifteen-foot drop to the outside. Bostwick shoved and pushed him up, then dangled him out and let go. A moment of vertigo, a gasp of fear, and Keith hit the dirt feet first. His legs gave out, and he fell back, splay-legged, then sat forward with his head in his hands. Bostwick wormed his way out the window and dropped down. Keith just barely rolled out of the way before the big man landed where he had been sitting.

Outside, the temperature was a good twenty degrees colder than in the chilly infirmary. Keith shivered and groaned. Something warm and unrelenting grabbed his wrist and dragged him to his feet, and then he was running, gasping, head pounding, trying to keep from throwing up. He looked for the fence and didn't see it anywhere. He looked back toward the prison once, suddenly realizing that the back wall of the infirmary was the only spot anywhere on the prison grounds without fencing. Instead, the high electrical fences abutted the back corners of the building, but the rear wall was not enclosed. His last thought before he turned his attention to their reckless departure through the forest was: *What idiot is responsible for that design?*

# Chapter
# Eight

JAYLYNN CAUGHT SIGHT of a flash of orange as she bent over the stack of firewood. With one chunk of kindling in hand, she straightened and gazed into the woods, beyond the dark tangles of roots and the shedding trees. Glancing over her shoulder, she saw Dez squatting next to the fire, which gave off puffs of gray smoke. She looked back to the woods, puzzled, then shrugged. *Must be a Baltimore Oriole.* She picked up another stick of wood and moved over to the fire, standing right next to Dez, and watched as her partner arranged wood and kindling, nursing a fledgling flame to life.

In a low voice Dez asked, "You think those two are ever gonna roll out?"

"Good question. I hope they're careful since their tent isn't looking so good. I think it needs some serious attention." She could tell Shayna and Crystal had been together a lot longer than she and Dez. No cries and whispers from *their* tent the night before. She smiled sheepishly. But Crystal had done a much poorer job pitching their tent last night than she had the first day out. Jaylynn didn't know what was wrong, but it looked none too sturdy.

Dez rose, towering over Jaylynn, and put an arm around her. Jaylynn snuggled in and surveyed the two tents on either side of the clearing. Dez's pale blue-and-gray lightweight tent was solidly anchored, the lines taut and the roof a straight line. The roof of Crystal and Shayna's red-and-black two-man tent sagged in the middle, and if Jaylynn didn't miss her guess, they hadn't pitched it square. She didn't think it was supposed to have a diamond shape, and she wondered how, when they moved on to another site, she or Dez could offer to help set it up properly without offending them.

The black zipper made a ripping noise as it opened. A booted leg emerged from the tent, and the rest of Crystal followed. Visibly shivering, she said, "Good morning, *chicas*."

From inside the tent came a plaintive wail. "It's free-ee-zing out there, Crys."

Even from a distance, Jaylynn could see Crystal roll her eyes as she strode toward the fire. Without responding to Shayna, Crystal squatted and rubbed her hands together near the flames. "Anybody got a shoehorn to help me get her out of that sleeping bag?"

Smiling, Dez pointed at one of the two packs hanging from a tree off to the side. "Once we get some coffee and food going, I think she'll come around."

"I can only hope so," Crystal said. She and Dez went over to the guy line and lowered the packs as Jaylynn rooted around in another bag which, among other things, contained a lightweight frying pan and cooking utensils.

As she opened up one of the big packs, Dez said, "I checked the water purifier, and it worked great."

"That's a relief," Crystal said, "though how Shayna is going to hold up without Pepsi is beyond me."

"I heard that!" Shayna's corn-rowed head popped out of the tent. She stepped out, adjusting the waistband on her jeans. "I had no idea how damn uncomfortable this camping BS would be. It's bad enough doing all that hiking, and now I've got kinks in my back that will take my chiropractor weeks to work out."

Jaylynn held up a spatula. "Look at the bright side. Once we eat a hearty breakfast, all of our packs will be lighter."

Shayna bent and reached inside the tent. "Yeah, Crystal's will be lighter right now." She stood, holding up a deep blue can, popped the top, and took a swig. "It's warm, but who cares."

Crystal stood, hands on hips. "Well, shit. No wonder my pack was heavier than I thought it should be. How the hell many cans of Pepsi did you bring?"

"One, honey, just one." Shayna took another sip. "And it was worth all the heartbreaking work you had to do." Grinning impishly, she shuffled over to the fire, her arms tight against her chest and one hand cradling the can. She lowered herself to a log and, at the tail end of a big yawn, gasped out, "What kind of bark and twigs are you serving for breakfast, Dez, honey?"

"Oh, brother," Dez said. "You're a piece of work, Shay."

"I know." She beamed at all of them. "At least I woke up in a good mood."

"Right," Jaylynn said, "God knows what we'd do if you

were all growly and snarly." She looked down at the pan in one
hand and the spatula in the other. "Let's get to work. At the rate
we're going, it'll be noon before we get out of here."

Half an hour later, they sat on logs close to the fire juggling
cups of instant coffee and paper plates stacked high with
scrambled eggs and hot reconstituted potatoes. Jaylynn took a
big bite and swallowed. "Not bad for that packaged crap."

Dez nodded. "You add a little fresh air, some smoke from
the fire and—"

"And good friends," Jaylynn said.

"Yup. It's a good recipe." Dez nodded and wolfed down the
last of her breakfast. "Later, if anyone's hungry, I've got the
world-famous Reilly Gorp, made with fresh raisins and even
fresher M&Ms."

"Gorp?" Shayna asked. "What's that? Goo mixed with
slop?"

Dez raised an eyebrow. "Good Ol' Raisins and Peanuts,
actually. But I add some other goodies."

Crystal sighed. "I'm sure I was carrying pounds of that in
my pack, too, right?"

"Nope," Dez said. "Actually, I'm packing the Gorp."

Jaylynn rose and collected the plastic forks and paper plates
from everyone. "Allow me to do the dishes." She tossed the
plates into the fire, tucked the white forks into the pocket of her
coat, and picked up the still-warm frying pan. "I'll be back. This
pan and I have a date by the stream."

Shayna said, "Sure you don't need help, honey?" then let out
a guffaw.

Over her shoulder, Jaylynn hollered, "You can do the next
round." She cut through the trees and onto a path covered in
pine needles. With every step she took, the flow of the water
sounded louder. Taking a deep breath, she let contentment flow
through her. *One more nice, long walk, then we get to the hotel. Soon
after, it's just me and Dez again, snuggling in a queen-size bed.*

She squatted next to the stream, careful not to get her boots
wet. Burnt eggs and pasty potatoes clung to the side of the pan,
and she let out a sigh of exasperation at having forgotten to
bring something to scrub with.

She tensed to rise, and in that instant knew something was
wrong. Before she could turn around, she smelled him. Bitter
body odor and then something cold and pointy jabbing her in the
back of the neck as she was grabbed around the middle, her arms
pinned to her sides.

A raspy voice next to her ear said, "Not a sound. *Not a word.*
There's five of us, and the other four'll do your friends." He

jerked her tighter and lifted her off the ground, slung her around in front of him, and trudged up the slope.

"You're hurting me." She tried to say it with anger, not fear, but it came out with less punch than she would have liked. He didn't respond. She looked at the bulging muscle in his forearm and the hand that held the cold metal tent stake to her throat, and suddenly it all made sense — the orange flash in the woods, Crystal and Shayna's sloppy-looking tent. She let out a yowl.

"Shut up!" He stopped at the edge of the clearing. Already Dez was on her feet, hastening their way. He brought her to a complete standstill with just one calm sentence: "Stop or I'll stab the bitch."

Jaylynn felt his rapid intake of air and even his heart beating against her back. His stench wafted over her again. Coupled with the tight grasp he had around her middle, she gagged, tasting eggs and fear in the back of her throat. Dez stood, shocked and white, halfway between them and the fire where Shayna and Crystal sat looking dazed.

"What do you want?" Dez said in a quiet, deadly voice.

The man didn't answer. He let out a loud whistle. "Randy! Get out here."

A rustle and the sound of footfalls came from the west side of the clearing. A compact man, also in an orange jumpsuit, burst into view. He stood tense and quivering, his eyes darting from person to person.

Jaylynn winced when the raspy voice hollered in her ear. "Goddammit, Randy! Follow the plan." He bent forward slightly, crushing her ribcage, and she groaned in pain. "The rest of you, get down on the ground. On your knees with your hands on your heads." When nobody moved, he yelled, "I said, get on your knees or I'll kill her!" The three women dropped to their knees, but only Shayna put her hands on her head.

The smaller man gave the kneeling women a wide berth as he headed to a pack and dumped out the contents. Hands grasping like a madman's, he hunted through the items. He gave a shout of success once, then again. "Better than you thought, Bostwick."

Bostwick let out a growl. "I don't need a fuckin' analysis. Just hurry up."

Dez, looking poised to spring, asked once more, "What do you want?"

"Shut up. You'll find out soon enough."

Jaylynn's eyes scanned the campsite, the tree line ahead of her, and as much of the forest as she could see. *Liar! There aren't five of them.*

She got a look at the smaller man, Randy. From what she could see, his face looked like hamburger — like he'd been in one hell of a fight. He rose and carried a handful of things across the clearing and dropped them off to Jaylynn's left. She craned her neck to see, and all the air went out of her when she realized that not only were there two jackknives and the hatchet in the pile, but also the Neoprene bag containing Dez's .45 Colt. *Oh, shit, why did she bring that? Why?* She watched as the skinny man peeled back the Velcro and pulled out the gun.

Bostwick said, "Gimme it, Randy. Don't be slinging it around like that. Check to see if it's loaded." He reared back, nearly giving Jaylynn whiplash. "Jesus! Don't you know how a gun works? Yeah, yeah, there ya go. Okay, bring it here and give it to me."

Jaylynn waited, rigid and ready. When the thin man passed in front of her, she planned to lever herself up to kick him, throw him off balance. She knew Dez would be on them in a heartbeat. *Even if I get cut, we'd have a better chance.* She glanced toward her partner. Eyes wide, Dez had a look on her face as though she was doing all she could not to spring up and attack. Jaylynn was certain Dez knew just what to do. *If only we can get our timing right.*

But the man gave Jaylynn a respectful margin of space, stepping around behind them, and coming up on the big man's right side. Before Jaylynn had a chance to act, the metal was gone, and instead, the barrel of the gun pressed into the soft spot behind her ear. She could actually see Dez's shoulders slump a little. Jaylynn made a face and mouthed, "Sorry." In response, Dez shook her head and frowned.

"Here's how this is going down, ladies. Listen up." Bostwick took two steps closer. "On your bellies. All three of you. Face down. Fingers laced together behind your back. Now! Don't make me shoot her. Lay down! Do what I say, and everybody gets out of here alive."

Jaylynn watched Dez's slow descent, eyes locked with her partner. She took in Dez's expression — the helplessness and utter desperation. Over her own panic, she tried to send back: *I'm okay, Dez. I'll be okay.* Dez arranged herself on the ground with her arms behind her and her back arched, head up.

"Randy, pull the stuff out of the two tents, then cut some of the tent line to tie 'em up with."

The smaller man scowled. "How many times do I have to tell you? My name is Keith, not Randy."

Bostwick grinned, his straight, even teeth looking out of place in his crooked mouth. "I don't give a shit, Randy. Just do your job."

Keith trotted over to the blue-and-gray tent and hauled out sleeping bags and piled them in a heap, then did the same to the other tent. He had to scurry back across the campsite for a jackknife.

His fellow inmate let out a sigh of exasperation. "Geez, are you stupid or what? Hurry up. We ain't got all day."

Jaylynn watched the tents collapse, and in seconds, Keith had several lengths of nylon cord. The man tightened his grip and jammed the barrel of the gun even harder against Jaylynn's head. She closed her eyes and tried to suck in a deep breath.

He said, "Tie up the big one first."

Keith looked toward the two women by the fire, then at Dez, obviously confused as to who the "big one" was. "Which one do you mean? They're *all* big."

"You stupid shit!" The man squeezed, forcing air from Jaylynn's lungs. She gasped as he screamed, "That one! The dangerous-looking one. Do her first—then the other two."

Keith hastened to do his bidding, and Bostwick relaxed enough to allow Jaylynn to suck in a breath of acrid, foul-smelling air.

Dez's eyes glittered. "You don't have to do this. If you want our stuff, just take it. Take it all, and leave us be. We promise we'll—"

"Shut up!"

"Please," Jaylynn gasped out. "Take it all, but—"

He slid his arm lower and jerked her upward. "Shut up." To his companion, he said, "Just do it, Randy. And don't let her pull any tricks. Hey, you! Amazon woman! Don't get any bright ideas. I don't give a shit if you jump Randy or kill him, but I bet you'll care if I blow away Blondie here." With his lips next to Jaylynn's ear, he muttered, "And you just keep quiet."

For the next agonizing minutes, Jaylynn could do nothing but watch and wait until her friends' hands and feet were tied, and they all lay facedown in the dirt. Shayna let her corn-rowed braids cover her face, but Jaylynn could tell she was crying silent tears. *Oh, Shayna, only a little while, and then they'll take our stuff and go.* Once the inmates were done, she thought she'd be trussed up and tossed into the clearing, too.

Once the small man finished his work, he rose and sorted through a backpack, pulling things out one at a time, and finally dumping the contents onto the ground. "Oh, look. Some duct tape."

"Too bad you didn't find that earlier, Einstein. Lots quicker than rope. Go wrap some of that around their hands. While you're at it, slap a piece over the big one's mouth. Hell, tape all their fat mouths shut."

Jaylynn saw Dez trying to inch away, but it did no good. The slim man leaned down with the duct tape. Dez spoke softly to him, but Jaylynn couldn't hear what she said. Obviously over her objections, Keith managed to cover her mouth with a strip of silver duct tape. Once Dez was silenced, Jaylynn's fear increased, and shooting pains ripped through her stomach.

When all three women were gagged, Bostwick relaxed his hold and came into the center of the clearing to the left of the fire. Jaylynn gave a mighty roar and tried to break free, but he just laughed and pulled her closer. "Not nice, you little pissant. Be good. Just remember, if you run, I'll put a bullet in the back of each of their heads. You don't want that, now, do ya?"

A thread of intense hatred boiled up from within Jaylynn. She hadn't even seen the man's face, and already she wished him dead. *If he gives me one opportunity, I swear I'll blow him away. I will.* The intensity of her feelings and the pressure on her midsection made her stomach roil. "No," she gasped. He laughed, as if he thought she was answering his question, but her stomach convulsed, and a warm rush of bile and coffee, eggs, and soft potatoes came up. Next thing she knew, she'd thrown up on his arm and down the front of her jacket.

"Eeew, shit!" he hollered. He loosened his hold for just a moment, and she squirmed free.

Through the duct tape, Dez let out a strangled yowl. Jaylynn heard it, but her legs had a will of their own, and she was already diving toward her partner. It was the click that brought her up short. On her knees, she clutched Dez's coat and peered upward.

Bostwick, looking like a six-foot-tall traffic cone, loomed above them both, the revolver cocked and pointed at Dez's head. His dark eyes burned in a head that seemed too small for the size of his body. His bald scalp, patchy with psoriasis, looked like someone had raked across it more than once with a dull razor. Both his upper and lower lips were split and healing, but the jagged red lines gave his face a frightening cast. In a calm, reasonable voice, he asked Jaylynn, "Is this what you want?"

Panting, tasting sour eggs, she shook her head.

"Get away from her now. Away." With a soft whistle, he summoned Keith. "You need to tie Blondie's hands. In front. Just duct tape her."

"Legs, too?"

"No."

"But—"

"She's coming with us." Still gripping the gun, the big man turned and stalked away toward the black-and-red tent.

Keith grabbed the roll of tape. There hadn't been much to begin with, and now it contained only another yard or two at most. He waited for Jaylynn to rise. With a worried frown, he asked, "You're not going to blow chips again, are you?"

She gulped and shook her head, knowing there was nothing left in her to vomit.

"Here," he said. He reached down and picked up a dirty t-shirt poking out of one of the packs. With surprising gentleness, he wiped away a streak of yellowish crud from the front of her coat. "That wouldn't smell so good in a few hours." He dropped the shirt. "All right. Hold out your hands." In a quiet voice, he said, "Geez, these coat sleeves are bulky. I can't really tape you up well."

He peered into her eyes, and for the first time, she got a look at him. *Good Lord, he's younger than Kevin.* And he reminded her of her good friend Kevin, too—same blond hair and blue eyes. He was much fairer-complected, as though he rarely got into the sun. Along with dark half-moons under his eyes, he had a fist-sized purple bruise on his left cheek, a big lump on his forehead, and some older bruising on the left side of his jaw.

"Hey, miss," he whispered. "Are you okay?" She nodded but didn't say a word, and he rattled on. "It'll be damn cold at night if . . . if this goes on that long, so I'm not going to make you take your coat off. Put your hands out like you're praying."

He wrapped two turns of tape around her wrists, half-covering the base of her palms, while whispering, "Don't get me in trouble. Just cooperate. He's not so bad if you cooperate." He grabbed her arm and tugged her toward Dez's collapsed tent where Bostwick was busy sorting through things.

Without turning around, Bostwick said, "We need to get a move on, Randy. Take that pack and fill it with food and any clothes you find. And while we're at it . . ."

He rose and tucked the gun inside his jumpsuit, then opened a jackknife and strode over to Crystal. He cut the cords tying her feet together, set down the knife, and reached to unbutton her Levi jeans. He was on the second button when Jaylynn saw what he was doing. "No!" she screamed. "No!" She flew across the clearing and launched herself at the big man's back. Using her taped hands like a hatchet, she hit him twice before he easily shrugged her off, laughing, then smacked her face with a huge paw and knocked her down. "I'm not planning on screwing her, Blondie. She's definitely not my type. You, on the other hand . . ." He stood leering, then closed his eyes, swallowed, shook his head.

His eyes popped back open. "No time for that now. If you're feeling so protective, *you* take her pants off. I want the pants." He stood and unzipped his orange jumpsuit. "Now!" he shouted. "I want 'em now!"

She looked up at him in amazement, then at her tethered wrists.

"Oh, shit," he said. He bent and picked up the knife. "Gimme." She extended her arms, trying to hide the fact that they were shaking, and he cut the tape. With the hand holding the knife, he patted inside his half-unzipped jumpsuit and located the gun. "Don't do anything funny or I'll blow away one of these friends of yours." He stood waiting as Jaylynn helped Crystal shrug her way out of her jeans.

"I'm so sorry," Jaylynn whispered, and a tear fell. Crystal's brown eyes looked at her with understanding, and she shook her head. Jaylynn was certain her Latina friend was telling her *Don't cry — don't give them the satisfaction of seeing you cry.* She wiped her eyes and said, "I won't cry anymore." Crystal nodded. "Oooo oh, errr." Even through the tape, she was certain Crystal had said, "You go, girl."

Bostwick said, "Hey! Tape her ankles again. Now."

Jaylynn shouted, "We can't leave her bare-legged. She'll —"

The roll of tape hit her in the chest. "Shut the *fuck* up. I don't need any girlie bullshit from you. Now do it!"

Jaylynn picked up the roll and wrapped a loop of duct tape around the Crystal's ankles, making sure to get as much dirt as possible on the adhesive. When she finished, all the tape was gone. She left Crystal shivering in the dirt and handed the pants to the tall man. He stepped out of his orange suit, wearing only shoes, socks, briefs, and a sweat-yellowed t-shirt. His legs slid into the jeans, and he pulled them up roughly. They fit fine around his waist but were at least three inches too short. He didn't seem to notice. After buttoning them, he rearranged the pistol in the front and went over to squat down by the sleeping bags Keith had heaped into a pile outside Dez's tent.

Jaylynn hovered, nervous, still sick to her stomach. She peeled the remaining strips of tape off her wrists and backs of her hands and thought, *What do I do? How do we get out of this?*

When the man rose, he tried to pull on a dark green sweatshirt belonging to Jaylynn, and she felt the rage surge in her again. *Who does he think he is? He can't take our things. How dare he!* When he found the arms too tight, he dropped it and donned Dez's blue sweatshirt instead.

"Jesus Christ, Randy. You gonna wear that fuckin' orange monkey suit all day? Find some clothes to change into!"

Keith's gaze darted around the campsite. "But they don't have anything."

"Don't you get it? We're sitting ducks in this color. Get some different pants. Take 'em off the big one if you have to." He turned away and bent over the food packs.

From the other side of the fire, Dez writhed and made growling noises, but Jaylynn couldn't tell what she was saying. She had a hunch, though. No way would Dez surrender her pants. She had another idea. "Wait! Keith, I think I can help." She hustled over to the pile of things in front of the tent and grabbed at the sleeping bags. She and Dez had zipped theirs together to sleep in, and for a moment, as she thought of the previous night's comfort, a sob of fear rose in her throat. She pushed it down and reached into the bag, searching until she found her flannel pajama bottoms stuffed inside. "These may fit you. They're baggy, and the waist is elastic."

He snatched them from her and headed toward the edge of the clearing.

"Hey, loser!" Bostwick shouted. "Where in the hell you think you're going?"

Keith's mouth dropped open, and from where she stood, Jaylynn could see his bruised face flood with red. "But...but I gotta change."

"Bullshit. We ain't got time for your fuckin' modesty, pretty boy. Shuck off the prison suit, and make it fast. How many times I gotta tell you, we ain't got all day?"

Keith did exactly as he was told. The gray-and-blue flannel pants fit tight around the waist, but he didn't seem to care. He stood shivering in a dingy t-shirt and the prison-issue tennis shoes as he rolled the suit into an orange ball. His hand twisted at the cloth, and his face remained red and angry. He stalked toward the dying fire and dropped in the orange wad, which sat amidst the dying embers, nearly squelching the fire.

All the while, Jaylynn had been edging across the clearing, moving closer to Dez. The big man's back was to her. She thought that if she could get near her partner, she could figure out a way to free her.

Bostwick rose to his full height and shouldered a pack. "Get your ass in gear, loser. I've got food here. Find another sweatshirt — or take a jacket off one of them."

Keith muttered, "You should've thought of that when you had me tie them up."

"What?"

The blond man turned away and went to rummage again. He came up with a flannel shirt of Crystal's. It bagged on him, but he buttoned it anyway. The red and white clashed with the pattern of his pants. Jaylynn thought he looked like a little Scottish dog gone crazy. A gust of cool wind hit her, and she stood in the middle of the clearing, shivering, still feeling shock and disbelief, while watching Keith unzip and roll up one sleeping bag, then another. He crammed them into Dez's emptied pack and put a variety of other items into another pack, which he shouldered. He picked up the two half-full canteens in the pile of stuff outside Crystal's tent and slung them over his shoulder. "I'm ready, I think," he said. "Here, put this on." He handed the large pack to Bostwick who threaded his arms into it and got it settled comfortably.

Bostwick, in his high-water pants, pulled the gun out of his waistband and checked the ammunition. He tucked it back in again and gave a toss of his head. "Take their boots."

Keith frowned. "I looked. None of them will fit me . . . or you."

"No, you stupid shit. You think they're just going to lay here and let the wildlife eat 'em? Minute we leave, they'll get free. Might take 'em an hour or two, but without shoes, we'll buy some time ahead of the cops."

Before Bostwick's explanation was finished, Keith was already kneeling at Shayna's side to untie her hiking boots. Dez tried to resist, but it was no use. In moments, he had all three pairs dangling from their shoestrings. He made his way over to them on the south side of the clearing, stopping only to bend and pick up a jackknife and the hatchet lying on the ground. He pointed at Jaylynn. "Should I take hers, too?"

"Of all the guys I get stuck with, it's gotta be an idiot? No, you stupid shit. Her boots stay on so she can walk." Bostwick cuffed Jaylynn on the back of the head. "Let's go, Blondie. You can carry something, too. Give her the boots, pal."

He glanced around the campsite, then stopped, wrinkles forming on his patchy forehead. He brought his index finger to his lower lip and tapped it. "So you girls hiked in. From where?"

Jaylynn wouldn't meet his eyes. She clenched her fists, trying to remember to breathe. *I won't tell. I won't.* She took heart in knowing that on the other side of the smothering fire, Dez's eyes followed her every move.

"Where'd you park, Blondie? Where!" He stomped toward the black and red tent and put the gun to Crystal's head. As though asking a child, he said, "Want me to start with her? You tell me now. All we want's the car or . . ." He took the pistol grip in both hands and waited, a cruel smirk on his lips.

Jaylynn met Crystal's brown eyes. In a voice hardly louder

than a whisper, she said, "We came in off the trail south of Lake Jeanette."

Dez's body went into convulsions. She managed to roll onto her side, tuck long legs under her, and rise to her knees. Bostwick strode across the clearing, backhanded her with his forearm and knocked her over. "Ah-ah-ah." He shook his finger at her. "Now cut it out. You're not following the rules." He turned and smiled at Jaylynn. "But you are, Blondie. That's more like it. Where are the car keys?"

*Can't give them the Jeep keys.* As though sleepwalking, Jaylynn moved away from Crystal's gear and to the jumble of things near Dez's blue-and-gray tent. She found her little canvas bathroom bag and unzipped a side pocket to remove her keychain. Biting her lip, she threw the keys at the man with all the strength she could muster.

He laughed when they hit him dead center in the chest and fell to the ground. The deep rumbling of his amusement went on longer than Jaylynn thought she could bear it. "I like a spirited woman. Yes, I do." He bent and picked up the keys. "Which way, bitch?"

Without a word, Jaylynn pointed east.

The man glanced toward his partner in crime. "Let's go. You, too, Blondie. We've got miles to travel."

THE MOMENT THE men left the campsite, dragging Jaylynn with them, Crystal rolled toward Dez, who was doing the same thing. Pebbles and sticks cut into her bare legs, but Crystal could think of nothing but her kidnapped friend. The vision of the brave, but shaken Jaylynn scared the hell out of her. What would those men do to her? Crystal didn't want to consider it. She and Dez had to get free. Go after them. Now.

Dez's eyes were wild and her face redder than Crystal had ever seen it. In her haste to get to Crystal, she had very nearly rolled through flames. The orange jumpsuit had finally caught fire and blazed merrily. It was clear Dez didn't care.

Inches from one another, Dez made oomphing and growling noises. She sat up, in profile to Crystal, and bobbed her head, then kicked up her bound legs, leaning more to the left than the right. Dez turned away from Crystal, kicked her legs up, and awkwardly tried to point with her bound hands.

"Mmm..." Crystal said as understanding came. She saw the lump in the side pocket of Dez's cargo pants. *Dez's Leatherman. They didn't get that!* With difficulty, she used her right elbow to lever herself up onto her knees and felt a sharp rock grind into her kneecap. She lifted the pierced knee and shifted. Just then, the tape on her ankles broke free. She let out a muted squeal uncharacteristic of her while silently thanking Jaylynn for the poor tape job she had done. Dez's head jerked around to stare with such intensity that Crystal's glee turned to a sinking feeling in her stomach. "I'm trying, I'm trying," she mumbled, but the words came out garbled by the tape, and she knew Dez hadn't a clue what she was saying.

With the tape loosened and pulling away, Crystal managed to kick apart her legs and stand. Shayna continued to wriggle her way over, too, and once she drew near, she lay panting on her left side, a look of hope on her face.

Crystal winked at her, then inched over to Dez, her bare calf against Dez's knee. Like a contortionist, she twisted until her bound hands came in contact with Dez's trousers. She groped for the edge of the pocket, found it, and pulled until the Velcro attachment ripped open. Thighs burning, breath coming out in snorts, she squeezed her hand into the pocket and felt the leather surface of the knife holder. Once she had it firmly in her grasp, she turned, feeling triumphant.

"Grrr-eeee!" Dez shouted through the tape.

*I am hurrying. I am.* Crystal worked her fingers under the snap and popped it open. *Why the hell did she have to get such a damned fancy thing?* She thought a long string of Spanish expletives as she struggled. Her hand felt cold and awkward, her fingers numb, but she got the metal tool to slide out. The case fell to the ground. Sweating and swearing, she managed to flip open the Leatherman and fumble for the various tools. With her hands so tight together, it took longer than she expected, but soon she had the blade out, locked in place, and clutched in a death grip.

She shifted on her knees again and sidled back toward Dez, who at the same time rolled over, facedown. They jockeyed to get lined up. Shayna scrambled over until she lay half curled around Dez's head. Crystal met her eyes, and Shayna tossed her head left. Crystal moved, and Shayna nodded in excitement. The tip of the knife touched something. Shayna's eyes widened as she tucked her chin against her chest and made deep guttural sounds. Crystal took that to mean to go lower, so she did, and then Shayna let out a squeal, widened her eyes, and raised her chin up and back.

*Ah, I see.* Crystal smiled behind the tape. *I'll follow your lead, sweetie. Keep talking.*

Minutes passed. Up and down she cut, up and down. Once Shayna wheezed in a quick breath, and Crystal knew she'd cut flesh, but not a sound came from Dez.

FOR DEZ, IT felt like eternities passed. Neck straining, body tense, she lay facedown trying her best to stay still. Something burned along her wrist, and she knew she'd been cut, but she didn't move. And then with a sudden snap of the cord, she was free. She nearly knocked her friend over in her haste to rise, and Crystal fumbled and dropped the knife.

Dez ripped the tape off her mouth. "Aaaah! I'll kill them!" She grabbed up the knife and sawed at the rope and duct tape binding her legs. "Oh, shit. Oh, shit, Crys." She panted as though she'd run a sprint. "We gotta hurry."

"Mmm!" Crystal shifted around and met Dez's eyes. "Mmm!"

Dez reached up, dug her fingernails into Crystal's face, and none too gently ripped away the silver tape. "Owwww! Get me loose, Dez. Hurry."

Two minutes later, all of them were free of their bonds.

"Gotta go . . . got to . . ." As adrenaline pumped through her system, Dez bit her tongue to keep from babbling incoherently. She was sweating and shaking so much, she could hardly close the Leatherman. She stuffed it in her pocket and started across the clearing. "I'll track 'em. You get the cops."

"Wait, wait, for cripesake. Wait, Dez." Crystal launched herself at her friend and grabbed her by the arm. "Stop! You're bleeding."

"It's nothing." Dez glanced down at her wrist. What was Crystal thinking, trying to detain her over a superficial slice that only needed a Band-Aid? Hadn't they lost enough time? Furious, Dez shrugged her friend off, but Crystal was never easily intimidated.

Wrenching at Dez's jacket, she yelled, "Listen to me. Three minutes, Dez. A three-minute plan. You need shoes. Water. And a gun."

"They took my damn gun." Dez pictured the Colt Commander with its wooden stock. A shock of rage shot through her. "That was my dad's gun."

Crystal gave a wicked half-smile and pulled Dez back to the now-dying embers of the fire. "They didn't get mine. Stand here and calm down. I'll go get it, okay?"

Dez couldn't trust herself to speak. The urge to lash out was as powerful as the urge to run. Struggling to control both, she watched Crystal cross the clearing and scramble into the tent, grumbling as she raked one bare leg painfully along the zipper. Dez heard her rooting about for what seemed like forever. Impatient, she strode over just as a pair of solid legs emerged from the flap. Backing out on her knees, Crystal held a lumpy

Neoprene case aloft.

"Oh, God, thank you." Dez reached for the weapon.

Crystal eluded her and stood up. "It's only my little Beretta."

"I don't care. It's something. Give it to me." She took a step toward the shorter woman, barely able to suppress the urge to shove her and grab the gun. But something in Crystal's eyes penetrated the fog of anger that had engulfed her. With a shock of awareness, Dez saw herself, poised and ready to lash out like a wounded animal. A terrible swell of emotion rose in her. Clenching her fists, she tipped back her head, and let out a long, throaty bellow that reverberated through the trees surrounding them. As the noise subsided, she met Crystal's fearful gaze, and said very quietly, "Just give me the gun. We don't have time for this."

"We *do* have time. Time enough, Dez." Instead of backing away, Crystal touched Dez's arm. "She bought us time with the lie about where we parked."

Dez shook her head and took a deep breath, forcing herself to think like a sane woman instead of the cornered animal she felt like. Crystal was right. Jaylynn had given them—and herself— a fighting chance. "I can't believe she told them the Jeep was at the Lake Jeanette Entrance. That's ten, fifteen miles away."

"Yes, but that's good, Dez. Smart of her. She gave us the time we need."

"But what the hell will they do to her when they find she's lied?" She brushed a hank of dark hair out of her face. "C'mon, let's go."

Shayna hurried around the clearing, cursing and muttering. She shouted, "Wait just one damn minute, Dez." She set several items on the ground and picked up the big convict's smelly orange jumpsuit. "Gawd, this stinks." She glanced toward the other two women. Crystal stood shivering in sweatshirt, underwear, and socks. "You want to wear this?"

"No! Gross!" Crystal answered. "I've got some lightweight long underwear." She moved to help Shayna root around in the mess of clothing outside their tent. "Here they are." She set the gun next to her foot, quickly stuck one leg in, and shimmied the thermal-wear up her legs one at a time.

"Hurry, Crys!" Dez looked at her watch, panic rising once more. "They're getting too far ahead of us. Listen. The three-minute plan is this. You haul ass to the Jeep and get help. I have to reach Jay before they get to the Lake Jeanette area. When they find out she lied—"

"Dammit, don't worry. We'll get there." Pulling at the skintight bottoms, Crystal winced. "Where's the map?" Dez patted her right cargo pocket and Crystal nodded. "Get it out."

Dez removed it with shaking hands. "I'll take the topo and you can have the trail map. I know the area well enough to get by."

Crystal handed her the weapon in exchange, saying, "Strap this around your waist. You do *not* want to lose it. There are only a few extra bullets in the front pouch."

Dez took the gun and immediately felt some confidence return. Maybe she didn't have backup or any other weapons but her wits, but this one small gun was something. "Okay. You and Shayna run like hell, and I'll track those assholes. Jaylynn will know to leave signs. You get back down the trail as fast as you can."

But Crystal was looking at her strangely. "We're in socks. Shit, Dez, listen to me. *You're* in socks!"

"They'll ditch our boots."

Crystal nodded. "That's right. Bet they won't keep them long. Jaylynn will drop them somewhere obvious when they aren't looking. Let's go together until we find where they dumped 'em." She shouted, "Shayna, let's go."

"I'm ready." Shayna thrust a backpack at her and said, "Here, I put a canteen of water in with all that Gorp of yours. Do *not* add stream water without the purification tabs. You've got the compass and matches, socks, first aid kit, a Gore-Tex hat, one of the dead cell phones, other things. I just grabbed stuff you might need. If any of it's too heavy, ditch it on the trail."

"Thanks, Shay." Dez felt her eyes prickle with unshed tears. Shayna reached out to pat her arm.

Crystal said, "Wait. The keys, Dez. I need to find my car keys. They were in the tent where my gun was."

"I'll get 'em." Shayna fell to her knees on the trampled tent and rooted madly through the piles of stuff surrounding the collapsed tent. "Here they are!" She threw the keys.

Dez leaned forward to catch them. "Enough talk. I'm going." She tossed the key ring to Crystal, who caught the jingling metal and looked at Shayna helplessly. Dez didn't have time for any further discussion. She turned and ran for the trees, thankful to be moving at last.

Dez could hear them shuffling swiftly behind her as she reached the nearly leafless maples. In her mind's eye, she pictured Jaylynn out there somewhere, terrified but also trusting her. She would know that Dez was coming for her, and being Jay, she would do whatever it took to survive until then. Of that,

Dez was certain. She sent the love of her life a silent message. *Be strong. I love you. I'm coming.*

# Chapter
# Nine

**Kendall Correctional Facility**
**Outside Buyck, Minnesota**
**Sunday, October 17, 7:07 a.m.**

A DUSTY RED half-ton Chevy pickup wheeled into the parking lot at the Kendall Medium-Security Correctional Facility and screeched to a halt in its regular parking space. Assistant Administrator Ralph Soames slid out, slammed the door, and walked hastily to the administration entrance. He knew he was late, and he was mad at himself for leaving his briefcase in the entryway at home. Now he would have to go back home at lunch to get the paperwork he needed. He was glad his boss was on vacation, though he envied the fact that Mike Martin and his wife were currently on a cruise in the Bahamas.

He stopped on the walkway halfway between the truck and gate to tug on his tie. It didn't feel right. He attempted to tighten it properly, but he needed a mirror to see whether it was crooked or not. Letting out a tired sigh, he decided none of the guards would care. With the Chief Administrator gone, everyone relaxed and let things go. With a final tug at the tie, he moved once more toward the entrance, but before he took two steps, a sound like a giant squawk came from the outdoor loudspeakers, and then all went silent. For one brief half-second, Soames was flooded with relief. Just an errant noise from the alarm system, he tried to tell himself, but then the ear-splitting wail blasted out, startling him, hurting his ears, nearly giving him a heart attack.

*Oh, shit. Someone's dead on my watch. Or escaped. Oh, God.*

"WHAT DO YOU mean, you don't know when they got out?" Ralph Soames gaze went back and forth between Morris and Schecter, two of the prison's security guards.

The two men studied the ground.

Soames grabbed at his tie, loosening the knot as he took a deep breath. His face was hot, and the pulse beating in his forehead actually hurt. "Goddammit, this is a disaster. How could you let this happen? Where's Buddy Boldt?"

Schecter and Morris both looked up. Morris frowned. "Buddy went home early. He was sick."

"And so did Franklin," Schecter hurried to say. "We got stuck here on double shifts, Mr. Soames. You gotta understand, we were seriously short of staff."

"Why the hell didn't you call me?"

Morris shrugged. "Why bug you? We thought we could handle it."

"Jesus, Mary, and Joseph! You sure enough did handle it! How did they get out?"

"Infirmary window, sir," Schecter said.

"And why the hell were they in the infirmary to begin with?"

Morris let out a sigh. "Big fight in the laundry. I'd stepped into the restroom. I wasn't gone more than two minutes, and when I came back, the two men were on the floor. Out cold. The doc drove in from town, gave them both a once-over around supper. Randall was in worse shape, but Bostwick looked pretty bad, too. In fact, the doc said he'd stop by this morning sometime." He checked his watch. "Should be here soon, in fact."

Soames asked, "When was the last bed check?" Neither man met his eye, and Soames had to force himself not to shout. "You didn't do any head counts?"

Schecter said, "Cursory, sir. They were cursory."

"What the hell does that mean? You look me in the eye and tell me what the hell you mean!"

Morris glanced up a brief instant, then seemed to deflate. "We did the hourly rounds, sir, but after midnight, I never bothered with the infirmary."

"Why?" It came out as almost a whisper. "Why not?"

Morris attempted a justification. "They were locked in there, sir, and geez, one of them was unconscious and the other very nearly so. We figured — well, how could two guys beat up so bad get into any trouble?"

Soames ran his hand through his hair. "Oh, my God, we're screwed. Just screwed." He reached behind him and found the edge of the desk, then sat back against it, sweating and shaking his head. "I want those two men's known associates pulled out of their cells and squeezed. You got me? Put them in solitary, and leave 'em there until somebody cracks. Some of these men had to know this was going down."

Morris drew himself up tall and squared his shoulders. "Lean on them, then?" Soames nodded. "You sure?"

"Yes. Do what you have to do. Within reason, that is." He balled up his fists and lowered his head with eyes shut tight. "What will Mike Martin say? What about the contract? What if someone is hurt? Shit, what if they kill someone?" He reached up and tugged again at his already loose tie again. "We're all going to lose our jobs."

From far off in the distance, the whine of multiple sirens sounded. Soames jerked his head up, surveyed the two men, and said, "We've got to get our stories straight here."

Morris shrugged again and grimaced. "What's to get straight? You're right, sir. We're screwed."

# Chapter
# Ten

DEZ HAD RUN the first hundred yards or so at top speed, stubbed a toe, and taken a header into the brambles. She got back up and forged on at less of a breakneck pace. She was conscious of the bruising her feet were taking, but she didn't care. Crystal huffed behind her, but not too close. Dez had already nailed her fellow cop in the face once with a branch that she'd pushed past and let swing back.

She wasn't sure how much of a lead the convicts had on them. Twenty minutes? Twenty-five? In the shock and fear, she had lost all track of time. How fast were they moving? She knew Jaylynn could probably outrun the two men. She just hoped the two convicts didn't realize that. A brown hump in some spindly bushes to her right caught her eye, and she skidded to a halt.

"What!" Crystal shouted from behind. "Oh, my God, is it Jay?"

Breathing heavily, Dez shook her head and reached down into the tangle to grab a boot—Shayna's. A few feet beyond, she found another. She waded into the prickly overgrowth and tossed boots toward the path until she found five, and by then Crystal was at her side, stomping through the vegetation, saying, "Of course, it would be my boot we're looking for. Here it is." She bent for it. Dez moved away, righted her boots on the path, and shoved her foot in one.

Shayna came jogging up then. "Hallelujah. You two were right." She leaned over, hands on knees, and took in great gulps of air. "At this rate, we're sure to catch up with them any minute." She frowned at Dez. "In your pack. Get out fresh socks, Dez. Sit down."

"Dammit, I don't have time!"

Shayna marched over, bulldozed the taller woman to the

ground, and unzipped the backpack. After digging a moment, her hand came out with a pair of clean socks.

She squatted and got in Dez's face. "Thirty seconds might prevent an injury and will definitely speed you up. For want of a shoe, the horse was lost." She unrolled the socks and handed one to Dez. "For want of a horse the rider was lost, for want of a rider—"

"Shut up! I get it, I get it!" Dez tore off the dirt-encrusted socks and replaced them, then jammed her feet in the boots and tied them as fast as she could. She was already rising when Shayna reached around her to re-zip the pack.

Crystal's boots weren't laced yet, but she shoved a hank of black hair out of her eyes and grabbed Dez's hand to pull herself up. "We'll head back—get help. We'll backtrack to the Jeep, find police, or at least drive south enough that we can pick up a cell signal. It's got to take them two or three hours—maybe more—to get to that lake, right?" Dez nodded silently. "You follow them. We'll drive around—figure out how to get to Lake Jeanette once we have backup." She bent to lace up.

Dez's voice was gruff. "Somebody has to know those men escaped. They *gotta* be looking for them. I just have to reach them before . . . before . . . "

Shayna put her hand on Dez's arm. "It's okay. We know."

Crystal bent and finished tying her boots. "Dez, listen to me. If you get lost, start a big fire. Burn down the whole damn forest so we can find you."

"I won't get lost. Now go. Take what you need from camp, and hightail it down to the Jeep. Get me some help, Crys, because believe me, if they hurt her in anyway, they're dead." She scowled, feeling a shiver run through her.

Shayna gave Dez's arm a squeeze, then bent to tie her own boots. Without another word or a look back, Dez took off.

JAYLYNN HUSTLED DOWN the trail, stepping around roots and over fallen branches. Desperate for some sign that they were being followed, she scanned the forest, searching, hoping. So far, all she'd seen were chipmunks and birds.

Keith set a swift pace, but Bostwick, bringing up the rear, kept hollering for him to hurry. She heard the big man's regular breathing as he stomped along behind her. "Hey!" he shouted. "Hey, numb-nuts! Get your ass in gear. This ain't no Girl Scout stroll." The creep chuckled to himself, obviously enjoying the panic he caused the smaller man.

Jaylynn put chilled hands into her jacket pockets and found a tissue and a few coins in the left, and a pen and four plastic forks in the right. The plastic pen was silky smooth, and she remembered it was blue. It wouldn't be much of a weapon, but she would keep it in mind. She thought she could use the forks as trail markers, too. Her Swiss Army knife and compass, tucked in her hiking pants pocket, pressed against the top of her thigh. Both would be helpful when she managed to break away.

She wished she had her watch. It had probably gotten lost in the mess of the tent. She hoped Dez would find it, that it wouldn't get crushed. A stab of fear ran through her, and her already upset stomach felt like lead. *Who am I kidding? Am I even going to get out of this alive? Okay, no use freaking out. What can I do?* None of her police training had ever prepared her for a situation like this. *What the heck would Dez do?* She thought about that for a few minutes, finally concluding that Dez would never have let herself be taken captive and forced to run through the woods. Not under these circumstances anyway. She figured that the two convicts would hardly have gotten half a mile down the trail before Dez would have jumped the big guy and disarmed him. *But I'm not Dez, and I don't have that kind of strength. As usual, all I've got in my bag of tricks right now is guile, and I guess that will have to do.*

She stole a glance over her shoulder.

"Move it, Blondie!"

Facing forward once more, Jaylynn was suddenly furious. Angry that these men had humiliated her, degraded her friends, and above all, that they thought she was a stupid, brainless woman to do with what they pleased. Her face burned. *I will not be a victim. I'll have some tricks in store for them.* She didn't yet know what tricks she could come up with, but when she thought of some, she'd play them. For starters, she wasn't going to hurry, and they didn't need to know that she was in great running shape. She let herself gasp a few times, hoping they'd think she was winded.

Another few minutes passed, and they came to a fork in the path. Keith stopped and turned to call out, "Left or right, man?"

"Ask the bitch." She came to a stop near Keith and before she could turn to look, Bostwick poked her between the shoulder blades. "Which way? And don't give me any bullshit."

She bent and put her hands on her knees. "Left," she said, panting harder than she needed to. When she straightened up, the big man was looking at her skeptically. "The next fork, too." She had no clue if this was true, but she kept her voice even, her chin in the air, and when she met his eyes, she couldn't help but glare. She dug her boot heel into the ground, twisting ever so imperceptibly.

He subjected her to an intimidating stare, as if to warn that a lie would have dire consequences. "Go on, then."

As she leaned and took a step, she dragged her heel. She couldn't check the results without garnering suspicion, but hoped she'd left a clear mark for Dez to follow.

CRYSTAL AND SHAYNA spent little time at the campsite, stopping long enough only to make sure they had the cell phone, the last canteen, and the keys to the Jeep. Near their destroyed tent, Shayna stopped with mouth slightly agape and shook her head. "I can't believe this is happening. I just can't believe it."

"Me neither." The sun's early morning rays were finally poking up through the branches of the partially denuded trees all around them, and Crystal was grateful. The chill in the air was gradually abating, though she still shivered. She wasn't sure if that was more from the chill or from fear. She reached out and cupped her hands on Shayna's shoulders, and her partner melted into her arms.

"Oh, God, Crys, this is awful."

They embraced for a moment, then Crystal pulled back. "Don't cry, *mi amada*. Save the feelings for when we have Jay back safe. Come on." She grabbed Shayna's hand and pulled her along. "Let's do our part—and fast. This isn't going to be fun. No fun at all." They took off toward the north trail with Crystal setting the pace at a slow trot and Shayna following.

"Maybe we'll get lucky and find someone with a CB radio or something," Shayna gasped out.

"Maybe. No way to know," Crystal huffed back. "Be prepared. We may have to—make it all the way—to the parking lot."

"That's what I'm afraid of."

DEZ RUSHED DOWN the trail, her strong legs eating up the path. She came to a spot with exposed tree roots, gnarled and bumpy, and realized Crystal and Shayna had been right to make her stop for her boots and gear. The roots would have hurt like hell. Instead, she barely felt the uneven surface.

Her head pounded at twice the rate of her footsteps. *I feel like I'm going to stroke out!* She focused on fighting her anger. She couldn't let it cloud her judgment. Actually, she didn't believe she could even afford to feel it. All she wanted to do was choke the two men to death. She was reminded of the class she took on hostage negotiations. What did the SWAT specialist who talked to the class tell them? Three criteria . . . what were they? What had he kept telling everyone to remember in a hostage situation?

What do they want?

How far will they go to get it?

How do I stop them?

*Okay, that's it. Those three.* Panting with strain and fatigue, she forced herself to think clearly, realizing she needed to consider carefully the answers to those questions. *What* do *they want?* Obviously to get away, to escape. That seemed relatively easy.

*How far will they go to get it?* She wasn't sure about this. *They could have killed us all, but they didn't. Would they have taken Jay if they could have just found a car on their own?* Dez's intuition told her that the big convict might have taken her no matter what. *So maybe there's a secondary thing he wants. She's not safe with him at all.*

She kept plodding along down the path, thoughts whirling in her head. *I can think of two things they want: to get away and to have their way with Jaylynn.* The thought made her sick, and she picked up her pace.

*So now, the key question — how do I stop them? Easy. All I have to do is catch them. I'll have to make it up as I go once I overtake them.*

She heard a sound and slowed down, then stopped abruptly, forcing down her breathing, listening. Every nerve in her body jangled and goose bumps rose as she shivered. She heard a skittering sound followed by a rustle. Letting out the breath she'd been holding, she panted as quietly as she could. *Only an animal in the brush. That's all.*

Dez lifted her foot, leaned, ready to step forward, but something moved in her peripheral vision. A black shape hesitated off the path in the bushes to the right. Jaylynn's name came to her lips, but she made no sound as she took quiet, careful steps backwards.

The shape shuffled from along the tree line, through a partially denuded thicket, to the edge of the meandering path.

*Oh, shit. A bear. A honking big bear.*

The tan nose went up in the air and sniffed at the light breeze blowing at Dez. Resisting the instinct to flee, she stood as still as she could hold herself. When the bear's head went down, she moved her hand toward the pouch at her waist.

*What does he want?* There were berries and roots all around, so she didn't think he'd be that hungry. Safety would be first on his agenda, just as it was on hers. *How far will this bear go to get it?* She hoped he'd run if he saw her, but there was no telling with wildlife. He could attack to protect himself. She fingered the gun grip. *If the bear gets spooked, how do I avoid being mauled?* Dez could only hope that she didn't have to kill the animal, but if he came at her, she'd empty her gun.

Eyes on the shambling black creature, she stepped back three slow steps. *Get outta the way. Outta the way.* The words ran through her mind like a chant. The huge head turned; the bear caught sight of her. For a brief moment, she met dark eyes and was struck at how intelligent they appeared. She looked down and away, hoping he would take that as a show of respect. It struck her that she was assuming the bear was male, but could it be female? A mama bear with cubs somewhere close by? She hoped not. How could she communicate that she meant the animal no harm?

Skin prickling, heart beating fast, she waited, feeling the eyes of the animal upon her.

When the bear moved, it was explosive. He skittered across the path much more nimbly than Dez expected and plunged into the trees on the left.

She was alone.

Listening, she crept along, easing forward one small step at a time, her hand still on the gun. As soon as she felt confident that the bear was gone, she pressed forward again, her mind and stomach in turmoil at how close she had been to four hundred pounds of deadly power.

For the next twenty minutes, she made steady progress down the trail as her stomach settled and her fear subsided by a notch or two. There had been no signs so far that anyone had gone off the path. She came to a place where the trail forked. Her eyes scanned automatically. There—a heel mark in the soft dirt. Farther ahead, she found another pair of heel marks. One she was sure was from Jaylynn's boot, and the other was smooth and wide, not nearly so deep. She thought it probably belonged to the big man. She sped up again.

*What will I do? Will I have to kill them outright?* She hadn't ever shot a man before. Jaylynn had—and she'd gone through hell trying to deal with it. That had been a matter of life or death; if Jaylynn hadn't fired, the man would have had a second shot at them. He had hit Dez in the vest as it was, so Jaylynn had saved both their lives. That had been small comfort for the rookie cop.

Dez rested her right hand on the holster pack strapped tight against her front. She'd left it half-unzipped so that all she had to do was stick her hand in, and the zipper would gap open the rest of the way. The handgrip poked up, ready for action. Her jaw went tense as she envisioned the big inmate holding Jaylynn off her feet, the metal stake pressing into her small neck. She breathed faster as she imagined shooting the sneering look right off the convict's face. She wasn't too sure about the shorter fellow, but she thought she might have to disable or kill him, too. This might be one of those times where shooting first and asking questions later was necessary.

She told herself to stop thinking about blood and consequences, instead wondering what kind of crimes this Keith had committed. He didn't seem like a hardened criminal, not like the cruel big man did. She bet if the police ran their sheets, Keith would be a white-collar criminal or some sort of petty crime aficionado, whereas the other man would be a whole different story. But then again, who knew? Some of the most despicable thugs looked like mild-mannered Caspar Milquetoasts.

Dez was grateful to feel calm and focused now. The first few minutes running through the forest had passed in a blur, and she knew that if Crystal and Shayna hadn't slowed her down, she'd still be in stocking feet and without gun, water, or a first aid kit. *What was I thinking?* She wanted to give herself a mental head-slap. *I'm on track now. That's all that counts.*

But what if Jaylynn were injured? Her chest felt like it was going to explode. *I have to hurry.* She forced herself ahead, then skidded to a halt at a fork in the path. The deciduous trees dripped gray and tan leaves, some of which covered the path, but clear as anything, she saw the indent of a boot and then a drag mark to the left. Two steps farther she caught sight of a strip of white plastic. The tines of the fork were broken off. *Good job, Jay. A fork in the path, literally.* She plunged into the overgrown left path, ducked to avoid a low-hanging branch, and sped up to a jog.

GRIGOR ROSSEL KNEW time was running out, and as the minutes ticked by, his tension increased. He jerked the SUV off to the left, onto what he assumed was a snowmobiling trail. It narrowed too much, so he slammed on the brakes, tossed a look over his right shoulder, and backed up until he was going thirty miles an hour. When he lurched onto the dirt of the regular road, he hit the brakes as he turned the wheel. The vehicle shuddered off to the left, skidding and sliding, until he was pointed north.

Just then, static from the CB radio increased, and he heard a faint female voice. Foot on the brake, he turned up the volume, and what he heard set his heart racing. The code words were vague at best, but the urgency in the dispatcher's voice told the tale. Something was going on at the prison. He sat listening as a male voice indicated he was sending units and 10-4'd the transmission. Other voices came on line and checked in. They continued to speak in garbled code that Rossel could only make sense of half the time, but within minutes, it was clear to him.

They were setting up a manhunt.

"Thank you!" He hit the gas at the same time he smacked the steering wheel with the heel of his hand. The Explorer jerked forward seeming as jittery with adrenaline as Rossel felt. He must hurry now, but he knew he would also have to be cautious. Before long, the woods would be crawling with cops.

He headed to the original meeting site while listening to both the police scanner and the SUV radio. The local Buyck radio station gave more information than he gleaned from the police band. A scratchy-sounding reporter said, "Armed escapees go mobile. These are words law enforcement officials never want to hear, but they heard them this morning when two convicts escaped from the Kendall Correctional Facility. Stanley Michael Bostwick, age 32, and Keith Sterling Randall, 26, are on the run, and people in the vicinity of Buyck are urged to lock up and stay in."

Already deputies from all over St. Louis County were on their way, along with backup searchers from Koochiching County to the west and Lake County to the east. Soon they could expect the National Guard, other local police search units, perhaps even the Feds. Rossel knew from his study of the Minnesota area that St. Louis County covered a lot of ground. It had taken him nearly three hours to get from Duluth, in the southernmost part of the county, up to Buyck. If he could locate Bostwick and the "package" in the next hour or two, he might be able to get away. If he didn't have some luck soon, roadblocks and heavily-manned cordons would put an end to his search. And to Leonid's life.

Rossel knew that Lukin, the lawyer, had told Bostwick to leave the prison and head northwest along the Vermillion River, but there was no sign of anyone there. Rossel had traveled every one of the roads near that river and even barreled down some of the paths marked for snowmobiles. No luck. Increasingly frustrated, he covered miles, stopping regularly to reorient himself with the GPS he carried. From the news reports, it was clear the prisoners had escaped sometime in the night. How far could they hike? Though the ground wasn't too hilly, the vegetation was thick and the man-made paths and deer trails confusing. Even if they managed to travel a mile or two an hour in the dark and as much as three miles an hour in the light, they couldn't possibly have gone more than fifteen miles—probably much less.

"Where are they?" He hit the steering wheel with both hands. "Where?" He skidded the Explorer to a stop, turned off the engine, threw open the door, and got out. He fumbled for his maps and GPS unit, then laid out one of the maps on the seat, the other half-hanging off the center console. He wished he had someone to talk to, a partner with whom to brainstorm. If only his phone worked. But it didn't. He had to solve the problem on his own. He scanned the topographical map and the Kabetogama State Forest trail map, his quick eyes darting, examining.

He let out a sigh and decided there were only three possibilities: Bostwick had been picked up by someone else and was long gone; he had gotten lost and was traveling in circles; or he had decided upon another plan and had thus betrayed the Gubenkos. The more Rossel considered it, the more his suspicions increased. *If the convicts were traveling in circles, by now the authorities would have found them. If they've already exited the area, there's nothing I can do. But what if they have betrayed us? What would I do to change the plan if I were them, and why? Bostwick would be paid well for the "package." Did he imagine he could demand more?*

Rossel contemplated this sobering possibility, lit another smoke, and gazed around him at the shedding arbor. He stuck the cigarette in his mouth, shoved the maps to the side, and got back in the Explorer.

He wouldn't have to study the maps again. He knew of hiking, camping, and canoeing recreational areas west of Crane Lake, on the south side of Echo Lake, and to the east in the Superior National Forest. Plenty of what Gubenko would call "easy pickings." How hard would it be to ambush some poor, hapless campers, take their gear, and disappear into the forest? If Bostwick made it to Canada—or anywhere else—with his "package," he'd have the Gubenko family over a barrel. He could name his own price.

Rossel started up the engine and debated for a moment. Far north to Crane Lake? Or East to Echo Lake and on into the Superior National Forest and the Boundary Waters?

He chose the path toward Crane Lake.

# Chapter
# Eleven

Kendall Correctional Facility
Outside Buyck, Minnesota
Sunday, October 17, 7:52 a.m.

ASSISTANT PRISON ADMINISTRATOR Ralph Soames
worked at the computer in his boss's suite. He could have
accessed the prisoner records much more easily from his own
eight-by-ten-foot cubbyhole, but then there wouldn't be room for
two St. Louis County deputies, two Rangers—one from the
Kabetogama State Forest area and the other from the Lake
Superior National Forest—and the City of Buyck patrolman, not
to mention Morris, Schecter, and the four day guards who stood
against the wall near the door, arms crossed, faces hard and
angry.

Crammed so full of people, the room was hot and reeked of
sweat. The ten men and one woman Forest Ranger stood staring
at him, their faces intense and impatient. A trickle of
perspiration ran down the middle of Soames' back. He wiped his
forehead with his jacket sleeve as he answered one of the
questions fired at him. "Yes, the entire prison is now in
lockdown."

Cabot, the female Kabetogama officer, asked, "And you're
sure it's just two escapees? Only two?"

"Yes. We've done a cell-by-cell count." He nodded toward
the six men at the rear of the office.

In a tight voice, Morris called out, "All others present and
accounted for." This information set everyone into side
conversations.

From his seat, Soames slipped off his suit jacket and tossed
it on the floor behind his chair. He turned back to the computer
and pulled up records for the two prisoners, Bostwick and
Randall. He hit the print button for one, then for the other, and
sat wondering how he would make it through the packed room

to pick up the printout in the utility room. Without the secretary on duty, little printing was ever done on weekends. He didn't even know if the printer was on.

With the exception of Ranger Cabot, who was actually assigned to their geographic area in Kabetogama, and the Buyck officer, a guy Soames had seen around town, he couldn't keep track of which officer was which. And they were all talking and interrupting at once. A pair of radios, each on opposite sides of the room, blasted out static. Both county deputies took bulky units off their belts and adjusted the squelch. One of them responded, and all Soames could make out was that the man spoke a string of 10-codes, then finished saying, "Yes, manhunt. Rural operation. The Feds have been informed."

Over the din, Cabot asked if the escapees could possibly be armed. Soames winced at her and shook his head. "No, they had no access to weapons."

"Not even, say, hypodermics or medical gear?"

"No. They went out the window of a locked room containing no equipment or medical supplies."

"Not locked too well," someone muttered sarcastically. Soames looked up. The speaker was a heavy-set county deputy sheriff.

The Buyck patrolman said, "How the hell did they jimmy the window?"

Soames blushed. He swallowed and took a deep breath. "We think they used a zipper pull to unscrew the window. Seems the heavy-duty metal grate outside had unobtrusively rusted away."

"Unobtrusive, huh?" the deputy sheriff said. Soames looked closer to see his name was Fraley.

"Look, Fraley," Soames said, "this is no time to cast blame. It's happened, and we can't go back and change it."

Fraley said, "The media is reporting that the inmates are armed."

Soames kept his temper, but it wasn't easy. "If they're armed, they got the weapons off-site." He caught Morris's eye. "They were searched, and they were kept in a stripped-down room with nothing in it. They didn't get any guns or knives here." Morris nodded once, and Soames was grateful for at least that one small detail.

The phone rang, and Soames picked it up and identified himself. He paused. "Yes. Yes, sir. Two convicts, unarmed. Yes, it is very possible. Right. Okay, we'll await your reports." He returned the phone to the cradle. "The Canadian authorities may send some men down. They're working with the Feds to tighten up the border patrol."

The Buyck officer said, "You think they've gone north?"

From the back of the room, Morris raised his voice. "All these guys talk about, day in and day out, is fleeing to Canada."

Soames nodded. "It's likely. But we have to be ready for anything—"

"There's no 'we' anymore, Soames," Fraley cut in. "You're out of this now."

"But, we can help. We have—"

"You've got squat!" Fraley's voice was filled with derision. "On behalf of the various authorities coordinating this fugitive retrieval, I am commandeering resources here at your facility. We'll settle up when this is over." He leaned down to the desk, and put his hands flat on the shiny wood. "You and all your civilian hacks just stay clear. Understand?" When Soames didn't answer, Fraley stood up, pulled at his duty belt to adjust it around his waist, and backed away.

Cabot, the female Kabetogama Ranger, met Fraley's eyes, then looked down at Soames. "Ralph, we're taking over your meeting room—to make it our situation room. We ask that you keep the prisoners in lockdown until this crisis is over."

Soames sat back in his boss's chair, suddenly wearier than he could ever remember being. "Certainly. So noted."

The phone rang again, and Fraley raised a hand. "Until we get our own lines in here, we ask that you and your men help with the phones—and get food and coffee as well."

He heard Cabot's closing words, requesting he print out the records for both escapees. Soames nodded and reached for the phone as all the officers filed out of the office leaving his half-dozen guards looking more defeated than he had ever seen them. "Shirley? It's on the news already? Yes, you heard right. A breakout. Get in here. We need you. Yes, you'll get time-and-a-half."

# Chapter
# Twelve

JAYLYNN HEARD A trill of laughter and nearly stopped in her tracks. Another voice called out, a girl's voice, and then a high-pitched cry of exultation. Over the thud-thud of Bostwick's boots behind her, she heard more noises—a shout, a lower-toned warning, more laughter. She felt a rush of elation. *Please let it be an entire pack of mountain men.* A figure appeared ahead of them seventy or eighty yards down the trail, and more people followed.

Keith stopped. He turned and looked at the big man, then met Jaylynn's eyes. She gauged the distance between the darkness of the forest and where she stood. Could she make it?

Before she could decide, Bostwick grabbed her by the back of her jacket collar and turned her around. In a low, hoarse voice, he said, "Not a word from you, Blondie, or I'll shoot these people. You just shut the hell up. Got it?" She nodded, and he released her. He pulled the gun out of the front of his waistband and shifted it behind him, tucking it out of sight. "Now just keep on moving." He pushed her and told Keith to get going.

The line of hikers continued to make their way toward them. The laughter and catcalls died down as six gangly-legged girls and two women examined them with inquisitive eyes.

Jaylynn estimated that the girls were eighth- or ninth-graders—maybe fourteen or fifteen years old. The two women looked to be in their early thirties. Every girl wore hiking boots, jeans or hiking pants, a vest or jacket, and each carried a daypack. The leaders' packs were bigger and bulkier.

Even if Jaylynn stepped to the side into the thick vegetation, the path wasn't wide enough for more than two people to stand side by side. Jaylynn stopped next to Keith and felt Bostwick loom behind her. After a moment, she could smell him, too, and the stink made her feel sick to her stomach once again.

The dark-haired girl in front of the line raised a hand. "Greetings and salutations. We come from afar." The girls behind her giggled. The line of hikers marched forward a few more seconds, then came to a stop ten feet away and crowded into a knot of curious faces.

Keith gave a half-hearted wave back but didn't seem to know what to say. From behind Jaylynn, an amazingly prissy voice said, "Well, hello. What have we here? Girl Scouts?" Something heavy pressed down on her shoulder, and the foul-smelling convict squeezed her shoulder through her jacket.

"Nah," the girl answered. "We're part of WAO."

"Wow?" Bostwick asked.

One of the adults, a tall woman whose short black hair had lines of silver in it, pushed her way to the front. Herding the girls aside like a watchful sheepdog, she said distractedly, "W. A. O. Wilderness Adventures Outdoors. We pronounce it wow."

"I see." Bostwick tightened his grip on Jaylynn. "You wouldn't happen to have a spare area map, would you? We came out hiking yesterday, and now we seem to be a bit lost."

"I don't think we have a spare, but we can give you some directions." The leader turned. "Laura, you're better at this than I am."

Laura stepped through the crowd of girls. She could not have looked more different from the other guide. Long blond hair cascaded down her back, and a pair of savvy blue eyes peered out from under her bangs. Her fellow group leader seemed preoccupied, perhaps focused on small details, as though she were in a tunnel. On the other hand, Jaylynn thought Laura sized them up shrewdly before asking, "Where are you headed?"

Bostwick nudged Jaylynn. "Honey, can you tell this nice lady?" He increased pressure on her shoulder.

"Lay off me, will ya?" Jaylynn rolled her arm to shrug away the unwelcome paw. He loosened his hold, but didn't remove his hand. She met Laura's eyes and tried to make her voice sound normal. "We parked in the Lake Jeanette lot—on the east side." She was just taking a wild guess about the parking lot. She only vaguely remembered Lake Jeanette as being east of Echo Lake.

Laura's dark-haired colleague frowned. "You must mean one of the two on the south? Or the west one? Or maybe you parked closer to Nigh Lake? There isn't any lot on the east."

Jaylynn's mouth went dry. "Oh, yeah. Maybe. I get turned around pretty easy, but I'll definitely know it when I see it." She looked away. Though she didn't know for sure how to go about doing it using only her eyes, she hoped to alert them to the danger they were all in. She sought out the eyes of the distracted woman, next to the first two girls, and decided not to look away. Bostwick wouldn't know if she faced Laura and spoke to her, but actually looked at the other woman. "Can you share directions?"

"Sure. Stay on this path," Laura said. She sounded hesitant, as if something had jarred her. Casting a quick look at her colleague, she continued a shade too brightly, "You'll come to a creek in about three-quarters of a mile. Cross over it, and take the path on the right—*not* the one on the left. That one loops around and ends up going north. After the path on the right, each time you come to a fork or a place where it seems to turn, make sure you keep going east." She paused. "Do you have a compass?"

Jaylynn had her brand new Suunto beginner's compass in her hiking pants and her knife as well, but she was not about to admit it. "No, but this one here has a good sense of direction." She elbowed Keith, who flinched. He cleared his throat, but didn't say anything.

"Okay, then," Laura said, still extra-perky. "Just keep on eastward. It's quite a ways, though, with a number of forks."

One of the girls said, "We've been walking for hours and hours!" The kids giggled again.

The other woman seemed to have caught on that there was something odd going on. Awkwardly, she shook her head and rolled her eyes. Her smile was so fake that Jaylynn worried Bostwick would pick up on it. Nervously she said, "We got started something over an hour ago from Hunting Shack River where we camped last night. Took us maybe two and a half hours to get there from Lake Jeanette. Probably take you folks less time. The girls goofed off a lot."

The tight shoulder grip was back as Bostwick, again in his prissy voice, said, "Okay. That's good to know. Maybe next time we should enter elsewhere. Where did you folks park—near here?"

Laura shook her head. She bit her lip and seemed to be debating. "No. We have a bus driver. He and some of the parents dropped us off yesterday at Lake Jeanette and will pick us up south of Echo Lake in a few hours."

The dark-haired girl giggled and said, "It's a forced march. We're pretending to be captives marching to our doom." Her friends laughed with her, and Bostwick let out a merry guffaw. Jaylynn was struck by how bizarre it was that the kids were laughing about the very experience she was actually having. Her gaze drilled into Laura's, and to her credit, the WAO leader didn't flinch or give any indication that she saw anything unusual.

"Oh," Bostwick said. "I see. Well, we don't want to slow you down. Thank you for your kind assistance, and you all have a nice hike." He shoved Keith to the side, and Jaylynn ended up taking two steps into the brush. The little troop of girls and women moved toward them, and as they passed by single file, some of the girls said "See ya," and "Have a good day."

When the quiet WAO leader finally broke eye contact, Jaylynn's heart sank. She didn't know if it would help her in any way, but she had a hunch that if the WAO group ran into Dez, Crystal, or Shayna on the trail, they would have plenty to talk about.

Bostwick pushed Keith and Jaylynn forward. "Shut up now," he said. "Not a word. Get going."

Keith looked back, frowning. "But, what about—"

"Get a ways down the trail, you moron! We'll talk when we're out of their hearing." Once they were out of the WAO kids' line of sight, he urged them to a trot.

For the next five minutes, Jaylynn dragged her feet as much as she could. Three times Bostwick grunted at her to hurry up. Panting and sweating, Keith was the one who finally pulled up. He bent over, hands on his knees. "Geez, Bostwick. They're three miles down the trail by now."

"Shut up, Randy. Voices carry in the woods."

Keith stood tall, still breathing hard. "It's Randall, not Randy, you stupid asshole! Keith Randall."

Jaylynn saw that the smaller man's hands were in tight fists, and as he turned to confront his companion, he looked ready to pop a vein.

Bostwick smiled and wiped his sweating forehead with his forearm. "Whatever." He glanced around, then said, "Blondie. On your knees."

She backed up a step, her heart beating so hard in her chest that she thought she would throw up. *I should have broken away back there. Should have run sooner. . .* Before she could move or speak or act, he rolled his eyes. "Listen, you dumb bitch, I gotta take a piss, and I'm not giving up the gun to Mr. Moron here. On your knees."

He stepped toward her, and she dropped to one knee, her other leg tensed and ready to propel her to her feet and away from this crass and frightening man. He let the pack slide off his shoulder, unzipped it, and hunted through it. "You got the hatchet?" Keith nodded. "Get it out." He bent slightly and pointed his index finger at Jaylynn. "Don't you dare try anything. Randall, get behind her there and watch her. If she makes a move, clobber her on the head with the hatchet."

He turned away and stepped off the path with his back to her. The gun was still tucked in the back of his jeans under the big backpack. He removed the weapon and set it to the right on a log. Too far away for her to lunge for it. In a moment she heard urine running onto the ground. When it stopped, Bostwick let out a sigh, made adjustments to his pants, and did an about-face. He bent for the gun and tucked it into the front of his jeans, then scratched at his scaly scalp. As he strode toward them, she saw flecks of dandruff accumulating on the blue sweatshirt he wore.

"Okay, up and at 'em," he said. "Let's get going." He looked up at the sky, gave a toss of his head toward the sun peeking through the trees. "We're running out of time. You gotta pee, Blondie?"

Shaking her head, Jaylynn slowly got to her feet. Bostwick smiled a wicked grin. "Wouldn't want to pull your pants down in front of us now, would ya?" He let out a cruel chuckle. "Did you see them sweet young schoolgirls, Randall? Now one of *them* would've been fun to get it on with, don'tcha think?"

Keith, who was drinking from one of the canteens, choked, spraying water down the front of him. Bostwick laughed again. "A little too much excitement for your tender heart, huh, Randall?"

The smaller man didn't answer him.

Jaylynn watched Keith screw the cap on the canteen. *I don't think he's quite as bad as this horrible Bostwick. Randall. Keith Randall is his name. I have to remember that. He's the weak link.*

Keith saw her looking closely at him and asked, "You want some?" Without a word, she shook her head. There was no way on earth she would drink or eat from the same container as either of them.

"I'll take some more." Bostwick stuck out a huge hand and snatched the canteen. "Jesus! There's hardly any left. Gimme the other one." He took the second canteen and let out a snort of anger. "What the hell are you? A water buffalo? How the fuck did you drink all this? Oh, hell. I don't care. She said there was a creek. We'll fill up there." He gave Jaylynn a push. "Move it."

She turned on her heel, leaving a nice deep impression, and passed Keith. She could already smell the water—a pungent, moist odor mixed with the scent of pine and something else unpleasant. *Probably dead rodents.* The image made her shudder. She wondered if she could make a break for it now, but she didn't think they were far enough from the WAO girls, and she couldn't live with herself if the two convicts caught up with the group and hijacked any of those kids in her place. *I'll wait a while, try to find another spot where I can escape.*

They came to the creek, which was really little more than a three-foot-wide brook. Cold, clear water burbled by, and Jaylynn suddenly realized just how thirsty she actually was. But she remembered how insistent Dez was that they use the water purifier.

Bostwick tossed the canteen at the other man. "Hey, water buffalo, fill 'em up."

Keith didn't say a word, just squatted next to the brook, opened the canteens, and submerged one after the other. When they were filled, he screwed the caps back on and handed one to Bostwick. "Carry your own, Bostwick."

The big man took it and looped the strap over his shoulder with an amused expression on his face. Jaylynn realized something had changed in the communication between the two men, but she wasn't quite sure what. The cooperative, compliant Keith was no longer taking guff from the big man. But why? He'd seemed so meek earlier, but with every mile they traveled, he grew less timid and more assertive. She wasn't sure if that was a good thing or not.

# Chapter
# Thirteen

SERGEI GUBENKO FIDGETED in his office at the Best Jobs Printing Company. The Chicago weather had taken a turn for the worse, and rain drummed on the roof as it had all morning. He leaned back in his chair, arms crossed and half-asleep, his drooping eyes fixed on a muted 13-inch TV on the top shelf of a four-drawer file cabinet. He had work to do, jobs to set up, accounts to settle, but instead he waited, watching the various news stations, hoping to see news of a prison break in Minnesota.

He passed a big hand across his sweating forehead. He hadn't heard from Grigor Rossel for three days, and while he knew that communication would be difficult, he hadn't expected a total blackout. The morning before, he had been so out of sorts that he'd sought out a safe phone line all the way across the city to put through a call to Vanya. No answer. The phone had rung and rung, but no one picked up. He supposed it was a good sign that Vanya was on the job, but this lack of information was killing him.

The phone rang, and the shrill sound jerked him out of his sleepy musing. He picked it up. "Best Jobs Printing."

A quiet, unaccented voice said, "This is a message about the delivery of the birthday package. The party has begun, and we are happy to report that you can expect the gift to arrive on time."

"You are sure?" Gubenko sat up straight in his chair. "Right on time?"

"Yes, sir. Thank you for your business."

Before Gubenko had a chance to respond, he heard a click. He hung up the phone and glanced up. CNN was reporting on civil unrest in Afghanistan, but the crawl line on the bottom gave him the information he wanted to see: *Federal authorities are working with Minnesota law enforcement to apprehend two escapees from the Herman R. Kendall Correctional Facility.*

The next entry in the crawl line was about a bus bomb in Iraq, but Gubenko couldn't see it through the tears in his eyes. He had the news he wanted and needed. Leonid might be saved after all.

# Chapter
# Fourteen

WITH GREAT RELUCTANCE, Dez bent at the waist, hands on hips, and surveyed the path ahead as she caught her breath. *Oh, shit, this is wrong.* She wheeled about quickly and retraced her steps. Before she'd traveled an eighth of a mile, she was back at a fork in the path. She took the other trail, moving slowly, looking for evidence. For a dozen yards, the hard-packed dirt yielded no noticeable footprints, but then she saw the familiar little half-moon wedge. *Thank God, I'm on the right path again.*

It was the second time she'd been thrown off the trail, and she realized all too clearly that every moment traveling the wrong way was time Jaylynn couldn't afford. She picked up her pace to a jog and hustled east, watching for footprints and scuff marks and wondering once again how the hell this could have happened to them. How could they be so unlucky?

She caught her boot on the edge of a root she hadn't seen and tripped. She fell forward, one knee bent beneath her, the other trailing behind, and both hands went flat on the path. The gun jostled in front of her, but didn't fall out of the Neoprene pack. She pushed herself back up and stood, wiping dirt off her hands as tears came to her eyes. The pace she was keeping was impossible to maintain. She had to slow down, even if just to make sure she didn't break an ankle or hit her head. *Balance*, she thought. *I need balance.* Panting, she took her canteen and downed a swig of water. It tasted unexpectedly sweet, so she took another big drink, then capped it and set off again.

She wondered how far she had traveled. A quick glance at her watch confirmed that it had been well over an hour since Shayna and Crystal had parted from her to head to Crane Lake. How far could Jaylynn and those bastards have gone since then? Five miles? Six? She had no sure way to estimate, but she had to catch up with them before they covered the miles between Echo Lake and Lake Jeanette. She must keep on, as fast as she dared, and find them. Soon.

She jogged forward, watching for half-buried roots and holes in the path, all the while wondering how the convicts had escaped. They must have come from the facility outside Buyck. Dez estimated that they had to have traveled a minimum of ten miles just to get from the prison to the campground by Echo Lake. *Oh, God, I hope they're tired.*

Now that her head was clear and she had plenty of time to think, she considered all the possibilities. The men had to have broken out of the prison, so surely a manhunt was underway. Help couldn't be far behind, could it? An uneasy shiver ran through her. Maybe they had broken away from a bus transfer. But if so, why no helicopters? Shouldn't the state police be overhead?

She slowed her pace to a walk and reached down into the cargo pocket low on her thigh to pull out the area map. Kendall Prison wasn't even on the map, but she knew it was west of Buyck near the Pelican River. There were so few roads in the North Woods. If they got a car, they'd have to take Highway 24 to go north or south; 23 to go west. But to the east, there weren't any two-lane highways—mostly just crappy old logging roads and snowmobile paths. It didn't make sense for them to go east when they could travel north to Canada, slip over the border, and get lost there for good.

She shook her head, wondering if there was a method to their madness. Maybe they *wanted* to get lost in the Boundary Waters Canoe Area. With 140,000 square miles to hide in, they might be the D.B. Coopers of the new millennium. But they hadn't gotten nearly enough gear, food, or supplies to last more than a few days in the woods. *No, they believe there's a car at Lake Jeanette, and they think they'll make their escape via some road there.*

After tucking the map away, she pressed on, despairing that she wasn't in better shape. Her legs were tired, and she knew she needed to eat something soon if she were to keep up this pace.

She heard a chortle up ahead and skidded to a halt, every nerve, fiber, and tendon on alert. Someone whistled a jaunty tune, and the sound came nearer instead of fading off into the distance. Neither side of the trail afforded any hiding places other than tall, thin trees and low brush. Still, she plunged off the path and pitched herself into the damp undergrowth. Panting, heart racing, she waited, her eyes searching frantically for a shock of short, white-blond hair.

The blond hair she first caught sight of was not short, nor

was it attached to anyone remotely resembling Jaylynn. Her heartbeat gradually slowed as her disappointment mounted. A troop of females approached. Seeing only eight calm women—no men in sight—she hoisted herself up from the slimy vegetation and called out a hello.

The woman at the front jumped back, her hand to her heart.

"Sorry," Dez said. "Didn't mean to scare you." She tried to keep her voice pitched calmly, but what she really wanted to do was run up, grab someone, and shout. "Have you seen her?" She waded through the brush and onto the trail, where she stamped moisture and leaves from her boots.

Recovering from her fright, the woman said, "What in the world is going on!" She held her hands out to the side, motioning for the girls behind her to stay put.

A second woman spoke up, one hand fidgeting with the fabric of her sweater. She seemed unsettled, or maybe she was just the high-strung type. "Are you looking for someone?" she said, the hand relocating to toy needlessly with her short black hair.

"Yes. Tell me you ran into two guys with a woman in a brown coat and tan hiking pants?"

Almost everyone in the group nodded solemnly. "Yes," the woman at the forefront said. "What's going on?"

"The woman with them—was she all right? Was she unharmed?"

The fidgety adult stepped forward. "I knew there was something wrong. I could tell from her eyes. She looked haunted."

Dez didn't like the visions that came into her head, and it took great effort for her to focus on the people at hand. "Did she seem all right otherwise—not roughed up or anything?"

One of the girls said, "She just looked nervous. That's all."

"Okay. Good." Relief flooded through her, and once again she had to steel herself to focus. "Listen, you're all in danger."

The girls squinted up at her as though she were nuts. One of them said, "Danger?"

The words tumbled out of Dez's mouth now. "She's in trouble. Her name is Jaylynn Savage, and she and I are both police officers. We were camping with friends. The men escaped from Kendall Prison. They hijacked our stuff, trussed up my friends and me, and took her hostage. I have to catch up with them. How far up the trail are they?"

One girl looked at her watch. "We saw them twenty-three minutes ago." Another girl elbowed her. "What? I pay attention to details, unlike you, Sweeney!"

"What did you tell them?" Dez asked. "Did you identify yourselves? Say where you were going?"

"No, not exactly. We didn't say too much. By the way, my name is Laura Hiller. My co-leader here is Emily Yates. We're part of Wilderness Adventures Outdoors, W.A.O.—or wow, for short. We told them we were with WAO, but nothing much more."

"Good."

Laura nodded. "We did tell them we're headed to Echo Lake. Our bus driver will meet us there. He's got all the tents and camping equipment we used last night. Later this afternoon, these girls head home to Duluth."

Dez passed a hand over her hair, dislodging a small leaf. She brushed it away and let out a breath. "That's bad if they know where you're going and that there's a bus there."

"Laura sort of exaggerated," Emily said.

"Yeah, I did. I told them the driver and the kids' parents were waiting for us. Actually, it's just the bus driver."

"Well, that's good. Perhaps somewhat of a deterrent. Let's see. You *could* take one of the south trails and hike southwest toward Buyck. They wouldn't expect that, and I'll bet they'll avoid the town."

Laura frowned. Her blue eyes met Dez's. "Shouldn't we just hustle back to Echo Lake and get the heck out of here?"

Dez swallowed. "When they get to the Lake Jeanette parking lot, they're gonna find out there's no car there for them to get away in." She took a deep breath and looked back at Laura. "They'll try to find another way out—and probably remember your bus. You've got a big lead on them, assuming that they kept going east on the trail while you've gone west. So yeah, if you take off now for Echo Lake, you better just hurry. You may find other hikers on the way. If you don't show up by the appointed time, your driver is going to get worried and call it in, too, right?"

Laura said, "Yeah, but our cell phones don't work up here."

In a rush, Dez said, "I urge you not to stay on this path. I can't be sure how dangerous these men are. I don't know whether they killed anybody to escape, but they *are* armed." A collective murmur rose from the group, and the girls were listening closely now. "The bald guy has a gun. They've got knives and a hatchet, too."

Laura's eyes went wide. "Okay. You've convinced us."

Dez reached out, then pulled her hand back, not wanting to scare the woman any further. "Just hurry, okay?"

Laura nodded. "We will."

"When you get somewhere with a land line, please call 9-1-1. Tell them you met me — Desiree Reilly — on this trail, and that the convicts have one hostage, Jaylynn Savage. Tell 'em everything you know, everything you saw."

"All right. Do you need anything? First aid kit? Water? Anything?"

"No, I just need to go. You hurry. Hurry out of here!"

"Thank you," a voice called out after her.

Dez raised a hand in an over-the-shoulder wave, but she was already running east. Her legs felt strong again, and she was filled with hope and energy. *She's still alive. She's not hurt!* She realized that at some level she had been bracing herself for bad news, but if Jaylynn had looked all right to the WAO group, it was something to be hopeful about. Still, she knew she had to get moving. A twenty-three-minute lead would not be easy to eclipse. *Drag your feet, Jaylynn. Please slow them down.*

# Chapter
# Fifteen

Kendall Correctional Facility
Outside Buyck, Minnesota
Sunday, October 17, 9:20 a.m.

RALPH SOAMES PACED in the Chief Administrator's office, coffee cup in one hand, phone pressed to his ear with the other. "No, I can't give out that information. No, sir. No comment. I'm sorry, but the media is not allowed anywhere—" He set his mug down on the cluttered desktop. "I'm sorry, sir. No. I have to go." He hung up without waiting for further entreaties. Reporters were driving him crazy. All media calls were being funneled to him in order to free up dispatchers and 911 operators. Aloud he said, "What a useless task."

Out in the hallway, a constant stream of officers and guards hustled by. That sick feeling he'd been experiencing for the last two hours washed over his midsection again. He reached for his mug, then reconsidered. He'd already drunk way too much coffee, and now he needed to visit the lavatory.

He walked meekly down the hallway, stopping in the doorway to the conference room. The facility's training cart, loaded down with a 32-inch TV, was parked at the rear of the room. Someone had pushed another table next to it upon which a smaller television sat. Local and national news played on the two screens. Four telephones and a tangle of lines sat at the corners of the large middle table, and seven of the eight chairs were filled.

At the front of the room, the county deputy, Fraley, stood at the whiteboard brandishing a red marker. An overhead projector cast up the image of a faded-looking Crane Lake Area recreation map. "Look," Fraley said. "We don't know when the hell they got out, but it had to be some time after twelve hundred hours. Let's assume the worst."

A man in a suit said, "We've already done that, Fraley. If

they got out at or about midnight, then they've a max of just over nine hours' lead. At one to two miles per hour while dark and three to four in daylight, they may have gone as little as, say, fifteen miles, and as much as twenty-five. Likely somewhere in the middle of that, don't you think?"

Fraley sighed. With the red marker, he carefully drew one big circle on the board. "Here's a thirty-mile radius. From this point—perhaps even in a larger circle," he said as he drew another red circle around the first one, "we should beef up roadblocks, and get squads better organized into road, off-road, and trail searches. We need more men. And I still think they'll have gone north, not over to Orr or Buyck."

Sally Cabot, the Kabetogama forest ranger, spoke up. "Local officials deployed their people to protect Orr and Buyck. Whether you think the escapees went north or not, Fraley, the townspeople *do* get first dibs on safety. We need to think about taking stock of who's out there in the parks, too. We've got a lot of campers and portagers at risk."

Fraley scowled. "You think I don't realize that?"

"I'm not criticizing," Cabot said. "But there are several hundred miles of forest roads and logging trails. The hiking and skiing trails alone are over a hundred miles spread throughout the various forest jurisdictions. We've got a lot of area to cover."

Fraley sighed again and shook his head. "They aren't going to spend time hiking around and hiding in the forest. I know how cons think. They'll hijack a car or steal someone's truck, and then they'll be on the road. If we take the men we have and focus on the roads, sooner or later they'll turn up, if only for lack of food."

"So you intend to wait, let them kill whoever they want, 'til they get a vehicle, then capture them?"

"No, of course not! We have to maximize the use of our men."

Soames didn't miss the reference to "men," or the glare Cabot shot at Fraley, who didn't seem to notice. The arrogant deputy twirled the red pen in his hand and opened his mouth, but before he could say anything, the man in the suit sarcastically said, "Not everyone thinks about food all the time, Fraley. They could go days without it, and there's plenty of water to be had. Besides, all they have to do is take provisions from one set of hikers or a canoeing party and they could hide in the bush for weeks."

Cabot said, "Guys, I'd be happy to coordinate forest search parties within that circled radius. Kabetogama has an on-duty dispatcher we could all report through, and—"

Fraley interrupted. "That's all well and good, but we don't have the manpower yet. And we need to operate from somewhere more centrally located and accessible."

Behind Soames, someone cleared his throat. A tall black man slipped past him, flipped open his leather ID holder, and said, "Jerome Giles, FBI. Who's in charge here?"

Fraley said, "County sheriff, state patrol, city police, and park rangers are working collaboratively."

Giles tucked his ID badge in his breast pocket and crossed his arms over his dark suit. "Well, that never works in an emergency. Someone needs to assume full authority. Where's the warden?"

All eyes turned to Soames just outside the doorway. For a moment, he thought he'd pee his pants. He gulped and coughed before squeaking out, "Yeah, that's me, Assistant Administrator Ralph Soames filling in for my superior, Mike Martin, who's on vacation. Can I help you?"

"Yes," Giles said, in a deep, rich baritone. "I happened to be in Minneapolis for a law enforcement conference, so I was sent up here in one hell of a hurry by charter chopper. I've had no breakfast and would like something to eat, preferably with fresh coffee and no eggs."

"Yes, sir."

"And you need to prepare for the fact that unless these escapees are found soon, then in approximately twenty-four hours, thirty dozen Feds from Chicago will arrive with a lot of gear. We need to start thinking about a staging area." He looked around the conference room. "And a much bigger meeting room."

Soames gave a nervous nod and stepped away from the doorway. Hustling down the hall, he felt like a three-year-old boy who needed to go potty before going outside to deal with the neighborhood bullies. He smacked open the door to the men's room and strode to the urinal.

As Soames finished washing his hands, the door opened and Morris and Schecter stood looming just inside the entryway, both glum-faced.

Morris said, "We've been looking for you, boss."

Soames reached for a paper towel. "Yeah? What's up? You got something for me?"

Morris shrugged. "Nobody has said much except the con nicknamed Swiff. Nothing like being blindfolded, shackled, and terrorized to get a bit of information."

Schecter gave a half-hearted chuckle. "Swiff's afraid of the dark. Probably say anything to get out, but after an hour, he talked his way back to the cellblock."

"Yes? Go on!"

"His exact words were that Stanley Bostwick told him he was gonna make a hundred thou—maybe a quarter mil." Morris leaned back against the wall. "And Bostwick told him he'd put money in an account for Swiff for when he got released."

Soames threw the paper towel in the trash can. "In return for what?"

"It was a set-up for Keith Randall and Stanley Bostwick to go to the infirmary. But that's all we've gotten out of anyone. Buddy Boldt and Franklin are down there now seeing if they can get anything else."

"All right. Thanks."

Morris cleared his throat. "Sir, we've both been on duty since six last night. The inmates are in lockdown, and we're not doing any good around here, and within an hour or so, you'll have a full staff."

"You're saying you want to go home?"

Schecter said, "Not exactly. Yes, we want to go off the clock, but we'd like to join the search efforts."

Soames leaned back against the edge of the porcelain sink and crossed his arms. "Man, I don't know if they'll let you."

Morris stuck his chin out. "They don't have a choice. And they don't know everything about this area and the way these cons think. We've got a chance to save face for our organization. So we're going, Mr. Soames, as soon as you give us clearance."

Soames shrugged. "Be my guest." He looked at his watch. "Wait until your replacements show up at ten, then run through all the Level One security measures. Once everything is under control, you can sign out. Oh, and when you head out of here now, will you stop at the kitchen and tell them to send up fresh coffee and some breakfasty type food—no eggs—for the FBI guy?"

"Okay."

"Come see me if you get anything else out of the inmates. Hell, come see me when you get ready to leave."

"Yes, sir," Morris said.

"And guys, just make sure you get back for your next regularly scheduled shift. This whole thing started because we were short of staff."

Schecter grimaced and said, "No problem. We're not on duty until four p.m. This better be wrapped up by then."

Passing a hand through his hair, Soames said, "I sure as hell hope so."

AS PART OF the first wave of women rangers, Sally Cabot joined the State Forest Service in 1972 after graduating from the University of Minnesota's forestry program. She had wanted to be a ranger ever since she first heard of Smokey Bear, who was saved from the ravages of fire on May 9, 1950, the very day of her birth. Even before she hit grade school, the family nickname for her had been "Smokey's Sal."

Cabot had braved fires, tornados, snowstorms, and sub-zero temperatures. She'd helped rescue stranded boaters, hikers, campers, picnickers — any number of people who'd gotten lost or trapped in difficult places. She'd survived multiple encounters with bears and once a rutting bull moose, but in over three decades of service, she had never actively participated in a manhunt for escaped prisoners.

She sat quietly in the meeting room, off in the corner, and listened to Giles ask questions and give calm instructions. If the escapees weren't found soon, his agents would arrive in Buyck later in the day. The National Guard from Duluth had just been contacted, and they would assemble and start traveling north in early afternoon. The Saint Louis County Rescue Squad and the state police had been called in, too. Unfortunately, due to rain and lightning, the nearest State Patrol helicopter was socked in 98 miles away in Ely, and bad weather was soon headed toward the Kabetogama area.

Ignored by all in the room, she drank her fill of coffee, wondering about her daughter Emily, a wilderness guide. *Was this the weekend Em was going to camp with a group of middle-schoolers? Or is that next weekend?*

Several minutes passed, and the men seemed to be rehashing old news. It didn't seem there was much else for her to learn, so she got up to leave. Her colleague from the National Park Service, assigned to the Superior Forest, had already taken off to monitor his territory, and her superiors had called to let her know she should do the same.

Checking her watch as she waited impatiently in the hallway, she realized she needed to make a quick trip to the ladies room. She hadn't been able to catch Ralph Soames before he disappeared from the meeting room a minute earlier, and she wasn't about to bust in on him in the bathroom. She wasn't blind; it was clear he was under a lot of stress. For all she knew, he could be in there throwing up.

With a whoosh, the door pulled open, and two of the guards came out, followed by Soames. "Oh, hi, Sal," the administrator said. His men paused in the doorway, curious looks on their faces.

She cleared her throat. "Ralph, I just wanted to let you know—"

He shook his head and raised a hand. "It's okay, Sal. This whole thing's a mess. Don't worry. I'm not upset with you. Everybody's doing what they gotta do."

"Look, that Fed fellow doesn't have a lot of use for a middle-aged forest ranger, and what my superiors are telling me to do is get some help and find out what's going on in the campgrounds and parks. We need to clear people out."

"These guys are off duty." Soames looked at Morris and Schecter. "Guys, I know you want to capture the escapees, but maybe it would be better if you helped Cabot."

She said, "I figure I'll call and find out who filed trip plans, then scout around and make sure those people are okay. I'm a little worried that my daughter Emily might be out there. I seem to recall that she was going on an outdoor camping trip over at Echo Lake. So I'm going to check for her trip plan first. I'm also going to break all the rules and take my Yamaha road bike just in case I need to hit the trails."

Morris brightened. "I'd sign on for that. I've got a Suzuki."

"Me, too," Schecter said.

"I could really use the help." Cabot brushed her silvering hair back and put on her ranger hat. "I'll check with dispatch to see who filed trip plans. Let me get my truck and meet you two in Buyck at the Gas-N-Go as quick as you can get there. Bring a pack with some food, water, and first aid supplies. I'll try to scare up some radios. I suggest you wear your uniforms. We need to look as official as possible." She looked at her watch. "Can you make it about eleven?"

"I can do that," Morris said, and Schecter nodded. "We'll see you there." They turned and hustled down the hallway.

"Thanks, Ralph. I'm glad to have the help and support."

He nodded, looking gray and weary. "This has been one hell of a day, Sal, and I'm betting it's far from over."

# Chapter
# Sixteen

**Minnesota North Woods**
**Sunday, October 17, 9:35 a.m.**

GRIGOR ROSSEL HAD exhausted his patience, the coffee in his Thermos, and most of his tank of gas. He regretted having traveled north toward Crane Lake. Before he got halfway there, the traffic on Highway 24 slowed to a crawl, and he soon saw the roads were blockaded with police letting people through only after a careful search. After several impatient minutes, he found a turnoff where he could get out of northbound traffic and back out on the highway going south. Along the way, he periodically left the highway to traverse dirt side roads, but he hadn't seen a single sign of the escapees.

He doubted that he'd find Bostwick hiking Highway 24. Granted, they could probably commandeer a vehicle, but it wouldn't be smart. Too easy to be spotted and captured. Ever since the radio began broadcasting news of the breakout, the number of trucks with rifles in hunting racks had increased exponentially. He wondered if any of these people had any sense at all. What were they doing out driving around? Didn't they know that desperate convicts were on the loose?

Now here he was, north of Buyck and near Echo Lake, approaching yet another choice. Did he dare travel into Buyck, go through the roadblock, and head south? Or should he travel east and head toward the Superior National Forest?

The latter choice won out, mostly because he didn't want to be stopped and remembered. His ID listed him as Gregory Russell, but it would stand only so much scrutiny. Later on, after all the hoopla was over, if the authorities went through information about the various people they processed through roadblocks, his fake ID would stand out. They'd find his hotel, perhaps discover information about the stolen SUV coming from Illinois, and know to look further. They might even be taking photos at a roadblock. No, he wasn't taking any chances, even if it meant failing to find Bostwick.

Driving east on the bumpy country road, he passed a dark purple minivan with two canoes on top. The van's occupants looked like tourists. Road signs showed up on the right side of the road as he drove along: Hanson Creek. The turnoff for Echo Lake. Lost Jack Creek. That brought a smile to his face. Now *there* would be an appropriate place to find those he sought. Wherever there was a dirt road off to the left or right, he nosed the Explorer in and proceeded. Many promising trails petered off into nothing or ended in clearings where perhaps hunters or snowmobilers parked their rigs in the winter.

Once he thought he saw a bear half-hidden in the red and gold foliage, but when he reached the end of the bumpy road and reversed to back out, the dark form was nowhere to be seen.

He returned to the country lane and pointed his hood east. Looking at his watch, he shuddered with fatigue and worry. Nearly ten a.m. and still no luck. He drove on toward Hunting Shack River.

CRYSTAL JOGGED METHODICALLY, concentrating on putting one foot in front of the other as she tried to block out the pain in her lungs and legs. Though she had not been a churchgoer for many years, when under extreme stress, she prayed fervently to God as she had been taught during her years at Catholic school. *Dear God, please . . .* A lot of her prayers faded off into internal incoherence, but she kept coming back to it, like a mini-chant: *Please, God, please.*

She thought of Dez, of the pain and anguish on her best friend's kind face, and of her bellowed howl of rage and sheer desperation. Dez didn't deserve to have this happen to her, especially not after what happened to Ryan Michaelson. She had already tragically lost someone dear. Before Jaylynn had come along, Dez rode most shifts with Ryan, and the tall cop had taken Ryan's shooting death especially hard, blaming herself, and suffering from post-traumatic stress disorder. The usually unflappable, clear-headed officer had had a devil of a time getting control of that, but with Jaylynn's support and a good counselor, the veteran cop eventually resolved the difficulties. And now this.

Yet another spike of fear drove into Crystal's heart. She was so relieved they hadn't taken Shayna—and that made her feel guilty. She didn't want them to take Jaylynn, either, but if it had been Shayna . . . well, she knew exactly how Dez was feeling right now. She almost never worried about Shayna's safety, but at the moment, the prospect of losing her made her quake in her boots.

She tossed a glance over her shoulder and discovered Shayna was nowhere to be seen. Crystal slowed to a stop and turned, bent over, and put her hands on her knees. Between gasps, she bobbed up, watching the trail. Nearly a minute passed before Crystal saw her partner dragging disconsolately along. It took another minute before Shayna caught up to her.

"I'm sorry, Crys," she huffed. "I can't keep at this pace. I just can't."

"You too cold?"

Shayna gulped in a big breath and pointed at the sheer long underwear Crystal wore. "Not as cold as you must be."

"They look thin, but they're fine. I know I look ridiculous. I've got those Carhartt overalls in the Jeep, though. Just gotta get there."

Still out of breath, Shayna said, "I don't mean to whine, girl. But I just don't have the stamina you do. And I'm getting blisters."

Crystal stood tall and spoke with a worried expression on her face. "You've got to stay with it, *mi amada*. Jaylynn's life may depend upon us."

Shayna's face squinched up as though she might cry. "I know! I know that. I'm just so scared and tired and—oh, God, it's awful!"

Crystal opened her arms, and Shayna fell into them, crying in earnest. "Shhh. It's okay. It'll be all right, Shay. C'mon, don't cry."

"I can't help it."

"I know you can't." Crystal held her tight, stroked the back of her hair, patted her between the shoulders, then loosened her hold. "We have to keep moving, hon."

Shayna wiped her eyes on the sleeve of her jacket. "You go on. Go like hell. I'll catch up as soon as I can."

"No. Not a good idea. I'm not leaving in the Jeep without you."

"I don't mind. I can wait. Maybe someone will be there, and—"

"No way! We're not separating. For all we know, they could come back this way. We can't predict Dez's—or Jaylynn's—success or failure. We aren't safe until we're out of here, and I'm not leaving without you."

Shayna looked at her, a plea in her eyes as though she didn't want to say it, but she did. "I'm nearly done in, Crys. I can walk, but I just can't lift my knees anymore. I can't run."

"Okay. No shame." She reached for Shayna's hand. "Let's go as fast as we can. That's all we can do, right?" They turned northwest together, and struck out at a determined walk.

# Chapter
# Seventeen

"WHEN THE HELL are we gonna get there, Blondie?" Bostwick gave Jaylynn a shove from behind.

She lurched forward, caught herself, and turned to face him. She was sick of him pushing her. His touch made her feel sick to her stomach. She didn't speak and just glared at him.

"I asked you a question. How much further?"

"I don't really know. We must be close."

"You stupid bitch — hiked in here, didn't pay any attention." He shook his head, and a pained look crossed his face. Rubbing his belly, he groaned. "Must've been something in that jerky I ate a bit ago." He reached out a big mitt and swatted at her. "Sit down. I gotta rest up."

Jaylynn lowered herself until her back was against a tree, her knees up almost to her chin. Warily, she watched him for a moment, then looked ahead on the trail. Keith stood there looking like an imbecile.

Bostwick stumbled over his own foot, reached out a hand for a tree, and steadied himself. "Jesus. This is a nightmare. First thing I'm doing when I get out of this godforsaken hellhole is soak in a tub for about an hour. Then I'm gonna take my money and go buy the nicest, most comfortable clothes — something a lot better than those shitty jumpsuits. Never wearing orange again. Not even to hunt." He crossed his arms over his stomach and leaned forward, making a grunting noise.

Jaylynn closed her eyes and listened for a moment. The trees rustled. Some small animal skittered in the bushes. She heard a bird's call. But nothing else. She sent out a silent, emotional plea: *Dez, where are you? I'd give a million dollars to hear your size tens come thundering up here now.*

Bostwick took a deep breath and straightened up. "I've had

enough of this shit! Get up, Blondie. Let's go. We gotta hurry."

When she rose and stepped back on the trail, Keith was waiting ahead, his eyebrows raised and a look of concern on his face. When he saw her strike out again, he, too, continued on down the trail.

Jaylynn started thinking of the performance she was going to have to put on when they reached the parking area and it became clear that there was no vehicle matching the keys Bostwick had. She hoped there were other cars there, other people, perhaps even Dez and Crystal. She allowed herself to think of her partner's emotional state, which was something she had been avoiding. *If something happens to me, Dez will never get over it. She'll blame herself. I can't do that to her.*

Behind her, she heard a strange gurgling, and Bostwick yelled, "Shit. Hold up. Randall, get back here."

"What's the matter?"

Bostwick actually blushed. He gestured toward the woods. "Gotta find me a log. Gotta take a shit."

Keith shook his head in amazement.

"Owww." Bostwick was flushed and sweating. "Down on your knees, Blondie. Randall, you know the drill." He wheeled around and stomped into the brush about twenty yards, dumped the backpack on the ground, and fumbled with his pants.

Jaylynn made sure to look elsewhere before he squatted. Down on one knee, she gazed up at Keith. His face revealed uncertainty and fatigue. He had yet to express any of the glee Bostwick kept harping on about their big escape.

When he finally turned toward her, he rolled his eyes. "This is nothing like I—Jesus, how did we get into this mess?" He passed the back of his wrist across his mouth and stared off into the distance.

In a soft voice, Jaylynn asked, "How *did* you get involved with him?"

"Him? I'm not involved with him. He—he took me. He just hauled my ass out of the infirmary. I've still got a headache." As if he'd said too much, he stepped back and turned away. Jaylynn took that lapse in attention as an invitation. In her best sprinter's form, she rocketed to her feet. Knees high, arms driving, she took off down the trail, her heart pounding like a bass drum. *Get away. Get away. Get away.* The chant beat in her head. *I can outrun them. I will outrun them!*

The path meandered to the right, and she slowed slightly and leaned into it, turning, turning, until she felt the sun on her left cheek. She knew it was the race of her life, and one she must win. She strained forward, gasping in great gulps of air.

A blur of blue came crashing out of the trees on her right, and she ran right into it. A stinking muscular arm caught her around the neck pulling her into a wide, flat chest, but she wrenched herself from his grasp.

Panting, he grabbed the front of her jacket and shoved her. "Thought you'd get away, huh? Worthless little bitch!" His breath smelled rancid as he stepped toward her, one big paw ready to strike.

"No!" she screamed and surprised him with a solid blow up to his chin. He grunted with pain, pulled back his right hand, and slapped the side of her face with his big mitt. He grabbed the front of her coat with his left hand and shook her like a rag doll. "Stop it! You run again, and I'll kick the shit outta you!"

"You beast!" Using her self-defense training, she twisted against his grip and knocked his hand away. He reached out, grabbed her coat collar, and lifted her off the ground. "Let go of me!" She kicked at his shins.

"Goddammit, girl! You—" She struck out at his face again. "Ow!" He shoved her away.

She dropped to the ground. He brought his right hand up to his face and loomed over her like a giant ogre, sweating, blood trickling from a cut above his eye. Jaylynn tried to scramble away, but he snarled and struck out, his fist catching her in the chin and lower lip. She hit the ground and frantically tried to crab-walk away from him. She heard flapping footfalls behind her, then actually felt them through the hard-packed dirt on the trail. As she sat up, she saw the other convict rush past. A pair of hands pushed away the sweating bully.

"Jesus, Bostwick!" Keith's voice was shrill. "Leave her be! What the hell are you doing?"

"Fuckin' bitch cut me! Poked me in the eye. I'll kick the shit outta her."

"No, no, no!" Keith shoved at him again. "Listen to me. We don't have time for this. And we might need her. Have you considered that?"

Bostwick shouted, "I don't need this fuckin' bitch!"

"Shit, Bostwick! You can't mark her up. What if one of us has to, like, be in the trunk, and the other two have to drive along pretending to be some happily married couple or something?" He slugged the giant convict in the shoulder. "We might need her. You hear me? You can't hit her. Not now."

Jaylynn got to her knees, feeling shaky. She listened to Keith as he continued to harangue the bigger man. If her head hadn't been spinning so much, she might have tried to run again, but it took all her effort not to throw up.

Bostwick was nodding. Grudgingly he said, "Yeah, yeah, yeah, all right." He reached behind him and pulled out the gun. "See this, Blondie?" He pushed past Keith. "I've shot people before, and I'm not afraid to shoot your ass. Got it?" When she didn't answer, he said, "On your feet, and don't try a trick like that again."

Keith reached down a hand, but Jaylynn ignored it. She put her palm down onto the dirt and pushed up, rising on her own. Her mouth was dry as dust, and she felt disoriented—not exactly dizzy, but close. When she put the back of her hand to her lips, it came away with a smudge of blood. The left side of her face where Bostwick had struck her was on fire, but she wouldn't give him the satisfaction of knowing that. Pulling down her jacket and squaring her shoulders, she tightened her fists, made herself go tense. She willed herself to have courage. *Don't give in to them. Never. I'll die first.*

"You okay?" Keith asked.

She let out a breath and willed herself not to respond to him. *He's the enemy. I can't let them play good cop/bad cop with me. Don't fall into this Stockholm Syndrome crap.* "I'm fine."

Bostwick laughed. "Yeah, fine. Right. Not as fine as you'd be if you'd gotten away. Lucky I'm a fast crapper." He grabbed her arm and shoved her forward. "Get going. But don't forget—one more move like that, and you'll get what's coming to you."

Jaylynn jerked her arm away, took a deep breath, and marched forward, past Keith. Tasting blood, she spat to the side of the path and was relieved that the inside of her mouth didn't seem to be bleeding too badly. She definitely did not want to touch it for fear of germs and infection. She fought tears. *I was so close, so close.* But she couldn't let it get her down. She resolved to watch for other opportunities, and she didn't intend to let them hurt her anymore.

Keith called out, "Hey, wait. Here." She turned to see him fumbling in his pack, and next thing she knew, his grimy fingers held out a steri-wrapped gauze pad. "There's some antiseptic in here, too. Do you want it?"

"Screw that, Randall!" Bostwick scowled. "She doesn't need that crap. Just get moving."

Jaylynn turned and stepped along again, but she did open the little package and take the gauze out. When she pressed it against the inside of her lip, it came back stained pink with blood. It wasn't too bad. Already the cut must be sealing up. She applied it again for another minute or so, then let the pad drop to the path. One more thing that might help searchers find her.

The two men hiked behind her for a time, not saying

anything, then Keith said, "Excuse me," and moved on ahead. She was back in the middle again with Bostwick nagging over her shoulder once more.

"Step on it, Blondie. Let's pick it up, Randall."

GRIGOR ROSSEL MANEUVERED the Explorer down the long lane to Nigh Lake as he thought of the Gubenko brothers. Rossel was not particularly close to Leonid, but Sergei Gubenko loved Leonid above all others. The two siblings had been through so much: starvation in Russia, the indiscriminate killing of most of their family, time in a work camp, a journey of hundreds of miles to a ship, and a terrible passage in order to emigrate. Rossel knew all this had happened long before he was born, yet the stories Gubenko told were so vivid, so powerful, that Rossel felt he, too, had been a part of the painful journey to the new world.

Sergei Gubenko had definitely been part of Rossel's journey, and he wasn't sure where he'd be without him. In 1965, when Rossel was only thirteen years old, he'd first encountered Sergei Gubenko. Rossel and his mother lived in New York then. The previous year, Rossel's father had fallen into a vat of boiling liquid at the paper factory where he worked. Rossel's stomach still turned at the memory of his father's injuries. He lingered for three days before dying from the severe burns. Rossel's mother worked 12-hour days at a laundry to pay for food, utilities, and rent for their two-room apartment. There were no extras.

Rossel was big for his age, and already he was wearing his father's clothes and boots even though they were a little too big. His mother often commented, not without a little pride, that he would eat them out of house and home. He tried to curb his appetite, but he was growing and most days he was ravenous.

One day, his mother planned to make *holubky*, a kind of baked cabbage stuffed with meats and vegetables. She discovered she was out of onions, so she gave him a dollar and sent him to the market. Late on a Saturday morning, there were long lines. Rossel stood in the queue, eight customers back, and waited patiently, watching people and hearing Russian, Yiddish, French, and English all around him. The man ahead of him wore a rumpled dark blue suit and held a package of throat lozenges. Leaning to the side, away from others, he coughed a deep, wracking bark. The line moved forward. In a flash of speed and agility, a skinny youth in a tight white t-shirt, jeans, and boots slid in line ahead of the coughing man. When the man in the suit stopped wheezing and turned back, he still stood bent over a little, looking weak and shaky.

The youth's arms were covered with tattoos: a skull-and-crossbones on the ball of muscle on his right shoulder, a snake on the left, and some sort of blood-and-flowers motif on his left forearm. His right forearm was obscured by the package of potato chips he held.

Rossel saw Tattoo Man's shoulders moving, as though he were laughing. He knew it wasn't his business—but then again, by cutting in, this lout was cheating Rossel, too. He reached around the sick fellow and tapped Tattoo Man on the shoulder. "Step out," he said, in his most ominous voice. "You know why."

The line cutter whirled around, a sneer on his face. "Fuck off."

People nearby noticed something was going on and edged back. The din in the store dropped a few decibels. The man with the cough turned to Rossel, a questioning look on his face. His hair was dark, and his eyes were bright blue, but watering from his ailment. He still looked weak and shaky from his coughing fit; however when he stopped slumping and stood upright, he was much taller than Rossel.

In a loud voice, Rossel said, "You cut in line. The rest of us have waited patiently. Go to the back and wait like a civilized human being."

A hum of approval around Rossel told him he had stated his case in such a way that other people supported him. Tattoo Man didn't see it that way. He reached into his front pocket and pulled something out. Rossel heard a click, spied a flash of silver, and realized the man held a switchblade. The checkers stopped checking, and shoppers ceased shopping.

Rossel didn't think. As if of its own volition, his left leg came up, and his father's heavy leather boot slammed into the man's knife hand.

"Yeow!" As Tattoo Man yelped and tried to back out of range, someone in the line stuck his foot out. The youth tripped and fell heavily, hitting his elbow sharply on the floor. The switchblade clattered to the side. The snack bag burst, spewing yellow-colored chips all over.

Rossel kicked the knife aside. He didn't wait to see it skitter across the floor, all the way to the wall forty feet away. Instead, he stood above the man, and in a calm voice said, "Get out your wallet."

The murmur of voices steadily rose as the man on the floor rolled to his side and reached for his back pocket. Rossel felt a thrill of satisfaction to see that the triumphant look of superiority on Tattoo Man's face had been wiped aside. Rossel nodded toward the checker. "How much for the bag of potato chips he has ruined?" The checker told him $1.09. "You will pay two dollars because somebody has to come clean up this mess."

Tattoo Man got to his feet and threw two bills toward Rossel. They fluttered to the ground. Rossel narrowed his eyes and stared at the man with what he hoped was the most evil and threatening look imaginable. "Get out. And don't ever come back in here."

In a flash of white t-shirt, the creep turned and fled. Rossel bent to pick up the two bills. He laughed out loud when he saw that instead of two one-dollar bills, one of them was a five.

"What's going on!" someone shouted behind Rossel. A fat, heavily-jowled fellow pushed his way through the crowd. Rossel was relieved to see it was the store owner.

A gray-haired Jewish man in a dark coat and skull cap said, "This young man thwarted an assault."

A shrill-voiced woman said, "The man pulled a knife! It's over there." She pointed toward the far wall.

The manager retrieved the knife and shouted loudly across the store for someone to bring a broom. Rossel fell back in line and attempted to blend in behind the coughing man. As the line moved forward, a clerk swept up the broken chips, and when Rossel finally faced the checker, he handed her the onion and said, "You may also charge me for his carelessness."

Wordlessly, she entered the two prices. He paid and walked out of the store almost five dollars richer. He could buy his mother a new dress at the thrift store. Or he could easily get an abundant amount of fruit for jam and preserves. Or he could replace his loose boots until he grew more fully into them. Dreaming of all the ways to spend the money, he tossed the onion up and plucked it from mid-air. At the same moment, he caught sight of a man standing a few feet from the store's entrance.

The man lifted an arm and coughed into the crook of his elbow, then said, "Fast reactions you showed in the store."

Rossel noted the man's thick accent. On a whim, instead of using English, he spoke in Russian. "Yes, sir."

The man's reddened face broke into a smile. He responded in Russian. "Ah, you are my countryman. That explains it. You are rather fierce when faced with opposition." Rossel didn't know how to respond to that. His face flushed with the praise. "Do you live around here?" the man asked.

Rossel nodded. "Two streets over. In the tenement."

"What is your name?"

"Grigor Rossel."

Now the man stepped closer and held out a hand. "I am

Sergei Gubenko." Rossel shifted the onion to his left hand, and shook with the stranger who then stepped back and coughed again. When he recovered, he said, "My brother and I own the printing company around the corner. Do you have a job after school and on weekends?"

"No, sir."

"I could use a man good with his hands." He looked down at the package of cough drops he held. "If you worked for me, I could have sent *you* out on the errand to purchase these, rather than me having to stand in the long line when I don't feel well." Rossel nodded. "How old are you?"

For a moment, Rossel considered saying fifteen or sixteen, but something told him to be truthful. He did, however, put the truth in the most favorable light he could think of. "I will be fourteen at my next birthday."

Gubenko grinned. "You are very big, son, very imposing. I like your style, your sense of fairness. Why don't you come with me, and I will make some arrangements."

Rossel was torn and his face must have showed it. Gubenko frowned. "What is it? You have heard something bad of me?"

"Oh, no! No, not at all. It's just that—well, you see . . ." He looked to the ground, embarrassed. "My mother is waiting for me to bring this home to her so she can make *holubky*."

"Ah, I understand." Gubenko was smiling again. "You have a family obligation. One's family should always come first."

"I could deliver this to my mother, then come back?"

"Excellent idea." Gubenko coughed again. With shaking fingers, he peeled open the package he held and rooted around inside. Between thumb and forefinger, he held a reddish-colored cough drop up to the light, then popped it in his mouth. He cleared his throat. "Perhaps later this afternoon, after your noon meal, you could come see me. Say, two o'clock?"

"Yes, sir."

And that was how it began. Gubenko took the young man under his wing and became the father Rossel had lost. When Rossel was twenty, and his mother fell ill from an internal cancer, Gubenko paid Mrs. Rossel's hospital bills. When she died seven months later, Gubenko made all the funeral arrangements and lent Rossel the money to pay for it. Nearly forty years had passed since that young boy had stuck up for a man coughing in a grocery line, but in all those years, the oath of honor and loyalty he had made to Gubenko never waned.

Rossel had never snooped into what went on in the Gubenko affairs. He was in his early twenties before he understood that the printing work done was not always on the up-and-up. One day he noticed that the company was printing a variety of state tax forms — not just New York's. After a time, he came to understand that the company's "accountants," and there were many of them, falsified tax returns and received reimbursement from the government through dozens of front companies all over the nation. Those fronts were usually small businesses that "failed" regularly, so by the time auditors and investigators had unraveled the complex messes presented in the tax forms, refunds had been issued and it was too late to recover the money. Poof — gone in the night.

In addition to the authentic printing jobs that were requested, the Gubenko employees printed documents, falsified verifications, completed tax returns, and couriered the paperwork to other locations where they could be mailed to appropriate government offices. There were many other fraudulent techniques, but that was the one Rossel understood best. He knew it was illegal, but he did not think it particularly terrible. After the first few years of working for Gubenko, he stopped getting paid in cash and instead received regular paychecks complete with state, federal, and Social Security deductions. He knew how much of his hard-earned money the government stole, and it did not bother him to take some of it back.

Rossel did whatever he was told, taking care to keep his mouth shut about the business. In all the years he had worked "security" for the Gubenko brothers in New York, and then for Sergei Gubenko in Chicago, he had killed only two men, both for clear betrayals. Others he forced to see the light by calm reasoning. If that didn't work, a well-placed beating followed up by a few days of captivity in a small, dark place usually did the trick. Most men were cowards, he had learned. He did not enjoy using violence to subdue them, but as Gubenko always told him, the ends justified the means.

Rossel was not a flashy mobster type. The fancy tracksuits and multiple tattoos other Russian "muscle" men wore did not appeal to him. He preferred the anonymity of slacks and a polo shirt or a plain dark suit, with or without a tie, and comfortable leather shoes or boots. He still remembered the foolishness of the Tattoo Man in the market all those years ago. How easily he could be identified. The two times Rossel had been arrested, back in New York, he had been respectful and quiet, and both times there had been insufficient evidence to hold him. Rossel prided himself on not being a loud-mouthed, bossy, power-hungry maniac. He did not require attention or recognition or even money. Gubenko's infrequent praise was all he ever wished for. He had found that his own quiet, focused methods worked best for him, allowing him to blend in, even though he was slightly over six feet tall and broad-shouldered.

And now it was time, once more, to protect his benefactor, his superior, his friend . . . his father. He had his doubts about the effectiveness of the plan, but that was not his concern. He would do everything in his power to insure success. He had purchased a few things before he left Chicago, hauled them out to the car, then driven all night to the tiny town in northern Minnesota, and he intended to do everything in his power to help the Gubenkos.

There were no cars in the flattened area up the slope from Nigh Lake. He pulled the SUV alongside a display board protected by thick plastic and capped by a protective eave. A covered garbage can sat next to it. He got out and stretched his legs, went around to the other side of the vehicle, and read the announcements and information from the Department of Natural Resources.

POISON & CONTAMINANT GUIDE
The DNR wants you to know:
Children under age 15 and
women who are pregnant, planning to be pregnant,
or who are breastfeeding:
Do Not Eat WALLEYE over 15 inches
in length from Nigh Lake
Thank You.

Rossel was sure he had never eaten walleye, whatever that was. He pictured a swordfish-sized creature with bulging eyes, like the bleary-blue ones of an old man he remembered from the neighborhood when he was small. One day he'd been walking down the street, holding his mother's hand, when Mr. Lipinski lurched up to them and tried to hug and kiss Rossel's mother. He hadn't understood the man's bizarre behavior then, but now he knew that Lipinski had probably been drunk. After his mother pushed the man away and tried to salvage her dignity, Lipinski bent and said, "Lucky little man. Kiss her for me." He'd staggered off and, not more than a block away, wandered into traffic and was hit by a car. Rossel had heard the horn, the thud, the cries of the driver, before his mother hurried him off in the other direction.

The memory gave him a terrible feeling of unease. Odd how such recollections surfaced at unusual times. With a shudder, Rossel quickly viewed the rest of the items on the display board, then returned to the car and collected a couple of empty water bottles and some sandwich wrappers. He stood next to the garbage can and surveyed the forest and lake. Clouds had moved across the sun. In the muted light, the tree trunks looked gray and the branches hung down like denuded, dying boughs. A gust of wind picked up a cluster of dry leaves and blew them toward the display board. Rossel felt a presence, something dark and evil. He hastily opened the garbage can lid, dropped in his trash, and jammed the lid back on. Rubbing his hands on his jeans, he returned to the SUV and stood shivering for a moment before he got in and started the engine.

In less than a minute, he was back at the turnoff, considering whether he should go east, toward Lake Jeanette, or head back to Buyck for gas and food. After pausing to examine the GPS and to listen to the radio and CB reports, he decided to make a quick sweep east. He wouldn't be able to face Gubenko unless he could say he had made every effort.

# Chapter
# Eighteen

**Minnesota North Woods**
**Sunday, October 17, 11:36 a.m.**

A CHILL WIND blew into Jaylynn's face. She jogged forward, dragging her feet or digging in her heels whenever they came to paths that shot off in any direction. Twice more her captor suffered intestinal problems and stepped off the trail, but both times he insisted she lie facedown on the path where he could see her. She was disgusted by his crass comments and sickened by the sounds and smells to which he subjected her. She was also miserable, tired, and hungry. Her thirst had increased to the point where it was nearly all she could think about. Despite their pace and the sun occasionally peeking out from heavy clouds, the temperature felt colder than it had when she had risen hours earlier.

She was watching the ground when Keith stopped ahead of her, and she took several more steps before she realized he had halted. She pulled up behind him, wearily focusing on his plaid lounging pajamas as they wiffled in the breeze.

"What?" Bostwick asked.

Keith pointed. "Through the trees there."

Jaylynn squinted. She hadn't noticed, but they were walking parallel to an open space on their left with only a stand of trees separating them from it. Not too far ahead, the path bled out into a wide apron of packed-down yellowish grass that surrounded a dirt lot. The clearing was a large circle perhaps twenty yards in diameter. She couldn't quite make out what was written on a tall signpost directly across the clearing. A dirt road led into the circle not far beyond where the path ended.

There were no cars in the lot. Bostwick bit his upper lip. "Well, Blondie? What have you got to say for yourself?"

She crossed her arms in front of her. "This isn't it."

"Don't you think I've fuckin' figured that out?" He bent so his face was level with hers, and she stepped back. "Do you know where your fuckin' car is or not?"

"Hey, hey," Keith said in a soothing voice as he stepped between them. "This is probably some side lot, you know, for snowmobiles or something. This isn't the right place, right?"

Jaylynn shrugged. Keith's eyes burned into hers. Before he could say anything further, Jaylynn heard the sound of car tires crunching on dirt and gravel. Bostwick's head jerked to the side. "Get the hell outta sight," he said in a stage whisper. He grabbed their arms and pulled them back along the path and over to the side behind a flaming red sumac bush.

A dusty, tan SUV rolled slowly along the lane and into the lot. Fluttering in the wind on the passenger side was a yellow flag on a white plastic post. All over the state Jaylynn had seen Vikings and Twins flags—even Green Bay Packer flags—but never a yellow one with a smiley face on it.

Bostwick tightened his grip on her arm. "Ah, this is great. Fuck your car, Blondie. This is a ride we can use." With confidence, he strode out, dragging her along with him. The car door opened, and a man emerged. He was as big as Bostwick, only not as broad-shouldered. Though rumpled, he looked a far sight tidier than Jaylynn thought the three of them did. His light brown hair was cut short and speckled with gray, and he was dressed in jeans and a red and tan plaid shirt, as though he were ready to go hunting. It occurred to her that if he was a friend of Bostwick's, perhaps he *was* hunting.

Bostwick called out, "About time you got here."

The new arrival narrowed his eyes and licked his lips. "Here is not where the exchange was to be made."

The big man looked startled. "Yeah. That's right. Uh—"

"Enough." The man raised a hand and turned his blue eyes to Jaylynn. "This is not the package." Jaylynn heard a funny lilt in his voice and wondered what sort of accent it was. The man tipped his head slightly and examined Keith who stood off to the side. "You are Keith Randall?" He rolled the R in Randall.

Jaylynn whipped around in time to see Keith's expression of surprise. He said, "Who wants to know?"

"Friends of your brother desire to make your acquaintance. Come with me."

"Wait just one minute," Bostwick said in a threatening voice. "Where's my money?"

Jaylynn looked back and forth between her two captors. Her eyes rested longest on Keith because of the confusion his bruised face revealed. Suddenly he turned and sprinted away, back toward the path they had just left.

"Shit!" Bostwick said. He slipped out of his bulky pack, dropped it next to the car, and took off after him.

Jaylynn saw her chance to go the other direction, but the man grabbed her arm. She tried to shrug him off, but his grip was strong. "Sorry, young lady, but I think you should stay with me until your friends return."

"They're not my friends."

"I see. You look very tired. Would you like something to drink?"

Jaylynn didn't know how to answer, so she said nothing. She very much wanted water, but she didn't want to accept anything from him.

Still gripping her arm, he leaned down into the open driver's door and fumbled for something next to the seat. The Ford's hatch popped open, and he pulled her to the back, stepping around the lumpy backpack that lay in the dirt.

"Sit," he said, gesturing to the tailgate. A 24-pack of Crystal Springs water sat unopened and shrouded in plastic next to another one containing seven of the original 24 bottles. He separated one from that case and handed it to her. "Be my guest. And be assured that nothing is expected in return."

She wrenched the plastic sani-wrap away from the top, twisted off the plastic cap, and sucked down a third of the 24-ounce container. She looked up at his amused eyes. "Yes, I was very thirsty. Thank you."

He gave her a nod, then gazed off toward the path. Bostwick had Keith in a headlock and was plodding toward them, trying his best to avoid the trapped man's wild swings. They were both out of breath when they reached the rear of the Ford. Bostwick's bullet-shaped head was shiny with sweat. "Listen, Russky, I want my money, then let's get out of here." He pushed Keith over near Jaylynn, and his hip fell heavily against the tailgate. He steadied himself and shifted to sit, panting, next to Jaylynn.

Bostwick wiped slime away from his brow and stood with one forearm against the raised hatch. "We had a deal."

The driver's eyes narrowed. "First, I would like to know why you did not meet me as planned."

Bostwick looked away, obviously trying to repress a tight smirk. The scabby line on his bottom lip broke open and a bit of red blood oozed out. "We can get into that later."

"Yes, we shall. For now, time is of the essence." The man returned to the driver's side of the SUV and reached in. He emerged and approached Bostwick holding a flat, rectangular item wrapped in brown paper.

Keith sagged like all the life was being sucked out of him. Jaylynn heard a little choking noise, as though he'd started crying, but when she looked at him, he sat stone-faced with his feet on the ground and his filthy hands shaking in his lap. The knuckles on his left hand were bruised, and she saw a spot of blood. He slipped off the backpack and let it drop behind him in the cargo area.

Jaylynn drank more water, watching, waiting. She put her hand in her coat pocket and found the pen, which she took out. No one paid any attention as she scribbled on the side of the water bottle.

Bostwick pointed at the object in the man's hands and sneered. "Whaddya take me for—an idiot? I'll kiss your filthy ass if that little stack is fifty thou."

Later, Jaylynn realized that was where everything went wrong. The Russian froze in mid-step, holding the packet tightly, and said, "You are most unpleasant, Mr. Bostwick. Mr. Gubenko will be dismayed."

"Fuck Gubenko." He reached behind him and pulled the gun from the small of his back. "The money or your life."

"Such a cliché. This *is* the money. I have personally overseen the counting of it, and it is all there."

"Gimme it." Bostwick leaned forward and reached. As the Russian held it out, the gun went off. Bostwick stared down at the gun in his hand with a look of disbelief on his face. "Oh, shit."

Jaylynn watched in shock as the brown-haired man grabbed his stomach and crumpled to the ground. She and Keith both sprang up from the tailgate and moved away from the back of the SUV.

Keith shouted, "You dumbshit! Why? Why did you do it? He was giving it to you!"

"I'll be damned. It just went off." He looked over at Keith in wonderment. "That's the last time I ever stick a gun in the front of my pants. I could've shot my dick off."

Keith pushed him aside and fell to his knees. The Russian lay on his right side clutching his abdomen, which was rapidly becoming soaked with red. "Oh, mister, oh, man, oh, my God. I don't know what to do for you." Jaylynn looked on in horror.

Bostwick bent and retrieved the money packet that had fallen to the ground. He ripped the end off and slid the money out. "Well. The Russky was right. Looks like the money *is* all here. Will you look at this? Who would ever guess so much money would take up so little space?"

Keith rose, clenching his fists. He had a smear of blood on

the right knee of the flannel pants. "You sonuvabitch! You greedy asshole. You didn't have to do that!"

Bostwick pursed his lips. "What's done is done. Nothing we can do now. Let's go."

Jaylynn slipped to the side of the SUV hoping to make a run for it, but before she could go any farther, Bostwick got hold of her. "Ah, ah, ah. You, too, Blondie." In a tight voice, he said, "Get in the fuckin' car."

She looked down at the man moaning on the ground. "We can't just leave him."

"Sure we can. He'd just get blood all over everything and die anyway. Get in the back seat. Now!"

"But why? You don't need me anymore. You've got a car. Just leave me with him."

Bostwick's face leaned in close and she smelled his foul breath. "It's like Keith said. What if we need you to get through a roadblock? Besides," he leered at her, his bloody grin cruel, "I've got some other fun in store for you. Get the fuck in the car!"

He shoved her, so she opened the door and reluctantly got in, still smelling the cordite hanging in the air. She purposely left the door open.

Outside the Explorer, Bostwick said, "Now Randall, you know I was never gonna give you up to them. I wasn't." Keith didn't answer. The convict went on in a half-pleading voice. "We were supposed to meet him north of the prison. If I'd been planning on turning you over, we would've gone that way. I took you east instead." Keith turned away. "Listen to me," he growled as he grabbed Keith's arm. "It's a killing you're part of now. We gotta get out of here. Get in the goddamn car." He moved toward the bulky backpack.

"You make me sick." The disgust in Keith's voice was clear, even inside the car, and Jaylynn agreed with him completely.

"Whatever. Let's go." Bostwick stepped over the Russian and moved around to Jaylynn's side of the car to slam shut the door. He went back around and opened the other rear door. "C'mon, Keith. We're outta here." Then suddenly he was in a hurry. "Oh, shit! Now!" He looked out toward the path. "We gotta go now!" He pushed Keith into the back, slammed the door, and jumped in the driver's seat.

DEZ FELT AS though she had run fifty miles. She was sore, and the rapidly cooling temperature didn't help her stiff muscles any. *Time for water.* She slowed to a walk and uncapped the canteen to take a sip. She'd been eating a few handfuls of Gorp every so often in an effort to keep up her energy, but the last time had made her feel sick. She didn't think she could stomach more of it.

She was swallowing the last of the water in the canteen when she heard a gunshot in the distance.

*Oh, my God. What was that?*

She dropped the canteen and ran. Her own breath echoed in her head. For a moment, she saw red and blue lights, then the white glare of a police searchlight. She shut her eyes tight for two beats, then opened them. The only glare was from the sun fighting to come out from behind the growing banks of clouds.

The three or four minutes she ran seemed like half an hour before she came to a stand of trees that bordered a clearing. She fumbled for the gun in her waist pack, felt the coolness of the grip, increased her stride.

A figure lay on the ground next to a misshapen lump she recognized as her backpack. A big man looked her way, then got into a tan Ford Explorer. Its grill faced her. She heard it rev and lurch toward the trail. For one split second, Dez thought they planned to run her down and drive the trail. Instead, they veered off to the left, backed up, and accelerated toward the dirt road. She skidded to a stop and tried to take aim at the tires. Through the SUV's side window, she saw a shock of blond hair and a surprised face. *Oh, God.* Her finger froze on the trigger. *What if I shoot high?*

Dez burst across the clearing and gave chase, the gun heavy in her right hand. Then she was breathing in billows of dust. She kept running after the vehicle until long after it had disappeared, then finally dropped to her knees in the middle of the lane. The Beretta fell into the dust beside her.

"Noooooo!" Her cry was dry and ragged, and when the tears came, they were a torrential rush from five hours of fear and frustration. She leaned forward until her arms rested on the ground, cradled her forehead in her hands, and cried. *I was so close.* Her mind whirled with scenarios: what if she hadn't gotten off the trail so many times? What if the bear hadn't slowed her down? *Why, oh why, didn't I run harder?*

After a few minutes, Dez lifted her head and slipped off the heavy backpack. Sitting next to it, she rooted around until she found the cell phone and turned it on. *C'mon. Please. Please work.* The phone lit up, but the display very clearly showed *NO SERVICE.* Just for good measure, she pressed 9-1-1, but nothing happened.

She wanted to throw the phone into the woods. Crush it beneath her foot. Break it with her bare hands. Instead, she turned it off, carefully folded it up, and put it away. The gun went back into the waist pack.

Rising, she dusted herself off as best she could and picked up her pack. As she walked back toward the clearing, her stomach tensed. Right there in the middle of the road, she bent and vomited. After that she felt better, though the bitter, acrid taste in her mouth made her squeamish.

She forced herself on, half-running, and made her way back to the figure on the ground. With knees pulled up, he lay in blood-spattered dirt, his flannel shirt drenched dark red. She gently put her hand on the knob of his shoulder, intending to ease him onto his back, but he groaned and shifted his hips slightly.

She didn't know him; hadn't ever seen him before. "Sir, are you shot?"

"Yes. Shot."

"Can I help stop the blood flow?"

"No." The word came out sounding wheezy. "Gut-shot." He gasped out. "I need hospital. Now."

"I'm on foot. I'll go for help in a minute. Keep pressure on the wound. You'll slow the blood loss."

She rose and trotted over to the blue backpack, knelt, and opened it. In it were a hatchet and sheath knife, a dozen packets of dehydrated food, a small Johnson & Johnson first aid kit, and a red knit cap. Stuffed down at the bottom were also a half-roll of toilet paper, a bandana, some thermal underwear, and Jaylynn's water-resistant wind/rain shell, which was rolled up and zipped into a kit about the size of a paperback book.

She picked up the backpack and brought it over next to the bleeding man. She slid off the pack she carried, unzipped it, and pulled out a shirt. It was all she had, other than her own jacket. She debated what would be best to do. Finally, she took out the thermal underwear and wrapped the legs over his midsection and shoulder. She opened the wind shell and smoothed out the wrinkles, then laid it carefully over him. The hat she pulled on over his head as gently as she could, but still he groaned in pain. She combined all the rest of the items from the two bags into her own, then zipped the empty one closed and fashioned it into a pillow of sorts to tuck under the man's head.

She sat back on her heels beside him. "Sir, what's your name?"

"Russell." Through gritted teeth he said, "Greg. Greg Russell."

"I'm an off-duty cop, Mr. Russell. What happened here?" He didn't answer. "Mr. Russell. Greg! Were you carjacked?" She pressed a hand into his hip. "Greg, wake up and tell me what happened."

"Shot."

She reached out and put her palm on his cheek. "Greg, can you hear me? Open your eyes. Can you see me?" His eyes popped open, unfocused and every bit as shiny blue as her own. The pupils were pinpricks. He turned his face away from the light shining through the clouds and squinted toward her. In a moment, he met her with a clearer gaze. "Greg, how many of them were there?"

"Two men," he choked out, his gaze growing clearer. "Blond girl."

"They carjacked you?"

"Pick up. Package. Gubenko."

"What?"

"Jail breakout."

"Yes, yes, they broke out of Kendall. Greg, stay with me. What else?"

"Tell Gubenko. Tell . . . " She waited. He closed his eyes and took a shallow breath. "Gubenko...my father...tell him..."

His body went slack. "Greg? Greg? Stay with me, man. Come on." She pressed her hand against his throat, searched for a pulse, and found a weak throb.

"Greg! Hang on, buddy. I'll go for help. Just hang in there."

She rose and went over to a wooden plaque posted at the edge of the clearing. The upper half showed the white outline of Lake Jeanette. Below was a loop indicating Lots A, B, and C, and where they were in relation to the lake. Apparently she was in Lot A, the westernmost—and smallest—parking area and the farthest from the water. Lots B and C were down around the western curve of the lake and to the south. From the tiny key in the lower corner, it was clear the road the SUV had departed on curved north, reached a T, and then ran east-west. She would likely need to travel west on it to find help.

She hustled back over to the man and stared at him from above. She was about to leave, but his eyes opened again. "Lipinski?" He frowned, then made a gagging sound and closed his eyes.

Worried that he had died, she squatted beside him and put two fingers against the side of his neck. After a moment of fumbling, it hit her that he was indeed dead. His chest no longer rose, and there was no pulse at all.

"Well, shit!" A chill ran through her. They'd killed this man—what would they do to Jaylynn?

This time she didn't pause. She shouldered her pack and

started to hurry away, but something shiny and cylindrical
caught her eye. She detoured to the right and bent to pick up a
partly filled water bottle. The taste in her mouth was awful, but
she wasn't sure the water would be safe. She rolled it in her
hand, and on the back, over the blue label, she saw something
that made her heart race. *Jaylynn Savage, SPPD. Kidnapped: IL
Lic#ARL3054.*

The date was scratched on the other side. *Good girl,* she
thought, tears in her eyes. *Good job.* Dez had only caught the
letters on the plate; now she had the whole thing.

She opened the twist top, took a little water, swished it in
her mouth, and spat it out. Then she drained the remainder
down her grateful throat. When it was empty, she stowed the
bottle in her pack. She looked at her watch. Five past noon. *Hit
the road,* she thought, and took off running.

SALLY CABOT SAT in her Chevy outside the Gas-N-Go,
listening to Kenny Chesney wail "A Lot of Things Different" on
the country radio station. The Forest Service dispatch radio also
crackled to life periodically, but at the moment it was silent.
After stopping by the ranger station in Buyck earlier, she'd gone
home and found her husband watching the local fishing channel
on TV while cleaning his hunting rifle. They had a quick
discussion about the escape news that kept breaking into his
morning show. He hadn't realized their daughter was out in the
forest somewhere. The news spurred him into action. He decided
to cruise the highways and back roads while she hit the trails.

They had each packed rain gear. Cabot put on insulated
underwear beneath her uniform, picked up a box of 9 mm shells
for her Smith & Wesson handgun, and selected a dry change of
clothes. She filled up a Thermos with hot coffee, kissed him
goodbye, and told him to check in with the forest service
dispatcher every so often.

She'd already been in the gas station to buy a few snacks.
Now she was waiting for the guys from the prison to show up,
and she wasn't happy that they were so late. As she watched the
highway, she saw a surprising amount of traffic for Sunday late
morning, and most of the drivers didn't look like they'd been at
church. A certain electricity hung in the air; it couldn't all be
attributed to the change in the weather. If she were a civilian,
she wasn't so sure she'd be out and about with convicts on the
loose. Her husband had the right idea in keeping his hunting
rifle handy.

She looked at her watch again and decided she'd waited
long enough. As she contemplated leaving, a black cycle came

roaring into the parking lot. Recognizing it was one of the guards, she opened the door and hopped out of the truck, a hand raised in greeting. She'd left the tailgate down and a ramp out, so all he had to do was coax the bike right up and into the back of her truck without crashing into her back window. He managed without incident.

"Morris isn't coming." Schecter took his helmet off and tossed it in the back. He hoisted in the plank and shut the tailgate. "He got home and found out the babysitter had called in sick. Wife was late to work, and he's stuck there with the three kids."

"That's too bad. Well, then, it's just you and me."

"I expect so." They got in the truck and took off southeast on Highway 24, which ran parallel to the Vermillion River. "What's your plan, ma'am?"

"Please don't call me ma'am. I know I probably *am* old enough to be your mother, Schecter, but still, just call me Sally. Or Sal."

"Yes, ma—I mean, okay, Sal. You call me Lou. I'll call you Sal."

"Glad that's settled. To answer your question, I don't have much of a plan. There are eleven groups unaccounted for—thirty-six people total—who are out canoeing, camping, and hiking. You probably heard there's a busload of girls and their two guides supposed to be hiking from Lake Jeanette to Echo Lake. One of those guides is my daughter, so obviously I want to check on their whereabouts first."

"Sounds like a plan to me."

"COME ON, HON," Crystal said. "You can make it. See? We're almost there."

"Thank God. You go on ahead," Shayna answered. She walked gingerly, favoring one leg.

"Good work. Keep coming. I'll go pull the car to this end of the lot." With renewed energy, Crystal broke into a trot and ran the last three hundred yards. When she finally got to the red Jeep, she fished the keys out of her pack and hit the power door button. It only took another minute to start it up and drive over to the sign that marked the trail entrance. By then Shayna was dragging herself around the corner and down the last little hill.

Shayna got in the Jeep and let out a huge breath. "Thank you, good Lord in heaven. Thank you." She patted the dashboard, then leaned forward and kissed it. "Thank you for being new and starting right up."

Crystal handed her a cell phone. "We're still out of service, but watch the display. I'll drive south toward Buyck." She put the car into gear and squealed out of the lot. "Put on your seatbelt, love. I'm driving like a bat outta hell."

True to her word, Crystal drove fast, though carefully. They hit the two-lane highway, and she kicked up the speed to nearly eighty.

"Aren't we traveling west?" Shayna asked.

"I hope not. We want to go south. Get out the map and see. Any cell service yet?"

"I can only do so many things at once." She looked at the phone. "No."

"Check it out, we've turned some." Crystal pointed at the Jeep's compass. "Now we're going south again."

"Good. That's a relief. Crys?"

"Yeah?" She hazarded a glance over at her partner.

"You think maybe we should just go right to the end of the trail? You know—by that lake the trail headed to?"

Crystal bit her lower lip. "I don't know." She squinted at the clock on the dashboard display. "It's past noon now. We're probably too late." They drove in silence for a couple of minutes. "Any cell service yet?"

"Dammit! Quit asking me that. The very second there's cell service, you'll be the first to hear my scream of delight as I dial 9-1-1."

Crystal put her palm to her chin and shook her head. In a quiet voice she said, "Don't yell at me."

"I'm sorry. Dammit, I always had a bad feeling. I never did want to come. I should have trusted my instincts."

"Oh, Shay . . . "

"Don't 'Oh, Shay' me!"

"Come on, *mi amada*. I'm just as, you know, jittery as you are."

"Yeah," she said with a sigh. "I'm sorry, too. I *am* watching this thing. Don't worry. Within five seconds of getting a signal, I'll be on it."

"When we get close to Buyck, we may get lucky." She swerved around a pothole in the road. "I sure as hell hope so, anyway."

MILES DOWN THE road, Bostwick also dodged potholes. Jaylynn held on to the head-rest in front of her. She and Keith, in the Explorer's back seat, were jerked from side to side as Bostwick drove like a crazy man. She didn't want to put on the seatbelt; the first time the vehicle stopped she planned to get out and run like hell.

Bostwick had been cursing nonstop, carrying on his own indecent soliloquy, which Jaylynn tried to ignore. He let out a strangled shout. "Jesus Christ! I told you that big one was dangerous, Keith."

"What?"

"That was *her*! Didn't you see her? That big, crazy bitch from the campground? Shit! She had a gun!" He slammed his hand on the steering wheel. "We came *that* close to getting caught. Another minute, and she probably would've shot us."

Keith didn't say anything.

Jaylynn closed her eyes, shocked and miserable to think how close Dez had been. Again her stomach turned over, but she took a deep breath. *Be strong. It's not over yet.* She looked out the window, her mind reeling with questions. Could she open the door and roll out—run for Dez? No, he was going too fast. She looked around the car for something, anything, she could use to strike Bostwick. Where was a car jack when you needed one? There was nothing in the back seat that could be used as a weapon.

Bostwick turned left onto the main dirt road and drove at a calmer rate for another couple of minutes, cursing and muttering to himself. Jaylynn reached over the back of her seat and felt around. Nothing. The only thing her fingers felt was the plastic over the top of the case of water bottles.

"Hey, Blondie!" Bostwick stared at her in the rearview mirror. "Get down. You don't—oh, wait. Gimme that. Gimme that water!" He stuck his arm back, and she passed him a bottle. There were plenty more where that came from. She got another and tossed it into Keith's lap, then took one for herself.

"Thanks," Keith said, obviously surprised.

Jaylynn opened hers and drank greedily, not caring that in a short while she would have to pee. She hadn't been so thirsty in ages, and the cool water restored her, soothed her, gave her a moment of serenity in the midst of the storm.

She hadn't seen Crystal with Dez, so Jaylynn assumed what Dez and their friends had probably done: Dez took the path; Shayna and Crystal ran the other direction for help. She wondered what would happen next—what Dez would do. How soon before the authorities arrived?

Bostwick pulled over, leaving the engine running. In alarm, Keith asked, "Why are we stopping?" He glanced at Jaylynn, concern etched on his face.

Bostwick opened the door, got out, then stuck his head back in with a grin on his face. "Search the car. You search this side. I'll go around and make sure Blondie doesn't make a run for it."

Keith opened his door and stuck a leg out. He paused and looked toward Jaylynn. "Hey. I know you aren't named Blondie. What's your name?"

She met his tired eyes, hesitated a moment. "Jay. Call me Jay."

"Okay. Nice to meet you, Jay. I'm Keith."

Jaylynn was alarmed and at the same time touched by his old-fashioned manners. *What kind of psycho is this guy?*

Bostwick opened the front passenger door and rooted under the seat and in the glove compartment. "For shit's sake. I smell cigarettes in this car. Where are they? There's gotta be a pack here somewhere." After a moment, he pulled the rear hatch release and yelled at Keith to get around the back of the car and see if the Russian had any food on board. Keith leaned out the door and dragged himself up and out.

"Well, looky here," Bostwick said merrily. He held up another rectangular package wrapped in brown paper. "Looks like I got me — we got *us* – a real sweet present from the Russky." He pressed the packet to his face and made a kissing sound. Tossing it on the seat, he bent and hunted around some more.

Jaylynn tuned him out, wondering what would happen next. She couldn't understand what their plan was. Were Bostwick and Randall operating with a plan? She didn't like to consider it, but after this much time, she was surprised she hadn't been raped. *They don't really need me. They must know that I wouldn't be much help at a roadblock. Why didn't they shoot and dump me at the parking lot with the dying Russian? This makes no sense.*

Bostwick opened up the Explorer's center console. "Oh, sweet. Maps. And hey, this is one of those GPS thingies. Got no idea how the hell this works, but we'll figure it out, right, Randall? Oh, we ain't gonna need this CB radio." He ripped it from the support unit and tossed it behind him and off the road. "Jesus, what I'd like to know is why the hell there's no fuckin' cigarettes! Fuckin' asshole didn't smoke? I thought all those foreigners smoked. Shit, somebody smoked in here! The ashtray is full. Hey! Have you found any food?"

Keith, rooting around in the back, said he hadn't. "No food in my pack. Just clothes and the sleeping bag."

"Dammit. For Chrissake! We left behind the pack with the food in it."

As he searched the car, he kept up a running patter about the SUV, Russians, money, and all the niches and hiding places there could possibly be in a Ford.

Finally he groped beneath the driver's seat and Jaylynn heard his triumphant cry. "Aha! What a nice gun." Her heart sank when she saw the 9 mm Walther he held up. "Here, Randall. Looky here! I'm keeping this one. It's a beaut. You take this." He pulled Dez's Colt from the back of his pants and shoved it at Keith.

"I don't want it." Keith's voice was flat.

"Don't give me that shit. Take it!" He insisted, and Keith reluctantly complied. "In fact, you keep watch on her, Randall. Time for another visit to the woods. If she tries to get out, shoot her." He reached in, shut off the engine, pocketed the keys, and marched off the side of the road into the woods.

A whiff of exhaust wafted through the car, a welcome change from the rancid smell of sweat. Jaylynn huddled against the door in silence.

Keith bent, hands on knees, and looked in at her. She didn't know where he'd put the gun, but she assumed it was in the back of the plaid pants. "I won't shoot you, Jay." He squatted down. "Please, you have to believe me. You know that, don't you?"

Unconvinced, Jaylynn didn't answer. She looked away, searching for Bostwick, wondering if she dared to open the door. Would Keith let her go? She wanted to believe Keith Randall might be an ally, but her experience as a cop had taught her to be wary of felons. Some of the worst could seem completely inoffensive, just as Keith did.

He stood up and looked toward where Bostwick had disappeared, then laid a hand on top of the doorframe. "I never planned this. I never—oh, shit. What a mess." He got in the car and slammed the door. "Look, we've got to figure out how to get away."

"We? What do you have in mind?"

"I'm not sure." He put his face in his hands. "I'm just so damn tired I can hardly think. All I know is I'm glad I didn't drink any of that swamp water in the canteens. He's been drinking that slime since we left the prison." He shook his head and muttered "idiot" under his breath. "I think it's about near run through his system, and we might not have many more chances to run."

"You've got a gun. You could always shoot him."

"True, but I don't want to have to kill anybody! I'm in enough shit without adding a life sentence."

"I could take the gun." His face went a little more pale and strained. "Or you could just let me go now."

"No, he'd know. He stays too close, and he'd kill me. I don't know what to do, Jay. He's a sick bastard. He's bragged about all kinds of killings. I always stayed far away from him on the yard. Like I said, I never wanted to come with him in the first place."

He looked at her, eyes imploring. "You have to believe me. He dragged me with him. I'm starting to think it's some sort of set-up. My brother works for some Russians, and I haven't heard from him for two months. I'm scared it has something to do with that."

A shiver of fear raced up her spine. *Russians? The mob? It couldn't be possible. Could it?* She made her voice low and calm. "What was the original plan?"

"What? A plan? There *was* no original plan. I just got the shit kicked outta me and wound up in the infirmary with him. It's all been hit-and-miss since then."

Jaylynn studied his face. He had a five o'clock shadow, so not only did he look bruised, but also dirty and unkempt. But still, an ally. He could be an ally — but could he be trusted? Jaylynn's doubts resurfaced. What if this was a trick? He opened the car door, but didn't get out. She sat, looking out the window, thinking hard about how to escape without getting shot.

She caught a movement in the distance, and Bostwick appeared from the shelter of trees. A gust of wind blew, and a dozen gold and brown leaves fluttered all around the convict's head. The wind blew hard now, and the entire sky was overcast. It looked like rain was on the way.

She turned back to Keith and quickly said, "By now, there must be quite a manhunt. It won't be long before we run into somebody — the National Guard, forest rangers, sheriffs, maybe even local yokels wanting to be heroes. I'm not the only one in danger here. You are, too." She hesitated, almost ready to tell him she was a cop, but the thought of Russian mobsters caused her to hang back. By then the big convict had slammed shut Keith's door and was swinging into the driver's seat.

"Let's get on the road." As Bostwick pulled his door shut, he put his hand on the headrest of the passenger seat and looked over his shoulder. "Ready to go, kids?" He laughed aloud, put the key in the ignition, and started the engine.

The SUV sprang forward. Bostwick let out a whoop and turned on the CB, which filled the car with static and crackly voices. Jaylynn glanced sideways at Keith. He sat slumped against his door, his head resting against the window and his face slack. Asleep. She couldn't believe it; he had fallen asleep.

Her heartbeat picked up as grim realization set in: *They don't really need me any more. They've got a car, money, guns. I'm expendable now.* Her eyes filled with tears as she thought of Dez and the brief glimpse of her face, then her figure, running behind the Ford, engulfed in dust, and dropping back as the vehicle sped away. *Oh, God, what do I do?*

# Chapter
# Nineteen

JAYLYNN PEERED OUT into the surrounding forest, looking for any sign of help. She still felt sick and in shock. For one brief moment, she had thought Dez made it in time, but no, she hadn't. *Why didn't I drag my feet just a little more? Oh, God.*

They jounced along the potholed dirt road until Bostwick slammed on the brakes. They skidded to a stop at a T in the road. The big convict let out a shout of happiness, hit the gas, and wheeled to the right, careening around the corner on two wheels. The narrow lane was paved, though it had its share of potholes, too. Bostwick pressed the accelerator to the floor and let out another whoop. Jaylynn felt a surge of hatred. He was a horrible man. He didn't deserve to live.

She glanced over at Keith, but he was still asleep against the car door. Even the bumps didn't seem to bother him. The Explorer suddenly made a strange clunking noise and the engine stalled. Bostwick swore and pumped the gas. For a brief instant, the engine sounded like it would catch, then it died for good.

They coasted to a stop, and Bostwick threw it into park, turned the key, and pumped the pedal. Nothing. The starter just made a whirring sound, and the vehicle didn't revive.

Bostwick turned, gun in hand. "You make a move to get outta this car, Blondie, and I'll blow you away before you reach the trees."

When he turned away, Jaylynn leaned forward, squinting, and with a mixture of dread and glee realized the gas tank was on E. She wondered how long it would take the brainiac in the front seat to figure that out.

She glanced at Keith again.

Stopping hadn't awakened him, but he was roused — with a start — when Bostwick let out a roar. "Get the fuck outta the car,

Randall! We're screwed again." Bostwick kicked open his door, and Jaylynn grabbed the handle to get out. He shouted, "Not you, Blondie! You stay right there or I'll shoot you." He beat on the steering wheel. "Shit!"

It was a cry of fury, and Jaylynn couldn't help the overwhelming surge of joy she felt. She turned her face away to keep from laughing, realizing that the Russian's car might possibly have bought her some extra time.

Bostwick got out, and with a sigh of fatigue, Keith joined him. They carried on a conference, most of which she could hear. It all narrowed down to one thing: they needed to get back to the parking lot at Lake Jeanette and get her car.

Keith opened the back hatch and used the bottled water to rinse and refill the canteens while Bostwick gathered up the maps, the GPS, and the packages of money. She watched his every move, but his attention didn't stray. Even when he moved around the front of the vehicle to the passenger side, he kept an eye on her. He laid a map over the hood and anchored it with the handheld GPS unit. Bostwick moved toward her door and gestured for her to get out. "Don't fuck with me now. Get out and come look at these maps."

Jaylynn hoisted herself out of the back seat. In the short time she'd been in the car, her legs had tightened up, and she felt sore and slow. Putting one foot in front of her, she did a hamstring stretch, then took another step and did the same for her other leg.

"We don't have time for you to do fuckin' gymnastics. Get the hell over here!" He jabbed an index finger toward the map. "Where are we, and where is your car?"

In her best imitation of helpless female, Jaylynn adopted a wan smile and said, "Gee, let me see. Hmmm. I'm not so sure." She bent over the map, memorizing as much of the area as she could. They had traveled south on the dirt road from Lake Jeanette, then hit a T where Bostwick turned right, so now they were going west. The road they were currently on had many hiking and snowmobile paths as offshoots, but it seemed to be the only way in and out for a vehicle. The paved lane to the west went towards Buyck. Going that way, one first passed Nigh Lake, then Pauline Lake, then much farther west, Hunting Shack River. It looked like over ten miles—maybe more—to Highway 24. If they had gone left and traveled east at the T, it would have led them deeper into Lake Jeanette State Forest and then into the Superior National Forest.

"What's the slow-up, Blondie?" he shouted. "It's not that fuckin' complicated!"

"Give me a second, will you?"

A big dirty index finger came down on Lake Jeanette. "Which lot?"

She saw they would have to travel north again, back the way they had just come, and Dez would be traveling along that path. Her heart lifted. *Dez. She'll find us. We can get out of this mess together!* But they had quite a distance to double back. Further north on the map, two lakes with funny names caught her eye— Hag Lake and Weeny Lake. She suppressed a smile.

"Well?"

"The car is parked by Lake Jeanette. That's all I know. I'm pretty sure it's not Lot A."

"No, it's not, you stupid bitch! That's the one we were already at."

She pointed a finger and picked Lot C, which she thought was farthest from them. Since she didn't have the keys to any car in Lot B either, going to Lot B would buy her time if they had to travel the extra distance to Lot C. "It's this one. I'm sure of it." She stepped back and let her gaze wander to the piss-yellow flag flapping in the wind. She thought about what a bizarre choice that was for a signal. She figured Bostwick must have picked it. No Russian mobster would advertise himself as a moron in that way.

The burly convict reached over, grabbed her forearm, and jerked her back to the hood. "How the fuck does this thing work?" He turned the GPS unit on and shook it violently.

Jaylynn shrugged. Although she'd had plenty of training with global positioning units, she wasn't about to tell him that. "It's all Greek to me."

Keith sidled up between them to look at the map, forcing Jaylynn to turn her face away for air. The two convicts smelled so foul she could hardly breathe. The smaller of the stinky pair pointed to a red line indicating paved road. "Seems like we ought to stay off this road. If anyone comes down it, they'll see us, and then we're in big trouble. And what about the woman with the gun? I don't want her to shoot me."

Bostwick smacked a hand down on the front quarter-panel. "Now you're thinking, Randall! Good point." He gestured toward a path across the road. "We'll take those back trails."

Jaylynn now wanted to kill Randall as well as Bostwick. Why couldn't her would-be ally have kept his big mouth shut? Once again, her stomach clenched, and if she'd had anything in it, she might have vomited.

Bostwick folded the map haphazardly, not paying any attention to the proper folds. "Let's push this sonuvabitch off the road. We don't want nobody to see it. Get the hell in the driver's seat, Blondie. You steer."

She had no choice but to do as he said. She put the Explorer into neutral and cranked on the steering wheel. Once they got it rolling, she was tempted to slam on the brakes and let her companions run into the back of the SUV, but she didn't think she could injure either of them enough for it to make a difference. Instead, they would just be mad — perhaps mad enough to hurt or even kill her.

Bostwick let out a shout, and she steered over to the left, off the road, and down a slope into some woody-stemmed juneberry bushes. The leaves were yellowed and the stand of juneberry had lost half its foliage, but the SUV wouldn't be immediately noticeable from the road. Jaylynn popped the hatch and crawled over the front and back seat. When she stuck out a leg to exit the hatch, Keith grabbed an arm and steadied her.

"Good job, Blondie," Bostwick said. He slammed the hatch closed and ripped away some shrub branches to pile on the back. "It'll be dim enough in a couple hours that nobody'll ever notice it. Let's get going."

Jaylynn moved up the short slope to the dusty dirt road, her legs protesting every step of the way. *As soon as I feel less stiff and sore — maybe even if I don't — I have to run.* From her study of the map, she estimated it was at least three miles back to the Lake Jeanette lots, and perhaps three times further to the main highway that led to Buyck. As she crossed the road, she made the mistake of glancing back. Bostwick's big ham hand immediately landed on her shoulder and he gave her a push.

"Let's go, Blondie. Looks like we have to do this the hard way. Don't make me hurt you." He chuckled. "Not yet anyway."

GRIMACING, CRYSTAL TIGHTENED her hands into fists and fought the urge to kick the man next to her right in the shins. They stood at the county sheriff's visitor's counter in a small satellite office in Buyck. It smelled like stale coffee. The only window was streaked with grime. Through it, she could see the Jeep with Shayna peering out the passenger window.

For the fifth time in less than a half hour, Crystal tried to get the county cop to understand the timeline. "Look, Deputy, they hijacked us, stole our stuff, and kidnapped my friend sometime around seven. They took off on the trail toward Lake Jeanette maybe twenty minutes later. We quickly got free and gave chase. Look at the map." She pointed at Echo Lake and ran her index finger to the right toward Lake Jeanette. "There are a lot of little paths off this main one, and I am sure Savage misdirected them as much as possible, but—"

"How do you know that?" Deputy Fraley looked hung over and smelled as though he'd had a little too much garlic and cilantro the night before.

"She's a cop! She's smart. She'll do whatever she can to slow them down."

"If she's so damn smart, how did she get kidnapped?"

Crystal wouldn't dignify that with an answer. She went on. "Even the little paths off the trails don't go anywhere except to these other various lakes." She pointed to Pauline, Nigh, Astrid, and Crelin lakes. "She very clearly told them our Jeep was at Lake Jeanette. They'd follow any trail markers there, and Savage—"

"I don't see your point."

*No, you don't, you idiot.* She restrained herself from telling him off and asking for a superior. Through gritted teeth, she said, "My point is that after misdirection and any other slowdowns Savage could arrange, they would eventually arrive at Lake Jeanette, but it would be hours. That trail winds around. It's bumpy. Even at a trot, they had ten or twelve miles to travel!"

"And your point is?"

"They have to be back there wandering around still, armed with a gun and being pursued by a cop with a gun. We need to find them before Reilly does—that is, if you want either one of them left alive."

Deputy Fraley hitched up his duty-belt, and gave her an odd look. "This doesn't square with the reports we got. They had to have made it to the lake, picked up the car, and gotten out of there. We've got some reliable reports that they're north at the Ash Lake area."

Crystal cleared her throat and took a deep breath. "I see. They *picked up* a car. So you're saying they're *carrying* somebody's goddamn car?" The deputy looked startled. Through gritted teeth, Crystal continued, "For the love of God, man, *we drove here in our Jeep.* Our Jeep was never there! Savage took 'em on a wild goose chase. When they find out, they're liable to kill her. Then they're going to find someone else to hijack. And you need to understand, no matter what, when Reilly gets there, those two men are in grave danger. Get it?"

"No need to shout, Miss Lopez."

"That's Officer Lopez to you! I'm a cop, and I *know* these two officers. I know how their minds work."

"That's all well and good, but the Feds and state and local forces are doing all we can. We'll get your friends back."

Crystal shook her head. "This isn't working. I need to talk to whoever is in charge of this manhunt."

"I'm the local liaison."

In disbelief, she said, "You don't even have regular communications other than by radio. I need to talk to the command center."

"I'm afraid I can't let you do that. Someone as involved as yourself, and," he pointed toward the window at Shayna in the Jeep, "a civilian, well, you can't be brought into this." He slipped behind the counter and reached for a coffee mug on the desk.

Stunned, Crystal stared at him. She had shown this idiot her police ID, so he had to believe she was a cop. What was with the attitude and the obstructive behavior? She narrowed her eyes as reality dawned. *Shayna's black. I'm Latino. And we're both women and therefore suspect.* Weighing her options, she gazed outside through the crud-encrusted window, then watched Fraley pour coffee into a blue mug. Realizing this conversation was a waste of precious time, she whirled and headed for the door. A bell made a *ding* sound as she pulled it open. "Thanks for your help," she said in a sarcastic tone as she left.

"Wait—don't you want—"

She didn't hear anymore. She slammed the door and jumped down the three steps to the ground, then headed for the car. When she got in, she let loose a string of Spanish invective while she started the Jeep.

Shayna waited until she drew a breath, then asked, "I take it the officer was less than helpful?"

"That's for damn sure." Crystal backed up in a hurry, then accelerated and squealed across the lot to the edge of Highway 23. No cars were coming so she peeled out into the road.

"What are we going to do?"

"We'll look for them ourselves."

Shayna reached over and laid the flat of her hand on Crystal's shoulder. "Sweetie, is that a good idea? These people—"

Before Shayna could finish her thought, Crystal hit the brakes and swerved over to the right side of the road toward a strip of rustic little stores. She brought the Jeep to a halt in the middle, in front of Dan's Sport Shop. To the left was a realtor's office, to the right, an art gallery.

Shayna squeezed Crystal's shoulder. "What are you doing?"

"We need gear. We need weapons." She opened up the door and burst out.

"Wait. Wait!" Shayna limped behind her. "But they're armed!"

Crystal bounded up the wooden plank stairs to the wide porch that served all three shops. "We can't just sit around, Shay. C'mon!" She yanked open the door to the sport store and stepped inside.

A man glanced at her from behind the counter, then looked back to the left where a 27-inch TV sat on a pedestal high in the corner. It was tuned to the local Buyck station, and a reporter in a yellow slicker stood in the rain, giving an update about the escapees. Crystal paused and watched as the reporter wrapped up his story. "No breaking news on this, huh?" she asked grimly.

"Nope. Still haven't caught the guys. What can I help you with?"

"I need a gun and some other gear."

The shopkeeper, an older fellow with thinning white hair, shook his head slowly. "You're the third person in here today. Everybody's spooked on account of those convicts getting out."

"Tell me about it."

The man pulled a thick binder out from under the counter and set it down with a *whump*. "You'll have to fill out some paperwork."

"I think I can circumvent some of that." Crystal slapped her police ID on the counter. "I'm a sworn peace officer from the Twin Cities."

# Chapter
# Twenty

Kendall Correctional Facility
Outside Buyck, Minnesota
Sunday, October 17, 1:30 p.m.

JEROME GILES STRODE down the hallway toward Ralph Soames. The administrator watched the man approach, thinking how much he resembled Morgan Freeman—not from the more recent movie, *The Shawshank Redemption*, but rather from the earlier 1980s prison film, *Brubaker*, which Soames had seen as a teenager. With shame, he realized Giles was everything he was not. So far, the FBI man had been calm, organized, fearless. He wore his crisp FBI suit with ease, never appearing to sweat. Meanwhile, Soames had soaked through his own shirt, and when he looked down at his gray JCPenney slacks, they were rumpled, the thighs creased into deep wrinkles. To the outside observer, he hoped it looked like he was holding it all together, but he was a quaking mess inside.

Giles met his eyes, and it took all the courage Soames could muster not to look away. "Mr. Soames, we'll soon be pulling out. Relocating to Buyck. Could we sit down for a few moments so I can update you?"

"Yes, of course." He entered Mike Martin's office and offered Giles one of the visitors' chairs, then felt like a fraud for settling behind the desk in his boss's chair. "May I get you some lunch or coffee—"

"No, no, that's all right. Thank you, by the way, for the breakfast earlier. This won't take too long, Mr. Soames. I want to thank you for allowing my men to interrogate the inmates. I'm leaving two agents to continue with that, so long as that meets your approval."

Soames blushed. This was sheer pleasantry on Giles' part. As a representative of the federal government and under these circumstances, he had every right to do whatever he wanted with the prisoners. Soames was counting himself lucky that he and his staff hadn't been thrown out or arrested. "Anything, Mr. Giles. Anything we can do — you just ask."

"State and federal authorities are on their way. I'm sure they'll be here by tomorrow. You're in for a real ordeal, I'm afraid, and there are two subjects I would like to broach, both of which they will likely address with you, too. The first is whether you suspect any sort of inside job?"

"Wha — inside job?" Soames shut his mouth to keep from babbling any further and took a moment to compose himself. He shook his head. "I'm sorry. I just can't see that. No way." Giles was examining him closely, watching his reaction. He forced himself to look the man in the eye. "I can't swear to anything, but all of this seems to be a bizarre set of coincidences."

"A confluence of events." Soames gaped blankly, and Giles frowned. "In my business, most of the time coincidences are highly overrated." He paused to stare out the window for a moment. "My second concern is one that I hope I can trust you to keep confidential. I'm relatively certain this breakout was not coincidental. Keith Sterling Randall is the brother of a federal informant. According to your records, last week Stanley Michael Bostwick was visited by an attorney close to the crime family involved in that federal investigation."

"What! I — that can't be true."

"I'm afraid it is. It would behoove you to look into this." He rose and held out his hand. Soames shook it without paying any attention at all. Giles took a business card out of his breast pocket and set it on the desk. "If you receive any information or think of anything at all, please call me. Now I must go and find out whether your escapees have helped themselves to a busload of schoolgirl hikers that was expected an hour ago at Echo Lake."

"Oh, my God."

"Good luck, Mr. Soames." Giles turned and strode out of the office without looking back.

Soames sank back in the executive chair, his mind whirling with confusion. "An inside job?" he said aloud, and buried his head in his hands.

# Chapter
# Twenty-One

**Minnesota North Woods**
**Sunday, October 17, 2:10 p.m.**

A FIERCE WIND blew in Jaylynn's face and whipped her hair straight up in the air. The cool, damp gust sent shivers through her. She looked up at the gap overhead between the walls of trees on either side of the winding trail. To right and left, tall birch, poplar, and elm towered and the width between served as a funnel for the cold wind. The slash of sky directly above and spaces between branches and leaves revealed darkening, battleship gray heavens.

The route they were traversing had narrowed from two feet wide to less than a foot and was rockier than the morning's trail had been. A hilly rise loomed ahead, and after a couple of hundred yards, they began a gradual climb along the side of the hillock. As they progressed, the trees thinned, and they waded through brush. The path dwindled, scarcely wider than a deer-trail, and in places it dropped off down the slope. Jaylynn stepped over a two-foot wide indentation that formed a channel to the left, down the hill. The last rain must have been a torrent because a lot of the path had washed away. Brambles from a bush on the hill to the right reached out and caught her jacket, and she had to jerk to pull her arm free.

Jaylynn glanced ahead at Keith. His cruddy prison sneakers slipped on the uneven ground, sometimes almost tripping him. It was clear he was exhausted. *Looks like he's moving on auto-pilot. He's flagging something terrible. I have to make a move soon.* Jaylynn felt a twinge of regret. There was no way she could help him or take him along. He'd slow her down, and she couldn't afford that. Bostwick was too big, too strong, and too cunning. She watched and waited for the one opportunity that she prayed Fate would offer.

As if answering her prayer, Keith stumbled. Shale and dirt

slid out from under his left foot. With a high-pitched cry, he lost his balance, hit the dirt with his right hip, and slid sideways down the hill a good fifteen feet.

"Well, shit!" Bostwick shouted. "You stupid moron. Whyn't you watch where you're going?" He stepped to the edge of the trail and angled his way down the incline, reaching for the fallen man. "C'mon, you asshole. You're not hurt."

That was all Jaylynn needed. She turned and fled, back the way they'd come, picking her way through the brush as fast as she could. She leapt over a four-foot-wide jumble of lumpy rocks, half-buried in the middle of the trail. As moist wind blew against the side of her face, she ran, certain that any second a big hand would come down on her shoulder and drag her to the ground.

"Hey!" She heard Bostwick's shout — far away — and ran with more confidence. She had a better lead on him this time. She reached the bottom of the hill. Tall trees loomed above. Her lungs burned with her effort, but the adrenaline rush impelled her forward. *Go! Go! Run like wind.* And as the path turned, the breeze was at her back, pressing her forward.

She couldn't hear anything behind her, but Bostwick had to be following. He wouldn't just let her go. As she rushed through the thick of the trees, she chanced a glance back, but saw nothing moving. Speeding up again, she wondered if she'd made the right choice by running downhill. Uphill looked like so much work, but that was the direction where they'd last seen Dez. She felt a pang of longing, but pushed it away. Dez wouldn't sit around waiting there. She'd have headed down the road after the car. By now, she was probably halfway there. Maybe, with a little luck, Jaylynn could get back to the road and meet up with her.

Minutes passed, and she heard another shout, this time closer. Her panic rose. Bostwick couldn't be too far behind. To the left she saw a tight copse of trees surrounded by fire-red sumac bushes three and four feet tall. She plunged off the trail, leaping high, then dove into the sumac and crawled up next to the trees. Scuttling along on all fours, she prayed that Bostwick wouldn't be able to see evidence of her flight. Behind the trees, she lay facedown with a bower of sumac blazing overhead.

She couldn't stop panting even though she knew she had to try. Shaking hands fumbled in her hiking pants pocket, located the Swiss Army knife. She snapped open the largest blade and held the little blue knife in a death grip. The minute she heard or saw him, she would hold her breath and pray she didn't have to use the knife. Heart beating wildly, she inched around to face the direction from which he would come. She had to meet him head-on. If he were to locate her, she didn't want him to find her cowering with her back to him. To minimize the chance of him seeing her white-blond hair, she tried to cover her head with the sleeves of her brown coat.

The quiet was broken without warning by a soft click, then another. Jaylynn stiffened and held her breath. Then a rattle of clicks and *plit-plit-plit* sounds started up. She wanted to cry when she realized rain was falling. Now the trails would be muddied, and Bostwick would find it easy to track her. She frowned. But that's only if he found her starting point. She wondered what would happen if she waited indefinitely, hiding until she was sure it was safe. She could even wait until after dusk. *But how can I be sure he won't figure out a way to track me?*

She heard his approach before she saw him. *Thud-thud. Thud-thud.* He ran heavily. The sound of breathing huffed nearer.

KEITH SAT HIGH on the hill, his back against the dirt of a shaly hillock. His left foot ached, and his right hip had hit hard upon some rocks when he'd fallen. He felt like he had dirt ground into every part of his body. Shifting his shoulder, he reached up to wipe a stray clod from his neck. *Jesus, how did I get into this? Am I even going to live to tell the tale?*

Down the slope that Bostwick had dragged him up, the rocks and brush looked gray-green under the darkening sky. He had no idea what time it was, but the thick storm clouds made it seem like dusk was about to fall. Far off in the distance, a deep rumbling started. Cocking his head to the side, he listened. *Thunder. Somewhere, close by, it must be raining. Shit. It's going to be miserable out here.*

He pulled his knees up close to his chest and leaned his left arm against the pack Bostwick had left behind. He hoped the girl had gotten enough of a jump to elude the big convict, but he wasn't sure. How much time had passed before Bostwick noticed she had disappeared? Certainly not more than fifteen or twenty seconds.

Energy spent, Keith closed his eyes and let himself float. He felt as though he was in a strange dimension, in a place where everything was shrouded in a dreamlike aura. His body ached. His head pounded. He slid to the side, nestled into the backpack, and slept.

SALLY CABOT EASED up on the trail bike's accelerator and steered around a ragged trench. She goosed the gas and hastened to catch up with Lou Schecter, who rode a couple hundred yards ahead. They'd covered all the trails around Echo Lake and over by Echo River and now were working their way south toward Picket Lake. Her legs were already sore. She decided she was getting too old for trail biking. *My butt's going to hurt for days.*

The wind had picked up, and the air was cool and damp. She looked up at the darkening sky a moment, then back to the unpredictable path. It was going to rain sometime soon. She hoped Schecter had brought along something water-repellent to wear.

Schecter slowed and pulled over, swung off the bike, and put the kickstand down. She stopped and waited for him to stroll back. Over the rumble of her bike, he said, "We're in for some bad weather. Thought I'd put on some rain gear."

"Good idea." She turned off her Kawasaki KLR650 and dismounted stiffly. She found her olive green hooded anorak and rain-resistant pants in the backpack and put them on.

"What do you think, Sal? Should we go east to Lake Jeanette? Go all the way down to Picket Lake?"

"I'm trying to think where my daughter would have taken her WAO girls. It'd be a flat hike, I'm sure. There are a lot of choices, aren't there?"

Lou shrugged. "Yeah. But you'll have to take the lead here. You've got a better idea of the lay of the land. I'm just along for the ride."

Cabot got her canteen out of the backpack and leaned back against the motorcycle's seat. "I thought of splitting up to try to cover more ground, but I'd rather not, to tell you the truth."

"I agree. I've got maps, but a guy could get lost up here, and with a storm coming, I don't want to have to hunker down for the night while it pours on my head."

"That's exactly what I'm worrying will happen to this group of kids and their leaders. It'd be pretty miserable."

"And possibly dangerous."

Cabot nodded. "Let me check in with base." She pulled her radio out of the backpack, turned it on, and called in their location. "Any news on any of the campers?"

The dispatcher's voice was breaking up, but clear enough for them to hear that two more of the eleven missing parties had reported in safely.

"How about the school kids? Have you heard from Emily?"

"Negative. No word." She asked for status on the manhunt, and the dispatcher said, "Units deployed north to Ash River for pickup."

"Great! Looks like it's only clean-up then?" She met Schecter's hopeful eyes.

"Affirmative. The Saint Louis County Rescue Squad is en route, and if there are injuries, Life Flight can fly out of Duluth with no delay so long as the weather cooperates."

"Okay, copy. I'm conserving batteries, so I'll check in on the half hour." They signed off, and she returned the radio to her bag. "I'm still concerned about Emily's school kids. They should have shown up by now."

# Chapter
# Twenty-Two

**Minnesota North Woods**
**Sunday, October 17, 2:44 p.m.**

IN THE RAPIDLY advancing gloom, Dez jogged along the dirt road. Her thirst was unbearable, but she'd dropped her canteen when she'd heard the gunshot earlier. She considered filling Jaylynn's empty water bottle from a brook or pond and adding the purification tablets, but didn't want to spare the time. Besides, if she stopped moving, she was afraid she wouldn't be able to go on. She was long past tired, but it was mind over matter now. Every so often she stopped jogging and walked for a couple hundred yards, but mostly she kept up the pace.

The Explorer didn't have a distinctive tire tread, but few other vehicles had driven the dirt track for some time, so all she had to do was follow the impressions she saw. Twenty minutes earlier, she'd come upon a spot where they had stopped. Footprints surrounded the places where the vehicle had come to rest, and one set of size fourteens led off the road and into the brush and back. She swallowed the fear that rose. For all she knew, Jaylynn could have been killed and carried into the sticks, so she followed the trail. But it stopped where someone had defecated. There was no sign of Jaylynn.

She ran from the woods back to the dirt road intent on continuing, but something caught her attention. Near footprints and a tire track was an odd little mound of dust. With her fingertips, Dez gently brushed fine dirt away from the top of the pile, ready to move back if some little critter was burrowed there. She saw a glint of gold, a small cylindrical object. Impatient, she grabbed at the pile and scooped up a handful of .45 caliber bullets. *What are these doing here?* Eyes scanning the ground, she tried to reconstruct what might have happened. *Could Jaylynn have – no. She would have kept these bullets and the gun and used them.* From the location of the pile, she decided it had been placed under the vehicle and hurriedly covered. But why? And by whom?

She had no way of knowing. She collected seven shells and tucked them in a cargo pocket, rose, and headed south.

Out in the woods, with only the trees, an occasional bird call, the scratching of little feet in the brush, and a gradually darkening sky to keep her company, Dez found her mind playing tricks on her. She tried to keep an eye on things all around her, but more often than not, she concentrated on the tire tracks, almost as though pulled along by an invisible force. Once she glanced down the road and swore she saw the outline of a tan car, and her heart leapt. She gulped in air and pumped her arms for two strides before realizing that what she saw was merely an unusual arrangement of tan leaves and gold bushes.

Tears welled, and it was all she could do to keep from stopping right there in the road and screaming, crying, and raging out loud. *I can't. I won't. It takes too much energy. I have to keep going.*

She tried to calculate how far she had come since leaving the campsite earlier. Ten miles? Twelve? She couldn't be sure. In high school, she had run cross-country, and she learned then to be patient. That was exactly the type of attitude she needed to take now. She also knew she would run until she dropped over dead before she'd give up on Jaylynn. But she couldn't help wondering where the authorities were. Why weren't cops and state police and rangers crawling all over? It had been hours — almost eight hours according to her watch — and that was just the time Dez personally knew about.

Where was a good SWAT unit when she needed it? Right now, she'd pay every penny of the rest of her salary for the coming years just to see any reinforcements at all. *C'mon, Crystal. Get us help!*

RALPH SOAMES GREW more impatient by the moment. He paced in his supervisor's office, monitored police dispatch on the radio, and watched the local television news coverage on a color TV that sat on a rolling cart. After the Feds had left, he'd surveyed the wreckage of his conference room, and steeled himself to keep from crying. He might have done so if Shirley, the secretary, hadn't come bustling in, complaining about what pigs men were as she started tidying up the mess.

"Ralph, Ralph, Ralph," she said in her nasally voice. "Thank the Lord you're not like most of these people. What's wrong with men? Such slobs." She was clad in a blue denim jumper with a white turtleneck underneath. Even with nylons, Shirley always wore sensible shoes—Rockports and Hush Puppies and sturdy sandals—just like the nuns at Catholic school. Shirley was a sensible woman all around, and her calm, no-nonsense demeanor was just what he needed now.

"Thanks for picking up, Shirl."

She patted her tinted red-brown hair. "Well, I won't say it's a pleasure or anything like that, but somebody has to do it. Might as well be me. I'll bet you've got a lot on your mind."

"That's the truth." He left Shirley to manage the mess, rolled the TV out, and returned to Mike Martin's office. Behind the closed door, he got out the work records of every single employee, both past and present, and stacked them up on the desk's left-hand pullout tray. With one eye on the TV and the other on the files, he passed a solitary hour. The news offered nothing helpful until three o'clock when the station cut into a commercial.

"Channel Six brings you new developments about the escape of two inmates from Herman Kendall Correctional Facility. Here's Alicia Alden with the latest."

A slender woman dressed in a trench coat, hair blowing in the wind, appeared onscreen trying to hold onto a microphone while struggling in a downpour with an umbrella. "Thanks, Ken," she shouted. "Authorities are tight-lipped, but CB and ham operators in the area are reporting that the convicts have been sighted on the northernmost edge of the Kabetogama State Forest near the Ash River Falls Trail area. We have unconfirmed reports that state police and the National Guard are on their way north to apprehend the escapees. Meanwhile, as you can see, the weather has taken a turn for the worse in a storm that stretches from miles south of here all the way up north of Crane Lake. A manhunt in these remote areas isn't easy, especially with sundown in less than three hours. Campers, hikers, and others living in the vicinity are advised to lock up. If you, or anyone you know, see anything unusual around the Ash River Falls Trail area, please contact your local authorities to report the information. Alicia Alden, for Channel Six News. Back to you, Ken."

The news anchor launched into a recap of what Soames had just heard, so he sat back in the executive chair and tuned it out. He wondered about the school bus and the kids near Echo Lake that Giles had mentioned. How come there'd been no comment about them or their safety?

Soames reached for the phone, then drew back his hand. He didn't think he could expect much cooperation or information anyway. He supposed he would just have to wait and see. Stuck behind prison walls, there was nothing he could do. He picked up the next file and went back to his review.

SURE SHE HAD traveled a dozen miles or more, Dez wondered when she would hit civilization. She hoped she'd come upon a place soon as she was nearly sick from fatigue and thirst. Doggedly, she ran, directly between the two sets of tire treads. Daylight slowly leaked away. Black and gray clouds clotted the sky. She didn't look forward to the coming rain, even if she could moisten her dry mouth with it. Rain would obscure the trail and make her search more difficult. As she had the thought, a drop spattered on her face, then another. Soon it was coming down hard.

She reached the end of the Lake Jeanette dirt road and came to the badly paved county road. The Explorer had obviously gone west, to the right. For perhaps a dozen yards, tread marks were evident, but the rain was quickly washing them away. After a while, she no longer saw any tire marks at all.

She moved on, concentrating on the sides of the road, her eyes sweeping back and forth. Less than a mile ahead, she approached a deep rut off to the side. She followed this to the graveled shoulder and found footprints and scuff marks rapidly filling with water. A vehicle had been pushed ahead and to the left. Down the slope, she saw the tan Explorer she'd chased earlier, hidden in a thicket of juneberry bushes.

*Jay! Oh, please, don't be in there.* She rushed down the embankment and swept some branches away from the top of the car. Frantically she peered in. No one in the cargo area. Squeezing into the bushes alongside of the Ford, she cupped her hands on either side of her face and pressed her nose to the glass. Empty.

For a few moments she felt exactly the same way she had the night Ryan died. She hadn't believed he was dead, even when one of the medics had quietly said, "DRT," not thinking she'd hear him. Dead Right There. The shock had been so great that she thought her heart had stopped beating. Ever after, she knew what people meant when they said their blood ran cold. A chill had come over her that took hours to lift.

And now, with the rain pouring on her head, she felt the same chilly lethargy coming on. *I can't let myself feel this. I can't give in no matter how tired I am, no matter how afraid I feel. If Ryan were here, he'd tell me to get off my dead ass and do something. Keep moving. That's what's important.*

Fighting the crush of bushes, she managed to wrench open the rear passenger door and lean in. The Explorer was definitely unoccupied, with keys still in the ignition. She extricated herself, and the door slammed shut. She hurried to the back hatch, got it open, and plunked down her backpack next to a case of bottled water, then scrambled over the back seat. It was tough to squirm into the front seat, but she contorted her six-foot frame several different ways until she finally managed. She turned the key. The engine whirred and caught, then made a ragged coughing sound and died. She tried again, even as she surveyed the dashboard. The needle on the fuel gauge sat a hair's breadth below the E, and a little orange symbol of a gas pump glowed on the display. Now she knew why they had ditched a perfectly good SUV. She turned the key to the off position and tried to open the driver's door, but the bushes pressed too hard against it. Rather than fight it, she wormed her way over the console again and crawled over the back seat to launch herself out.

"Dammit!" Her chest pressed tight, and she squeezed her eyes shut. For a moment she saw the blue and red lights again, felt the panic rise, but she forced it all down and opened her eyes. She kicked the rear tire as she screamed, "Where are you, Jaylynn! Where?" Her words were lost in the wind, and the only answer was an increase in rainfall. But moving around, expressing her feelings out loud, made her feel more in control.

She sat back against the Explorer's bumper and immediately regretted it. Beads of water soaked into the formerly dry seat of her cargo pants, one of the areas on her body that hadn't been rained on. She clambered into the vehicle and hunched down, cross-legged and out of breath. She took her Leatherman knife out and cut away the plastic encasing the bottled water. She opened a bottle and drank half of it in thirsty gulps. She made herself stop, not wanting to over-do it right off the bat.

Dez sat back, letting the water settle, before opening her backpack and stuffing in six containers. *Oh, geez. That'll be way too heavy.* Two came back out before she re-zipped it. She drank some more. It revived her, and she felt some strength return.

With the hatch open, she was protected from most of the rain, and she paused a few moments to consider what course of action to take next. The only thing to do was continue down the road and hope to overtake them on foot or pray that help would come along. How far could they have gone? She looked at her watch. How long ago did the car conk out, and how far could they have traveled since? She assumed they'd only have a lead of a couple miles.

Sooner or later, somebody had to come back this way, didn't they? *I'll probably have to run all the way to Highway 24.* She drank some more water, finally feeling somewhat sated, and

watched the rain come down. Realizing she had rain gear in her
pack, she reached in and dug to the bottom, thanking God once
more for Shayna's quick packing. She paused and realized that
Crystal would be urging her to eat now. She could almost hear
her friend's voice. "You've been on foot for hours, Dez. Be smart.
Take five minutes to feed your own engine."

She didn't think she could stomach the Gorp, so she pulled
out some of the items that had been in the pack left at Lot A. One
silver packet was labeled "Santa Fe Chicken with Rice" and
another, "Trailside Tetrazzini," neither of which could be
prepared without hot water, so she stuffed them back in.
Another contained "Crisp Crackers & Spread," so she opened it
and found that the "spread" was creamy peanut butter. That
suited her fine, but once she'd eaten that small portion, she
realized she was ravenous. She opened a package of "Mashed
Potatoes and Gravy" and found two separate containers, one of
gravy powder and the other potato flakes, which didn't taste too
terrible, though she had to wash them down with a lot of water.
When she went to put the gravy container in the pack, she
noticed a picture of an ice cream bar on a silver package, pulled
it out, and ripped it open. The smell of vanilla wafted around her
as she bit into the small rectangle without hesitation. It didn't
taste too bad, but the idea of unchilled "milk product" seemed
odd to her. She consumed the little bar in three bites, thinking
that ice cream just wasn't all that good if it wasn't cold. She
almost laughed. Freeze-dried ice cream. *Yeah, right.* This
particular purchase had to be Jaylynn's idea.

*Oh, Jay.* A sob bubbled up, and once again, she felt
overwhelmed. She let herself consider that her partner, her
lover, her best friend might be dead. She could be anywhere
along the highway ahead. Or behind. They might have dumped
her somewhere along the paved road, and Dez might not have
even seen her. Without any tire tracks on the cement, Dez could
not have told where they had stopped. Anguished, she brought
her forearm up to her eyes and wiped away the tears, then felt a
burning fury suffuse her body. *Whatever evil they've done to her, I
will visit upon them a hundred-fold.* It occurred to her that shock
was cold while rage scorched and blazed. The old adage was that
revenge was a dish best served cold, but it felt hot and blood-red
to her. A horrible, primal thirst for vengeance rose, feeling like
an all-consuming fire of violence burning in her chest. She
understood how — and why — a kind and compassionate person
could kill another to avenge the death of someone dearly loved.
She curled her hands into fists.

*I could do it barehanded.* The visions of blood and violence shocked her.

*Oh, my God. What would I become without her?*

Through the maelstrom in her head, she heard Jaylynn's voice. "Stop! Just stop and think, Dez. You can't give in to this now. Think!" She opened her fists and stared down at the silver package in her hand, feeling some of the helpless rage slip away. She stepped out and away from under the hatch, into the storm, tipping back her head to feel the cold rain beat against her face. *I will find her. I will!* Breathing heavily, she ducked out of the deluge and waited a few moments until her heart stopped racing.

Her stomach felt better, so she gathered up the packaging remnants and stuffed them into a plastic catch-all above the wheel well, then turned her attention to her rain gear. With difficulty, she got the rain-resistant pants on over her wet cargo pants, then pulled the anorak over her head, making sure that the Neoprene waist-pack and gun were protected from the moisture. Now clad in light blue, she thought she ought to be more visible than in her former clothes. As dark as it was getting, it was just as well to be dressed in light colors so any driver coming down the road would spot her and not run her over.

With a final sigh, she shouldered the now-heavy pack and stood, feeling wooden heaviness in her legs. She didn't bother to close the Explorer's hatch, but left it open so it would be more noticeable to searchers. Up the muddy incline she slogged, a bottle of water in each hand, and worked up to a jog heading west.

JAYLYNN HAD NO way of knowing how long she lay nestled in the shrubs under the cover of spindly branches. She had seen Bostwick run by, traveling south, some time ago, but she remained motionless on the cold ground, afraid to rise lest he suddenly come back. Finally, her breathing returned to normal. She hoped none of the plants around her were poisonous. Even though it was long past flowering time, residue on poison ivy and poisonous sumac could still get on the skin and start itching and burning. She felt itchy, too, as though she were lying on an anthill, but not a single bug was anywhere to be seen. She took that as a good omen.

She spent some time considering her predicament. *Lost in the woods, no food or water, a rainstorm getting worse by the minute, and a psycho killer hunting for me. Well, I suppose it could be worse.* A little voice in her head asked, "How in the world could it possibly be worse?" *I could be naked.* For some reason, this struck her as funny. For the first time in hours, nervous laughter bubbled up, and she had to suppress the sound. It would do her no good to come this far and have Bostwick find her because she giggled.

She wished she knew what time it was. *How frustrating it is when you can't be sure how to gauge how much time is passing.* She knew it was at least a couple of hours past noon, but since the clouds had rolled in, it was difficult to estimate anything. Fumbling with the Velcro on the lower pocket of her hiking pants, she pulled until she could worm her hand in and remove the Suunto compass. Jaylynn was glad that Keith was too inept to have searched her properly. She had been concerned that her compass could have been damaged when Bostwick jumped her, but there were no cracks and the needle floated perfectly. Without a map, she wasn't sure how much it would help, but if she followed the trails and kept traveling east, eventually she figured she'd run into Highway 24.

A bank of even darker clouds had moved in, cutting her visibility. *If I can't see, then neither can he.* She shuddered, wondering if she was hidden well enough.

As if to answer her question, she both heard and felt the thud of heavy footsteps coming back. This time she didn't cradle her head. She peered through the thicket in front of her, her eyes searching for any movement beyond the tangle of leaves and stalks. A flash of Levi blue shot by, and the sound of heavy breathing gradually grew fainter. In hope and disbelief, Jaylynn raised her head slowly. Off to her right, Bostwick's running form grew smaller as he lumbered north in the light rain. She held her breath. Waiting. Listening. *Can it be a trick? Has that horrible man really given up? And where is Keith?*

Rain dripped from the trees overhead, down over the sumac, and onto her head. Cold water worked its way inside her collar and down her neck. She felt it, damp against her collarbone, and shivered.

When she could bear it no longer, she emerged from her hiding place. Her body felt heavy, as though her arms and legs were weighted with lead. She looked down at the dirt and grass stains covering her hiking pants. *Oh, well. Forest fashion is going to have to do.* Her stomach growled, and she felt lightheaded for a moment. Once the dizziness passed, she waded through the brush and crept out onto a trail awash with trickling water. Without a look back, she took off south, away from Lake Jeanette and the two men. Where she could, she tried to run on the weeds and grass alongside the dirt path, partly because it would leave fewer marks by which to track her, but also because the trail was growing more slippery by the minute.

She ran until her fatigued legs begged for relief, then slowed to a labored jog. She didn't know how much time passed. The trail circled past huge stands of elm and conifers, regularly changing course. Each time she checked the compass she was meandering a different direction. She finally put the compass away, realizing it was of no use. If she traveled in a straight line, she wondered if she would reach the road in half the time. She looked around for landmarks but didn't recognize anything. It was all the same: trees and brush, grass and weeds. About the time she slowed to a walk, she came to a slight incline. The path widened to reveal a swath of muddy brown dirt that ended perpendicular to a road. Beyond that, there were trees, trees, and more trees.

Jaylynn stopped, suddenly frightened. What if someone was on that road? What if Bostwick hijacked someone else's car and suddenly came rolling toward her? She walked, listening carefully now. All she could hear was wind and water and her own heart beating loudly. When she got within a hundred yards of the end of the trail, she crossed to the west side of the path and inched through brambles and brush until she reached a stand of sodden maple and elm trees. As she stepped into the darkness they afforded, something wet and creepy-crawly hit her face and clung to it. She realized she'd walked into a large and intricate spider web.

"Oh, yuck!" She brought her hands up and batted away the webbing, then ran her hands through her hair. She almost wiped her face against her right coat sleeve, but realized all that would do is apply a patch of mud. "Good God, I'm a mess." With the back of her hand, she patted at her face, hoping no spiders had taken up residence anywhere on her head. Shuddering, she bent to pick up a stick, which she held out in front of her like a sword as she advanced into the darkness. Her stick took down another spider web before she veered off and headed toward the road, taking care to keep the noise down, an effort made easier by the damp earth, moss, and a thick layer of fallen leaves.

Though there was plenty of rain making its way through the thicket of trees, Jaylynn savored the quiet and protection from the wind. She took a moment to utilize the benefits of what Dez called Nature's Outhouse, then picked her way to the road, stopping periodically to listen. The wind was muffled, and even the birds were silent. When she drew near the edge of the tree line, she hung back and surveyed what she could see of the road. Rain fell lightly, splashing in puddles. East or west, there was no one and nothing in sight.

She squatted next to a giant elm and waited until she was sure all was clear. Then she rose and walked down the slope and up a slippery grade to the dirt road. To the west, she saw faint light shimmering. *Are there searchers off the road?* Excited and hopeful, she crept forward twenty paces before she realized the light was coming from the open hatch of the tan Explorer. She recalled that Bostwick had closed it and covered it with branches. How had it popped open? *What if somebody is in there?* That spooked her, and she ran for the trees, feeling exposed and vulnerable.

She waited and watched for a few minutes, and when nothing moved in or near the vehicle, she approached it, creeping between trees and bushes that sparkled with jewels of water. Finally she had to make a decision whether to bypass the SUV or investigate. Remembering the bottled water in the back was enough to drive her forward. She plunged into the thick brush around the front of the vehicle and worked her way circuitously to the back. Just as she suspected, the Explorer was empty. She crawled in over the bumper. The carpet was damp. *Someone has been in here. Who? A passerby? Maybe Bostwick?* The thought scared her, but she didn't think he would come back again. He and Keith were probably halfway to Lot A by now.

She grabbed at the nearest bottle of water and opened it. Reclining against the back wheel well, she downed gulps of the liquid.

With a sigh of fatigue, she reached for the back hatch and pulled it closed, shutting out the rain, the wind, and the outside world. For the first time in hours, she felt cozy and protected. With a bottle of water in each hand, she crawled and squeezed her way to the front passenger seat. She figured Bostwick hadn't missed anything, but just in case, she looked under the seats, in the glove compartment, and in every nook and cranny. When she got to the center console, she realized she had left a big muddy footprint on it. Ordinarily she would be concerned about something like that, but she was too fatigued to care. Besides, by now, the owner was probably dead.

She opened the console and rifled through the contents. CDs, a phone cord to plug into the cigarette lighter—but no phone—three different kinds of lip balm, and a pad of paper with gas mileage notations on it. A search of the back seat yielded nothing but an oily rag.

Discouraged, Jaylynn settled herself on the passenger side. She put the water bottles on the console, turned the rearview mirror toward her, and took in her begrimed appearance. Her normally white-blond hair was plastered to her head and looked brownish-yellow in the low light. She touched her lip, which felt fat and ragged inside. When she pulled it down, she saw a crooked line where her teeth had cut through with the force of Bostwick's earlier blow.

She was more pallid than usual, and her left eye was slightly bloodshot, most likely due to the swollen purple-and-blue knot on the top of her cheekbone, near her temple. *Whoa! He must've whacked me harder than I thought.* She touched the bruise with the tips of her fingers. *Must have been a lot of adrenaline running through me not to feel that! Power of suggestion, though – I sure feel it now.* Aware that she was damn lucky to have gotten away with so few injuries, she shuddered and twisted the mirror away.

The keys were still in the ignition, so she turned them one notch and the *Buckle Seatbelts* sign lit up on the dash. The radio came on, faintly, so she increased the volume. An announcer on the local station was finishing the weather forecast. "Rain, rain, and did I mention rain?" he said in a merry voice. "Just be relieved it's not snow. Yet. Overnight you can expect a low of 20 with the highs tomorrow reaching only 40. Currently, the temperature is 38."

*No wonder I'm so damn cold.* Jaylynn shivered and wished the heater would work. Without the engine running, though, it would just blow cold air, so she didn't turn it on. She shifted sideways in the soft seat, her back to the door, and pulled her knees to her chest. A commercial for roto-tillers finished, and the announcer came back on. "The search for the two escapees from the Kendall Correctional Facility has taken a new twist in the last few hours. Based on multiple reports of sightings near Ash River, authorities have been focusing the manhunt north of Buyck and stretching up toward Canada. But new reports received offer conflicting information. Of particular concern is the fact that a Twin Cities bus of students and their guides did not make it to their checkpoint at Echo Lake by noon. Rangers are out searching for the eight members of that party. In addition, police are close-mouthed about reports that a female St. Paul police officer was kidnapped by the escapees. Her name and the circumstances of her abduction are not being released at this time."

*Yes! Crystal and Shayna, I love you!*

"The search is now complicated by the weather, but the governor has called out the National Guard." He went on to recap the facts of each man's convictions and ended by warning people to lock their homes and cars, then ran another commercial before introducing a new Faith Hill song.

Shivering from fear as much as from being cold and wet,

Jaylynn wondered how a person went about counting lucky stars. While Keith Randall had been convicted of drug possession and burglary, Bostwick had a string of offenses dating back to the mid-eighties. Multiple assaults, attempted murder, and the latest, armed robbery. *What an awful man.* She thought about Keith for a moment. He was a miserable, indecisive wimp, probably a permanent low-life. She almost felt sorry for him. Bostwick was sure to murder him—or get him killed.

Jaylynn peered around the seat and looked out the hatch window. A crack of lightning illuminated the sky. The rain beat down so hard on the hood and roof that it sounded like a thousand little feet stomping. She had no desire to go back out into the storm, and with it raging all around her, she doubted anyone would come near the Explorer. She hoped that with the hatch down, the SUV would blend in well with the brush and not be easily noticed in this weather. Unless Bostwick was crazy, he'd be watching the road, not looking for a tan tailgate in the encroaching brush.

She left the radio on, crawled over the console and back seat, and sat in the cargo area, looking out the hatch window. She contemplated taking off down the highway, but decided to stay in the car and wait out the storm. There was a chance that Dez could go by at any time—and so might the convicts or other drivers. She wanted to see and be prepared for whatever happened.

WHEN KEITH AWOKE, he could barely get his eyes to open. Someone stood over him, shouting.

Although the world wouldn't come into focus, he knew it was Bostwick bobbing and weaving above him in the rain. "Wha-what?"

"...finds her? I should've left her dead on the ground with that Russian! What if some asshole hikers pick her up? Or even worse, if someone comes along with a car, we're fucked!" He kicked at the backpack and leaned down. "Get up, Randall. We've got to go. Now!" Stepping over Keith, the big man yelled some more, and finally Keith was awake enough to attempt to rise. He let out a groan as he straightened his kinked and aching body.

"Why?" Keith asked. "Why don't you just go along and leave me behind? You'll make better time."

"Oh, yeah, you'd like that, wouldn't you? I suppose you'd want me to leave the supplies, too. With all the money in it!" He leaned down and picked up the pack.

"Take it. Just leave me a canteen and go."

"Oh, right." Bostwick's voice was scathing. "So you can run off to the cops and tell them I took you against your will? I know how you think. Don't be an asshole. If you haven't figured it out yet, you're worth a helluva lot more to me alive than dead. Now come on."

"No."

Bostwick crossed his arms over his chest. "You've got two choices: move on down the trail, or I shoot you here and now." Keith glanced all around, searching the ground, but Bostwick laughed. "Look all you want, but I've got both guns, you little weasel. You couldn't even be trusted with that, you stupid jerk."

Keith's face burned. He had stopped thinking about the gun. He supposed he'd lost it when he fell, but he really had no clue.

"This is your fuckin' fault, buddy boy. You fall off the path like some fairy-ass dipshit." He shook his head. "I can't believe what a fuckin' fairy you are."

This filled Keith with fear and resolve. He straightened up and met Bostwick's eyes. "You're a real piece of work. Just shut the hell up!" He stood, eyes boring into the other man's.

Finally Bostwick looked away, wiped at his face and jaw, and muttered, "All right. Enough. Come on. We still got a chance to get outta here." Without another word, he turned and stalked off.

Keith drew in a deep breath and took a tentative step. He hoped the man ahead of him never figured out how right he was. For the last three years, Keith had carefully hidden his sexual orientation. Until recently, he had even hid it from himself. He wasn't proud to be gay, but he wasn't proud of how he'd hidden it either. He just felt confused.

He didn't know what to think, but being in prison had made him come to terms with his feelings. During all those long nights lying in a lonely bunk, thinking about his past, he had come to realize all the reasons he'd never fit in, never enjoyed dates, never wanted to get close to anyone. Instead, he took drugs, and to finance that habit, he stole. He wasn't proud of that either, but in less than a month, his whole world had been scheduled to change. He was supposed to get out and start a new life, and now it was all ruined. He gazed at the broad back ahead of him and felt anger burn deep and wide. *I'll do my time – and whatever else they tack on – but this man, this* animal, *will not break me!*

His whole body ached, but he knew he had to go on, if only to keep Bostwick from doing anything terrible to anyone else they met on the path.

# Chapter
# Twenty-Three

**Outside Buyck, Minnesota**
**Sunday, October 17, 3:30 p.m.**

CRYSTAL REVVED THE Jeep's engine and inched forward. She and Shayna sat impatiently, waiting behind a logging truck that was loaded down with giant tree trunks chained to the flatbed. Shayna reached over and grasped Crystal's arm. Her hand was warm and moist. "I can't believe this damn phone still won't get a signal. Why did we bother with it? I'd like to throw it out the window."

"No, don't do that," Crystal said. "Just wait. We must be almost to the town."

"What the hell is with this traffic jam anyway? We're in the flippin' wilderness! I'm getting out to look." Before Crystal could object, Shayna was out of the car on the side of the road. She shielded her eyes with her hand and gasped.

Crystal leaned to the right and ducked down, trying to see out the open passenger door. "What?"

"We *are* near the town, I think. It's a roadblock up ahead!"

"Hallelujah! Get in." She put the car in gear, nosed it to the right shoulder next to the logging truck, and sped past the line of waiting vehicles. One driver honked, then a series of others. "The cops here won't like this, Shayna. Get your hands up on the dash where they can see 'em."

Shayna did as she was told, and Crystal was glad she had because as she steered the car along the shoulder, suddenly she saw men in black uniforms moving and running. Red and blue lights flashed. She heard the bullhorn: "Stop the car! Stop or we open fire."

Crystal slammed on the brakes and hit the automatic power window button. She put her hands on top of the steering wheel and waited for further instructions. "Just sit tight until they tell us to get out, *mi amada*. And then do it slowly. No sudden movements. They might manhandle us a bit. They'll be nervous at first. Be patient, okay?" Shayna nodded.

In seconds the car was surrounded, and Crystal found herself looking up the barrel of a Colt AR-15. She stayed very still. When one of them shouted at her to get out, she calmly said, "Lopez. St. Paul Police Department. Badge number 433. We're both getting out now, and we're not carrying."

She reached down slowly and pulled on the handle, opened the door and shoved it wide. Keeping her hands in plain sight, she stepped out, repeated what she'd said before and added, "My companion is a civilian, and we need help immediately."

One of the men came forward while others kept their rifles trained on Shayna and Crystal. Two others slipped cautiously over to the Jeep to look in the windows.

The leader's name badge read *WERTEL*, and his insignia indicated that he was a Buyck city patrolman. "What the hell is going on, lady? We could've shot you. Why not wait in line with everyone else?"

Crystal let her arms down slowly but still kept her hands out, palms up. "At approximately 0700, while camping south of Echo Lake, three friends and I were accosted by two escaped convicts. Three of us were tied up, our gear was stolen, and Officer Jaylynn Savage, St. Paul Police Department, was kidnapped."

By this point, the officers lowered their weapons, and Wertel said, "That's impossible. Last we heard, they'd been sighted up north fifty or sixty miles away."

"They hijacked us, so I'm sure they could carjack somebody to head that way."

Shayna came around the side of the car, and Crystal thought she looked near tears. "Aren't you cops going to do *something?* They've got our best friend!"

One of the cops strode over to a police car and reached in for the radio to report to dispatch. Crystal tried to keep her cool when, in the midst of the codes, she also heard a few editorial comments, the most offensive of which was "not sure if they're a couple of fruit loops or what."

Wertel frowned. "You said you and three friends. Where's the fourth?"

Crystal shrugged. "She went after them."

"She, who?"

"Officer Desiree Reilly, St. Paul Police." He started to say something but she interrupted. "Three of us are St. Paul cops, and this civilian is Shayna Ford. So we've got two problems. The convicts have Officer Savage, and Officer Reilly is somewhere in the woods, chasing them. Believe me, this is a bigger problem than you think."

SALLY CABOT'S TRAIL bike slogged through another puddle and splashed a wave of muddy water up at her. She looked down at her rain gear, thankful she had thought to bring it. She was stained with sludge. Though she and Lou Schecter had stopped every mile or so to clean the muck off their helmet visors and face shields, there was nothing they could do about the muddy water, and they both looked like drowned muskrats.

They'd already checked out Hunting Shack River and Pauline Lake. Now they were on their way to Astrid Lake, neither one of them feeling much hope or energy.

Schecter was considerably ahead of her. Getting close to his bike's spray was out of the question, so when Cabot cleared the trees and putt-putted down an incline toward Astrid Lake, he was already off his motorcycle and staring out at the lake. To his right, farther down the shore, was a small brown building no bigger than a shed. During the summer, the Department of Natural Resources people or forest ranger staff could leave gear there overnight or lock up a canoe or bicycle while hiking the surrounding trails.

Schecter's tan rain gear was liberally coated with dark brown, and his red-and-white helmet hadn't escaped much dirt either. As Cabot got off her cycle, he removed his helmet and dunked it in the water.

She sighed. "I'd hate to see what all this water is doing to the innards of our helmets, Lou."

He turned, shaking his head. "No kidding." His sandy-colored hair was plastered to his head, and he shivered. "There's no way to tell if those kids or anyone else was ever here."

"Yeah. I know." Cabot let her pack slide off her back to rest on the bike's seat. "Let's go over to the storage shed and get out of the rain for a few minutes. I don't know about you, but I need something to eat." He gave a curt nod, tucked the helmet under one arm, and they both made their way over the slimy ground.

As they approached the shed, Cabot wasn't sure why, but suddenly the hair on the back of her neck stood on end. She glanced up at Schecter, but he seemed oblivious. She hesitated, and then she heard a voice. "Don't come a step closer. We've got a gun." Though pitched low and hoarse, the voice was a woman's.

Cabot reached up slowly to push her helmet off her head. "Sally Cabot, Kabetogama State Forestry Department. I have ID."

Schecter called out, "We're looking for lost campers and hikers."

The storage door inched open, and the top half of a blond head peeked around. "Thank God it's help, not harm."

"Mom?" asked another voice.

"Yup," Cabot said, her relief so strong that she felt a little shaky. "A cavalry of two has arrived." She reached the shed with Schecter right behind her, and the door swung wide. Pale light from the sky shone into the dim interior, and Cabot saw a circle of pinched, bedraggled faces staring back at her. The shed was large enough for perhaps two canoes, but that wasn't much room. There was no insulation, and the eight people crammed in the small space didn't look any too warm.

The blonde said, "I'm Laura Hiller."

Emily emerged. "Thank God you're here, Mom."

"This is excellent," Schecter said with a big grin on his face as he shook her hand. "Everyone present and accounted for?"

Emily nodded. "We're cold. We're tired. We're hungry. But we're all here." She hugged her mother tightly. Schecter moved past them and out of the rain, leaning against the wall just inside the entrance.

Cabot stood in the doorway surveying the group. Their faces looked fatigued, but all of the girls met her eyes. It was obvious they were chilled to the bone, but nobody had the spacey look of hypothermia. "You altered your trip plan."

"Yeah, big time. Mom, we ran into two escaped convicts on the trail, and they've got a hostage."

Alarmed, Cabot's glance shot to the kids. They'd shifted back against the wall and sat on lumps a few inches off the ground. As Cabot's vision adjusted, she realized they were perched, shivering, on their backpacks. "Not one of the kids—"

"No! No, the girls are all fine. They kidnapped someone else. A female cop." With occasional interjections from the girls, she sketched out their morning encounters, and with each word, Cabot felt more uneasy.

"After those three walked on," Laura said, "we met another woman. She said she was a cop looking for the convicts. Her name's Desiree Reilly—she's the one who told us what was going on. Apparently she was camping with her friends and those two convicts tied them up and took their stuff. That's when they kidnapped that poor woman."

"Her name was Jaylynn Savage," Emily chipped in. "Wait, I wrote everything down once we were well away from them." She produced a scrunched piece of paper and gave her mother a small grin. "See, all those lectures on paying attention and having presence of mind finally paid off!"

Cabot laughed. "Em, you were smart to get off the Echo Trail and hide. Those convicts are bad news, but don't worry, we'll get you out of here. First, let's warm up." All of the WAO group were soaked through and through, and she was worried about that. "I've got something you kids might find useful." She retraced her path out to the motorcycle and got her pack. From the saddlebags, she also pulled out four packages and a bottle of water. As the rain picked up again and the wind blew a sheet of it at her, she hustled back to the shed, shook off the water as best she could, then entered.

Once inside, she said, "I'd like you to pass around this water and everyone drink a little." She handed the container to the closest girl. "I think it would be best if you all stayed in here for a bit where we can conserve warmth. I'll radio in and get your bus or some other vehicle to come down and pick you up. In the meantime, these are heat sheets—you know, survival blankets." She handed three of them to Emily and ripped open the packaging on the fourth. "You girls are doing a good job huddling for warmth, but use the blankets." She moved over in the dim light to a pair of shivering girls and wrapped them up. "There, now a good eighty to ninety percent of your body heat will be conserved, and not only will you feel warmer after a while, but your clothes will start to dry."

The WAO leaders set to work helping the other two pairs of girls. "Ooooh," one kid said, teeth chattering. "This is definitely better."

Cabot asked, "When's the last time you had something to eat?"

"We finished our snacks a couple hours ago," Emily said. "We were supposed to have a picnic lunch at Echo Lake. The food is in our bus, but of course we have no clue where that is."

Cabot squatted and rooted around in her pack. She handed over some packages of M&Ms and peanuts to the girls. "Share those. They'll give you some energy and help you stay warm." With a toss of her head, she met Emily's eyes. "You and Laura ought to get under that last heat sheet."

Laura said, "I feel fine. I've been so nervous and uptight—"

"Me, too!" Emily said. "This has been a bizarre day."

Cabot peered up at Schecter. "Hey, Lou. Will you anchor the door shut? Just lean on it."

He said, "Geez, it'll be pitch dark in here."

"Not for long." She removed a battery-powered portable light from her pack and turned it on. "I've got all sorts of great stuff in this bag." He shut the door and slid down into a squatting position against it. Though dim in the shed, it was light enough to see faces.

Laura said, "Too bad you don't have a double latte."

"Ah, but I do!" Cabot pulled out her Thermos. "Actually, it's not quite as good as that, but it's strong coffee, and you two are welcome to share it with us."

The two leaders backed up and sat upon their packs. With shaking hands, Laura opened the container and poured some coffee into the capacious lid. Cabot took out her radio and turned it on. Dispatch sounded distant, but she got a clear signal and called in their circumstances. After she signed off, she said, "ETA is twenty minutes," and the girls let out a cheer.

The four adults passed the coffee around while the leaders, with occasional interruptions from the kids, talked more about the day's events. Cabot had them go over the encounter with the convicts multiple times.

Laura said, "I knew that young woman was upset and something was wrong."

One of the kids piped up. "Me, too. She looked really scared."

"And then we went on down the trail," Laura continued, "and another woman showed up. She scared the hell out of us, coming out of the bushes. I nearly had a heart attack. But real quick, she told us we were in danger and what to do."

"This is a bad business," Cabot said. "I'm just so thankful you're all safe. Is everyone feeling warmer?"

The girls' quick responses were heartening. Cabot shot a sharp look over at Schecter, who was squatting sleepily against the door with his arms crossed over his chest. She stood. "Lou, let's go check our gear."

He got up slowly, and they squeezed through the door, trying not to let too much cold in. She pulled the door firmly shut, and they stood in the rain.

He shivered. "Christ, it's cold out here!"

"It's always worse when you've started getting warm and have to go back out in it. I'll make this quick. It sounds like the convicts were heading east mid-morning. Even at a fast clip, they couldn't have gotten to Lake Jeanette any earlier than noon — possibly much later, depending upon the trail and the hostage's condition. Think they're still back there?"

Schecter scratched at some chin stubble. "Could be. Hard to say. How come the authorities keep saying they tracked them north?"

She shook her head, feeling perplexed. "There's been damn little traffic back here, and other than a few canoeists portaging through, none of the parties we're looking for were camping at Lake Jeanette. But if the policewoman led them there with the expectation of a vehicle, and they didn't get one, what would they do?"

"I don't know. What's further east?"

"There's the road that goes through the forest—maybe a five-mile trek—and then another ten or fifteen miles through Superior National Forest. Sooner or later they'd cross state lines over into Wisconsin."

"I wonder how well they know the area. I mean, I didn't grow up here, and I don't know the backwoods very well, so how could they?"

"Good point. Well, I do know the lay of the land. If they had half a brain, they'd travel north toward Loon Lake and cross over into Canada there at the finger of land that juts down. But they'd need a map. And brains. Convicts aren't always known for an abundance of those."

Schecter shivered again. "Damn right about that. I just can't believe they've eluded capture for this long."

She chuckled. "Like the old song—we've been looking for love in all the wrong places, or in this case, looking for cons. Do me a favor, would you, Lou? Escort the WAO group back to town and round up whoever will listen and come back out here and hunt the woods with me."

"Sure, but what are you going to do?"

She let out a sigh. "I've just got a bad feeling, Lou. I can't help it. We've got law enforcement personnel—at least one, perhaps two—in danger, and I hate to think of that. And every hour that goes by, these guys have to be getting more and more anxious—more dangerous."

"All the more reason why you shouldn't do this by yourself. Come with me, and we'll come right back with reinforcements."

"I'll call for help, Lou, but so far, we peewee rangers—all two of us—haven't been given much credence by the rest of the searchers, even though the Superior ranger and I know this area a lot better than anyone else. The state police are doing one thing. Fraley and the county boys are off on their own tangent. City cops are running scared, worried that Orr and Buyck aren't adequately protected, and the FBI isn't on top of it yet. It's a recipe for disaster. So I say, you take this group into town and try to get hold of the media. Maybe they'll listen."

"I've just been along for the ride, Sally. You should get the credit for finding the kids."

She gave a snort of laughter. "You prison guys can use all the help you can get. You already have a black eye because of the breakout. Go take some credit on behalf of that poor guy you work for. Besides, wouldn't you rather save face than ride around in this horseshit weather?"

A grin split his face. "Well, there is that."

"Stay on your toes, and please keep your weapon with you, okay? Make double-damn sure the bus doesn't get hijacked. Then when you get into town, grab some dry clothes if you like and meet me at Lake Jeanette. Bring your truck this time. And hurry."

"All right." He glanced to the right, then raised a dripping arm and pointed. "What do ya know. Here's their ride." A yellow mini-sized school bus plowed through the mud puddles at a rapid rate. Brown water splashed six feet high on either side of the bus, and each bump the wheels hit caused the vehicle to bounce. "Man, this guy's rolling."

"I'll say. Made it here in record time. Good for them."

The vehicle rolled to a stop, and a silver-haired man opened the side door. In a frantic voice, he said, "Where are they? Are they all right?"

Neither Cabot nor Schecter had a chance to answer. The shed door burst open and six girls, all speaking excitedly, tried to get out at once. Somehow they managed to exit and ran toward the bus carrying their backpacks and dragging silver heat sheets. Laughing, the two leaders trailed them out the door, and Emily said, "What an end to an unusual day."

"Oh, it's not over," Cabot said, gratified to think of her daughter coming out of this business safely as well as looking quite heroic. "Your media awaits."

"What?"

"You've been all over the news. When you get to town, the press will want to know what happened."

Laura said, "Oh, God, just what we need. And we look like hell."

"Get in the bus. Head into town and get cleaned up. And good luck with all your future hikes."

"We'll need it." Laura reached out a hand. "Thank you for finding us. And for your kindness."

"My pleasure."

Emily gave her mom a big hug, then turned to Schecter, but before she could say anything, Cabot interrupted. "Don't say goodbye to him. He's your escort into town."

Picking up on her unstated misgivings, he assured her, "Don't you worry, Sal. I'll meet you at Lake Jeanette as quick as I can."

"Attaboy."

THE SKY GREW darker by the moment with thunderclouds gathering as if to wage war in the heavens. A gust of cold, wet air buffeted her, but Dez ran on, trying not to take the increasingly bad weather as an omen. With the rain gear, she didn't get wet to the skin, and with the exertion, she was plenty warm. She wished she had spent a little time looking at the map when she had been under cover back at the SUV. It was in her cargo pants pocket, under the rain gear, but with the torrent blowing all around her, she didn't think it was wise to get it out. Instead, she tried to summon up a memory of the map. This road—which was really no more than a forest and logging access—just kept going west until eventually it hooked up with Highway 24 south of Echo Lake and north of Buyck. How many miles was it? Six? Eight? She couldn't quite visualize it. All she knew was that she had a long way to go.

She told herself over and over to stay strong. And she did feel renewed strength and energy. She was tired, but the overwhelming fatigue from earlier had passed. *It was smart to eat. I'm glad I did that.*

A flash of lightning far ahead of her illuminated the gray sky, and for a moment, the woods looked bright and yellow, charged with a strange luminescence that reminded her of the old sepia print hanging in her mother's den. The picture had been her father's—an ancient shot of several buildings in the small town in Ireland where the Reilly ancestors had lived. Her father had liked the picture because the little structure wedged between two bigger buildings had a tiny sign on the front that read *Constable*. Michael Reilly liked to say that his great-great-grandfather spent so much time at the constabulary that it was family legend that many of the Reilly clan had been conceived in that tiny police house. "You've got blue blood running through you, Dez," he'd say. "The law is your heritage."

She had, indeed, always felt comfortable being a cop. Her father's death when she was young had left her a pair of big shoes to fill, and being on the police force had always made her feel close to him. A lot of the old timers had known him well, and it was a comfort to hear their war stories. She wondered what he would think of her current crisis. What would he tell her to do now? She wasn't sure. It was easier for her to conjure up the voice of her long-gone partner, Ryan. She thought of his laughing face and imagined him shaking his head and saying, "Well, Dez, looks like you've gotten yourself into a *situation*. All you can do now is run your ass off." Then he would have laughed, and she would have joined in.

Thinking of the two most important men in her life gave her

a feeling of balance. Both were strong men, physically and ethically as well. She could almost hear them cheering her forward.

She estimated that she had run more than a mile since leaving the SUV, and she soldiered on. The backpack bumped against her spine, and under the rain gear, the Beretta pressed against her abdomen. She was still holding out hope that nothing had happened to Jaylynn — but if something had, she was afraid of what she might do with the gun. She only had so much blue blood running through her, and at this point, she thought it was running mighty thin.

# Chapter
# Twenty-Four

**Minnesota North Woods**
**Sunday, October 17, 4:20 p.m.**

JAYLYNN HAD TO fight her fatigue. The only thing keeping her awake was the music and periodic news reports on the radio. For what seemed like at least an hour, she had watched out the back window of the Explorer. Twice the window had fogged up, and she'd wiped it clean with her sleeve, but the third time it happened, she finally crawled to the front and pressed the rear defrost button. Now, where the metal wires ran across the back glass, she could see out. She hoped the Explorer's battery would hold out for quite some time.

All she wanted to do was curl up in the back cargo area and sleep. She leaned against the side of the car and closed her eyes, but she wouldn't let herself rest for more than a minute. She didn't want to miss seeing potential rescuers.

She peered out at a soggy world illuminated now and then by cracks of lightning. The thunderstorm was spectacular, and if she lived, she'd have quite a tale to tell. Another silent flash of lightning came, followed two seconds later by a giant rumble that shook the ground. "Wow." She was reminded of her littlest sister Erin, almost sixteen years younger than she. Their other sister, Amanda, two years older than Erin, never seemed bothered by the rainstorms that often hit Seattle where they all grew up. Tough, swaggering Erin, who wasn't afraid to climb the cupboards, chase dogs, or scuffle with any of the bigger kids in the neighborhood, was deathly afraid of thunder. It was the one time the normally fearless little girl turned to Jaylynn for nurture. Amanda slept through storms, but Erin woke up no matter what. During Jaylynn's senior year in high school, she often found the squirmy two-year-old in bed with her.

The thought of her sisters made her smile, and then, just as quickly, tears filled her eyes. Would she ever see them again?

They would never understand if something happened to her. She remembered how lost she had felt at age eleven when her father, an over-the-road trucker, died in an accident in his semi. She didn't want to put them through anything like that. Amanda and Erin had only just turned sixteen and fourteen — far too young to understand and cope.

Pressing back the tears, she let out a sigh and resolved to make it through the ordeal. There were far too many people who loved her, and she never wanted to let them down. If she had to stay in the car all night, she'd hold out.

RAIN KEPT POURING from the ominous sky, and wind cut through Keith's thin, wet clothes. He slid and stumbled on the path.

"You dumbshit. Why the hell did I get myself involved with a fuckin' weenie like you?"

Keith wanted to say, *Believe me, we're not involved. When this is over, you're the last person on earth I ever want to see again!* But he kept his mouth shut and continued on. Each step was an effort. He didn't look at his anklebones anymore. The prison-issue canvas tennis shoes had rubbed the skin raw, and he thought he might even be bleeding. The wind whipped at the wet flannel pants he wore, and he was cold clear through. He wondered if you could get hypothermia when the temperature wasn't freezing. He tried to ponder that, but decided his brain must be frozen. Nothing made sense. "How much further?" The words came out with effort, but Bostwick didn't seem to have heard. Keith turned and repeated the question.

"How the fuck would I know? Oh...wait." Bostwick pointed ahead. "There's the sign for Lot A. Not going there." He rumbled with laughter and wiped his dripping face. "I think we head off to the right up ahead." As he walked, he pulled up the back of his pants and resettled the pack on his shoulders. "We get us the car, and we're gone."

Keith had many questions, none of which he would ask out loud. *Where are we going next? What will happen to me? What do we do if we get stopped? What's Bostwick going to do with all that money?*

He was too tired to consider. The only bright light of the day had been when the girl, Jay, had broken away. He was glad his fall had given her the opportunity — even though he now had a mass of bruises on his right hip that hurt more with every step. He wondered where she had ended up. Would she be able to summon help before something terrible happened? He realized he was not afraid to die. But he had never thought he would have to die for such an appalling reason—over something as stupid as someone else's greed. It was crazy.

*I was a month away. One short month. Now I'll probably die in a shoot-out with the police, and I'll never see my mother again. Yup. Call me a mama's boy. I let her down so badly, and now she'll never know the real truth – that I was ready to go straight and be a good son.* He nearly laughed at that. He was going to go "straight" while admitting his homosexuality. It was an odd juxtaposition.

"Randall, get your head outta your ass and get going. We're almost there."

The excitement in Bostwick's voice made Keith feel even bleaker. The last thing he wanted was to be stuck in a car with the stinking bastard. Still, being out of the rain actually sounded quite appealing.

When they came upon a muddy dirt lot, Keith plodded toward the only vehicle parked there, a white Chevy Nova. He stopped and turned to face Bostwick. The big man fished in his pocket with a puzzled look on his damp features. The keys he pulled out and dangled in front of Keith were on a blue and white keychain. For the first time Keith looked at them and realized that the keychain was adorned with a gold badge-like detail. He reached up and took the keys, then examined the wet plastic and leather. SPPD. *Something-or-Other Police Department.* A laugh bubbled up. *God help us now. Bostwick really picked the wrong group to tangle with. Someone – maybe all of them – might have been with the police.*

As he'd gagged the tall, dark-haired one back at the campsite, she'd whispered through gritted teeth, "You hurt her, and I'll personally track you down and kill you." Such intensity. It hadn't clicked at the time, but now it made sense that she'd be a cop. He shook his head and grinned, knowing he should fear for his own hide, but the thought of that menacing woman's hands around Bostwick's throat was downright heartening.

"What's so fuckin' funny?" Bostwick asked.

"These keys are for a Toyota. This car is a Chevrolet."

Bostwick bellowed, "And you think that's funny? Fuck you! It's not funny. That stupid bitch told us the wrong lot." He stalked over to the car and tried the doors, but they were locked.

"Can't you break in and hot-wire it or something?" Keith wanted to add, *And you call yourself a criminal?*

"I don't know how to do shit like that. I don't care about cars—never did. Jesus Christ, I wish I had now!" He reached over and snatched the keys from Keith and stuffed them in his pocket. "Now we got to double back to Lot B. C'mon."

Keith followed him back down the lane to the trail.

Somehow he had known before they got close that the day's walk had been a ruse. It was obvious now why the young woman had been so desperate to ditch them. She had to have known that once Bostwick figured out he'd been duped, she would be in grave danger. *And what kind of danger am I going to be in?* He shivered once more, as much from fear as from the cold.

# Chapter
# Twenty-Five

**Kendall Correctional Facility**
**Outside Buyck, Minnesota**
**Sunday, October 17, 5:10 p.m.**

RALPH SOAMES HAD tried all day to reach Mike Martin, the facility's administrator, but it wasn't until five o'clock in the afternoon that Martin had called him back from somewhere in the Bahamas — he never got the name of the island — and Soames was almost sorry that he'd acted so responsibly in informing his boss. After taking a tongue-lashing like no other, he got off the phone and decided it would soon be time to spruce up his résumé. Right then he decided that even if he didn't get fired, he was going to quit. Pack up his wife and kids, sell the house, and move down to the Cities. He was sick of working with depraved people all day. *And that's the administrators.* He laughed with a sour taste in his mouth, feeling like he might be sick. He'd drunk far too much coffee and decided he needed something to eat to calm his nervous stomach.

Things had been quiet all day. Shift changes at noon, two, and four o'clock had gone without incident, and though they were currently short one guard, it didn't matter because the entire prison was in lockdown. Because of this, the hot meals had to be delivered to the inmates in their cells, and the food would likely be cold. It served them right. He hated them all.

With a sigh, he packed up all his papers, the staff files, and the Styrofoam coffee cups scattered around the administrator's office and shuffled over to his own small cubbyhole. Shirley could field any phone calls now. If he was needed, they could come find him. He dropped off the paperwork in his own office and wandered down the hall to the staff break room. Somebody had done a competent but unflattering pencil sketch of the baldheaded convict. The red tack that held it to the bulletin board was placed in the center of Bostwick's forehead, and a fine drop of blood had been drawn with a red felt pen.

The candy machine had not been recently stocked, and the only items left were mints, Lifesavers, Snickers—which he couldn't eat because of peanut allergies—and some small packets of Tylenol. He'd already taken more than the recommended dosage of aspirin, and candy wasn't going to assuage his hunger, so he passed on the machine items.

In the corner sat a very old refrigerator that one of the guys had donated. Soames opened the door and peered in. Various lunch bags and pop cans littered the shelves. He would never touch someone else's lunch, but there was also a tray that had once held a dozen chocolate muffins. Three were left. He pulled out the tray and set it on the break table.

"Hi, Ralph." Shirley came breezing into the room with a coffee mug and went to the sink to rinse it out.

"All quiet on the western front?"

"Yes. The phone has *finally* stopped ringing—for now, I suppose. You think they'll find those men?"

"I sure hope so." He took a napkin from the dispenser on the table and selected a muffin. "I'd like to tan their hides, too. If I have my way, they're going into solitary for the rest of the year."

"Good idea." She took a paper towel and wiped the mug as she turned and leaned against the sink counter. "Oh, no, Ralph. Don't eat that."

"What?" He looked down at the muffins. "They're yours?"

"No, silly. One of the guys brought them in. I ate a bite of one yesterday and got called away. Before I got back to my desk half an hour later, I had stomach pains. Must've been food poisoning. The cramping was terrible." She blushed. "I won't go into details, but I threw the muffin away and warned people, but it was too late. I'm glad I only ate one bite. A couple of the others chowed down, then had the same experience and had to go home sick. I'll never eat anything from the guards again."

Soames dropped the muffin and wiped his fingers on the napkin. "Who brought them, Shirley?"

"Someone on the afternoon shift, I think." She waved a hand, then held it in the air to examine her bright pink fingernails. "Oh, no. My nail is cracked again. Now how did that happen?" She rolled her eyes. "You men are so lucky. You probably never have trouble with fingernails, but I swear, I need to bring a manicure kit in here." She clucked and shook her head all the way out the door.

Soames had been hungry, but now his appetite left him, and he stood over the break table, thinking. A few minutes later, when he finally left the break room, he'd wrapped the chocolate muffins in a brown paper bag to take with him.

# Chapter
# Twenty-Six

**Minnesota North Woods**
**Sunday, October 17, 5:35 p.m.**

JAYLYNN WOKE WITH a start when she heard a peculiar-sounding horn on the radio. News time. *Dammit! I didn't mean to fall asleep.* She decided she couldn't have slept for very long because she was sitting upright. *I must have just winked out for a few minutes.* Outside, it was still gray and stormy, so nothing had changed.

The announcer came on the air with the latest report, and right in the middle of the update, his voice took on an excited tone. "We've just received information that the busload of teenagers missing since late morning has been found. There are no reported injuries, but the girls are being taken to the Buyck hospital for examination."

Bleary-eyed and exhausted, Jaylynn was heartened to hear that the WAO troop was safe, but also disappointed because it didn't sound like Bostwick and Randall had been apprehended. She hoped the WAO girls would give information that would help the searchers.

*For cripesake! Why haven't they started searching over here? Where are they?* Another crack of lightning hit. *Well, that explains why there's no air support.*

She shifted from her cross-legged position, pulled her knees up under her chin, and leaned against the back of the seat behind her. She was struggling to keep her eyes open when a faint light shone on the road. Traveling toward her from the right, the light grew brighter and turned into twin beacons. A dark shape came to a stop at the top of the embankment.

She hated feeling like an animal in a cage. The only quick way out of the SUV was through the back hatch and it was exposed. If she exited the Explorer that way, she would be seen, and she didn't want to risk that. What if Bostwick had found a car, and he was back?

She launched herself toward the front of the car, bumping her head against the ceiling on the way. Sprawled over the center console, she rushed to power down the passenger's side window. Now the rain and the whistle of the wind filled the car and drowned out the loud pounding of her heart. Could she get out through the window? She decided that even if she had to crawl on top of the SUV's roof and slide into the brambles on the hood to get to the woods, she would do it. She scrunched down, knees on the floor on the passenger's side, her forearms on the leather seat, and watched out the back window.

A dark form emerged from the driver's side of the car, but she couldn't make out whether it was a man or woman. The person moved across the road, and then for a few strides was illuminated by lightning. A man—and not Bostwick. He was of much smaller stature. A little of Jaylynn's terror subsided.

"Hellooooo. Does someone need help?" The man picked his way over to the SUV. He held something in his hands, but through the streaked windows Jaylynn couldn't tell what. Over the rain, she suddenly heard the irritating news horn on the radio and snaked her hand over to punch the OFF button. She held her breath as the back hatch was raised.

There was a moment of silence, then the man must have shivered. He said something in another language and released a fractured, "Ohhh," then noisily shook the rain off himself and started humming.

Very slowly, Jaylynn moved her head to peek around the side of the seat. He stood by the hatch light looking at something in his hands. In a soft voice, she said, "Hey."

The man jumped and dropped whatever he was holding. When she met his eyes, for just one moment she thought she saw anger and malice, but then the man reached up with his right hand and placed it on his heart. "You scared the devil right out of me!"

"Who are you?" She tried to say it politely, but it came out rather flat and hurried.

"Me? I would be the not-so-proud possessor of this stolen Explorer."

"What?"

He reached down and picked up whatever he had dropped and shook it up in the air. It looked like a Game Boy. "Wonderful new technology. This Skyrunner vehicle location device has worked flawlessly. I have tracked this car all the way from Chicago."

He spoke with the same lilt to his voice as the man shot by

Bostwick. This made her wary, but she said, "Someone stole this car from you?"

"I am afraid so. Here is a lesson I must impart: never leave your keys in the ignition. Do you see my keys anywhere?"

"Yes. They're here." She pointed toward the dash. "But it's out of gas."

"Ah. I see. Did they leave anything—or have they stripped it completely?"

"The stereo system still works, but there's not much of anything left. Believe me. I've looked. I could have used something to eat, but there's nothing." As an afterthought, she added, "Other than the water back there, that is."

"How did you come to possess my SUV?"

"No! No, sir, I didn't take it. I got separated from my hiking party. When I saw it here off the road, it seemed like a good place to get out of the rain. I assure you, I didn't steal it."

"Of course not! I would have thought no such thing. But I must tell you, there is a manhunt in these woods for some very unsavory characters. I would advise you to get out and come away with me to safety." When she didn't answer immediately, he said, "You will come to no harm, miss. That I can promise you."

She pulled at the lever to raise the power window until it closed, then wormed her way between the seats and over the back into the cargo area. "Was this your water?"

He shook his head. "I have never laid eyes upon it."

She grabbed a fresh bottle as well as the half-empty one she had started. "My name is Jay."

"I am Konstantin Ivanov, but you should just call me Vanya. Everybody calls me Vanya."

"Nice to meet you, Vanya."

"Shall we brave the storm?"

Jaylynn nodded, her heart in her throat. The man was polite—a perfect gentleman—but something felt out of line. The only thing that gave her any solace at all was the fact that he was small-boned and not much taller than she, and though he could probably overpower her, she would give him one hell of a fight and use her knife if she had to. His clothes—Dockers and a windjacket—were slicked against him, and she couldn't see a single weapon bulge anywhere on his body. She stuck a leg out over the wet bumper, slid out of the cargo area, and stood under the dimly lit open hatch. She was far stiffer than she thought she'd be. The bottoms of her feet felt bruised and tender.

He cocked his head to the side and frowned. "You bear the mark of a brute. Who hit you?"

Bostwick's dirty smell and poisonous breath came back to her, and she flushed with embarrassment. "It's nothing." If she had thought more quickly, she could have told him she got hit by a tree branch, but her brain had stalled with the image of the big man's fist flailing in her direction.

"Nonsense. Are you sure you are all right? Who did this to you?" When she didn't speak right away, he said, "Come. Let us get out of the cold." Turning, he gestured for her to follow.

She slammed shut the back hatch and limped up the hill. "What are you going to do about the Explorer?"

"I will go to town and get a tow truck to come retrieve it." He opened the passenger door of a dark four-door sedan, and she slid in next to a small, leather valise with a map resting on top. The interior of the Buick LeSabre was spotless. "Now if I could only find that big lout who stole my vehicle."

The voice. It very much resembled the other man's. The door shut gently, and she closed her eyes, trying to block out the vision of the brown-haired man on the ground, writhing, his abdomen covered in blood.

Vanya got in the driver's seat. He had left the car running, and it was toasty warm. Jaylynn clutched her water bottles and breathed in the scent of the man sitting nearby. Instead of Bostwick's stench, he smelled of expensive cologne. She opened her eyes and looked at him. He gazed through the windshield and down the road. She shivered. "Do you think you know who took your car?"

"Oh, yes. An acquaintance who is not very honest."

"What did — does he look like?"

"Big fellow. Brown hair and blue eyes. Soft-spoken. Comes from my neighborhood and is a cousin of a friend of mine."

Jaylynn debated, but her concern for the injured man overrode her desire to keep her mouth shut. "I think I know where your friend's cousin is. I — I, well, I haven't told you the full truth about what happened."

Vanya didn't look her way but kept staring off into the distance. "I had a feeling there was more involved than you felt comfortable to say, miss."

"The truth is, some men hijacked me on the trail. They wanted a car."

"Did you give it to them?"

"No. I didn't have one to give."

Now he looked her way, sympathy on his face. "These men — they didn't violate you, did they?"

She shook her head. "One of them is a sociopath. The other is weak, but seems to have some principles. He kept the psychotic one off me. However, I have bad news. The man who took your car? They shot him and left him near the lake. I think he's probably dead." She gulped and let out a whoosh of air.

"Were you there?"

"Yes. But I ran." She didn't bother to tell him all the details. She let her head drop, and fatigue washed over her.

"This is not good. Are you sure he is dead?"

"No. But they shot him in the stomach. I'm not sure how long it's been. Maybe two hours ago? Before the rain started."

"We should help this man. Can you show me where it happened?" Fighting back tears, she nodded. He folded up the map lying on the valise between them and unzipped the leather satchel to pull out a towel. "Here. Don't cry. None of this is your fault. Take this and dry your face and hair. You look miserable and cold."

She took the towel from him, pleased to find that it felt as though it had been warming in an oven. She wiped her face and neck, pressed it to her hair and then blotted her eyes. Breathing in, the scent was familiar. Gun oil. The faint odor of cordite, too. She lowered the towel slowly to her lap. "Thank you. You are very kind." Her heartbeat had picked up, and once again she was on edge.

He didn't seem to notice, but gestured for the towel, which he zipped back into the leather bag. "Where do we go, Jay? Even if my friend's cousin is a vile thief, no one deserves to be shot and left bleeding in the rain."

The blunt assessment took Jaylynn's breath away. She'd been trying hard not to think of that, but it was true. While she hid in the car, protected from the rain, another human being lay out in the elements, his life slipping away. Ashamed, she realized she should have kept going down the road and tried to get help for him.

She teared up again, and when Vanya looked over at her, he said, "Tsk-tsk-tsk, it is not your fault. You are but a slip of a girl going up against bad men. Don't think of the shooting. Think of these men who surely must be the escaped convicts of whom they talk much on the radio. One was large, you say? And the other weak?" She nodded. "Let's avoid them then. Which way do I go?"

Jaylynn pointed. "Straight ahead. Make a left at the next turn."

He put the Buick in gear, pulled forward, and drove carefully to the T in the road. She sat in silence, slumped against the door, wondering if she had jumped from the frying pan into the fire. *Who is this man? Is his story true? Why do I feel so uneasy?*

She couldn't chalk it all up to exhaustion and stress; every synapse in her body told her something was off.

"I was dismayed to learn that cell phones won't work this far north," Vanya said in a conversational voice. "I had no idea that the telephone people only have towers in the more heavily populated areas. Seems such a shame. I would think that out here people would need phones as much or more than in the city." He reached over and pressed the button for the radio. "Lucky the radio still works. Let's listen to see if they have caught your assailants."

Other than a pause for a multitude of commercials, the announcer on the AM station talked solely about the prison break. At first, Jaylynn listened half-holding her breath, but after five minutes it was clear there was nothing new. With her head leaning against the window, she let weariness wash over her. She was sure she'd never be an adrenaline junkie. After the crisis passed, the letdown and fatigue were too much.

"Miss, if I remember correctly from the map, each of these lakes has at least one parking lot."

"Yes. Lake Jeanette has three. Lot A is where we need to go to. I could show you on the map."

"You may point the way."

"Okay, keep going."

With a nod, Vanya pressed harder on the accelerator, and they bumped along at about thirty miles per hour. They came to another turn, but he passed it. Jaylynn raised a hand and started to speak, but Vanya said, "I think we should scout the area—make sure there are no convicts in the vicinity. What do you think of that idea?"

"I've got no desire to run into them again."

"This is good." He drove on and soon came to another turn, but bypassed it, too. The end of the road turned into an open area. Three vehicles sat in the lot: a red Dodge truck, a green Subaru, and a boxy, black Honda Element. The latter two had double canoe racks on top. The area looked deserted. Vanya drove carefully around the square of the lot. His headlights shone into the trees. "I see nothing. You?"

"Me neither."

He repeated their search in the area of Lot B. All they found there was a white Chevy Nova and a lot of wide, sloppy mud puddles. Finally, he turned the car and rolled toward Lot A. Jaylynn's anxiety level shot through the roof.

THE LIGHTNING AND thunder were fierce, and even a veteran ranger like Sally Cabot was spooked by it. In a perfect world, she would have stayed holed up in the shed until the worst of it passed, but she had a bad feeling. So instead of warmth and safety from the storm, she rode along on the motorcycle, avoiding the biggest puddles and getting colder by the minute.

As near as she could tell, traveling over fifteen miles per hour was too dangerous, so she picked her way along the dirt trail from Astrid Lake until she reached the smoother road that went west toward town and east to Lake Jeanette. Now she could pick up the speed a little, but it was still slick and treacherous, so she never got much over twenty-five miles an hour.

Traveling down the middle of the lane, with wind blowing from the north and rain pummeling her, she noticed a grayish form up ahead. She pulled back on the throttle, acutely aware that her service weapon was on her hip, under the rain gear. She couldn't get to it without taking her hand off the throttle. Gearing down, she squinted into the darkness, then pulled the bike to a stop at an angle to the left side of the road. If she had to suddenly dismount, she wanted to put the bike between her and the oncoming person.

The runner drew closer, moving in short, quick steps, almost mechanically. The gray form gradually brightened until Cabot saw a person dressed in light blue rain gear. *Oh, shit. This guy's big. Is it one of the escapees?* She couldn't take any chances. She was off the bike in a heartbeat, stripping away her right glove, reaching for her gun. She got down behind the motorcycle, her arms balanced on the rapidly soaking leather seat. "Halt! Police! Put your hands up."

Arms went up in the air, but the person continued to jog forward, though slowly.

"Stop, I said!"

"I need help." The voice was low, but definitely female. "Desiree Reilly, St. Paul Police Department. Please put the gun away." She ran in place now.

Cabot relaxed and dropped the gun down by her side. "I'm glad to find you. My daughter is one of the WAO leaders you ran into today. She sent me out looking for you."

"Finally. Have you heard if Jaylynn Savage has been found?"

Cabot shook her head. "Sorry."

The tall woman jogged closer. She was at least a head taller than Cabot. Tendrils of dark hair spilled out from the hood she wore, and her pants were covered with splotches of mud. She came to a stop. In a breathless, hurried voice, she said, "My partner was abducted by the convicts. I gave chase. Almost caught them back by Lake Jeanette. They shot a man, stole his car, and headed this way. I found the car abandoned on the side of the road a couple miles back. I'm assuming they're now traveling this direction. You didn't see two men and a woman, did you?"

Cabot shook her head again. "No. I don't know where they are, but I just got on this lane. They could already be down the road halfway to Buyck. What about this man who was shot? Is he okay?"

"He died. His ID said his name was Greg Russell. I tried to give what little first aid I could, but he was shot in the stomach. He probably bled out internally. I had to leave him." With a pleading look, she said, "Can I take your bike?"

"No, but I can still help. I'll call in. By the way, I'm Sally Cabot, Kabetogama State Forestry Department." She put her gun away underneath her rain gear and slid out of her backpack so she could get out her radio. "What time was the shooting?"

"Shortly before noon."

Cabot called in to dispatch and relayed her location along with the other details, then said, "We need an ambulance out here pronto."

"Copy. Ambulance on the way."

"Isn't there a blockade at Buyck still?" Cabot asked.

The dispatcher said, "Affirmative. Nobody gets in—nobody gets out."

"I'm on County Road 116 near Astrid Lake Trail. Please inform authorities that we have a confirmed altercation with the escapees at Lake Jeanette, and we have confirmation that they have at least one hostage—" She broke off and looked at Reilly, eyebrows raised.

With effort, the woman in blue said, "Jaylynn Savage, age 29, white, female, 5'4" and 125 pounds, blond hair, hazel eyes. She's a cop, too."

Cabot could see the strain on the woman's face and quickly relayed that information. "You've got to get cops out here, and a lot of them. The escapees are definitely out here—I can almost feel it. Are the Feds on the scene yet?"

The crackle on the radio reported, "No firm ETA yet."

"Okay." She finished her report to dispatch and signed off. The radio was wet, so she pulled up the waist of her rain gear top and tried to dry it off on her inner sweater. No luck. She hastened to put the radio in her backpack, hoping that no water would seep in. "I've got an obligation to go check on the injured man, Reilly, just in case he's not dead. You can ride with me to Lake Jeanette if you don't mind it being tight. I'm expecting to meet up with reinforcements there."

"No, thank you, ma'am. I don't want to lose any more time. I've already been back there, and I need to keep moving, find my partner."

"I can understand that, but you shouldn't be running around in the woods. Those men are armed."

A crooked smile came to Reilly's face, and she pulled up her anorak to display a blue lump against her belly. "They're not the only ones packing. I bet I'm a better marksman than they are."

Cabot frowned. "Okay. No time to argue. I'm heading to Lake Jeanette to check on the dead man. Please be careful."

"I will." She reached out a wet hand and grabbed Cabot's forearm. "Thanks." She whirled and moved away, loping west, her broad shoulders moving rhythmically as she pumped her arms.

"Bless you, kid," Cabot said softly, then kick-started the motorcycle and went in the opposite direction.

CRYSTAL AND SHAYNA tried to monitor the radio, but the local station's information was secondhand and not particularly timely. Crystal said, "Damn! I wish that sport shop had had police band radios in stock." Rain came down in sheets as she carefully steered south along a paved road that crossed Hunting Shack River.

Shayna held a brand new .38 pistol in her lap. "I wish we weren't out here at all. I wish this had never happened. I wish I didn't have a gun in my lap. I wish a lot of things."

"I know. Me, too." Crystal looked over at Shayna, noting the scared expression on her face. "We can only hope and pray."

"Well, even though it took an hour and an exorbitant amount of credit card cash, I'm hoping and praying that I don't have to point this gun at a real, live human being and pull the trigger."

Crystal sighed. "I know what you mean." She reached the end of the narrow road they were on and came to a stop. She squinted into the deluge raining down upon them. "So this is County Road 116, right?"

Shayna picked up the map. "Yeah. Here's that Hunting Shack River we just crossed. Go right to head back to Buyck. Go left and we'll come to some lakes and then the Lake Jeanette State Forest."

"How far are we from the prison?"

"A long ways. But as the crow flies we're only about five or six miles from our campground. Crys, they would have gotten a lot farther than this, wouldn't they?" She leaned over, holding the map between them. "See what I mean?"

"Good God. It's so hard to know." With her right index finger, Crystal pointed. "Here's the trail from the Echo campground to Lake Jeanette. They must have reached it by now, huh? And they should have figured out there was no car."

"And then what? Where's Dez? And what would they have done to Jaylynn when they got there and found no vehicle?"

"Don't even say that, Shay." She pushed the map away. In a grim voice, she said, "I guess we better go take a look over at Lake Jeanette."

"Wait." Shayna let the map drop and turned up the radio volume.

In an excited voice, the announcer was saying, ". . . to bring you this special bulletin. The prison escapees who were being sought north of Orr have now been reported as sighted near Lake Jeanette. Police band radio communications have erupted in a flurry of communications and indicate that someone has been shot. An ambulance is on its way to the scene. No word yet on who the injured person is, or whether the convicts have been located. State police and county sheriffs are on their way south, but are encountering traffic and roadblocks. We're still awaiting information regarding the St. Paul police officer allegedly taken hostage, and we'll bring that to you just as soon as we have more to report. Please stay tuned to your own country hit radio."

"Oh, shit," Crystal turned the volume down and looked at Shayna.

"Go! Take off."

"My thoughts exactly." She hit the gas, and they careened around the corner heading east. They hadn't gone more than a mile when a tiny figure appeared up the road. "Whoa!" Crystal's heartbeat went up. "Is that—"

Shayna shrieked, "It's Dez! Slow down!"

Crystal hit the brakes and skidded to the right. The blue-clad figure kept shuffling woodenly toward them, her knees hardly rising. Shayna set the gun on the floor and was out of the car before Crystal shifted into park. Crystal didn't get out. She felt like she might cry. Here was Dez, but no Jaylynn, and Crystal felt heartsick.

Crystal sat watching as her partner raced ahead to the jogging woman, gesturing wildly, and grabbed hold of her. Dez kept moving toward the Jeep with Shayna pulling on her arm, and the two of them tumbled into the passenger side, with Shayna in the front, and Dez breathing hard in the back seat next to her soaked backpack. Crystal turned and met Dez's eyes. Neither of them spoke. The look on Dez's face said it all.

Shayna said, "Let's go. Hit it, honey." Crystal put the Jeep in drive and goosed the accelerator. "Oh, Dez," Shayna said, "you're drenched clear through."

"It doesn't matter." In a quiet voice between shallow breaths, Dez said, "I almost had her. Almost. They drove off. Up ahead here. The car they took is parked. Out of gas. Now I can't find her. Where the hell is she?"

Crystal was already white-knuckling the steering wheel. The hopeless tone in Dez's voice was almost too much to take. Somebody was shot. Was it Jaylynn? She prayed that Shayna didn't mention it. She didn't want to lie to her friend, but then again, maybe someone else had taken the bullet, not Jaylynn. In her most official, most cop-like voice, she said, "Snap out of it, Dez. We just now got radio reports that the convicts are over at Lake Jeanette. Backup is on the way."

"I hope they're sending an ambulance. A guy was shot."

"What? How do you know —"

"That happened hours ago. I found the man. I think he's dead. They shot him before they ditched the car, and now I don't know where the hell they are."

Crystal let out a sigh of relief. She sought Dez's eyes in the rearview mirror. "They're still out here, Dez. Don't give up yet, buddy. Wherever they are, Jaylynn is with them. We just have to find 'em."

Shayna was turned in her seat looking back toward their friend. She asked, "Have you had anything to eat? You look done in."

Dez put both hands up and slid the dripping hood off her head causing sparkling rain drops to splash all around. "I did eat a little bit ago. I'm not hungry now — just thirsty."

Shayna produced bottles of Pepsi and 7-Up. "Want one?" She swayed to the side as Crystal went around a wide puddle.

Dez shook her head. "I don't think I could stomach it." She reached into her pack and pulled out a bottle of water.

"Where'd you get that?"

"Long story. Stole it from a car." She reached up and brushed her hair back with her right hand. The long French braid, originally tucked up, had long ago come out, and wisps of hair curled here and there. "I can't believe this is happening." She took a drink from the water bottle, then met Crystal's eyes in the rearview mirror again. As if the water had poured strength into her, she took a deep breath, and her voice came out strong. "Okay, there are things you should know. I ran into a forest ranger a short while ago. You're traveling faster than she is, and she's on a motorcycle, so watch out for her." She went on to tell them the sequence of events as swiftly as she could relate it all. When she got to the part about the shooting, she closed her eyes and shook her head slowly. "Damn, if I just hadn't stopped so long to talk to those girl hikers. Or if only we'd hurried faster at the campsite. Or if we'd managed to get free quicker. Or—"

"Stop!" Crystal called out. "You can't do that, Dez. No second-guessing. This isn't over. Hang on now." She took the turn to the Lake Jeanette Trail without slowing much. The deluge of rain gradually lessened as they sped through the sloppy mud, and Crystal was relieved that she could see farther down the road. She watched for signs of a motorcycle or anyone on foot.

They were approaching Lot A when a pair of headlights came at them. Crystal jerked the Jeep to the right. "Oh, crap!" A muddy dark sedan sped past, narrowly missing them. She looked into the rearview mirror. In trying to get a good look at the car, Dez had launched herself across the back seat. "Who was that?"

"I don't know. Didn't get a good look."

Crystal asked, "Should we go after them?"

Dez straightened up and returned to the seat on the right. "No, I'm worried about that forest ranger's safety. There!" She leaned forward to point over the front seat and slightly to the right. "Turn in. That's where I left the guy they shot."

# Chapter
# Twenty-Seven

**Chicago, Illinois**
**Sunday, October 17, 5:42 p.m.**

IN CHICAGO'S POURING rain, Sergei Gubenko cut across the street and got into his Lexus. His hand shook when he tried to insert the key into the ignition, and it wasn't from the cold. He hadn't heard from his people since the first news reports of the prison break in the early morning. By now, he should have received a telephone call, but he had heard nothing. With every hour that passed, he became more and more certain that something was terribly wrong. He drove carefully and stayed well below the speed limit. Today was not a day for accidents or speeding tickets.

The clouds and rain obscured what little light leaked from the sky, making Gubenko feel like he traveled in the swirling fog of a bad dream. All the way across town he drove aimlessly, keeping an eye out for a telephone booth or a "Phone" sign where he could make a quick call. With the advent of cell phones, he was dismayed to see public pay phones disappearing right and left. It was difficult to find one outdoors, but he didn't want to go into a shopping center or bank facility.

As he drove, he thought of his family—most of whom had been lost in Russian pogroms—and of his older brother and his devoted helper and friend, Grigor. *When this is over,* he thought, *I ought to adopt Grigor—make him a son and heir. He has no one. No wife, no parents, no children. He has been like a son to me, and far more present in my daily life than my four daughters. I should have done this a long time ago.*

He turned near Wrigley Stadium and drove slowly down the long avenue. Across the street from the stadium, he caught sight of a bank of phones lined up underneath an eave. With relief, he pulled over into a No Parking zone and hustled out of the car. There was no way to get out of the rain, so he stood in the drizzle and pressed the damp buttons to call his party. When the phone was answered, he spoke in Russian. "S.G. here."

"Ah, yes, sir. No news."

"This is not what I want to hear."

"No news is good news."

"No! You are wrong. No news is *no news*. I want information. Now!"

"Wait—wait a moment." Gubenko heard a whispered conference, but he couldn't make out what was being said. The man came back on the line. "I am not sure how to impart this news—"

"Just spit it out and be done with it!"

"Some number of hours ago—we are as yet unclear—your brother fell ill. An ambulance came to take him to the hospital. We know nothing further."

"You will find out!"

"Yes, sir. We will."

Gubenko hung up the phone. A cold shiver started low in his spine and traveled upwards to his shoulders and neck, which broke out in goose-bumps. He felt nauseous as he walked back to the Lexus. *What am I to make of this? What is happening?*

# Chapter
# Twenty-Eight

**Minnesota North Woods**
**Sunday, October 17, 5:45 p.m.**

DEZ GRIPPED THE back of the passenger seat as Crystal rocketed down the road. A wake of water sprayed behind the Jeep. The dim light from behind the clouds provided little illumination—less every moment as dusk fell. They barreled into Lot A, splashing through puddles. Dez squinted through the front windshield, certain she could see movement. "Watch out, Crys!" she shouted.

"Uh oh!" Crystal swerved off to the right to avoid hitting a group of people.

Three men and a woman who was dressed in yellow rain gear stood arguing in the middle of the parking area. Greg Russell's body lay on the ground next to Ranger Cabot's motorcycle.

The three men, all much bigger than Cabot, were obviously worked up, making wild gestures, and shouting. Dez noted that nobody held a weapon. Before Crystal brought the car to a full stop, Dez was out, the gun in her hand pointed toward the dirt. She stalked over as Crystal got out of the Jeep and hastened to join her.

"What's going on?" Dez asked.

"Goddamn guy hijacked our gear—"

"He took our canoe—"

"Gimme that gun. I wanna kill him!" The last one's eyes were wild, and he shook his fist in the air.

Sally Cabot waved her hands. "Shut up! All of you, just shut up." She turned to Dez, glancing at the gun. "You want to put that away, Reilly?" Dez pulled up her rain gear and stowed it in the Neoprene holder.

Cabot gave a nod. "Who are these people?"

"I'm Crystal Lopez, St. Paul Police. A friend, Shayna Ford, is in the car."

Before anything further was said, Dez asked, "Were the escapees in the car that just peeled out of here?"

"No," one of the men said derisively. "I don't know who the hell that was. The cons took our fuckin' canoe! The guy who jumped us was a total asshole. They're gone — out on the water!" He pointed toward the trees beyond which the lake lay.

Dez scowled. "Who was that in the car then?"

Cabot said, "I don't know. They drove in, saw us, and hightailed it out of here. Middle-aged white male was driving. I didn't get a good look."

Dez leaned over the body on the ground. She reached out to touch his neck, which was cold as ice. The rain gear and knit cap hadn't helped him much. There was no pulse. She looked up at the forest ranger. "I hoped I was wrong, but he's definitely dead."

Cabot nodded. "The ambulance is coming anyway."

Dez glanced over her shoulder at Crystal, then took in the appearance of the three men. Two were muddy, as though they had lain facedown in a dirty bog. One of them held his hands out, dripping brown water, and as the raindrops came down, he made washing motions to clean them. The third man was wet, and he didn't appear quite as angry as his friends who continued to rant.

"I just got here," Cabot said over their loud voices. "I don't exactly have the story straight myself."

Dez yelled, "All right, one person at a time. What happened?"

The loudest one said, "We came in off the lake because of the lightning. We were in such a hurry. Dave and me," he pointed to the hand-washing guy, "came out of the water first. We hauled the canoe up on the shore and headed for cover. A big, bald guy came out of the trees with a gun and demanded a car. We told him we didn't have our car here. Shit! We portaged in miles away. At first he didn't believe us, then he marched us over to a mud hole and made us lay down in it. Says he'll shoot our heads off if we move a muscle."

"How many were with him?" Dez asked.

"There was someone else down the slope."

"A woman?"

He shrugged, and his face grew stormy again. "We were down in the mud by then, dammit!"

The quiet man said, "It was blowing hard out there. I was alone in my canoe and ended up a lot further behind these guys. By the time I struggled to shore, their canoe had gone back out. I thought they were crazy, but it so was far away, I couldn't make out details."

The hand-washing man cut in. "Goddamn asshole. Who the hell does he think he is?" He wiped his hand on his thighs.

Dez said, "He's a prison escapee, and you're lucky to be alive." She pointed down. "This guy wasn't so fortunate."

Dave said, "We saw that—him, I mean. There was nothing we could do for him."

Crystal said, "I know this has been an ordeal, but we need you to stay calm and watch this scene here. Make sure nobody comes along and does anything to mess it up anymore than it already is."

The angry guy looked at her like she was crazy. "Screw that. We're getting the hell out of here, getting a gun, and killing that guy!"

Dez took a step toward him. "No, you're not. Not unless you want to walk a shitload of miles back to Buyck. You'll all give your car keys to the ranger here." He opened his mouth to protest, but she was done with the men. "And we're taking your other canoe. Now."

"What!" The angry man shook his head. "No way. We've already lost one canoe. We're not losing anoth—"

Dez got in his face. She was taller than him by two inches, and he stepped back. "I'll buy you a brand new one if it comes to harm. But those cons have a hostage. So get the hell outta my way and do what you're told!" She pushed past him.

Cabot said, "Wait a minute, Reilly. Hold up just a sec." She fumbled in her pack for her radio. "We need to report in—get backup."

Dez's words tumbled out in a rush. "Good idea. You do that. Then you take the bike around the lake to the north and try to head them off. We'll follow them in the canoe. Shayna!" She waved at the woman hovering near the Jeep. "Stay here with these guys and give directions to any emergency vehicles that show up."

"Gotcha," Shayna replied. "Here, take your packs."

"Thanks." Dez accepted the backpack and shouldered it. "Cabot, make sure you get details on these guys." She eyed the big-mouthed one. "They're either going to come off as heroes or jerks, so we need their names." She met the Latina cop's eyes. "C'mon, Crys. Hurry!" She turned and ran for the edge of the parking area, cut through the trees, then slipped and slid down the muddy incline. She saw the rust-red aluminum canoe twenty yards down the shore. When they got to it, Crystal cursed in Spanish. They found five or six inches of standing water in it as well as a waterproof deck bag, a cooler, and another insulated bag bungee-corded under the stern seat.

Dez ripped bags and items out and tossed them aside like flotsam. "Help me flip it!" With almost superhuman strength, she grabbed the bow and the front crossbar and turned it. Crystal grabbed the gunwale at midship and guided it to the side. Water sloshed all over, soaking their legs and boots. They plunked the canoe back on its bottom. Dez threw in the two paddles and shoved the craft into the water. "Get in!"

Crystal stepped into a half-foot of lake water and let out a yowl. The other foot stamped into the center of the craft as she reached for the side thwart. Dez gave it another push, and Crystal nearly lost her balance. She grabbed the bow thwart and threw herself down into the bottom, which righted the canoe. "Holy shit, Dez! Be careful. We can't dump it."

Dez steadied it from the point at the stern deck. "We won't. We can't."

Crystal scrambled forward on her knees to the bow seat. "Give me a second, Dez." She got a leg over the seat, then hoisted herself up in front with her feet under the bow deck. Dez lay over the stern deck, gave a last push, and slithered into the seat in the back as the canoe cut through the shallow water. She grabbed a paddle as Crystal did the same.

The trim was good. They rode high in the water with more than a foot of freeboard, though Dez didn't know how long that would last. It continued to rain, and now that she was saturated up to mid-calf, every part of her was soaked and cold. She couldn't think of that though. *Mind over matter.*

They quickly got into a rhythm. Dez thanked God that Crystal was strong—and more rested than she was. Her friend was paddling like a madwoman. Dez yelled encouragement, but a gust of wind ripped the words right out of her mouth, and she didn't think Crystal heard.

They pulled away from the shallows near the shoreline, and now the water would be deep and unforgiving. Neither of them wore a life vest, and their packs would weigh them down, so dumping the canoe was not an option. Paddling her J-stroke with all her strength, Dez hoped they were on the same basic course as the prisoners. She wondered if Jaylynn's extra weight in their canoe would slow them down—or capsize them. *Oh, no. Don't let their canoe go under!* She paddled even harder.

The breeze picked up, and long ripples rose, growing larger, as if someone underneath pushed the water into furrows that looked like rolled rugs.

"Whoa!" Crystal called out.

"Paddle into it," Dez shouted.

Air and water warred, and though the treetops bore the brunt, a straight-line gale crashed down from the clouds. Suddenly Lake Jeanette erupted into what seemed like Class Five rapids of bucking water. A gray swell crashed over the bow, drenching the Latina cop. The next wave came at them, coiled and twirling like a giant sea serpent.

Dez screamed, "Turn into the wind! Into the wind!" She and Crystal paddled furiously, crested a wave, then dropped into a trough. Over and over they adjusted and readjusted. The canoe took on water from both the waves and rain, and soon it was up to their ankles.

Through the fog and rain, Dez saw a flash of silver ahead. "Look!" She redoubled her efforts, shouting, "There they are! We can get 'em. Hurry, Crystal!"

Ahead, a rocky point of land, a finger of safety, jutted out and beckoned to them. But there was open water ahead, and that's where the other canoe traveled. Dez remembered that there were a couple of small islands in Lake Jeanette. She shouted, "Stay away from the island. Veer to the right!"

Crystal shouted back assent, though Dez couldn't hear the exact words. Far ahead, she thought she glimpsed a flat brown line. The fog obscured it. But there—there it was again a half mile away. "Almost there. Keep it up!"

Wind whistled in her ears and cold fear rose. The silver canoe had already grounded, while she and Crystal were still fighting rising waves. For every stroke they took, the lake pressed them back what seemed like a canoe length. Reach, dig, pull, rest for a split second. Repeat. Reach, dig, pull, rest . . . reach dig, pull, rest . . . And suddenly they were out of the churning cesspool of water. The canoe was half full of water, but floating on merely choppy waves. As quickly as the storm had come up, it had spat them out into sluggish swells that rocked the bow.

Through the stinging needles of rain, Dez saw movement on the shore, but they were too far off to discern who—or even where they went. She screamed. "Hurry! Hurry!"

Now the canoe cut through the water with as much efficiency as it could, considering they sat in cold water up to their shins. No longer were they battling waves. Perhaps another three minutes passed, and then the keel hit dirt and stone. Before Dez could rise, Crystal launched herself up and over the bow deck and landed on all fours on the hard dirt beach. She got to her feet and grabbed hold of the slick gunwales, steadying the boat for Dez, who was already pitching forward.

"Whoa, Dez. Careful." She leaned to the side, and Dez launched herself up and out, landing in much the same way Crystal had. Crystal pulled the canoe farther up the beach, banging it against her leg. "Shit, this is hell on knees."

"Yeah, but just ignore it," Dez answered. She turned and ran along the shore, past boulders and denuded brush. She felt for the bulge of the gun at her waist and was relieved to find it still there.

Molding pine needles, damp from the lake water, dirt and lichen on the granite bedrock — all of these registered distantly in her mind. Crystal huffed behind as Dez lifted exhausted legs and forced herself forward. With each stride, what she heard in her head was *Jay – lynn. Jay – lynn. Jay – lynn.*

JAYLYNN WAS CERTAIN that the red vehicle Vanya had just swept past was Crystal and Shayna's Jeep. Her heart leapt as she looked over her shoulder at the rapidly retreating SUV. Vanya had entered the parking area only seconds earlier. As they'd rolled in, she had seen the Russian man on the ground and four people in outdoor gear standing over him. Vanya had slowed and started to roll his window down. As they drew near the group, one of the men howled, "But they stole my goddamn canoe!"

Vanya punched the gas, wheeled the car around, and blasted out of there like a shot.

"What's the matter?" Jaylynn asked.

"This is not good. In fact, this is going from bad to worse." His voice was tight, as though he was barely suppressing rage.

"But...but...why?"

"Like you, I have been less than forthcoming, Jay. You see, the men who stole my car have something belonging to me, and I must get it back."

*The men? Or the man? Is he talking about the Russian guy? Or Bostwick and Keith? Someone took off in a canoe. It's got to be the convicts — who else would be so stupid?* She wracked her brain, trying to figure out what it was that was off-kilter about this whole situation. None of it made sense. And then it came to her. *Oh, God, the money. Keith knew he was in trouble. Maybe it was a sell-out, so he ran. Bostwick must have made some sort of deal with the Russians. But why would some Russians care about two escaped cons?* Some major piece of the puzzle was missing, and without it, Jaylynn couldn't get the whole picture in context. But it was clear to her she was now in grave danger. She no longer thought it a coincidence that Vanya and the man Bostwick had shot both had the same accent.

Because talking was her strong suit and had gotten her out of trouble before, she said, "So Vanya, you're on a recovery mission?"

"Yes, exactly." His hands gracefully steered the Buick around potholes, but the car still hit bumps and bounced. After one unexpected dip, her head hit the ceiling. "Sorry about that, miss. We must hurry. Put your seatbelt on."

She didn't think buckling up would hurt, and if they went off the road, it would help, so she snapped herself in. "Will I be able to help you, Vanya?"

"Perhaps. Tell me more about the men."

"There's not much to tell. I know they escaped from the prison. When they first got to us, they were dressed in orange jumpsuits. Then they stole clothes from us and changed."

"Us? Who constitutes *us?*"

"My girlfriends and I were camping by Echo Lake. Those creeps left them tied up. I hope they got loose." Having seen Dez earlier, she knew full well they had done so, but he didn't need to know that a dangerous cop was somewhere in the vicinity and gunning for whoever had her.

"Is there more you can relate about the men?"

She shrugged. "One was big and mean—verbally abusive." She shuddered. "On the radio they said he was one evil man with a lot of violent offenses. The other was small and not a bad sort at all." She purposely kept it vague.

"And they are both armed?"

"I think maybe." She debated what she should divulge, then said, "I know the big bald man—Bostwick was his name—he has a gun. He shot your friend's cousin. He's the one you have to be careful of. The other man isn't like him."

"I see." They reached the turnoff to the paved road, and Vanya went east and away from Buyck.

Jaylynn opened her mouth to ask what was happening and decided not to question. The speedometer climbed. Thirty-five. Forty. Fifty miles per hour. She felt as though they were in a rain tunnel, speeding through a never-ending car wash. She prayed no deer—or people—strayed onto the road.

Vanya took one hand off the wheel, fumbled next to him, and came up with a map. "Would you be so kind as to look at the map and see where this road goes?"

Jaylynn unfolded the map and found Lake Jeanette. She reached into her pants pocket and removed the clear Suunto compass and laid it on the map.

He glanced over. "You must be a Girl Scout. You have come prepared."

"Don't expect miracles. I'm also a neophyte." She squinted into the dim light shining in from the window. The north, west, and south sides of Lake Jeanette were ragged, and the road followed the coastline somewhat. "We're going due north now."

"That explains the straight-line winds." The car struggled into the wind and torrential rain. Vanya reduced the speed.

"I see where we must be—heading along the side here. I can't tell where this road goes. It's not on the map. If you want to get around to the north side of the lake, we actually end up doubling back southeast."

"How far from here?"

"I think anytime now. If we pull away from the water, then we'll be traveling away from Lake—"

He jammed on the brakes, came to a jerking halt, threw his arm over the seat, and looked back over his shoulder. "This is good timing. I see what must be the right road." He threw the gearshift into reverse and rolled backwards, wheels crunching, gears whining. Then Jaylynn saw what she had missed while she was looking down at the map. To the right was a road marked with a brown forestry sign that read *Lake Jeanette Inlet, 4 miles*.

Vanya rolled forward and turned right. It was hard to maintain any speed. The road wound all over the place, and every couple hundred yards or so, Vanya had to hit the brakes. After they had skidded three times, he slowed down. "Is our route coinciding with that of the map?"

"Yes. The road's a little more twisty than the map actually shows, but we should hit the inlet any time now."

"Thank you."

"You're welcome." Jaylynn looked over at him and noted the tightness of his jaw. He was totally focused on maintaining a high speed. *Is he a good man? Or bad? And why is it so hard to tell? He looks and sounds fine. But he* feels *bad*. A war went on inside her. On the one hand, she wanted to help—but on the other hand, would her help get her—or someone else—killed?

He said, "We have traveled four miles. I see no inlet."

Jaylynn consulted the map. "I don't think there's a parking lot or anything like that. Just look for a wide spot on the road." She squinted through the murky windshield. "Up ahead. See there?"

He nodded and pulled over. The shoulder of the road was only just wide enough for the car. Leaning down, he tried to look past her out the window. "Where is the lake?"

"I suspect you've got to hike through the trees, maybe down the slope to get to it." He said an unintelligible word, something in Russian, and Jaylynn noticed beads of sweat on his forehead.

In a weary voice, he said, "Let's go." He turned off the car, pocketed the key ring, and grabbed the satchel from the seat next to him.

She cocked her head to the side and gave him her most engaging smile. "Would you mind if I just stayed here? I'm still soaked and—"

"No. You must come with me." Cold blue eyes glared at her. For a brief second, she saw a glimpse of something evil. Just as quickly, he stifled it and gave her a weak smile. "I may need your help, miss."

"Sure." Still holding the compass in her hand, she opened the door and got out into the drizzle, her heart racing. *So that's the way it is.* She had hoped to stay in the car until he was out of sight, then disappear into the woods, but no such luck.

"You seem to have a good nose for direction. Will you lead?"

"I'll bring the map. That might help." Jaylynn reached back into the car and grabbed it, then slammed the door loudly. She put the compass back in her left pocket and wondered how she could surreptitiously get the knife out of her right thigh pocket. *Fat lot of good that will do if he plans on marching me into the woods and shooting me.* Her hands shook as she folded the map down to just the square of it that showed the Lake Jeanette area, then tucked it inside her jacket, out of the rain. She hoped that if he noticed her quivering, he would think it was from cold and not fear. "I have no clue where to go, Vanya, but let's give it a whirl."

She stepped forward, the back of her head prickling and her whole body aching and tense. All she wanted to do was get away. She heard something that sounded like the dissonant music in the movie *Psycho* along with the word *RUN! RUN! RUN!* It kept repeating in her head, but she overruled it, praying that she was making the right decision.

"Ouch!"

She turned and saw that he had slipped, perhaps turned his ankle in the mud. "You okay?"

"Yes. I am not attired in proper shoes."

She looked down at the leather oxfords he wore. "No, you won't get much traction. Just take your time."

"We do not have the luxury of time."

At that, she strode on, thinking that his poor footwear was one of the few advantages that might play in her favor.

They weren't on much of a path, but she saw light through the trees ahead and assumed that they would come to a clearing or a beach area near the lake. But then what? She plunged forward through a thicket of branches and then meandered along what could only be a deer path. The trees thinned, and she stepped out into a swirl of rain and wind onto a path that ran only a few feet from the edge of a bluff. The mini-cliff she stood on was only about twelve feet high, running at irregular levels along this northern edge of the lake. Below, down a slope of wild grasses, she saw the raging lake. A jagged bolt of lightning split the heavens and illuminated everything with startling clarity.

A canoe was beached below to the west, perhaps half a mile away from her vantage point. For a brief moment, Jaylynn saw two figures scuttling like maggots up the slope. With the next lightning strike, she saw another canoe bobbing in the water. She wasn't able to discern the shapes of anyone below. Though she didn't think it possible, she hoped Dez was one of them.

Vanya fell out of the bushes, and she gave a wave. "Look." She pointed down the hill, hoping he couldn't see the red slice of canoe and would concentrate on the silver one on the beach. "Men down there."

In a forceful voice, he said, "I can't see them. Take me there."

"This way." She picked her steps carefully, staying away from the edge, and not giving him any reason to look out at the lake, where the second canoe would be beaching soon.

After a good four hundred yards, the bluff petered out, and now they walked along the edge of the tree line with brush, shrubs, and wild grasses to their right. Her legs hurt, but she prayed that if she needed to make a break for it, adrenaline and fear would carry her to safety.

It was so dark that unless she missed her guess, it was near sunset. The cloud-covered skies didn't make it easy for her to estimate, but the sooner night fell, the better.

Vanya made a noise, and she glanced over her shoulder. "Wait," he said, pointing down the hill. "I see one of them."

Jaylynn shook her head slowly when she caught sight of the figures slogging up the incline. The big dummy had hold of Keith's arm and was trying to haul him up the hill without being able to attain any speed or balance. If he had looked thirty or forty yards to either side of him, he would have seen that the slope was more gradual there. Though they might have had to travel a bit farther, it actually would have been faster. Just seeing the ugly convict made her shiver.

Vanya came up behind Jaylynn and gripped her shoulder. "Easy now, miss. He won't hurt you. I won't let that happen."

She didn't mention that Bostwick probably weighed as much as both of them together, or that he didn't have any conscience at all. Breathing fast, she was ready to run when the first opportunity presented itself. A flash of lightning lit up the area, and in her peripheral vision, she saw a dark object on the path to her right. Trying not to appear obvious, she peered at it out of the corner of her eye. Another crack of lightning illuminated the path. The leather satchel gaped open. Vanya had tossed the bag aside. *If he has a gun, he's holding it now.*

Her legs turned to jelly, and for a few seconds, she felt lightheaded. *Oh, God, help me.*

# Chapter
# Twenty-Nine

**Kendall Correctional Facility**
**Outside Buyck, Minnesota**
**Sunday, October 17, 6:00 p.m.**

RALPH SOAMES PACED from one side of his tiny office to the other. Files and papers were stacked all over his desk with the package of tainted muffins off to the side. His rumpled jacket lay on the floor next to the desk. He'd been puzzling through things for what seemed like hours. On-duty records and sick leave forms were scattered here and there, and try as he might, he kept coming up with the same conclusions.

He reached for his jacket and stuck two fingers in the left breast pocket. It was empty. He frowned. *Now where did I put that?* He sorted through papers, moving things into orderly stacks. *Where is it?*

Five minutes later, he was still searching high and low, but finally gave up and sat back in his chair. He mentally retraced his steps. *Bathroom. Break room. Mike's office.* He got up and plodded into each of those places. It wasn't until he got to the administrator's office that he remembered that the FBI guy, Giles, had left his business card on the corner of the desk.

Soames strode across the room and snatched up the card. It was made of a very thick paper with a shiny, embossed insignia. *Two of my crappy Kendall cards aren't even this thick.* He shook his head and looked at the phone number. The man had said, "If you think of anything at all, please call me." It could be a bum steer, but Soames didn't want to take any chances. He felt he already looked like a damn fool, so what did it matter if he did one more stupid thing. Besides, if it turned out that his hunch was right, but that he'd sat on the information, he knew he would never forgive himself.

Soames left Mike Martin's office, returned to his own, and shut the door. He did not want to be interrupted.

He tried repeatedly to get through to the FBI man. Each time he dialed the Chicago number on the card, the call had to be routed through the Minneapolis office, then patched through to land lines in and around Buyck. One time he was connected to Fraley in the county sheriff's office, and Fraley wasn't helpful at all. Other times he was connected to state patrol dispatch, and once to the Buyck police station. Every time he talked to someone, they either told him they didn't know where—or who—Giles was, or that Soames was not allowed to talk to him. He kept begging people to give Giles a message to call him back, but he doubted anyone passed it on.

"Dammit!" He threw a wadded-up piece of paper across the room.

He heard footsteps behind him, and Shirley came running into his office. "It's on the TV, Ralph. They've got them cornered now up by Lake Jeanette!"

"No kidding?"

"Come see."

He followed her plump figure into the administrator's office and watched the TV coverage for a few minutes. The authorities were trying to keep a lid on events, but the news reporters were in a frenzy. They smelled the exciting climax of the story, and like a cloud of angry hornets, they swarmed any official or cop who crossed their paths.

Arms crossed tightly over his chest, Soames grew increasingly agitated. Something just didn't feel right.

Shirley asked. "What will happen to them once they're apprehended?"

"I don't know. Certainly they'll be removed to another facility—one that's more secure. And Shirley, I'm not so sure this place will even stay in business."

Her expression became wistful. "I sort of thought that, too, Ralph. This has been such a good job for me. I like working with you guys. There isn't a one of the men who isn't really nice to me."

Soames nodded. "I think it's out of our hands." He looked at his watch. "Will you do me a favor, Shirley?"

"Sure. Anything. Need some coffee or something to eat?"

"I need for you to go down to the staff sign-in desk. Hang around the supervisor and gossip for a few minutes. Then get a look at who's reported for shift and who hasn't. Can you just do that, you know, sort of sneaky?"

Her plump face split into a big smile. "Sneaky, you say? Why, sure. Sneaky is my middle name. I'll be right back."

At least ten minutes passed. Soames watched the TV

coverage the entire time Shirley was gone. He learned that the thunderstorm prevented any helicopters from flying, or, as the reporter put it, "Authorities aren't able to put a bird in the sky at this time." Neither were bloodhounds effective since their handlers had not been able to get them up to the remote region before the rainstorm began. The National Guard had just arrived, though, and the news people were all but salivating with excitement as they filmed the six dozen troops in the back of six big green transport vehicles that would soon make their way to Lake Jeanette.

"Ralph!" Shirley was out of breath when she burst into the conference room. "They don't want to come up and face you, but it looks like we're running short shift again. Buddy Boldt is on the phone trying to locate those due in and reach the others who might be able to cover."

"Who signed in?"

"Everybody but Morris and Schecter."

His heart nearly came up into his throat. "Oh, no. Oh, God, I hope I'm wrong!" He reached into his shirt pocket and pulled out the FBI man's business card. "Shirley, take this. Call these people. Keep calling until you reach this Jerome Giles and speak to him personally. Tell him what you just told me."

"But wait," she whined. "I don't understand!"

Soames paused a moment. "It's like this: I think the breakout may have been more of an inside job than we thought. So give Giles or his people our staffing details and answer any questions he asks. Tell 'em who didn't show—and explain about the poisoned muffins." He handed her the FBI agent's card. "Don't give up, don't stop. You may not reach them, but if you don't, I'm on my way down to Buyck. I'll see if I can find someone in person." He bent and looked into her eyes. "This is the most important thing you've ever done in this job."

Wide-eyed, she said, "Okay, boss."

"Lock yourself in your office. Don't let anyone in, Shirley, no matter what. Just keep calling." He slipped past her and ran toward the conference room door. "Thank you. I won't forget. I'll personally get you a new job if need be." He went through the doorway, veered around the corner, and ran to his office for his coat.

# Chapter
# Thirty

**Minnesota North Woods**
**Sunday, October 17, 6:15 p.m.**

SALLY CABOT SKIDDED and nearly lost control of the Suzuki. Only by luck, and because she knew her bike well, was she able to put a foot down, lean, goose the gas, and right the cycle.

*Aw, shit! That was too close for comfort!* She slowed down, but not for long. Even though dispatch told her the National Guard was finally in the area, she couldn't rely on them. Anything could happen to those women in the canoe. What if they capsized? What if the convicts shot them? The women had seemed to know what they were doing, and they *said* they were cops, but what did she know? She urged the bike forward, skirting as many puddles as she could.

Would she ever be warm again? It wasn't so much that she was wet — her rain gear did afford some protection — but her feet, hands, and neck were chilled. The wind blowing at her and the water that fell on her or slopped up from the road was icy cold. And it was worse going thirty miles per hour into the dark gale.

Up ahead, she saw the county road and breathed a sigh of relief, but as she turned the corner, a series of lightning flashes lit up the sky and blinded her. Now that she was on the wider avenue, she wasn't protected by tall trees on either side. She hugged the side of the road, hoping that if lightning struck, it would hit a tree and not her.

Grimly, she recalled that people believe lightning can't hit them if they are riding on rubber tires. It isn't true. In a car, the electrical current travels along the outside of the body of the car, and the occupants inside aren't injured — usually — because the current dissipates into the ground through paths that actually include the tires and the rainwater. But on a cycle, there was no protective metal shell. If she were hit now, chances were she'd lose the bike out from under her, and if the charge didn't kill her, the subsequent wipe-out could. The thought nagged at her, but she forged on.

As she slowed for a wide furrow in the road, thunder shook the ground and another blast of lightning lit the sky. She forded the eight-inch stream of water bisecting her path and realized the ground was still shaking and bright light lingered. With a backward glance, she saw a welcome sight: a big, dark-green military vehicle, a five-ton truck, sluicing toward her on the watery road.

Cabot pulled to the right and waved madly as the behemoth drew near. Seven men in helmets and camo rain outfits poured out of the back of the truck and aimed their rifles at her. She held up her hands and shouted, "Sally Cabot! Kabetogama State Forest Ranger." She wanted to add, *I'm with the good guys!* But she thought she had better play it straight.

The man closest to her let out a shout, then raised a hand in the air and made a circular motion with his index finger. The men lowered their rifles. Over the storm, he hollered, "We've been looking for you. Bring the motorcycle to the rear."

She accelerated and sprang forward, then turned the bike around. When she met them at the back of the truck, she said, "We've got to get around to the north side of the lake. The convicts fled over the water approximately twenty minutes ago. They were followed by two women, purportedly police officers, so we can't be trigger happy. Also, there are still three canoeing and hiking parties out in the woods that we haven't located yet."

"Yes, ma'am. Understood," the leader said.

Just then she heard the distant whine of a siren. When she looked toward the sound, far off in the distance she saw flashing red and gold lights. Abruptly they disappeared, and Cabot knew the emergency vehicle had reached the dirt road and turned to go to the south side of the lake.

One of the soldiers said, "Turn off the cycle, please, ma'am." She did as he asked and dismounted. Four of the men shouldered their rifles and lifted the bike as though it weighed no more than a kid's bicycle. They hefted it up and shoved it into the back of the huge truck, where more hands reached for it and rolled it forward and out of sight.

Two at a time, the soldiers on the ground grabbed the perpendicular tailgate rail and scaled the back end, leaving her standing there with only the sergeant. He looked past her and said, "Here come some more of us."

She turned and saw an approaching green vehicle followed by another. "Excellent! How many troops?"

"Four dozen. Get in and let's go."

She grabbed the slippery, cold bar, stepped on a metal rung, and hoisted herself up and over. Hands reached to pull her in and help steady her on her feet. The men scooted down and made room for her on the bench on the right side of the vehicle. She had barely gotten seated when the truck lurched forward, and another bolt of lightning cracked the sky, followed by a giant rumble of thunder.

In a loud voice, the man across from her said, "Bet you're glad you're out of that weather! It's scary as hell out."

The soldier to her right said, "You're safe with us now, ma'am. Even if we get hit, the tires will ground us."

She suppressed a smile. Though she would love to give them a lesson on electrical storms, now was not the time. She simply said, "Thanks, guys. You're life savers."

JAYLYNN HELD HER breath as Bostwick came barreling up the slope, dragging Keith along behind him. The big man still wore a backpack, but it was almost as dirty and soggy as both of the men were. From where she and Vanya waited in the shadows, she heard Bostwick say, "You're a goddamn nuisance. You hear me? A hundred percent nuisance. Why the hell did I ever get myself into this with you?"

He blasted up onto the flat plateau about twenty yards away from where Jaylynn stood, and she tried to draw back. Vanya nudged her forward, keeping her between him and the convict. Bostwick looked behind him, still muttering curses at the listless Keith. With so little light, neither man had seen them yet.

When they were a mere twenty feet away, Vanya called out, "Mr. Bostwick, I believe you have something that belongs to me."

Bostwick was so startled, Jaylynn swore she could almost see the whites of the creep's eyes. "Who? What—"

Vanya said, "Do not move or I will shoot you where you stand. You will play nice. This transaction requires no violence."

Keith stepped behind Bostwick looking for all the world like he wanted to roll back down the slope and run away. The big convict froze in place. "I thought—"

"Yes. You believed you had gotten the best of us, but you are sadly mistaken. You have yet to complete your side of the exchange."

In a jolly voice, Bostwick boomed, "I'd be happy to finish up. In fact, I'll trade you a little extra for that blond bitch there. How's that sound?"

Vanya didn't answer his question. "You will step aside. I

found the Explorer. I do believe you have probably taken an extra portion that does not belong to you."

Bostwick grunted out a nervous laugh. "You know that once I managed to get to safety, I would've called your boss."

Vanya's voice was icy cold. "You don't even know who employed you."

"I would've figured it out."

"I see. Well, it appears you may skip that telephone call. Finish the exchange now. You will give me the package—and the extra money, too."

Bostwick slowly removed the bedraggled backpack and let it drop in front of him. Keeping his eyes on Vanya, he reached down, unzipped the pack, and rooted around in it. Jaylynn held her breath, expecting the worst, and he met her expectations. Instead of pulling out the brown package, his hand emerged holding a glint of silver. The gun came up as he dove and rolled to the side. Jaylynn expected to feel a round hit her. All she heard was a crack of lightning and the rumble of thunder.

With a shout, Vanya pressed past her. Bostwick tumbled down the hill. Vanya squatted on the edge of the plateau. Shots rang out—three in a row, then another, then a few seconds later, another. By then, Jaylynn had turned and run—back the way they came, back toward the car. She heard a slap-slap sound behind her, glanced over her shoulder, and saw that Keith had somehow gathered up enough energy to make a run for it.

"Stop!" a voice yelled behind them.

A bullet whistled by.

Jaylynn dove to the left into the long grass. She tumbled down the slope through wet and slimy grass and rolled to a stop. She prayed that the storm would obscure the shooters' vision and hoped she was dirty enough to blend into the hillside. She almost screamed when something grabbed her ankle. On all fours, dragging her leg, she tried to pull away.

"Shhh! Stay down!" Something heavy fell against the back of her legs.

*Keith's voice. It's just Keith.*

Footsteps thundered by just a few yards up the hill from them.

Keith squirmed forward, scrambling alongside her. His voice rasped in her ear. "We have to play this smart if we want to get out alive."

"Downhill," she whispered. "To the canoes."

He crawled up next to her in the slime, and placed one arm over her middle. "Too easy to pick us out of the water."

She lifted her head and tried to look up the hill where she'd last seen Vanya. A dark figure stood there. She squinted and thought she saw him moving. She went rigid and let her head drop.

They huddled for several minutes, partially hidden in the grass. Keith shivered against her. She was cold, too — and half-soaked — but he wore far thinner clothing than she and was probably close to hypothermia by now. At least her jacket was keeping her torso fairly warm. She whispered, "Can you do the kamikaze crawl over to that stand of shrubs?"

He nodded, and they each began the slow process of inching their way. Jaylynn felt increasingly vulnerable. The only solace at all was that with each advancing moment, it grew darker.

A BOLT OF lightning brightened the sky and illuminated the slope, followed almost immediately by a clap of thunder. With each running step, Dez swore it grew darker. She nearly tripped over a chunk of granite protruding in her path, then abandoned the meandering east-west trail and ran directly north, uphill, through scraggly grass and bushes. The incline wasn't steep, but in her weary condition, every step seemed slower. Every place she planted a foot felt slicker. Every stride robbed her of strength.

Even with the wind moaning in her ears, she very clearly heard three rapid-fire gunshots. A surge of adrenaline raced through her. She heard another shot and looked to her right. Crystal was running up the hillside a little behind, keeping pace. Another shot rang out, followed by three pulses of lightning, but no thunder.

*Where are they? Where is she?* She shifted to the left and ran in the direction toward the sound of the shots.

She tripped over a long, soft log and went down on the other side, landing on her left hip and sliding downhill on a hillock of wet grass. With an elbow, she levered herself up, pushed off the soggy dirt, and was halfway to her feet when the log moved. An ugly, freak-show figure sat up and launched at her. Mud on his face. A gaping, bloody wound on his cheek with bits of grass stuck to it. A gun in the air. He reached out and locked his left hand on the front strap of her pack. She went back down, with him crushing the breath out of her. She used the incline to her advantage, rolling toward it and shoving him at the same time. He had a death grip and hung on. They rolled twice before coming to rest against the branches of a honeysuckle bush at the edge of the bluff. He landed on top, and the pack formed a lump under her back.

Up went her knee. He howled with pain. Dez peppered his

face and shoulders with blows as she struggled to buck him off. His gun hand clutched his middle, but he sat straddling her waist. This pressed her own gun into her abdomen. She couldn't reach the Neoprene pack.

Still holding tight to the front of her, he threw a roundhouse with his right arm. She turned her head and leaned away. The gun he held struck a solid blow to her left shoulder. Dez gasped in pain. She brought her fist up and jammed it into his nose, then punched wildly wherever she could.

With a groan, he let go of her rain gear and put that arm to his face. The gun in his right hand came around, and he jammed it into her neck. The hammer clicked, and she heard a gunshot. For a split second, Jaylynn's face came to her. A wave of grief washed over her.

She realized she felt no pain.

Dez grabbed Bostwick's arm, wrenched it away, and tried to push him to her left, but it was uphill, and he had the advantage of weight and leverage. "Bitch!" he roared. The gun hit a glancing blow to the top of her skull.

A slant of silver rain flashed in lightning over his head. Crystal's arm appeared from out of nowhere. It bashed into the side of Bostwick's head, and he fell away into the honeysuckle bush at the edge of the bluff. Dez spun a quarter turn on her butt and smashed the heels of her feet into his torso, but he didn't move.

"Where is she?" she screamed. She rolled up onto her feet and pounced on him, knees first. Grabbing the front of the sweatshirt he wore, she jammed her fists into him, shaking his limp body. "Where? Where is she?" All she could see now were visions of Jaylynn lying on the ground, bloodied, dead eyes staring up at her. She rose and kicked at the unconscious form. "Where did you leave her? Where is she?" His chest rose and fell, so she knew he wasn't dead.

Suddenly, his eyes popped open. He gave a mighty growl and grabbed her around the knees. She toppled over him. Squirming, he pulled her so close she could smell his rancid breath.

"Agggh!" She fought, punching, squirming, trying to get out of his grip. He rolled farther into the honeysuckle brambles, and she went under him, pressed into the mud and roots. He had his hands at her neck. She couldn't breathe. Using the hill to her advantage, she tried to keep rolling, to shove him off.

"Die, you bitch!" he roared. He tightened his grip on her neck, locking his elbows.

She bucked upward, rolled to her right, and jammed the

heels of her hands under his chin. Bostwick's head snapped back, and he let out a yowl. His grip loosened. The ground shifted under Dez. For a moment she slid, and one leg extended out into empty space. He slid, too, then with a sudden lurch, he fell over the bluff. He let out a startled shriek when she wrenched herself out of his grasp.

Crystal pulled at the pack still strapped to Dez and dragged her away from the edge. "Dez! Dez! You all right?"

For a moment, Dez fought her, and then she took a deep breath and tried to calm herself. *Breathe. Breathe.* "Yeah, yeah. I am." Crystal grabbed her left shoulder and a streak of pain burned from Dez's neck down into her upper arm. She closed her eyes and blinked. Panting, she coughed and swallowed. "What took you so long?"

"You two kept rolling — I was afraid to shoot. Didn't want to miss him and hit you." She stepped over closer to the edge of the bluff. "I'd like to take off *his* pants — *my* pants, that is — and leave *him* to die! I hope he's already dead."

"Me, too. Probably no such luck." She drew in a ragged breath. "Come on. We don't have time. Let's go."

"Wait. I think that's your gun!" Crystal picked up the .45 and checked the clip.

Dez rose, feeling shaky and still breathing hard. "Where's the other convict? Where's Jay?"

"Shit, Dez. There's no bullets in your gun."

Dez, who stood slightly up the hill, was still panting. She looked down at the outline of her friend. "Crys, we don't have time. Where is she?"

Her friend pressed wet metal into her hands. "Dez! Focus. Take this."

Dez accepted the weapon in one hand and put the other against her throat and coughed. "Okay, I hear ya. Thought I was a goner. He tried to shoot me." She remembered the gunshot she *had* heard. "Somebody's still up there with a gun. We gotta go, Crys."

"What do we do about him?"

Dez threw up her hands. "Hope that he dies a slow, painful death? We know where *he* is. Right now, it's Jaylynn I'm more interested in." She turned and took a shaky step up the hill, then started running.

JAYLYNN'S BREATHING HAD returned to normal. She and Keith huddled half-exposed under a juniper bush, facing up the hill. So far she hadn't heard or seen anybody for several minutes, but despite the pouring rain and the darkness, she didn't feel the slightest bit well-hidden. She whispered, "We have to get to better cover. The next lightning could—"

A bolt of lightning made a jagged line overhead, and they both jumped. The crash of thunder came a second later. They lay rigid, trying not to be seen. Darkness returned, and after a few moments of lying motionless in the slime, Keith shifted. Teeth chattering, he gritted out, "Which way should we go?"

She leaned in close to his ear. "I think they'd expect us to go the easy way, down the hill. But you're right. We'd be sitting ducks near the lake. We'd have nowhere to go—nowhere to hide. Let's go upwards gradually and over that way toward the path I came in on." She pointed off to the left. "If we cross that path at the top of the bluff, the woods are on the other side. It's somewhere to hide. But we have to be quiet. And stay low."

"Don't worry, I'll *crawl* a mile if I have to." On his knees, he started off to his left, slipping and sliding. Before he'd gone more than ten feet, Jaylynn could no longer make out his form. She realized that somehow, in the last few minutes when she wasn't really paying attention, full night had fallen, and there wasn't a single vestige of light from the sky.

She followed in the direction Keith had gone. The stringy, wet grass, slick leaves, and mushy soil were gooey under her hands. Cold liquid seeped through the knees of her hiking pants, chilling her legs to the bone. She had thought she was saturated before, but now it felt like slimy worms crawled up the legs of her pants. The thought made her shudder and move faster.

Something loomed over her, and her head and shoulders bumped into a thorny bush. She bit her lip and muffled her desire to scream. Backing up to slide downhill a few feet, she went around the bush, stopping once to rub a hot, stinging spot on her brow. *Now that was a bad idea! Probably just got dirt and germs in it!* She couldn't tell whether it was bleeding or not, but it stung like it was.

She'd lost track of Keith, but then she heard a squishing noise ahead of her. She wondered how far she had to go, angling uphill, before hitting the path she and Vanya had traversed. On the other side of the flat area above the bluff, the forest beckoned. The trees would be their salvation. Darkness would shroud them; lightning wouldn't illuminate them nearly as much. If she had to wait all night in the woods for help, she didn't care, just so long as she escaped from the menacing Vanya and got away from Bostwick's guns.

Another twenty yards and she reached the edge of the plateau. After a particularly spectacular crack of lightning, she hustled across the muddy trail and slogged on. She wondered where Keith had gone, but she couldn't slow down to look for him. All her thoughts were on getting into the woods, away from the open area.

She made a dash across the deer path and into the weeds and brush. The undergrowth grew thicker along the edge of the trees, and she plowed through prickly waist-high bushes. Her heart beat with elation. *Almost there!* The dark tree line was in sight. But before she could get to the forest cover, she heard a whooshing sound. Grabbed from behind, she was lifted off the ground. A large hand covered her mouth. She tried to scream. Nothing but a strangled squeak came out, and then she was bumping along, arms flailing.

"Shhh! It's me!"

The hand came away from her face, and Jaylynn gasped in shock, but didn't speak. Her back pressed against Dez's torso, and Dez's other arm gripped her so securely that Jaylynn's eyes filled with tears. The sense of relief that flooded through her was strong and immediate. She thought it was lucky Dez had scooped her up because if she had instead just confronted her, Jaylynn didn't know what would have happened. *I might have fainted. Ha. I should give myself more credit.*

They reached the tree line, and for the first time, Jaylynn realized there were footsteps hastening behind them. Dez released her, and Jaylynn was happy to find that her legs weren't as shaky as she had thought they might be. Grateful that Dez kept a grip on her frigid hand, she stayed close to the tall figure in front of her. They plunged into the trees. Branches whipped back at her. Stinging cold water and wet leaves slapped her in the face as they pressed in. Jaylynn forced back tears, realizing she needed to continue to be tough. *I can't let down yet. Not yet. Stay strong.*

She didn't know how far they'd gone before Dez suddenly halted, spun, and enfolded her in a crushing embrace. Jaylynn stood under a dripping tree, wrapped in warmth and safety. She heard a hoarse whisper in her ear. "I was so worried, so damn worried. I can't believe we found you."

"I'm okay. It's been hell, but I'm okay. How on earth did you find me?"

"Long story. Too long to tell." She lifted her head and whispered, "Hey, Crystal. I don't hear anything. Do you?"

Never letting go of Dez's middle, Jaylynn turned and looked at Crystal. "I could just hug the two of you," she gasped out in a whisper.

Crystal drew closer and leaned in, the outline of her face only barely visible in the darkness of the forest. Jaylynn felt hands on her shoulder. "You just keep hugging this maniac, Jay. I'll catch one from you later." She patted Jaylynn's back. "*Dios mio!* You're soaked."

She felt Dez's hands traveling over her, and her raspy voice said, " 'My God' is exactly right!"

Crystal leaned so close that Jaylynn could feel her warm breath against the side of her face. "Did you fall out of the canoe?"

"What? I was never in a canoe."

"Oh. Well, are you hypothermic?"

"No. I'm cold, but I'm mostly fine—especially now. I'm warm at the core and my feet are okay."

Dez gripped her right shoulder and Crystal her left, and Jaylynn felt encircled in warmth and safety. Dez said, "We'll sort it all out later. We've got to get you out of here now, Jay."

Jaylynn nodded. "Believe me. I now have faith that it will happen. I wasn't so sure a few minutes ago."

Arms around one another, they stood nearly forehead to forehead and discussed their options. Every couple of minutes, they heard thunder. Jaylynn tensed and looked around each time lightning filtered its way through the partially denuded trees. The time between thunder and lightning was increasing; the storm was moving away.

Crystal reminded them that Cabot, the forest ranger, was on her way and had called for reinforcements. Dez said, "Who knows how long they'll take to arrive. We've gotta get out of here."

A tremor of fear ran through Jaylynn. She brought her hand to her mouth. "Oh, no. Where'd Keith go? How could I forget him?"

Dez bent, obviously trying to see into Jaylynn's eyes, but it was too dark to make anything out. Jaylynn couldn't even see her lover's face. "What do you mean—*forget* him? Is he one of the convicts?"

"He saved my ass—I saved his ass. Now I've gone and abandoned him, and he's the key to this whole mess."

"Babe, you're not making any sense. What the hell are you talking about?"

Jaylynn's words spilled out end over end, and she wasn't sure whether Crystal or Dez would understand. She was glad the rain and wind covered the sound of her voice because she couldn't whisper this so both of them could hear. In a rushed voice, she said, "Bostwick—that's the mean, ugly one—he took Keith from the prison to turn over to some Russian guy who brought packages of payoff money. Bostwick shot the guy in the lot by Lake Jeanette. Then we ran, but I escaped when I realized Bostwick didn't need me anymore and would kill me. I almost got away, but this Vanya, another Russian guy, showed up and even though he *seemed* safe, he's plenty dangerous himself. I came around the lake in his car. Turns out he's after the escapees, too. Bostwick has his money — and something else of his that he wouldn't tell me about. He shot Bostwick — or at least he shot *at* him. I'm not sure he hit him. Keith ran away. I got free of Vanya in the shootout. Keith and I found each other, and up until you grabbed me, we'd been making our way together."

"What the hell?" Dez's voice carried a tinge of disbelief.

"You have to trust me. We have to find Keith. If they get him — oh, my God! He'll be dead."

Crystal said, "But why? This makes no sense. Why should we — or they — care about him?"

Jaylynn said, "That piece I don't know. But you have to trust me when I say that Keith is as much a victim as I am. We have to help him."

Dez's warm, wet hand palmed Jaylynn's chilled cheek. "It's more important to get you to safety and medical care, Jay. You've had hypothermia before. We can't take any chances."

Jay stamped her foot and hissed, "Stop! Dez Reilly, you're not listening to me." She grabbed the front of her partner's rain gear. "We're sworn peace officers. We can't leave the man out here to die. Besides, what about the ranger?"

Dez said, "Yeah, you're right. I don't want Cabot to get ambushed. Wonder how much ammo this Russian has left?"

Crystal grabbed her arm. "We also don't know what havoc Bostwick could wreak. We can't be sure he was dead when we left him. We should have tied him up or something."

"Left him?" Jaylynn said. "What do you mean?"

"Long story," Crystal said. "He jumped Dez. We knocked him over the bluff and hope he's dead. We didn't have time to check his status. We just ran. I can't believe how lucky we were to find you."

"Let's focus," Dez said, "We've only got two guns and limited ammuni—"

Crystal interrupted. "*Three* guns. Give Jay my Beretta that you're carrying. Then you have your .45, and I have a whole backpack full of .45 shells."

Dez sputtered. "Where'd the third gun come from?"

"Bought it at a gun shop in Buyck."

"Today?"

"*Si, señorita.*"

"Glock?"

"Nuh-uh. A .45 Tactical Smith & Wesson."

"Damn smart of you."

"Thanks, Dez. Means a lot coming from you." Crystal and Dez slipped off their backpacks and squatted. Jaylynn followed suit. Dez laid a hand on Jaylynn's knee. "You won't have many shells, Jay, but at least you'll have—let's see." Jaylynn waited, her legs starting to spasm from the cold. She stood and bent over, stretching her hamstrings and calves, then rubbed her hands together and squatted back down.

Crystal fumbled in her pack. "I can't see a damn thing. Here, I found a flash. Dez, can you shield this little penlight?"

In a few seconds, a tiny ball of light appeared, shining through Dez's cupped hands. They all huddled tightly around it.

Crystal met Jaylynn's eyes. "Okay, Jay, you've got all eight rounds left in the Beretta and a few spares, but that's it."

In a low voice, Dez said, "That'll be enough. She's gonna be with me anyway."

Crystal nodded and whispered, "Dez, you and I are flush. We've got 75 rounds between us."

"And I have seven more shells in my pocket."

"Good. You take one box—I'll take the other—and I've got some loose shells here from when I loaded up at the store." Jaylynn accepted the Beretta and also the box of .45 shells so Dez could keep holding the light. "Jay, you be careful with my Beretta. Once you run out, you're out completely."

"Got it." A wave of fatigue washed over her. She rose to her feet, the Beretta in her right hand and Dez's box of shells in her left.

The light below winked out, and they were shrouded in blackness again. Jaylynn reached over, seeking Dez's solidity. When her forearm made contact, she moved closer to her partner.

They all reacted to the rustling noise at the same time. Dez grabbed Jaylynn and pushed her back and behind her. It didn't occur to Jaylynn until later that Dez hadn't even put any bullets in her gun yet. She palmed the Beretta, dropped to a crouch in the brush, and pointed the weapon toward the shuffling noise.

Even through the trees, a flash of lightning illuminated everything, then disappeared as quickly as it came, leaving her even blinder than she'd been before. But for the briefest moment, she had seen the outline of the person coming their way. "No! Hold fire," Jaylynn said in a stage whisper. "Don't shoot! It's Keith." She rose, stuck the gun in her coat pocket, and pushed past Dez, who was squatting in front of her.

"Jay! Don't—"

"Shhh. It's okay," Jay whispered. "Keith. Psssst. Over here." He didn't move, so she went to him. She could smell him when she got within a few feet. Even the rain hadn't eradicated the strong body odor. "Are you okay?"

"I think." His voice was low and sounded exhausted.

"Did anyone follow you?"

"N-n-n-n-n-no clue."

She grabbed his arm and dragged him toward Dez and Crystal. She found Dez loading her Colt and Crystal in a shooter's stance, gun at the ready.

Impatiently Jaylynn said, "Put the guns away, and let's get the hell out of here."

Dez pushed close to her and grabbed the front of the man's shirt. "No funny stuff. You hear me?" He didn't answer—just gave a half-hearted groan. "Geez!" she said, "You are wetter than a dead dog."

Jaylynn grabbed at his face, put a hand to his forehead, touched his shoulders and chest. "This isn't good. You thought *I* might go hypothermic. I think he already *is*. Keith." She shook him. "Keith! Can you hear me?"

He shuddered. "I'm t-t-t-trying. Everything's fuzzy."

Dez handed Jaylynn the gun she held. Next thing Jaylynn knew, she got smacked with a flailing arm, then realized it was Dez pulling off the anorak she wore. One-armed, Jaylynn helped Dez put it over Keith's head, then gave her partner back her gun. She pulled the anorak down over the shivering man's midsection. "This isn't much, Keith, but maybe it will hold in some warmth. We've got to get moving. Can you stay with us?"

"I'll do my best," he muttered.

Dez whispered, "Everybody get down. We're sitting ducks if someone sees us." The four of them squatted, and she went on. "One more thing. Here's a pair of socks for him. It's all the clothes I have left in my pack. You want to wear them on your feet? Or maybe as gloves?"

"G-g-g-gloves."

Jaylynn and Crystal helped Dez put them over his hands. The tall cop said, "It's the best we can do. It will help if you keep moving."

Now Dez shoved something spongy and slick into Jaylynn's hands. "Here. Help him eat this."

"What is it?"

"Freeze-dried ice cream. You want one?"

"Are you flipped? Of course I do. I can't believe you had this and didn't offer it the moment you found me."

She accepted another package as Dez whispered, "Yeah,

right. Sorry if I wasn't able to attend to your gastronomic needs. I was a little busy carting your ass off to safety."

Jaylynn stifled a giggle and used her teeth to rip open the first packet and shove the interior contents up and out. She handed it toward Keith. "Eat this." His hands came up, swathed in the socks, and he fumbled. She barely kept from dropping the sandwich. "Forget it. Open your mouth." He did as she asked, and she fed him. In three bites he had consumed it all. She ripped open the other package and crammed it into her mouth. She hadn't eaten in so long that food was now all she could think of, and the freeze-dried ice cream did nothing to quell her hunger. "You don't have any more of those, do you, Dez?"

"No." She sighed. "I have a little bit of Gorp left."

"I'll pay you ten thousand dollars for it." She heard Crystal giggling in the dark. "Seriously. Take my car. Any sexual favor is yours. Everything I own. Take my little sisters. My mother—"

"Yeah, yeah. Hang on."

Jaylynn heard a zipper rip open, and then a plastic bag was pushed into her hands. In a suspicious voice, Dez said, "Aren't you the one who disparaged my Gorp?"

Jaylynn's mouth was full. Crystal said, "Uh, no, that would be *mi amada*, the sweet love of my life. My dear Shayna is the one who made fun of it. Please don't hold it against her."

Trying to cover her mouth, Jaylynn laughed.

"Shhh. Keep it down," Dez whispered. "Sound carries. Hurry up and eat that stuff so we can go."

Just that little bit of food was gradually making a difference in Jaylynn's energy level. She was sure it hadn't even hit her bloodstream yet, but the mere act of eating, of being nourished — both physically and emotionally — gave her renewed vigor. She turned to Keith. "You should have some of this Gorp."

"I'm okay. Y-y-you eat it."

She shook her head and scooped out a small handful. "Open your mouth." She shoveled in peanuts, raisins, and M&Ms. "Let me know when you're ready for another hit." She ate some more herself and picked through the bag to get M&Ms to feed Keith. She squatted, bent forward over her thighs, with Dez pressed up close behind her and was actually starting to feel a bit warmer.

Something flashed neon-blue across from Jaylynn. Crystal had pressed the Indiglo dial on her watch, and she said, "It's not even seven o'clock yet."

In disbelief, Jaylynn muttered, "You're kidding, right? It's gotta be at least midnight."

Crystal whispered, "The sun just went down about half an hour ago."

Over the rattle of the wind and the soughing of the rain, Dez said, "Let's go." Dez rose first, shouldering her pack, and the others followed. "I think we should go north through these trees, then wait and watch for Cabot and whoever she brings with her."

Jaylynn agreed. "If we pick our way north, we'll hit the road no matter what. Take my compass." She pulled up the flap to her cargo pocket, took out the compass, and in its place stuffed in the plastic bag with the remaining bits of Gorp.

Crystal came near and held a whispered conference with Dez. She took the compass, held her lit-up watch near it, and said, "This way."

With strong hands, Dez held Jay back and pushed Keith after Crystal. "Follow her, mister, and if you cause any trouble, just remember I'm behind you." Without responding, he shuffled forward.

"Dez!"

Dez pulled Jaylynn close and in her ear, she said, "I don't trust the guy, Jay. Keep an eye on him, and I'll bring up the rear." She released her. "Go on. Let's get out of here."

# Chapter
# Thirty-One

RALPH SOAMES WAS spitting mad. With all the roadblocks, he'd already spent half an hour getting from the prison to Buyck, but when he arrived at the tiny State Forest headquarters, it had been locked up. He had hoped he'd be able to talk to the Kabetogama or Superior ranger, but no such luck. Then, in the county sheriff's satellite office in Buyck, he had to wait twenty minutes while the county deputy was out "on rounds." *Ha. Rounds. The deputy sheriff didn't have rounds. The incompetent left his post for dinner and left no sign or note so that anyone could find him!*

Now Soames stood at the visitor's counter arguing with Deputy Fraley, who sat at a grungy desk drinking coffee. Fraley's lined face was marked by fatigue, and as far as Soames could tell, the man was even more dimwitted than usual. *How the hell did this man pass a peace officer's test?*

"How many times I gotta tell you, Soames? You're a civilian. You got no right to contact any of the searchers or negotiating team."

Soames was on the edge of losing his temper, but he knew it would do him no good. Fraley had always been a moron. "You don't understand, Officer. I *must* speak to Jerome Giles. It may be a matter of life and death."

"That's what everyone says." Fraley pulled out the bottom drawer of the desk, rested his dirty boots on it, and leaned back in the chair. "Whyn't you tell me what it is. I'll take care of it."

There was no chance Soames could trust this fool with any information. He had no way of knowing who had connections to whom. Not only might it be dangerous for the people out in the woods, but it could be deadly to Soames or his family. He simply didn't know. He'd already been burned by misplaced trust.

The phone rang, and Fraley snatched it up, speaking in low tones for less than a minute. When he hung up, he looked over at Soames as if surprised that he was still standing there. "Anything else I can do for you?"

Soames debated. He figured his career was shot, and he wouldn't stay much longer in this town after this was all over. He took a deep breath and stared daggers at the cop. "Yeah, Fraley. There is. Start preparing for the fallout when this gets reported. I hope you get suspended. Better yet, fired." He turned and headed for the door.

"Hey! You just wait one damn minute." Fraley stood up next to his desk, pulling his sagging pants and duty belt up over his protruding gut. "You walk out of here, and I'll smear your name all over town."

With one fierce twist of the handle and a mighty shove, Soames was out the door. It swung wide and smacked against the railing that ran around the porch. He didn't even bother to close it. He plunged headlong down the slippery stairs into the rain and ran to his car. Next stop was the Gas-N-Go where he used the phone on the counter inside to call the prison. "Shirley! Any news?"

Her voice sounded far-off and thready. "No, Ralph. I've been calling every five minutes and leaving the message. I hope it gets through, but no matter where they patch me through to, it ends up being a dead end."

He sighed. "Okay, keep trying. And by the way, if you get patched through to Deputy Fraley, don't tell him anything, okay?"

"No problem. Never liked that man anyway. He's been a jerk to me since grade school."

"Thanks, Shirley."

He hung up, looked out the plate glass windows at the downpour, wondering what he should do.

"Want something, sir?" the clerk asked.

"No, thanks. Appreciate the use of the phone though."

"You're welcome anytime," she said.

He pushed through the glass door and walked to his car, feeling utterly defeated. By the time he was settled in the driver's seat, his suit coat was beaded with water, and his thin hair was wet—soaked to the scalp. "I wouldn't want to be out in this miserable weather," he said aloud.

He turned the key in the ignition. Warm air blasted out of the heater, and the radio clicked on. "And there's no word yet in the search for escapees from the Kendall Prison. Still on the loose are burglar Keith Sterling Randall and his accomplice in this morning's escape, Stanley Michael Bostwick, a dangerous felon convicted on four counts of armed robbery and aggravated assault. In a strange twist, two men assumed to be the escapees, who were arrested near Crane Lake earlier this afternoon, have been released. Authorities reinstated the search and are now concentrating their efforts on the area around Lake Jeanette. If you live in that area, take precautions. And now this."

Soames tuned out the commercial. He closed his eyes and tried to think, all the while labeling himself a failure. When he reopened his eyes a minute later, a thought occurred to him: *Lake Jeanette.* It might be foolhardy to drive out that direction, but what else could he do? Hastily he flipped the wiper switch and cleared the windshield, then pulled out of the parking lot.

Several minutes later, wheeling down Highway 24, he considered that he could be on a wild goose chase and perhaps should go back. Staring out through the rivulets of rain cascading down his windshield, he almost missed seeing the big green form ahead. He sped up, hit the high beams, and was gratified to see a National Guard transport vehicle lumbering along. *Yes! I'll just follow these guys. They're sure to lead me where I need to go.* He dropped back as the five-ton truck lurched and splashed through puddles like a giant green sea turtle.

# Chapter
# Thirty-Two

**Minnesota North Woods**
**Sunday, October 17, 7:15 p.m.**

DEZ PLACED HER steps carefully, trying to keep an eye on the dark forms ahead of her while also watching the trees and listening for any sounds. It seemed the others were trying to do the same, but still, to her ear they sounded like a pack of lame dogs stumbling through the woods. She could only hope they were far enough away from their pursuers not to be heard. Swallowed up in the forest, sound had a strange quality, muffled, almost like they were walking in a bubble of air surrounded by deep water. Dez processed every sound, attuned to those that were normal, and alert to any that were not. Without much vision to speak of, she had to depend on her hearing.

Every time her eyes finally adjusted to the extreme darkness, a flicker of far-away lightning lit up things enough to filter down into the trees, and she was left half-blind, struggling once more to see. She hadn't heard any more gunshots but was on edge, waiting and wondering how much time had passed. She felt like she'd been on her feet for days. The ever-present fatigue—coupled with a strange electricity—kept her going in a kind of weird atmosphere that didn't quite seem real. She couldn't believe her luck—the incredible good fortune—of finding Jaylynn safe. A part of her was focusing on the danger of their escape; another tiny part marveled, filled with glee and thankfulness. Still another stream of thoughts and fears rose to the surface, cutting off the positive emotions. She tried to ignore those fears and concentrate on the data her senses took in. But the pictures in her imagination wouldn't stop: *Click.* Jaylynn's face early this morning, wild with fear as the big convict held her off the ground. *Click.* The pain on the face of the dying man in the parking lot. *Click.* Seeing the back of the tan Explorer pull away, taking Jaylynn with it. *Click.* Visions of Jaylynn bloodied, beaten, bruised, crying, dead.

She pinched her eyes shut, gritted her teeth, shook her head to try to rid herself of the thoughts. She wondered what Marie, her PTSD counselor, would say. *You're all right now, Dez. Focus on breathing, on telling yourself that you can manage this. You can handle it.*

Dez took a deep breath, then another. She felt for the solid steel of the gun tucked in the Neoprene bag under her wet sweatshirt. Peering ahead in the darkness, she made out Jaylynn's shape as the smaller woman shuffled forward. *She just went through twelve hours of hell, and look at her.* Marie had once commented that Jaylynn was exceedingly resilient both emotionally and physically: "You would do well to emulate her, Dez."

She thought of the SWAT course and the training advice once again. The key questions to assess a situation came to mind: *What do they want?* She wasn't so sure now. With the information from Jaylynn, it sounded like they wanted something from this kid—or to kill him. Two Russians? Neither Bostwick nor the kid were Russian, were they? The whole thing smacked of something mob-like, but the Russian mob in Minnesota?

*How far will they go to get it?* Without knowing what exactly "it" was, she couldn't be sure. All she knew was that Bostwick had already shot one man. She didn't plan to give him or anyone else the opportunity to shoot anyone in her party.

*How do we stop them?* It appeared that the best way to answer that question was to get the hell out of harm's way and let it all sort itself out in daylight.

Her boot hit a root. She caught herself and managed to avoid a nasty ankle twist, glad they were moving at a slow rate. Ahead, Jaylynn stopped, and Dez slid up and wrapped her arms around her from behind. She wished she could hold her and beam up to a ship somewhere, anywhere else. Jaylynn was drenched, and Dez wanted to get her out of the elements and into a warm car. Like now.

The skinny man stood meekly to the side as Crystal pushed past him and murmured something. Dez asked her to repeat it. "I thought I heard the sound of a vehicle. I think we're almost to the road."

"Okay, extra quiet now."

Crystal grabbed Keith's arm. In a harsh voice, she whispered, "Listen now. If you do anything stupid, you could get us all killed."

"Don't worry," he said in a tired voice. "I'll behave."

"You better. Dez, how about I crawl on ahead and scout the road?"

"Good idea. And I don't need to tell you how careful you have to be."

Crystal turned and moved up the trail with considerably less noise than the four of them had been making.

Jaylynn turned in Dez's arms and pressed her face into Dez's sweatshirt. "I can't wait to get warm again."

Dez drew her close. "Soon, sweetie. Soon. Just hang in there a while longer. Did you eat all that Gorp?"

"No, but I'm too tired to monkey with it now. I just want to concentrate on getting out of here."

With her chin on top of Jaylynn's damp head, Dez squinted into the darkness. All her senses were on alert. Keith's outline, a few feet away, was motionless. Now she heard sounds she hadn't picked up when they were on the move. Scurrying in the underbrush. An irregular pattern of water plopping onto the leaves. The coo of some far-away bird. She jumped when Crystal suddenly appeared in front of her. She hadn't heard her at all.

"The road is clear. No rescuers yet." Crystal's voice was raspy as she stepped close to Dez and Jaylynn. Crystal whispered, "You poor thing, Jay. Other than my feet, I'm not nearly as wet as you, and hey, I'm *freezing*. How can you take it?" Dez felt her friend's hands on her waist and the two of them encircled the shivering woman.

"It's okay." Jaylynn's teeth chattered. "Won't be long now, right?"

Dez nodded and patted her. "That's right. We're almost there."

Jaylynn giggled against Dez's front. "Would you call this a cop sandwich?"

Crystal whispered, "Now don't be getting any kinky ideas. Shayna wouldn't like that."

Dez smiled and shook her head. "I hate to break up this *ménage à trois*, but we've got to move on."

Crystal let go and turned, followed by Jaylynn. Dez felt a moment of alarm. With a start, she realized she had completely forgotten about Keith. He still stood, silently, off to the side. As she moved toward him, she swore she heard his teeth chattering, too.

As they reached the trees at the edge of the road, a light drizzle began to fall, and Dez realized she hadn't seen lightning or heard thunder for some time. The moon was out, but concealed. The faintest light shone through the clouds in the dark night sky, and for the first time since they'd entered the woods, she could actually make out more than mere outlines of dark objects.

They crouched together at the edge of the trees, facing the road. Dez was careful to place herself between Jaylynn and the brisk breeze, and Crystal squatted on Jaylynn's other side, her back against a tree. Ahead and to the left of Dez, Keith went down to his knees, sitting back on his heels. With his arms crossed in front of him and his body leaning forward, he looked like he was about to pass out and topple over. *He must be in another realm. The guy is hardly responsive. We have to get him to safety soon – before he's no longer able to walk.*

A slight incline led up to the dirt road thirty feet away. Dez wondered where they had come out—on the west end of the road? In the middle? To the east? She had no way of knowing. *How long until the cavalry shows up?*

As if in answer to her silent question, she heard the sound of tires on dirt and gravel. To the right, a vehicle slowly approached. She tried to get a mental image of the map, of Lake Jeanette, and of the east-west road that ran north of the lake. Buyck was to the west. Whoever was driving along came from the east.

She waited, breathless and tense. The sound of tires rolling over sticks and gravel grew louder, and Jaylynn clutched her knee. Dez held her breath, straining to hear. A faint glimmering lit up the road, and she saw two pinpoints of light—headlights.

SALLY CABOT SHIVERED as she jounced along in the back of the five-ton truck. Each gust of wind blew rain in on her, and she was colder now than she had been on her motorcycle. She wasn't sure if it was because the wind had picked up or the temperature had suddenly dropped, but she felt like she was riding in a meat locker on wheels.

She looked out the back at the two vehicles trailing them and estimated they were going only twenty miles per hour, slower than she had been traveling on the motorcycle. The road was bumpy and filled with potholes. She figured they were also keeping a close lookout for people and animals.

Someone across from her cleared his throat. "What'd you say your name was?" Even with the headlights shining in from the truck following them, she couldn't really see the man. He sat in shadows, the brim of his guard cap shielding his eyes.

"Cabot. Sally Cabot, Kabetogama Forest Ranger."

"I always wanted to be a ranger," the guy said. "How do you apply?"

"It's a very tight field now. You have to go to school and get a degree in forestry."

"Oh." He sounded discouraged.

The guy sitting to his left elbowed him. "Hear that? Probably have to read a book!"

Somebody else said, "Maybe two books."

"Shut up." There was no rancor in the first man's voice — obviously he'd been teased before.

Cabot said, "If you ever want more information, track me down through the forest service office and —"

She didn't get to finish. The truck jerked to a stop. So did the vehicle behind them. She heard the scratchy sound of a radio in the front cab, but couldn't make out any words. The truck sat idling. Someone got out of the cab, strode back to the truck behind them, and carried on a brief conversation.

Cabot knew the lay of the land well enough to know they were nowhere near the north side of Lake Jeanette. "Why are we stopping?" she asked no one in particular.

Nobody answered. After a long pause, the kid next to her said, "Ours is not to question why."

Two more minutes passed, and the sergeant stepped away from the second vehicle. "Right!" she heard him say, and the other soldier hollered, "Exactly. We don't answer to the FBI. Let's move on."

The sergeant hustled back to the truck, got in, and slammed the door. The convoy rolled forward again. Cabot wondered whether there was some new development. *What was that about the FBI? Are the various law enforcement agencies still squabbling?* Wanting to know what was going on, she pulled her radio out of her pack and called dispatch. The attention of all the guardsmen was on her as she reported her whereabouts and asked for an update. The dispatcher had nothing new to tell her — except that the storm was dissipating. From her perch at the back of the truck, Sally couldn't have agreed with the dispatcher's weather report, but she hoped he was right. She signed off and put away the radio.

The man next to her said, "You know this area well, correct?"

"Yes. I've been stationed her for years. I've hiked every trail, canoed every lake, portaged all over the place. Why?"

"How much further 'til we get there?"

"Not long now."

"Bet we could walk faster," said one disgruntled voice.

She gritted her teeth as the big truck slowed again and rumbled to a stop. "Could be true."

Nobody in their truck moved, but someone leaped from the

truck following them and hustled up to the front of the lead vehicle. "What's going on?" Cabot asked.

"Ask Radio," said the guy sitting next to her.

"Who?"

A voice came from the front of the canopied area. "Ma'am, I monitor the radio transmissions. We're being ordered to wait now — something about the FBI."

*Good God, if we wait for the FBI, the convicts will escape and who knows what will happen to those women.* "What's the deal with the FBI?"

"Just sit tight, ma'am," Radio said. "Hold tight. We'll get orders here in a minute."

"But every minute counts."

"Yes, ma'am. We have our orders."

She shook her head. Trying not to sound impatient, she said, "How 'bout you roll my cycle this direction, and I'll go on ahead by myself?"

"Negative, ma'am." She jumped. The voice came from behind her, over her left shoulder, and she realized the sergeant had come around to the back of the truck. "There've been some complications, and we're waiting to rendezvous with the Feds and our other three trucks." In a louder voice, he said, "Men, ready your weapons and ALT equipment."

ALT. She wished *she* had that sort of equipment right now. Ambient-light technology, otherwise known as night vision goggles with specialized gun sights for night sniping — not something the typical forest ranger had at her disposal. All around her, she heard shuffling and the sound of zippers and Velcro. "Look, sergeant, you guys have to be careful. I think I told you there are civilians in the woods as well as at least two armed policewomen."

"Yes, ma'am. My men will be briefed. But I can't take the chance that any of my soldiers will be injured either. Please don't interfere or I'll have to take you into protective custody."

Cabot's mouth dropped open. Resigning herself to silent compliance, she sat back while the sergeant barked out orders. She heard the same thing going on in the transport vehicles behind her. And then she heard the sound of a vehicle approaching followed by yet another guard truck. Apparently the guardsmen knew the oncoming minivan wasn't dangerous because they let it drive right up next to the second guard truck behind her. It couldn't get any farther because the lead truck straddled too much of the narrow dirt road.

Six men in business suits climbed out of the minivan, illuminated only by the headlights of the third and fourth five-ton trucks. Cabot stifled a laugh. *I'm sure these clowns will be a great deal of help. How long will it take before they've got mud in their expensive shoes?*

The sergeant and four other soldiers converged upon the men, and they stood talking in a close knot. Nobody spoke loud enough for her to make out what was being discussed. She rose from the hard bench and stuck one leg over the back, searching for the jump-step. Feeling herself slip, she grabbed at the slick tailgate, then clutched the metal bar. She swung her other leg over and managed to drop the few feet to the ground without falling over.

As she marched toward the group, the sergeant said, "Ma'am! Please return to the vehicle." He pulled away from the circle and came toward her.

"Wait just one damn minute," she said, trying to keep her cool. "This is *my* forest. It's Kabetogama State Forest, and I don't see a soul here who answers to the name of Kabetogama State Forest Ranger. None of you have jurisdiction over me." She crossed her arms over her damp rain gear.

"Ma'am, if you would—"

"Hold it," a deep voice said. A black man, tall and dressed in a perfectly tailored suit, stepped toward her. "Jerome Giles, FBI. And you are?" He held out a hand.

Cabot put her very cold, very damp mitt into his warm clasp. "Sally Cabot, State Forestry Service. I was with that crowd at the prison this morning."

Somebody said, "She's exactly who she says she is."

Cabot recognized the voice of the prison administrator. "Soames," she said, surprised. "What the heck are you doing out here?"

Giles said, "Good to see you again, Ranger Cabot. Mr. Soames is one of the few people who can actually identify who's an escapee and who's a guard."

"Guard?"

"Yes. It appears we have some guards running around loose in the woods trying to track the escapees."

"Ah, I see. And you don't want to take any chances that the guards would be confused with the inmates?"

Giles shook his head. "It's more than that. Why don't you get in the car with my assistant and me, and we'll explain. C'mon Soames." With a nod to the sergeant, he said, "Let's carry out the plan."

"Yes, sir." The sergeant and his men turned and ran back to their vehicles. No sooner had they disappeared into their trucks than the elephantine lead vehicle revved up and rolled forward.

Giles opened the driver's side slider, and three of the men in suits squeezed into the minivan's rear seat. "Hop in, Ranger."

For the first time in hours, Cabot could actually feel warmth. She shifted a little as Giles sat down next to her. Through the fogging windows, she saw the downpour had slacked off to an occasional sprinkle. *Figures it would stop raining now that I'm finally out of it!* She fantasized briefly about the hot shower waiting for her at home. It had been a long day and it wasn't over yet.

Giles said, "Let's go, Charley." The driver hit the gas, and they pulled away, spraying dirt and water.

"WHERE THE HELL are they?" A man's voice carried surprisingly well through the drizzle.

Dez couldn't see who was driving, but as the truck rolled closer she realized a man dressed in a yellow slicker and shiny, yellow cap walked alongside a white pickup truck. He held a flashlight, which he was pointing at the trees.

Crystal jumped first. "Move it!" she whispered. The three women backed up into the trees.

It wasn't until Dez got situated behind a maple that she realized Keith hadn't followed. He still knelt, doubled over and motionless. "Shit!"

The truck was about two hundred yards down to the right, crawling along slowly. If the searchers didn't shine the flashlight forward and to their left, Dez might have time to haul the young man out of the limelight. She crept ahead, grabbed him by the scruff of the neck, and pulled. He was lighter than she expected. He didn't resist as she dragged him back, over brush and brambles, and into the woods.

A man's voice called out, "What was that? You hear that?"

The truck stopped and a head poked out of the cab. "Probably a deer."

"Sit tight for a minute." The white truck idled, and the man alongside it shone his high-powered flashlight down the incline, up and down the trees on both sides of the road, systematically searching.

In the headlamps, Dez could just make out the unmistakable silhouette of a gun in his right hand. Were these guys friends or foes?

"See anything, Mike?" the truck's driver called out.

"Naw. You were probably right." He walked on ahead, and the truck rolled after him.

Dez couldn't be sure, but it seemed like both Crystal and Jaylynn held their breath. She kept her hands on Keith's shoulders, hoping he would remain motionless.

He turned his head. "Guards."

"What?" Dez whispered.

"Guards from the prison."

"Shhh. They'll hear." She leaned in close and wrinkled up her nose at the harsh smell emanating from him. "You're sure?"

He nodded emphatically, then shivered. Dez didn't know if he shook more from cold or fear.

As the truck moved ahead, the illumination from the headlights dimmed, and within just a few seconds, they were once again shrouded in darkness.

The three women huddled for a conference. Crystal said, "Maybe one of us should approach."

Jaylynn said, "We need to do something soon."

Dez grasped Jaylynn's arm. "Not you."

"Yeah, I know," she whispered, "but I can cover you guys. What if one of you just walks up on the road? Call out to them for help?"

Dez had a bad feeling, but then again, everything about the whole day had tested her judgment and intuition from the very start. "I don't know. I think maybe we should wait for Cabot. I'm surprised she isn't here. I thought she would have left on her cycle soon after we took the canoe."

Crystal said, "She's probably up or down this road somewhere. We just haven't seen her yet."

Jaylynn said, "All I know is that we have to get some help for Keith. He's obviously in bad shape. If those are guards, they could take him for medical help."

Dez took a deep breath. "Okay, that's true. Crys, it's me and you. Let's cross the road and call out to them from there." She slipped the backpack off and dropped it behind a tree. "Jay, stay with him, no matter what, okay? If anything strange happens, you stay hidden and wait for help."

"Mission accepted."

"Promise?"

"Don't be silly."

The warmth and good humor in Jaylynn's voice seemed so normal that Dez felt a wave wash over her of what could only be described as gratitude for her partner's life and love. She gave a final squeeze to the wiry arm, and she and Crystal hustled up the incline. They cut across the road and started to step down the embankment. It was steeper there, and the mud was thick. "Forget it," Dez said in a low voice. "Let's just stay in the middle of the road and catch up with them. You call out when we get close."

As they made their way along the dirt road, she reached under her sweatshirt, fully unzipped the pouch, and fingered her dad's Colt Commander. She couldn't quite believe she'd gotten it back. He'd bought it in 1978, the year before his fatal heart attack, and she had always treasured it. Her hand wrapped comfortably around the gun's grip, and the wood was smooth against her palm. She thought it an odd sort of security blanket, but that's exactly how it felt to hold her father's gun. She wrapped both hands up inside her sweatshirt, hoping it would look like she was just keeping them warm.

They trotted to catch up with the truck. Dez watched the walking man's flashlight bob and spray light. They slowed to a walk when they got within fifty feet. Crystal let out a whistle and in a high voice said, "Guys! Help us, will you?" Dez approved of the delivery. No gender confusion with that voice.

The brake lights went on, glowing blood red. The flashlight did a one-eighty and pinpointed them. "Who's there?"

"We need help. Me and my friend were hiking." Crystal let it go at that.

The driver got out of the truck, and the two men approached. Dez went still and tense. This was the most dangerous moment. She squinted away from the light as it fanned quickly over both of them. A deep voice said, "You look like drowned rats."

Crystal smiled. "We *feel* like drowned rats."

The flashlight beam settled on the mid-section of Crystal's rain gear and cast enough light for the strangers to examine each other. The driver wore tan rain gear. His head was bare. The two men were roughly the same height, and Dez looked at them eye to eye.

Mike, the man in the yellow slicker, waved a hand. "Neither of you is injured, right?"

"Nope," Dez said. "Just cold and wet."

"Have you seen any men in the woods?"

Dez hedged. "Today? Or yesterday?"

He frowned. "We're looking for two prison escapees. Don't you know there's a manhunt? They're reported to be in this area. You're lucky you haven't run into them."

The driver glanced at the guy in the slicker, then spoke for the first time. "You want to get in the truck and warm up? We can get you into town in a while." Both men seemed uncomfortable.

Dez nodded toward the gun in Mike's hand. "You're packing some firepower there."

"I am. These guys are dangerous."

The driver cut in. "We don't want to be caught unawares. Gotta be safe. By the way, name's Lou Schecter. This here is Mike Morris. We're guards at the prison."

"I'm Dez. This is Crystal. We're from St. Paul."

"You picked a tough day to be out," Schecter said. He tipped his head back and looked briefly skyward. "But at least it's slowing down."

Morris said, "Look, we can't wait around. Do you have some gear? If so, get it and we'll transport now."

Crystal met Dez's eyes, obviously waiting for her to decide what to do. Dez unwrapped her hands from the pouch, pulled them out from under her sweatshirt, and rubbed her palms together. "We've got a couple more in our party. Think you could give us all a ride in?"

"Four?" Morris asked. "You'll all freeze in the bed of the truck."

Crystal said, "We're already frozen."

There was a pause as the two men exchanged an uneasy glance. Again, something gripped at Dez's gut—an intuitive warning. She wished she had asked for ID.

Schecter said, "See, it's our fault these guys escaped. We don't want to quit searching. We could lose our jobs and—"

"She doesn't care about that!" Morris's voice was sharp. He brought up his index finger and pointed it at Crystal. "Go get the others. We'll run you up to Highway 24, but then you're on your own. We gotta find these creeps."

"Thanks," Crystal said with false enthusiasm. Once more she glanced at Dez as if for confirmation. "I'll go get Jay."

Dez nodded and tucked her hands back up under her sweatshirt. She found the gun grip. "So you guys know these escapees pretty well?"

"Oh, yeah," Schecter said. His thin hair had absorbed all the water it could take, and a rivulet of water ran down his forehead and into an eye. He brought up a hand and wiped his face. "I'd like to kick their asses, too. Pardon my French. We've had one hell of a day."

The flashlight beam wandered to Dez's left, and Morris elbowed Schecter. "Holy shit. Do I believe my eyes?"

Crystal and Jaylynn flanked Keith, holding his arms. He moved with the sleepwalking gait of the half-frozen.

The two guards pushed past Dez. In a deep growl, Morris said, "Where the hell is Bostwick?"

Keith didn't respond, and Morris grabbed for him.

"Hey!" Jaylynn moved forward, preventing the guard from getting close to Keith. "Easy there! The guy's hypothermic."

Morris reached for him again, but Keith hung back, mumbling, "Get away from me."

Crystal and Jaylynn each held up a hand. "Wait," Jaylynn said. "He needs medical attention."

Morris said, "The hell with that. He's fine. You're going back to the prison, buddy boy. Where's your big, ugly friend?" He succeeded in grabbing Keith's arm.

"Wait a minute." Dez pushed the guard away. "This man is in our custody."

"Who the fuck you think you are?" Morris said. "He's in *our* custody now."

"I don't think so. I think my peace officer license trumps your private guard status." She stepped between him and Keith.

"You're no cop," Morris said.

"We'll just call this in — settle it with help," she said. "Get out your radio."

Schecter said, "I don't have a radio in the truck. It's my personal vehicle, and we —"

"Shut up, Lou." Morris brought up his gun. "I think my gun trumps your phony ID."

Dez's hands were lightning quick. She twisted the gun upward and knocked the man back. Gunfire exploded in the silence. The shot was loud in Dez's ear, and the ringing started immediately, even before she stomped on his instep and twisted his arm. The weapon fell to the ground. He let out a yowl. He was strong. In a burst of energy, he jerked away from her.

Crystal dove for the gun.

Schecter hollered, "Shit, Mike! Cut it out!"

Jaylynn held out Crystal's .380 and said, "Freeze or I'll shoot." The man hesitated.

By then Crystal sat splay-legged on the ground sighting along the barrel of the guard's weapon. "And if she misses, I sure won't."

"And I won't either," Dez said. She held her .45, barrel tipped slightly upward. "Get up, Crystal. You guys keep your hands where I can see 'em."

Schecter raised his hands to shoulder level. "C'mon, ladies. Aren't we all on the same side?"

"If we were on the same side," Crystal said, "I wouldn't have water up my ass and mud all over my overalls. Dammit!" Mumbling, she tried to wipe away some of the mud.

With Crystal on her feet, Dez stepped back. "I thought we were on the same side, boys, but now I'm not so sure." Without taking her eyes off the guards, Dez said, "Crys, where's Keith?"

"Right here behind us."

"Okay, good." Dez kept her eyes on the two men. "How 'bout you loan us your truck, and we'll take care of this guy?"

"No way!" Morris shouted. "He's ours." He took off his shiny yellow hat and threw it to the ground.

"Wait a sec," Schecter said. "You can't take my truck." He sounded like a petulant child.

"I'll be sure it gets back to you safely," Dez said. "I promise you that."

"No fuckin' way," Morris yelled. "We don't know who the hell you are. You could be convicts yourself!"

"I'll show you my ID," Dez said, but she could tell Morris wasn't interested in the truth. There was some other agenda going on for him, and the stakes were obviously high or he wouldn't have waved his gun, especially at someone who identified herself as a cop. Dez decided this made him dangerous.

Morris shook his head, "Fuck that. Fuck you!"

Jaylynn raised her voice. "Everybody calm down. You two—" she gestured at the guards, "back up. Back up there. Keep going." When they reached the truck's gate, she said, "Okay, down. Sit on the bumper, hands up."

They lowered themselves, one on either side of the hitch that stuck out from the back of the still-idling truck. Schecter said, "Geez, this is *cold!* Cold as hell."

Jaylynn gave a little snort. "You should've thought of that before you threatened to kill us."

Schecter said, "He wasn't going to—"

"Shut up, Lou!" Morris sneered. "You talk too goddamn much. Just *shut* your trap."

Keeping an eye on the men, Dez leaned toward Crystal. "Why don't you and Jaylynn take off. Get Keith to the hospital in town. I'll stay and keep an eye on these two."

Jaylynn glanced over her shoulder. "I won't leave you here, Dez. No way."

She had been afraid Jaylynn would say that. "Get him in where it's warm then, Crys. Turn the heat up to high." Dez weighed their options as Crystal tugged at Keith, pulling him toward the truck cab. They didn't have a lot of choices. She would rather have one of the two women drive and the other ride shotgun with Keith. *Once Jay and Crys are down the road to safety, who cares about these two yahoos? And I can survive out here for hours. Besides, won't Cabot be bringing the cavalry any minute?*

Dez and Jaylynn faced the two men sitting silently on the bumper. Morris had an especially dark look on his face. Schecter just looked like he was sick of being rained on.

Dez waited for Crystal to deal with Keith. Crystal stood on the passenger's side of the truck, reaching for the door handle, when a figure rose by the left front quarter panel. "Don't move, bitch!" A meaty arm held a handgun out over the driver's side of the cab.

Jaylynn and Dez dropped behind the tailgate, but not before Dez got a glimpse of his face. Bostwick looked like death warmed over — scowling, bloodied, dripping wet, and pissed as hell. The two prison guards hit the ground and scrambled away. Dez didn't care about them. They weren't armed and probably wouldn't help anyway.

"What do you want?" Crystal's voice was reasonable. "You can have whatever you want."

"Drop the gun. Drop the fuckin' gun!"

"Done. Whatever you want. It's yours." Dez heard something fall to the ground.

"Gimme the kid. Give him to me or I'll shoot your fucking head off."

"Okay, sure. He's yours." Crystal stepped back slowly. She inched behind Keith, putting him between her and the enraged convict.

Dez caught Jaylynn's eye and gave a toss with her head. She gestured for Jaylynn to crawl toward her, nearer the passenger side. She got a frown and a shake of the head. Dez grimaced. *Don't play hero, Jay!* Jaylynn made the OK sign with her left hand, then mouthed, "Wait."

Dez gripped the edge of the bumper, ready to run, dive, stand — whatever she needed to do. From her vantage point on the ground, she could make out Crystal and Keith to the right, but the only way to see Bostwick clearly without coming in the line of fire was to look under the vehicle. To her left, Jaylynn had a better sightline on the convict. The smaller woman sat on her haunches, right shoulder pressed against the truck's bumper. No matter how Dez looked at it, any shot the right-handed Jaylynn could take would be awkward and expose her to return fire. Warm exhaust filled the air, and Dez resisted the urge to cough.

"Bostwick!" A voice shouted from somewhere in the brush up the road to Dez's right.

"Who's there?" Bostwick's voice sounded raspy. "Who is that?"

"It's Morris. I've got a bead on you right now."

There was a click, and something bumped the truck. Bostwick had opened the driver's side door. He hollered, "Bullshit."

"We want what you promised."

Bostwick shouted, "I didn't even get what I was promised!" In a lower voice, he said, "You! Put him in the truck. Now!"

The truck shifted slightly to the right as Crystal opened the passenger door and shoved Keith in.

"Shut the door," Bostwick said. "And don't move or I'll shoot him and everyone else."

The headlights went out.

A gunshot blasted from the driver's side of the truck. Crystal dove toward Dez.

Return fire came from the trees to the right. Dez and Crystal had nowhere to go but close to the tail end of the truck. Crystal shouted, "Stay low!"

Dez grabbed at Crystal as they scrambled behind the truck. Now Jaylynn wasn't there. Dez held onto the bumper and squat-walked to the driver's side. She peeked carefully around the rear. No Jaylynn.

She looked out toward the dark woods across the road. *I'll be damned. We should have searched them both. The other guard must have had a gun, too.* The vehicle sank down. *Uh oh, he's in, and he's got Keith.* She whispered, "Where's Jay? You see her?"

The truck's engine went dead.

"Shit!" Bostwick howled. "Gimme the fuckin' keys, pansy boy!" The truck shifted from side to side as Bostwick struggled inside, screaming, threatening, obviously hurting Keith.

Dez didn't know if Jaylynn was responsible for the lights going out or the ignition going off, but even as quick as her partner was, she didn't think she could have gotten past Bostwick. *It's Keith. It's got to be him. One less criminal to worry about if he truly is on our side.* The only light in the dark night came from the dim overhead light inside the truck. She avoided looking that way, hoping her eyes would adjust more quickly to the blackness all around her.

*Where's Jaylynn?*

Enveloped in darkness, Dez waited, Crystal by her side. Inside the truck, Bostwick muttered and cursed. The truck rocked as he yelled at Keith to give him the keys.

Dez whispered breathlessly, "Crys, do you see Jay?"

"No, but she usually takes the fall-back position. Whenever she rode with me, I went point, and she usually backed me up."

Dez let the thought register and gave one last hurried look all around. "I'll go point. Follow my lead."

Crystal whispered, "You got it."

Keeping low, Dez eased around the rear of the truck to the driver's side. *Where is she?* Her eyes scanned the side of the dark road, hoping Jaylynn had taken a sniper position off to the left.

Her heart beat rapidly as she searched for any sign of her companion. It was too dark to see much, and the faint light bleeding from the truck cab made it all the more difficult to discern anything. She listened for any sounds to the right from the prison guards, but her ears were still ringing from the gun going off. "I can't hear a damn thing. Keep an ear on the guards, will ya?"

"Shit, now they're a wild card to worry about."

"Yeah."

There was a howl from inside the truck, and Bostwick stuck a leg out, burst from the truck, and ran around the front to the passenger's side. With a click, the doors power-locked; apparently Keith was awake enough to manage this much in self-defense. Bostwick yanked on the door handle, then let out a roar. Peeping up over the back of the truck bed, Dez saw Keith throw himself to the driver's side of the truck and try to pull the door shut. For such a big man, Bostwick was fast. He got around the front of the truck and jammed his gun in the frame closest to the windshield. Instead of closing, the door bounced back open into the big man's gut. "You little sonuvabitch!" He leaned in and dragged the much smaller man out the door, allowing him to tumble to the ground.

Bostwick kicked him. Keith let out a choked cry. Bostwick kicked him again. "You fuckin' sonuvabitch! This is all your fuckin' fault! Every bit of it. Gimme the keys and get in the truck!"

Keith rolled over and tried to crawl away, but his head ran into the bottom of the door. Dez was tempted to shoot, but wasn't sure if she'd hit Keith. Bostwick grabbed the smaller man by the neck of the blue anorak. He lifted him up and slammed him face-first into the edge of the truck bed. He went limp, crumpled to the ground, and lay motionless.

Bostwick bent over Keith. With a nod, Crystal and Dez rose, and before the convict knew what was happening, they had guns on either side of his head.

"Drop the gun." Dez's voice was low. "I'd think nothing of blowing your head off."

He let the weapon go, and it fell on Keith's back, then slid partly under the truck.

"Spread 'em." Crystal kicked at his legs and pushed him against the side of the truck. One-handed, she reached to pat him down.

"Ooooh, baby," he said. "Bet you'll like what you find there."

"Shut up!" she said. "What I'd really like is to tie your sorry ass to a tree and call in some bears. And you can give me back my pants."

He chuckled. Looking over his shoulder he said, "You girls are a real laugh riot."

"*Besa mi culo.*"

"What?"

"Kiss my ass! Drop 'em. I'm not kidding." She jammed her gun into his ear. "Now! Take my pants off."

His voice was incredulous. "You gotta be kidding. You're holding me up for pants? It's cold out, lady. Come on!"

"Cut the crap. Give me back what you stole."

Dez thought Crystal must have struck him with her gun because he let out a yowl, but he did do as he was told.

"And don't bother putting those shoes back on either. You won't be needing them."

Crouched behind them, Dez laughed bitterly, but her eyes searched the darkness relentlessly. Had the prison guards run? Or were they merely watching and waiting to ambush them? She knelt, put fingers to Keith's neck, and hunted for a pulse. She found it, and not only did it feel strong, but she could tell he was breathing regularly. She didn't know if he'd sustained any major injuries, but she didn't have time to find out.

Crystal said, "Wish I had some handcuffs."

"No kidding. I agree. I've got some cord in my backpack—" Dez caught herself. "It's back in the trees. I'll go for it if I have to, but let me look in the truck. Get him on the ground."

Bostwick reluctantly went down to the mud, complaining every inch of the way about the cold, the water, the heartless bitches.

Dez reached behind the truck seat. On the passenger's side she found a mother lode of gear: a tool box, rope, heavy leather work gloves, some rags, and more. She was out of the truck with the rope immediately, and she and Crystal trussed up Bostwick. They made him rise and move toward the truck bed. He protested with every step. "Goddamn it! You can't do this. Let me go! You wouldn't shoot me anyway!"

Crystal leaned in. "I would do it with glee. You just give me *one* small excuse."

The tone of her friend's voice actually gave Dez a shiver. Even she believed Crystal.

The man was a huge load, but they managed to half-push, half-carry him to the tailgate. They opened it and shoved him onto the rippled truck bed. Once Bostwick lay facedown, Dez tied his ankles together. She anchored his hands to a hook that was obviously meant for a fifth-wheel trailer and used the trailer hitch at the back to tie off his legs. While she finished that, Crystal hopped over the side and managed to get Keith back into the cab.

Now that Bostwick was subdued, Dez paused and in a hoarse voice called out, "Jaylynn! Jay, we're clear!"

"Jesus!" Bostwick said. "It's cold. You can't keep me here without pants! At least put me in the cab! You bitches!" He continued to shout and scream, struggling in the rope binding him.

Ignoring his tantrum, Dez went over the side and squatted down to look for Bostwick's gun. She was surprised it was a Walther. *Where the hell did he get this?*

"I got the keys," Crystal said as she dropped down next to Dez. "The kid's locked in the cab. Now what?"

"Crys, you only brought your Beretta on this trip, right?"

"Yeah, why?"

"Where did this Walther come from?"

"I don't know? One of the prison guards?"

A feeling of dread washed over her. For the first time since the shooting in Lot A, Dez felt like she might vomit. "Where's Jay?"

Crystal had no answer for her. The rain slowed to a drizzle, and Dez was struck with fear. "Jaylynn!" she called out. "Jay!" She clutched the Colt tight in one hand, the Walther in the other, and peered out into the night.

JAYLYNN HEARD HER name being called, but she didn't dare respond. When Bostwick and the guards had first started shooting, she dove off the road and skidded down the slight incline, then scurried back around and got a bead on Bostwick's back. For a moment, she felt a shiver of fear, a memory of the big convict's cruel eyes as he struck her on the path earlier in the day. Her finger tensed against the trigger, but she didn't fire.

It was hard to see because of the drizzle, but the longer the truck lights were out the more her eyes were able to take in. She saw the convict's outline against the white truck. She could also make out — ever so faintly — Dez and Crystal at the rear of the vehicle. She felt guilty about wanting to shoot the man. She knew it was her duty to avoid pulling the trigger, and she would, reluctantly, do her duty.

While taking in great gulps of air, she maintained a steady aim. As she watched Bostwick's antics, her breathing returned to normal, and she sighted down the barrel of the gun with confidence. When Bostwick started kicking Keith, she very nearly pulled the trigger, but suddenly a dark blur came from the right. Crystal and Dez jumped the bald convict, and he was quickly under control.

Jaylynn relaxed, but continued to hold her position, only gradually becoming aware that she was lying half-sprawled in some sort of brambly bush. Drops of water spilled off a branch and poured down her neck. She shuddered and moved to the right slightly. Now the drops poured onto her shoulder instead. She shifted a bit more, and that was when she saw the figure creeping up the incline to the right about thirty feet away. His approach was soundless. He didn't seem to have noticed her. She lay very still, watching. Bostwick was making such a racket that the noise could have covered any number of stealthy guerillas. She extricated herself from the bush and scrambled to the right on her knees and one hand.

The dark figure reached the road forty feet behind the white truck and darted across. He started down the steeper incline on the other side, and when she couldn't make out his head anymore, Jaylynn crossed the road, too. Near the edge, she got down low and peered into the dark murkiness ahead. *There! He's moving toward the trees.*

She didn't want him to look back and see her outline against trees or sky, so she lowered herself, legs still on the road, upper body lying in the muddy weeds. Cradling her gun hand in a very cold left palm, she watched.

"Jaylynn! Jay, we're clear!"

She flinched but dared not answer.

"Jay!" The voice now had an edge of panic to it. *Dez, I'm okay.* She willed her partner to relax, to know all was well. She rolled off the flat surface and lay parallel to the road so that both the rear of the truck and the tree line to her right were in her sightline.

From the trees, Lou Schecter called out, "If you're taking my Chevy, can we at least ride to town with you?"

*Say no, Dez. Those guys are snakes!* Squinting toward the truck, she couldn't see either of her friends. Bostwick was no longer shouting. *Probably chewing through the ropes with his fangs.*

The hair went up on the back of her neck, and Jaylynn knew it was more than the cold. Something was about to happen.

A gunshot shattered the quiet. A man screamed. Somewhere ahead of the truck and to the right, she heard a commotion in the woods. A male voice in the trees shouted, "No!" and she heard crashing and huffing.

"Jay! Jay!" Dez's voice.

Another shot rang out. Another tortured shout came from near the truck. "Jaylynn!"

Jaylynn very clearly heard an *oomph* sound somebody made, and a figure rolled out of the woods and into a flat area ahead to the right. It lay there, a dark lump in her peripheral vision.

There was a scuffle at the truck, and she thought Crystal was probably restraining Dez. Jaylynn put her fingers to her lips. Wincing at the thought of all the dirt and grime on her hands, she let out a two-tone whistle. She paused, then did it again. All went quiet. She could hear her own heart beating, feel the cold, soggy ground under her. The wind had died down, and with a start, she realized it had stopped raining. Jaylynn was surprised she hadn't noticed before.

She held her breath a moment, then forced herself to draw in some air. If she could kamikaze-crawl across the road to Dez and Crystal, maybe they could all get into the truck and get away. Before she could move, four shots rang out. They made pinging sounds as they hit the truck.

Crystal let out a shout.

*Oh, shit. Vanya or the prison guards . . . which is it?* Jaylynn didn't dare move now.

Dez's voice carried from the other side of the truck. "What the hell do you want? What?"

No answer from the woods.

Something moved along the tree line. For a brief moment, Jaylynn thought a very large elk or deer had emerged. She couldn't discern anything at all when staring right at the dark form, but strangely enough, looking a little off to the side gave her a better view. Someone approached. Two someones. One slipped and let out a grunt. A deep voice muttered. The man in the rear helped pull the fallen man to his feet, and they advanced up the slope toward the passenger's side of the truck. The figure in front moved hesitantly, held by the other man's left hand.

When they got close to the rise where the road leveled off, a familiar, musical voice said, "One man is already dead. You can prevent the sacrifice of this one."

Dez's voice called out, "What do you want?"

"Toss the keys over the top of the truck and back away."

"What if I don't care if you shoot that moron there?"

"Oh, you must care, miss. If you are, indeed, an officer of the law, it is your job to preserve life, is it not?"

"Fine. Give me a moment to get these people clear—"

"Oh, no. On the contrary. Pardon me, but you must leave those two men exactly where they are."

"What?" Dez's voice sounded different, a little farther away, and Jaylynn surmised that she and Crystal had fanned out, one to the front and one to the rear of the truck.

A flurry of movement exploded from the bed of the pickup. "Hey, Russian!" Bostwick shouted. "I kept *my* part of the deal. You fuckin' better keep yours!"

"Oh, yes. You will get what is coming to you, Mr. Bostwick."

Jaylynn shivered. She couldn't believe she had sat in a car and carried on polite conversation with this man. His voice now sounded diabolical. "You will deliver the keys to me, or this man will suffer the consequences." He kept the prison guard in front of him. Jaylynn saw the light-colored rain gear on the guard and realized it was the one named Lou, not the man in the yellow slicker. She squinted into the night. The guard seemed to be leaning forward, as though injured. She assumed that Vanya held a gun in his right hand, though she couldn't see it.

*Where is the cavalry? Where is this forest ranger Dez kept talking about?* Jaylynn slid onto the muddy slant, and away from the rocks and gravel on the road. Using her elbows and her right leg on the slope, she pulled herself forward in the muck and lined up her target, aiming carefully. If Crystal was at the rear of the truck and Dez at the front, neither would have a good shot. Jaylynn's angle was more oblique, but the darkness hindered her. If she fired, she could just as easily hit the guard, not Vanya.

"Well?" Vanya said. When no one answered, the timbre of his voice shifted, and he sounded angry. "I expect action. Now!"

Jaylynn heard a quiet *clunk* sound. The light inside the truck came on. She looked away, but it was too late. Just that little bit of light affected her vision. It would be long seconds before her eyes adjusted. She could only hope that Vanya was in the same situation.

"Very clever of you," Vanya said, "but I want the keys."

"First let the man go," Dez said.

"Very amusing."

Bostwick hollered, "Make 'em untie me. I'll help you." Nobody answered him. "C'mon! I'm freezing my ass off here. Make 'em let me go."

Vanya shifted, with his back angled toward Jaylynn. He and the guard scuttled sideways until they were even with the rear corner of the truck. For a brief moment, Crystal was in Vanya's sightlines. Jaylynn almost shouted, but she'd never seen the husky Latina move so fast.

Crystal scrambled around to the driver's side and said, "I'm going to give you the keys, but first put the gun down."

"This is not a possibility. Do you think I am as stupid as the fat man there?"

"Hey!" Bostwick shouted. "I'm no dummy! I delivered the goods. Now get me out of here so we can settle up."

In a cold, quiet voice, Vanya said, "I am going to give you a count of three. If the keys are not in my hands by then, this man dies. One."

*He can't afford to shoot the man. If he does, he has no shield. But he could shoot Bostwick. Fine by me.* Jaylynn got her feet under her and moved to a crouch. Her first step put her on the road.

"Two."

In her best sprint form, she catapulted forward, aware of her body, of the air she displaced and the way she sliced through the wind like an arrow. She rammed Vanya with stunning force. His gun went off. Then she was rolling, skinning her hand. It flitted through her mind that people would be shocked to find out what an effective battering ram a 125-pound woman could be, especially if the target was already off-balance.

A blur of motion. Another gun shot. Jaylynn rolled, her legs twisting under her. Stabs of pain exploded in her right knee and ankle. She felt the cold ground under her butt, brought her gun up, sighted with care. Lou Schecter knelt in the road near the truck, bent over with one hand on the ground as he clutched his middle. Dez struggled with Vanya. He squirmed loose.

From the rear of the truck, Crystal dove. With a loud roar, she landed on Vanya. His gun went off again. He let out a shout, then made a choking sound.

Jaylynn never took her eyes off the tangle of arms and legs in front of her. She rose, her gun at the ready, and limped closer with careful steps. Dez held the man's gun arm to the ground. Crystal lay across his torso. Keeping the guard in her peripheral vision, Jaylynn sighted down her barrel. "Vanya! Stop it or I'll blow your head off. Let go of the gun."

His blue eyes were desperate. "Aaaah!" Gritting his teeth, he writhed and squirmed like a trapped rodent. His left arm came around and struck a glancing blow to Crystal's side. She grunted.

"Got it," Dez choked out in a hoarse voice. The gun went skating off the road a few feet down the slope.

"Stop," Jaylynn said. "It's over, Vanya. Quit struggling." He flung out his arm, tried to hit Crystal again. She struck him in the face with her gun. A surge of blood shot from his nose, and he lifted his free hand to cradle his face.

Grappling one-handed for a better hold, Crystal said something in Spanish. Even with her rudimentary Spanish, Jaylynn knew she'd said, "You don't deserve to live." Vanya didn't seem to be nervous at all about the fact that the two cops held guns. Dez pressed down on his shoulders, and Crystal straddled his middle. He kicked with his legs.

Crystal grunted. "Stop it! Holy mother, Jay, how do you know this worm's name?"

"He's the reason I wasn't in a canoe. He gave me a ride over here."

"Oh. I see there's a story in that." Crystal giggled, then in a loud voice, she said, "Well, we've got him. Now what do we do?"

"Hell if I know," Dez answered. "Wish we'd just shot him."

Jaylynn heard a noise in the distance. She jerked her head around. Schecter still knelt silently near the truck. The sound grew louder. "I'll tell you what we do," she said. "We just wait."

Dez shot a look at her. "Huh?"

"Can't you hear that?"

"All I hear is ringing in the distance."

Crystal said, "Me, too. Heavenly choirs of strange tunes."

The sound of gears grinding carried on the light wind. Jaylynn turned to the west. Two pinpricks of light grew brighter and rumbled toward them. She smiled. "I don't think it's a choir, but they might have been sent from heaven."

# Chapter
# Thirty-Three

AFTER TWO DAYS holed up at his office, Sergei Gubenko finally went home. The three-story, eight-bedroom manor was silent, cold, and drafty. He walked through the formal living room area, across a solarium, and into the entertainment wing of his home. Entering the enormous kitchen at the back of the house, he tossed his jacket over a chair near the door.

The servants had left for the day. Gubenko's personal bodyguard, who had been awake as many hours as his boss, was sleeping in the front room. Gubenko's wife, who was visiting friends in New York, had left instructions for the cook to prepare meals. When he opened the silver walk-in refrigerator, Gubenko found two pre-made dinners, yesterday's and today's, on a shelf for him to select from. After a moment's hesitation, he chose the *Bosartma,* a stewed lamb dish with onion, tomato, vegetables, and cherry plums.

Gubenko was a man who had grown used to being waited on, but today he wanted privacy. He had rarely ever used either of the microwaves, but he had no desire to call anyone to help. While he waited for the serving bowl of stewed lamb to heat, he opened both doors to an immense cupboard on the far end of the huge kitchen and examined the array of unopened bottles of California wines, vodka, drink mixes, liquor, and fine Russian wines. One bottle caught his eye: *Odjaleshi,* a Georgian red wine. *Odjaleshi grapes . . .* they brought back a memory from long ago of sitting with his grandfather on the banks of the Tskhenis-Tskali river.

He had been no more than five years old at the time. They sat leaning against a tree with branches swaying overhead in the warm breeze. His grandfather had a fine linen handkerchief spread in his lap, and he separated grapes from tough green vines and dropped them onto the kerchief. "One for you, Sergei, two for me." When he protested, his grandfather had laughed and presented him with an entire handful. The grapes were sweet — like nothing he had tasted before or since.

He reached into the cupboard and grabbed the neck of the wine bottle. The microwave dinged, but he spent the next couple of minutes hunting for a corkscrew. At long last he found one, opened the bottle of wine, and poured a crystal tumbler full.

He lumbered around the kitchen to find hot pads, a bowl, and utensils with which to serve the *Bosartma*, then took food and drink to a dinette table in an alcove where the servants usually ate. In the corner of the small nook sat a 19-inch TV on an elegant oak stand. He moved around the table, manually clicked it on, then returned to his seat. With a linen napkin in his lap, he took a bite of the lamb stew. He didn't know where the remote for the TV was, but the channel that came up was CNN. They were recapping information about a storm that had battered the Florida coast and caused severe damage to an entire fleet of fishing boats.

Feeling fatigue settle into his bones, Gubenko put an elbow on the table and slumped over the bowl, shoveling in the stew. After a few bites, he decided the cook had made it too bland, and he sat back.

"And from Minnesota, now this." The picture switched to a reporter holding a microphone and huddled under some sort of overhang outside a cabin. The picture was dim, though the reporter was well-illuminated. Gubenko looked out his window. *If it's dark here, it's dark there.* On closer inspection, he realized from a blurry sign to the left that the reporter stood on the porch outside a state forest office. "I'm Dean Cross, reporting from northern Minnesota where the frenzied search for two escapees from Kendall Correctional Facility has just taken a turn for the better. Earlier we reported that an unidentified man had been found dead near Lake Jeanette. Authorities have since identified the man, but are withholding his name pending notification of family. A few minutes ago, we received word that the convicts had been captured, and in a short while, the National Guard is expected to deliver them."

Three tones rang out sharply across the kitchen. Gubenko jumped. He rose and strode to his suit jacket and fumbled to find his cell phone.

A man speaking in Russian said, "Sergei, I have bad news."

He recognized the voice of his cousin, Alexei Zhukovich, from New York. "Alexei, I will call you back from another phone."

"No, no, wait! This is personal. Sergei, I don't know how to say this any other way. Please sit down."

"What is it?"

"It's Leonid. Your brother. He has died."

Gubenko's heart rate kicked right to an alarming pace, and the stew rose from his stomach and burned his esophagus. He choked it back down. "I—what? I don't understand."

"Leonid had a heart attack earlier today. He has died."

Gubenko walked across the floor and sank down in his chair. He pushed the serving bowl and stew dish away. "My brother . . . dead?"

"Yes. I am sorry, Sergei."

"All for nothing. Nothing. What about Grigor?" There was silence on the line. "Alexei! What about Grigor? You will explain!"

"There is no hope."

He shouted, "But—but, what about Grigor?"

"He is no more. Please call me back, Sergei. I cannot address that now." The line went dead.

On CNN, the reporter was still speaking in excited tones about the impending arrival of the authorities. Gubenko sat in shock. *Leonid is dead? Grigor, too? Oh, my God.* He was not a crying man, but tears sprang to his eyes. Elbows on the table, he put his face in his hands and tried to quell the sobs that shook him. *My son. Son of my heart.*

After a few moments, he sat back and wiped tears from his face. *Someone will pay.* He reached for the tumbler and took a large fortifying gulp of wine. The *Odjaleshi* was bitter and burned all the way down his throat.

# Chapter
# Thirty-Four

**Minnesota North Woods**
**Sunday, October 17, 7:45 p.m.**

FROM HER KNEELING position, Dez looked back at bright lights and armed men. The National Guard soldiers advanced and surrounded the strange tableau at the northeast end of the road around Lake Jeanette. There was nothing she could do to turn and face them. Vanya struggled even now, and neither she nor Crystal dared to let go.

A loud, distorted voice exploded from a bullhorn. "Throw down your weapons and get on the ground."

Jaylynn's gun slipped from her grasp. She raised her hands in the air and dropped to her knees. "Jaylynn Savage, St. Paul Police. Don't shoot. We three women are police officers."

The soldiers inched forward. When Dez and Crystal didn't comply with their order, it was repeated. By this time, Dez thought it was safe to release the Russian. No way would he get away from all these men. She hollered out, "We have weapons to relinquish. Don't shoot. We're both going to put them down out of this man's reach. Please retrieve them immediately." She slid the Colt and the Walther in the mud as far as she could. Crystal did the same. The three guns lay there. Jaylynn's was closer to the lead transport vehicle.

A woman's voice called out, "If those women say that guy is dangerous, believe them."

Dez grinned. *Cabot. She finally got here.* She shouted, "About time you showed up, Cabot."

"My sentiments exactly," the ranger answered.

A nervous male voice said, "The man there kneeling by the truck—he's one of the guards who was part of the inside job."

"Okay," another voice said. "He's not going anywhere."

Irritated, Dez said, "Come on, people! We can't let this guy go until someone retrieves the weapons."

The soldiers moved in another step, and then one of them came forward, snatched the handguns and faded back.

Dez said, "One more. Down the slope there." She moved her hand, pointing to Vanya's weapon which, in the bright lights from the guard truck, she could see was a very expensive H&K .45. The soldier seemed slightly more confident. He jogged over and collected the gun.

Dez said, "C'mon, guys. Let us know when we're clear."

A moment passed. In the harsh light, the man they held stared up at them with eyes full of hatred. He bared his teeth and made a growling sound. There was blood in his mouth. She didn't know if he'd bit his tongue or what.

"Clear."

Crystal and Dez looked at the dozens of armed soldiers with their rifles ready and then at one another. Dez took a deep breath. "Let go and get the hell away from him. He can just do whatever he wants." Over her shoulder, she called out, "When we let go, this guy may run. Shoot *him*, but please don't shoot us." She put her left foot flat on the ground, raised her arms, and pushed up slowly as she backed away. Crystal did the same, though she stumbled and nearly fell over the man's legs. The soldiers tensed. For one brief, scary moment, Dez hoped no one had an itchy finger, but they held their fire.

Dez kept her eyes on the man on the ground. He sat up, got a knee under him, and shakily rose to his feet. He put his hands in the air. "These crazy people accosted me. I am a law-abiding citizen. I did nothing to deserve their treatment. I demand—"

The deep voice on the bullhorn interrupted. "On the ground! On your knees, all of you, hands on your heads!"

Dez knew this was procedure, but she didn't like it. She sank down, hands laced over her wet hair. Soldiers with rough hands grabbed her and Crystal. Jaylynn was far enough away that Dez couldn't see what was happening to her. Over and over, she said, "I'm a cop. Reilly, St. Paul Police Department." She heard Crystal saying the same thing.

A man near Jaylynn shouted, "Clear!"

The soldier searching Dez said, "Clear!" It was a woman's voice. Dez looked at the baggy unisex guard gear. She wondered how many of the "men" here were actually women. Another group cleared Lou Schecter.

Her searchers stood back, looking like they were trying to be respectful. One reached out a hand. She grabbed it and levered herself up, suddenly realizing her thighs, calves, and knees hurt like hell. *Come to think of it, my neck and shoulders and back and left foot—geez, practically everything hurts.*

The knot around Crystal hollered, "Clear." She got to her feet and faced her friend. "Holy shit, Dez. Is it really over?"

The soldiers waved them back and they both turned, moving away from the rear of the truck, as the soldiers swarmed the vehicle and pulled Keith Randall from within.

In the glare of light from the five-ton trucks, Dez watched Sally Cabot as she seemed to swim through the guardsmen milling around, squeezing past one, stepping around another, saying, "Excuse me. Excuse me."

When Dez finally got a glimpse of a bedraggled blond head over the ranger's shoulder, all she wanted to do was go to her. But first she held out her right hand to Cabot. Crystal shook hands with Cabot next as Jaylynn limped toward them.

Dez said, "Thanks for coming and bringing the entire Minnesota Guard."

"My pleasure," Cabot said. "You all okay?"

Dez reached past the ranger and grabbed her lover. "Yeah. I am now." She turned away and pulled Jaylynn to her, enfolded the wet woman in a tight hug, and leaned into her. "Thank God you're all right," she whispered. Tears filled her eyes, but she fought them back. She reached up to Jaylynn's neck and put her palm against it. "Whoa. I thought my hands were cold, but next to your skin, they feel warm!"

Jaylynn shivered. "I truly cannot *wait* for a warm bath." She tipped her head back and sought out her partner's eyes. "I'm so glad you're safe."

Dez scowled and brought the back of her hand around to Jaylynn's face. "Jay! Look at you!" Even in the harsh light, she could see blood caked on her forehead. Her lower lip was split, she had a red, swollen goose-egg on her left cheekbone and various scrapes and bruises on her face. "Are you all right?"

"Nothing a little time and ice can't improve."

Dez held Jaylynn away from her. "And you're filthy. I've never seen you so dirty in my life."

"What can I say? I crawled through mud. I got smacked around a bit. I probably hid in deer shit." She giggled.

"I can't believe you can laugh about it."

"The whole day has been absurd. What else can we do?"

Dez tightened her grip, not wanting to ever let her go. *It's over. It's over. She's okay. It's over.* But it didn't feel over. Her heart had begun to race, and once more, in her mind's eye, she saw grotesque and frightening images of death and dismemberment. She didn't want to think about it. Over Jaylynn's head, she met Crystal's eyes. Cabot was waving toward someone over by the lead truck.

A sergeant jogged toward the ranger and Dez heard him smartly say, "Yes, ma'am?"

Cabot said, "Are ambulances on the way?"

"Yes, they are."

Even as the ranger said that, the whiny sound of an ambulance made itself heard. "Good. We need them."

Crystal came to stand near Dez, who continued to hold her shivering partner. They watched as Bostwick was untied and handcuffed—manacles courtesy of the FBI—and Dez had to suppress a smile when the soldiers helped him out of the truck bed. Shoeless, and without pants, he was a ridiculous-looking figure. Still, Jaylynn shuddered and nuzzled in closer.

"It's okay, sweetie," Dez said. "He can't get to you. Not ever. You never have to see him again." She didn't add that after all that had happened with the Russians, he wasn't likely to last long in prison. She'd lay odds he wouldn't survive a year inside. But that wasn't something she cared about in the least. "Reap what you sow."

"What?" Jaylynn asked.

"Bostwick is an evil man."

Crystal said, "You can say that again."

The ambulances somehow managed to make it around the giant guard transport vehicles. Dez was relieved when they turned off the sirens. Her ears still rang, and she had the beginnings of a headache. She reached up and touched a pulsing spot on top of her head and found a large lump there. *Bostwick. He marked us both up.* She pulled Jaylynn tighter and felt a wave of rage and hate pass through her. She was glad the soldiers had hauled him off to one of the trucks. Right now he might not be safe in her custody.

Someone flipped on another spotlight from one of the guard trucks, and the area was illuminated in harsh, yellow light. She counted the guard vehicles. *Wow. Three—no, four loads of soldiers.* Two sets of paramedics hustled into the center of the light. A soldier pointed their way, and one pair came toward them.

The EMT in the lead said, "Ladies, we need to check you over—"

"Oh, no, you don't," Jaylynn said. "Where's the man they took out of the white truck?" The medics stared at her blankly. Jaylynn turned to Dez. "Did you see? Where is he?"

Dez shrugged. "I didn't notice."

Crystal said, "I think they took him over to one of the army vehicles."

Jaylynn let go of Dez's hand. With what looked like painful effort, she limped past Schecter's Chevy and over toward the lead truck. Dez and Crystal trailed along behind. "Excuse me!" Jaylynn said. "Who's in charge here?"

A handsome black man stepped out from behind two solders. "Miss?"

"I'm not 'Miss.' My name is Jaylynn Savage, with the St. Paul Police Department. I want to know who's in charge?"

"I believe that would be me. Jerome Giles, FBI."

"Where's the man who was in the cab of the Chevy?"

"We have him under guard and ready to transport back to the prison."

"What!"

The FBI man seemed taken aback. "He's a federal prisoner, Officer. No need to worry. He won't escape now."

"Is he getting medical care?"

Giles frowned.

"Agent Giles, that man saved my life. Not once, but twice. He should *not* be treated like a common criminal."

"I'm sorry, miss, but the man *is* a common criminal."

Dez reached out, but grabbed thin air. Jaylynn was too quick for her. She confronted the FBI agent. "For God's sake. He's injured. He's hypothermic. He could die in your fine care. Do you realize that?"

Giles cleared his throat. "I'm not a medical expert."

Jaylynn put her fingers to her mouth, and whistled. "Hey! Paramedics! Over here." As the medics rushed toward them, she turned to Giles and said, "You can trust me on this. I did not spend the last fifteen or whatever hours out here freezing my ass off in the woods to discover that the *one decent man* I ran into ended up dying while I got medical attention for cuts and scrapes."

Giles raised a hand. "I see your point, ma'am." For a brief moment, he met Dez's eyes, then gestured to another man. "Charley, have the EMTs examine Mr. Randall."

"Yes, sir." Charley disappeared around the side of the guard truck with the medics in tow.

Jaylynn called out, "Even if he begs, don't bother with Bostwick!"

Giles laughed. "Ma'am, you, too, look a little worse for wear. Please allow the EMTs to take a look at you. Perhaps all of you should go to the hospital as well." Dez nodded. He went on, "And I've got work to do. Later, though, I need to talk to all of you. Once you get to town, please go to the Blue Iris Hotel. My assistant and the local authorities will want to take statements from all of you."

Dez said, "All right."

"Take good care of her."

Dez gave him a funny look. "I will." When she turned and saw her mud-encrusted companion, she suddenly realized what Giles had been referring to. Jaylynn stood staring blankly and seemed to have completely run out of energy. "Uh oh." Dez bent and caught hold of her. "Time for you to get in a nice, warm ambulance. Come on." She put an arm around her. "Jay, honey. You're limping. What happened to your leg?"

Jaylynn let out a sigh. "I was fine 'til I tackled Vanya. Now my knee and ankle are hurting like hell."

"Just lean into me."

Crystal shuffled past Dez and got hold of Jaylynn's other side, and they half-carried her toward the flashing lights.

As Dez passed some guardsmen, she heard one of them say, "That was no fun. We didn't even get to use our ALT gear."

The man who answered said, "If it's all the same to you, I'm getting a little old for this. And that guy down by the trees won't be getting any older. I'm just glad we're getting outta here alive."

Dez felt a guilty twinge. She had forgotten all about the other prison guard.

RALPH SOAMES WAS grateful it had stopped raining. For the last twenty minutes, he had paced next to the FBI's minivan, skirting the mud holes, waiting for the three-ring circus to wrap up. He knew he was superfluous — just some civilian guy whose incompetence had resulted in two deaths. And those were the killings the authorities had uncovered so far. For all he knew, more bodies could show up. His stomach remained queasy from having identified his employee, Michael Morris. Morris's body, covered with a stained tarp, still lay off the side of the road, down the slope near the tree line. All Soames could think of was how much blood there was.

He wasn't sure he would ever recover from the events of the last day. He didn't think his career would. Considering that, he straightened his back and squared his shoulders. *I'll face it like a man. That's all I can do. I just hope they understand that I had nothing to do with this.*

He saw Sally Cabot squatting next to the two paramedics working on Lou Schecter. Though he was nervous, he was also curious so he moved closer. Schecter lay on his back, his face white and grim. The medics opened his coat and peeled his shirt away. Even through all the blood, Soames saw the ragged hole in Schecter's right side. *Oh, Lord! He's been shot! How did he even manage to kneel?*

Soames met Cabot's eyes, and she shook her head slowly. "Ralph, this is such a shock."

"Tell me about it." Soames thought about how long he had worked with Schecter, how much he had trusted him. He felt cold through and through.

Cabot said, "Lou helped me find those WAO kids and my daughter and get them on the bus and safely to town. I just can't believe this."

Soames thought about how many sides there were to people. He'd always thought Schecter to be an upstanding guy, a trustworthy guard. How wrong he had been. From his standing position at Schecter's feet, Soames watched the paramedics staunch the blood flow and then set up an IV. They spoke in their own peculiar jargon, and he tuned them out, looking instead directly at his employee. "Lou. Lou, look at me. Tell me why?"

The man on the ground closed his eyes. Looking closer, Soames saw tears running down the sides of his face. "It was stupid, Ralph. I should never have listened to Mike."

"And you never will again, Lou. He's dead."

Schecter made a choking sound. "Yeah. I know."

"But why? Why would you get involved in this?"

Schecter turned his head to the side, then let out a groan as the medics worked to wrap something around his middle. "Greed," he gasped out. "Did it for the money." His voice was bitter and slow. "All for the fuckin' money. If I die now, my kids will know. My wife will leave me. Jail. Aw, shit."

Cabot said, "For cripesake, Lou, I feel like I'm in the movie *Fargo*. You're telling us this was all for a little bit of money?"

Schecter gasped in pain. "It wasn't a little bit. Mike and me were supposed to split twenty-five thousand bucks."

"Jesus!" Soames said. "You couldn't even buy a car with that, much less anything else valuable."

"Seemed like a . . . good idea. At the time." Lou Schecter scowled, then lowered his head. Both Cabot and Soames tried to talk to him further, but he closed his eyes and refused to respond.

Soames stepped back. Out of the corner of his eye, he saw Jerome Giles' assistant, Charley, striding quickly toward him. "Soames. Ambulances and the rear transport vehicles are preparing to head back to town with your guards, the convicts, and the policewomen. If you insist, you can stay on-site, but I'd prefer you accompany me."

"Okay. Fine."

Charley turned, let out a whistle, and held up two fingers. Two National Guardsmen jogged to the minivan and got in the back. Soames hadn't expected that. He wondered why they were needed on board. Charley got in the driver's seat while Soames slid in the passenger side. He looked over his shoulder at the two soldiers, then saw that the three policewomen were squeezed in the van's third row of seats. The blonde one in the middle was muddy and appeared totally done in. He put on his seatbelt and asked, "Where are Bostwick and Randall being taken?"

Charley started up the van and maneuvered back and forth to turn around. "Hospital first, then probably back to your prison — to solitary. Tomorrow they'll be moved elsewhere. Don't know the details yet." He edged over to the side of the road to get around the trucks.

A siren went off behind them. Soames tried to see out the back window. Through the condensation, he made out a lot of flashing lights and the outlined hulk of one of the trucks beyond the medics' vans. The two soldiers eyed him curiously, and suddenly he realized he was riding in the lead car of the caravan. *Duh, what a dummy I am. Of course some of the soldiers are coming with us. Geez, they're transporting criminals, and we've got injured law enforcement.*

The heater pumped out warmth, and the car smelled of dampness and body odor. Nobody spoke. As the van swayed and jounced along, Soames relaxed against the seat and took a deep breath. He was exhausted. He checked his watch. He'd been on duty for over thirteen hours.

The ride into town took a lot longer than he expected. The road was slick and full of muddy potholes. Charley covered the ground efficiently, but when they finally reached Highway 24, Soames was glad to travel on a smoothly paved road.

Another thing Soames didn't expect popped up as they approached town. Scores of cars — both parked and driving around — crammed the entire area. Despite the crummy weather, there were people on foot all over the place. They turned off the highway and down a side road. The normally empty lane leading to the hospital overflowed with parked cars. No less than a dozen news vans clustered in the parking lot.

People standing in the drizzle formed a ring at least three deep. They faced the entryway to the emergency entrance, pressing forward. Four local police officers in tan outdoor gear stood under the overhang trying to keep the reporters and bystanders from getting too close. Charley steered the minivan toward them, and they parted to let him through. He stopped beneath the overhang. He pulled up to the farthest edge of the sidewalk that ran next to the ER entrance. As soon as they stopped, the soldiers sprang out. Somebody blew a whistle, and Soames heard a loud, male voice saying, "Back, people. Everybody, back up now."

Soames got out of the van. Both ambulances, sans sirens, lined up directly behind the minivan, but nobody got out. The National Guard truck brought up the rear, stopped, and a half-dozen soldiers poured out the back. They took positions in a semicircle and herded people away from the hospital and from the driveway to the ER. Only then did the hospital doors open. An orderly Soames recognized from around town came out with two nurses, and they hustled to the curb. A guard exited from the first ambulance, then the paramedics muscled out a gurney. Soames realized his guard, Schecter, was on the stretcher. They whisked him up the walk and in through the sliding doors. Keith Randall was removed next. By this time, two FBI agents were guiding a shackled Stanley Bostwick toward the hospital. Someone had given him a pair of green fatigue pants, and he limped in stocking feet toward the hospital, flanked by two soldiers every bit as big as he was.

Charley came around to the passenger side of the van and pulled forward the middle seats so the policewomen could get out. Soames stepped away from the vehicle to give them room. Charley cut past him and followed Bostwick into the ER, but Soames stood and watched the grimy-looking blond woman as she emerged from the minivan. The dark-haired cop, Reilly, and the one named Lopez half-supported their friend as they stepped up onto the curb.

Two nurses, one a tiny lady, the other a very tall, hulking man, pushed a wheelchair quickly along the walkway and approached the van. The injured woman said, "I can walk. I don't need that damn thing!"

As the broad-shouldered male nurse locked the brakes on the wheelchair, Reilly bent and said something in her friend's ear, obviously talking the reluctant woman into getting into the chair. The hospital personnel wheeled her off through the entrance with the two other women following.

The moment they disappeared, Charley came through the hospital's sliding glass door. "Soames! You ready?"

"Huh? Ready?"

"Yeah. There's a bathroom inside, through the waiting room on the right. Go clean up, and get back out here."

"Wha—why?"

Charley moved closer. "Come on, man, the sheriff and my boss are ready. We've got to face the press. Go comb your hair, take a leak, whatever." He consulted his watch. "Be back here in five and we'll go do our duty."

Soames entered the sliding door with his stomach trying to get out through his navel. *Face the press? Me? Oh, my God.* The doors closed behind him, and he made himself keep walking.

# Chapter
# Thirty-Five

ST. THERESA'S HOSPITAL, a compact two-story facility, didn't have much of an emergency room. Three curtained bays took up most of the right side, the large trauma area with bright lights overhead was in the center, and a wall of equipment and cupboards was arrayed to the left. Right now, the place was jam-packed with people. Jaylynn thought every doctor and nurse in the region must have been called in. The nurse behind her rolled the wheelchair past Bostwick. He sat shackled in the hallway with three soldiers surrounding him. *Cops get first care,* she thought as she looked away from him.

Ahead of her, Keith's gurney was rolling toward one of the exam tables in the center of the room. The injured prison guard was already on the other table. Two paramedics shouted details that were unintelligible to Jaylynn. She wanted to pay closer attention, to find out about Keith, but she felt so tired. The last thing she saw of the blond escapee, medical personnel were moving him from the rolling cart onto the ER table, and then he was surrounded. Her view was further blocked as the paramedic walking beside her was met by a man in a white coat. The medic gave him an update on Jaylynn's vitals, and the doctor pointed to the far corner on the right. She was rolled into the bay.

A semi-reclined exam table sat in the middle with perhaps three feet of space on either side of it. A counter ran along the wall at the head, with cupboards above, and the small room was ringed by a curtain. The nurse pulled the curtain partway closed. He squatted down next to her. "Okay, we've arrived, miss. You're going to get cleaned up and examined. Another nurse will help you." He patted her forearm and rose, taking with him the scent of cinnamon gum. Jaylynn closed her eyes as a wave of fatigue washed over her. She was pretty sure she could fall asleep right there in the wheelchair.

The curtain made a shrieking noise as it was pulled aside and then shut again. "Jaylynn Savage? My name is Mindy. I'll be your nurse. You know where you are?"

Jaylynn opened sleepy eyes and nodded. "Hospital."

"That's right. St. Theresa's Hospital in Buyck, Minnesota. I'm going to help you undress."

Jaylynn nodded and reached for the zipper of her sodden jacket. She got it down, and the nurse helped pull off the coat. She struggled out of the second sleeve, which clung to her like Velcro. "Yuck. It's filthy. Guess I ought to dump that, huh?"

Mindy said, "Oh, I don't know. Maybe a good industrial wash will clean it up." The nurse's voice was warm and laced with humor. She dropped the coat into a heavy-duty plastic bag. "You can decide what you want to do with it later. Now, can you stand?"

Little by little, the muddy boots and clothes came off and were replaced by a hospital gown. Jaylynn stood shivering and barefoot until the nurse helped her up on the exam table. Mindy wrapped her in heated blankets. It felt so good to be warm and dry that Jaylynn nearly started crying. Another nurse entered the room, and the two of them systematically uncovered parts of her, examined her limbs, asked her questions, took her temperature and blood pressure, and drew blood. They sponged away the dirt and mud as best they could, and Jaylynn told them how much her knee hurt.

Mindy said, "It's swollen, but I'm more worried about your ankle. I hope it's not a break. I can't be sure, but I'll bet you've got either a sprain or strain. We'll have the doctor check you out further, Officer. We'll need to dress the cuts on your forehead and lip—get some antibiotic on both. I don't think you need any stitches, but the doctor will examine you. You're really banged up, kiddo." She touched Jaylynn's left cheekbone with the tips of three fingers. "This is going to be quite a bruise. Hope the other guy looks half as bad."

"I tried."

Mindy smiled, and for the first time, Jaylynn got a look at brown eyes in a kind, middle-aged face. "You're a tough gal. You're going to be fine."

"Thank you." Jaylynn felt so grateful for the tender care, but other than thanks, she didn't know what else to say. They placed a hot pack over her chest. It was deliciously warm. She had to laugh because it felt every bit as big as a catcher's chest protector. "Do you do x-rays in this, too?" Mindy looked at her curiously. "I just mean it's huge and heavy."

"Yes, it is. Wouldn't work well for x-rays though."

Jaylynn closed her eyes. She didn't mean to, but she drifted off to sleep.

DEZ AND CRYSTAL maintained they were each fine and fit, but the nurses insisted on checking them over. Dez spent a few minutes being examined and questioned in one of the two remaining ER bays with Crystal in the bay on the other side. Dez knew she was bruised in odd places, but other than expressing concern about the marks on her neck and the goose-egg on the back of her head, the nurse seemed satisfied that she was all right.

Dez was patient for just enough time to allow them to take vitals and pronounce her free to go. They were happy to dispense Ibuprofen for her headache, and they made her promise she would put ice on various bruises as soon as possible.

"I need to be with my partner," Dez said to the nurse who had checked her over. The nurse looked toward the entrance of the bay.

Mindy, who stood in the opening of the curtain, leaned to the left and looked into the cubicle where Jaylynn was. "Officer Savage has fallen asleep. I'd prefer that we leave her there quietly while she warms up. When things calm down, the doctor is going to check her ankle, knee and forehead. Once he does that, I'll get her cleaned up and out of here." She leaned closer to Dez and patted her forearm. "I know you're concerned, but she's perfectly fine. I'll take good care of her."

The nurse looked trustworthy, and Dez knew she needed to stand aside and let them do their job. Reluctantly she said, "All right. May I at least look in on her?" Mindy led her from the middle cubicle to the corner bay, and Dez peeked through the curtain. Jaylynn lay swathed in warm blankets. Even her head was surrounded by a halo of cloth; only her face was visible. "She's for sure all right?"

Mindy nodded. "Just cold, exhausted, and banged up. She'll be fine once she gets a few hours sleep — maybe a little food in her. Go on — take a minute with her."

Dez moved into the little bay, amazed at how small and defenseless Jaylynn looked. Tears filled her eyes. *This is my fault. Those guys never should have gotten to her.* She stood next to the exam table thinking about the morning kidnapping. She closed her eyes and tried to rid herself of the vision, but still, she kept seeing the look on Jaylynn's face — a look of pain and fear — as the big monster held her up off the ground.

Warm fingers wrapped around her wrist. Dez opened her eyes.

"Hey, sweetie," Jaylynn whispered. Her lips turned up into the tiniest of smiles. "We're safe now."

Those strong fingers tugged at her. Dez bent and touched her lips softly to Jaylynn's, but her partner had other ideas. Jaylynn raised her arms and encircled her to deepen the kiss. When Dez broke it off, she nuzzled her face into her lover's neck, struggling not to burst into tears. Jaylynn's hands rubbed against her back as something very warm permeated her sweatshirt. She inched back, her elbows on either side of Jaylynn head. "What is this? The world's biggest heating pad?"

Jaylynn giggled. "No, that's *you*. But this thing works pretty good, too."

"Are you all right?"

"I am, Dez. I truly am."

"I don't want to let go of you, just in case."

"They'll have an interesting time with x-rays if you're lying here with me." As Dez smiled and pulled away, Jay protested, "Hey, I'm not saying I object!"

"I'll be right here."

"No, you won't. News about this is going to be all over the airwaves. Please go call Luella and your parents. Mine, too, sweetie."

Gruffly, Dez said, "You know I'm no sweetie."

"I have to disagree. Anybody who runs fifty miles to save my ass is a sweetie in my book."

Dez leaned in for another kiss, and the warmth of Jaylynn's mouth fired her, assured her, gave her strength. She stood back, holding her partner's wiry hand. "I'll go make those calls. I'll be back when they're done with your exam."

Jaylynn yawned. "Okay. I'll just be lying around here, catching some Z's."

Dez bent to kiss the scuffed knuckles, then tucked the small hand under the covers and retreated.

Outside the cubicle Dez ran into Crystal. "She okay, *chica*?"

Dez nodded. "I think they'll keep her a while for observation—check her over. We'll let her sleep a bit."

"How can she sleep with all this racket?"

Dez chuckled. "This is Jay, remember? She can sleep through a hurricane."

The nurse pulled the curtain closed and said, "Officer Reilly, I'll come out to the waiting room in a while. As long as there's no five-car pile-up to deliver more patients to us, you'll probably be able to take her home in the next couple hours."

Crystal said, "Bet you're not used to this kind of Sunday night."

"Uh, that would be a big no," Mindy said with a smile.

"Thanks," Dez said. "Please let me know if she needs me." Dez shifted forward, then stopped as a gurney rolled by toward the bay Crystal had vacated. Keith Randall lay swathed in blankets much the same as Jaylynn, except he was also hooked up to an IV drip. His tired eyes bored into Dez's as he went by. Though his expression didn't change, she saw a flicker of recognition, but he looked away, almost as if ashamed. They wheeled him into the exam area and transferred him from the rolling gurney to the table.

"Is that kid okay?" Dez asked Mindy.

"Off the record, he's dehydrated. Hypothermic. A bit concussed and definitely exhausted. Other than a few cracked ribs and a broken cheekbone, he ought to be good as new in a few days."

"I'd like to have a word with him."

Mindy glanced around. "Make it quick before the doctor kicks the two of you out."

Dez ducked into the room. The convict's face was wan and his face sported bruising, some of which looked fresh and others that were a darker purple. She stepped up to his bedside. He met her eyes and this time didn't look away. "You seem to have acquired a fan," she said.

"Huh?"

"Unless my partner is having hallucinations, she claims you saved her life."

He nodded solemnly. "She saved my life. I guess we're even."

"What are you in for?"

"Burglary. Marijuana possession."

"Any violent crimes? You use a gun?" He slowly shook his head. "I can look it up. You're telling the truth, right?"

"Second-story man all the way. I stole to buy booze and pot. I kicked the habit in jail. If it weren't for all this, I'd be out in about a month."

"Hmmm." Dez nodded. "Well, if what you say is true, Savage and I will stand behind you."

He frowned. "Savage?"

Dez gestured toward the curtain. "That's her last name."

"Oh, you mean Jay." He blushed and met her gaze, looking a little embarrassed, like it was hard to say what he said next. "You and she—you're like, partners, right? On the force and in real life?"

She didn't think it was any of his business, but she knew her hesitation told him all he wanted to know. He gave her a little half-smile, then closed his eyes, and she turned away feeling a little off-balance. *A gentleman crook,* she thought. *Not many of those anymore.*

She found Crystal hanging around outside Jaylynn's cubicle and gave her a wave. They made their way to the ER door. She watched the commotion in the center area as they passed. Schecter, the prison guard, lay unclothed on the table, a towel across his hips. She couldn't see the bullet hole she knew was in his abdomen. He was hooked up to monitors and tubes and drips. Somebody said, "OR—stat!" Dez didn't wait to hear anymore. At least he was still alive.

They made it to the ER door, and it hissed open. Bostwick still sat glowering in the hall. Dez hesitated for the slightest moment. She wanted to kick him, to knock him to the floor and bash his head in. But she couldn't do that. She wanted to tell him what a good witness against him she planned to be, but in the split second of hesitation, she decided he could just wait and see.

She walked away, following Crystal, and reached out to tug on her friend's arm. "Where's Shayna?"

"Good question. I'm not sure. I figure she'll turn up before too long."

Dez scowled and stopped. "How can you be sure she's safe?"

Crystal shrugged. "Why wouldn't she be? I told her if all else failed I'd track her down at that hotel. Once the ambulance came for the dead man, she said she'd try to drive around to the north side of the lake, but I'll bet they wouldn't let her. Our fallback plan was for her to book a room and watch the news to see what was going on."

"What if something happened to her?"

"What could happen? She's in a car with a gun, and she had three very pissed-off canoeists there with her for protection. What could go wrong?"

Dez didn't respond. They headed out into the waiting room. An elderly woman and bald man sat along one wall to the right. There was a dark head ducked down behind the high counter surrounding the welcome desk, but otherwise, nobody had been allowed inside the ER waiting area.

A police officer stood at the far end of the room, legs apart, with his back to them. With his six-foot frame blocking the sliding glass door, it was clear no one would get past without first answering to him. As Dez approached, she saw that an impromptu press conference was set up outdoors to the side of the cement apron surrounding the entrance. Dez and Crystal moved across the glossy-surfaced tan floor. Before they arrived, the cop glanced back and wheeled to face them. "Is everything okay?"

His blue eyes searched hers, and Dez nodded. He took a moment to introduce himself, and then Dez asked, "What's going on out there?"

"Press has been champing at the bit." He nodded and pointed past her. "Over in the back corner you can see it all on TV. I prefer to observe it soundless from here."

Crystal frowned. "Are you *loco*? Check it out!" She turned and hurried past the two people sitting in the waiting area. Dez followed. The TV was mounted in the corner next to the ceiling. Crystal looked around for a remote. Dez walked over to the set, reached up, and hit the volume. The two women stood and stared up at the TV.

"...from FBI officials in a moment, but first, let's hear from Ralph Soames, the administrator at Kendall Correctional Facility. Mr. Soames, can you give us the timeline of events as best you know it?"

The reporter yielded the microphone to a slender man in his mid-thirties. A cowlick in his brown hair stuck up in back, and he looked scared to death. His voice was firmer and smoother than Dez expected.

"At approximately 12:30 a.m., central standard time, two men escaped from the facility, just like, uh, as the reporter here said." He paused to swallow, looking like he was trying to down an egg. "Upon discovery of the inmates' escape, authorities were contacted, search parties were formed, and a diligent manhunt was undertaken. The fugitives were captured earlier this evening by three off-duty St. Paul policewomen."

As he paused for breath, a swell of shouted questions could be heard from reporters outside the angle of the camera. "Mr. Soames! Mr. Soames!" One woman's voice overpowered the others. "Why was the search originally concentrated to the north of the Ash River area instead of around the area where the escapees were found?"

Soames looked like the proverbial deer caught in the headlights. An officer in tan pressed in, stepped slightly in front of Soames, and said, "Deputy Sheriff Roger Fraley here, folks." He gave a hokey smile. "Let me fill you in on that part of the search..."

Dez crossed her arms. *As usual, the powers that be sure have an interesting spin.* She looked at Crystal and rolled her eyes. Crystal frowned up at her with an enraged expression on her face. "That phony asshole! He's the reason Shayna and I bought guns."

"And it's a good thing you did." She glanced at her watch. "I'll be back. I need to make some phone calls." She turned and headed for the bank of pay phones over on a side wall.

Crystal called out, "Hurry up with that, then let's get out of here and change clothes!"

Dez thought that was a thrilling idea. Not only was she dirty and wet, but occasionally a boggy stench wafted up. She wasn't sure if the smell was her—or her clothes—but she wanted to shower in the worst way. She wanted to lie down. She wanted to lie motionless, not moving a single aching limb. She wanted to do that with Jaylynn safely in her arms. *Could I ever be as cavalier as Crystal is? She isn't even worried about Shayna.*

She opened up a ratty phone book hanging by a thick wire from the enclosure surrounding the telephone and found a local number. She fumbled around in her left thigh cargo pocket and pulled out her police ID. Inside the thin leather folder was a calling card she used to dial the Blue Iris Hotel. She asked for Shayna Ford and was promptly connected. The phone didn't even finish a whole ring before it was picked up.

"Shay? It's Dez."

"Oh, good. I was *hoping* you guys would call soon. I saw you arrive on TV!" She very nearly crowed with excitement. "I tried to drive over to the hospital, but it's a mess there. Where's Crystal?"

"Keeping an eye on the TV news."

"What about Jay? I saw you put her in a wheelchair."

Dez felt a wave of emotion, but she forced it down. "She's all right. Banged up. Mostly cold."

"Oh, and we know how much our girl hates being cold."

"Yeah. You called anybody yet?"

"Just my mom to let her know everything was fine. She didn't even know anything was going on." Dez had to laugh at how indignant Shayna sounded. "She spent the afternoon at my cousin's baby shower."

"Did you, by chance, reserve a room for Jay and me?"

"Sure did. You can get the pass-card at the desk. The place is nuts. Full because they're putting up the National Guard overnight. While I was checking in, the cops came to search the room of the guy we found dead."

"What!"

"Oh, yeah. They've got his room all cordoned off. I told them that was one room you wouldn't want to stay in. Our rooms are on the next floor up at the other end of the hotel, thank you very much."

"Okay, Shayna. I've got some other calls to make. We'll be

over whenever they finally let Jay go."

"What a relief. See you in a bit."

They hung up, and Dez stood there feeling conflicted. How could her two friends be so nonchalant? Even now, with Jaylynn safe and under doctors' care, Dez's stomach still clenched with fear. As the minutes passed, instead of feeling more relieved and relaxed, she grew increasingly tense. Spoiling for a fight. She'd like to have someone's head on a proverbial platter.

She dialed the number for her former landlady, Luella Richardson, whom she had known for well over a decade. A rich, pleasant voice answered.

"Luella?"

"Dez, honey. What a relief. Vanita and I have been watching on the news."

"We're okay," Dez hastened to say. "Jay's a bit bruised, but she's going to be all right."

"Thank the Lord for that. How are *you*?"

"Not so great. Actually, a wreck in every way." She wasn't proud to admit any of her feelings, but it all poured out then — her worries and fear and nervous energy. Luella listened, occasionally making little clucking noises. Dez ended by saying, "It's been hellish, Lu. I'm so damn stressed I can hardly bear it."

"Listen to me, girl. You go tell the medical folks that you're taking off for an hour. Get Crystal and go somewhere to clean up. You'll feel a hundred percent better once you shower. Then come back to the hospital, get your girl, and go rest. Tomorrow or the next day is soon enough to come home, you hear me?"

"Yes, ma'am."

"And once you get home, let us know. You two can come over for dinner and further unwind. I'll make you something yummy."

Luella's meals were legendary. Jaylynn would never pass one up. "All right. Gotta go. I need to call Jay's parents, just in case they caught any news. Oh, and I guess I better call my own mom."

"Good idea. And you'll do what I said." It wasn't a question.

"I will. You're right. I'll feel better."

They said their goodbyes, and Dez called Jaylynn's mother first and then her own as well. Both had been monitoring the news, and though each had seen a brief clip of the women arriving at the hospital, they'd still been worried sick. After updating and assuring each, Dez hung up. She stood with her hand against the wall, feeling fatigued and old.

"Officer?"

Dez turned to find the FBI agent from the capture scene. "Yes?"

"Jerome Giles, FBI." He held up his ID, then quickly pocketed it. "My agents will be questioning you further, but I wanted to touch base with you personally before I head out." Dez looked him in the eye and waited. "Off the record, if you don't mind."

"Yes, sir. Perhaps you can explain a few things."

Giles raised an eyebrow. "I'll try. We're still piecing it all together, but we have identified the dead man. He was an enforcer for a man named Sergei Gubenko, a Chicago printer with ties to organized crime, specifically the Russian mob. But his bunch has always flown low under the radar. They've long been suspected of involvement in stock fraud, various cons and swindles, penny stock scams — that sort of thing. There have been a few deaths and disappearances traced back to them, but nothing that has ever stuck. Sergei Gubenko has been bad news for a long time, but we've never nailed him. His brother, Leonid Gubenko, is the scarier of the two — a fellow you would *not* want to tangle with. We finally got him and a batch of his New York cronies on racketeering and RICO charges last year, and Leonid has been awaiting trial. He died this morning in federal prison."

"Murdered?"

"Heart attack. Too bad it didn't happen a few days earlier. I doubt this whole fiasco would have happened — the breakout and all — if not for Leonid's predicament."

"How do Bostwick and the Randall kid figure into this?"

"Randall is the younger brother of David Cromwell Randall, the accountant in charge of finances for Leonid Gubenko's operation. We nailed him, and he turned state's witness to testify against Leonid. Apparently the Gubenkos wanted to use the brother as a hostage."

"I see."

"Looks like things went wrong because Stanley Bostwick was a loose cannon. My men have talked briefly with Keith Randall. He said he thought Bostwick intended to spirit him away and hold him for a higher ransom than what Gubenko was paying, and that's where it all fell apart. If Bostwick had followed the plan and met the gangster as he was apparently supposed to, it's unlikely you and your friends would ever have been involved, the guards wouldn't have been shot, and the whole crew could possibly have gotten away with the jailbreak. Bostwick isn't talking yet, but he may when he's charged with the murder of Grigor Rossel. We'll see."

"Once again — it's all about money." She sighed and shook

her head. "I overheard the injured guard saying he and the dead guard were supposed to split twenty-five thousand dollars."

Giles nodded again. "Exactly. The National Guard will canvass the woods tomorrow, but already tonight they found a bag stashed close to where you captured the men. It contained a hundred thousand dollars in cash."

"Figures."

"That's the extent of what I can confide at this time."

"Okay. Makes sense. Thank you for the update, sir."

"My pleasure, Officer. Who is your commanding officer?"

"Lieutenant Malcolm, St. Paul Police Department."

"Good. We'll be in touch, and by the way, your firearms will be returned to you after the investigation has been completed." He held out a hand. "I have to go now. Best of luck to you and your companions." He wheeled around and walked toward the exit.

Dez leaned back against the wall to the right of the pay phones feeling conflicted and confused, still not believing all that had happened. Fear flooded through her, making her heartbeat race. She heard the ER entrance door slide open, then close. People came and went, and still she leaned against the wall trying to calm her rushing heart.

The door slid open again, and footsteps grew louder as they drew near the phones. Dez looked up. A slender man in an ill-fitting suit reached for the receiver of the phone furthest away from her. His pant legs were water-stained and splashed with mud. The faux leather shoes he wore were ruined.

The prison idiot. It's that fool who let the convicts escape.

Rage filled her. She wanted to hit him, shove him against the wall, scream in his face. She took a deep breath and reached out with her right hand to grip the top of the shelf surrounding the pay phone.

"Yeah, I know," he murmured into the phone. "Put her on the phone." There was a pause, and then he spoke again, his voice tender. "Hi, there, honey. I know. I know. I'm sorry. Daddy will be home as soon as he can. I'll read you *four* books tomorrow night to make up for it, okay? Mmm hmmm. I love you, too."

Dez felt the rage trickle out of her. She was glad to be gripping the board over the phone because she suddenly felt so tired that her legs felt weak. The man finished his conversation and said goodbye. He stood clutching the receiver with one white-knuckled hand. When he finally hung it up and turned around, the sight of Dez close and staring obviously startled him. "Oh, excuse me, ma'am."

"Wait." She put up her free hand. "You're from the prison."

All the color drained out of his face, but his chin went up. "Ralph Soames, assistant administrator." He looked like he expected her to hit him.

"That's what I thought."

"You—you were out there?" Dez nodded, and he hastened to say, "I'm so sorry."

"It's not really your fault. You know that, right?" The man's eyes went wide. He looked like he might cry. "It's a hard job, Mr. Soames. Things go wrong when the system breaks down, and you just do the best you can. Don't beat yourself up. It'll kill you inside."

"I didn't get your name."

She let go of the frame she clutched and reached out her right hand. "Officer Desiree Reilly, St. Paul Police." His hand was warm and sweaty. A closer look revealed to Dez that he was shaky. She let go of his hand. "I bet you haven't eaten for hours."

"No, I guess I haven't."

"The worst is over, Mr. Soames. Take an hour, see your family, get a big meal, change clothes. Maybe even take a nap. You can come back later. This might go on all night, probably a lot of tomorrow, too."

"I suppose you're right."

The beginning of a smile graced her lips. "I know I'm right. Take it from an expert. You go take care of yourself, and the show will go on without you. You'll feel better when you come back."

He straightened his tie and shot his cuffs. "Thanks for the advice. Thank you." Nervously, he started to walk away. "Take good care of yourself, too, Officer Reilly."

"I will. You just remember: the world's going to keep on turning."

With a bob of the head, he went past her, and she watched him hurry across the tile toward the door. The crowd outside had thinned, but there was still a flotilla of news vans in the lot. The torrent of rain was falling in sheets again. The sky looked just as ominous and heavy as before, but somehow Dez felt lighter.

# Chapter
# Thirty-Six

FOR DEZ, TIME had passed in a blur of relentless questioning and exhaustion-inducing waiting. She had managed to slip away earlier after her phone calls. Her spirits had lifted immeasurably by taking a shower, washing the mud out of her hair, and changing into clean-smelling clothes. Then when the FBI agents were done with her for the evening, she had gotten Jaylynn and gone to the hotel, where they had been pleasantly surprised to find that the National Guard personnel had somehow located their Echo Lake campsite, packed up their gear, and delivered it to their room. Now she and Jaylynn and their friends were hiding out, comfortable with the knowledge that the local cops and National Guard were monitoring the hotel's entrances.

The connecting door to Shayna and Crystal's room was open, and all four women were in Dez and Jaylynn's room. Crystal and Shayna lounged against pillows on top of the multicolored bedspread on one of the queen-sized beds. Jaylynn had swathed herself in the covers on the other bed, and leaned against the headboard. Dez lay half-curled around her.

"I can't *wait* to eat," Jaylynn said. "I've never been offered so much coffee in my life. And bad coffee at that. Here's a tip for you two." She pointed a finger first at Dez, then Crystal. "If you ever have to question innocent bystanders after a disaster, give them food!"

"Are you sure you can stomach pizza?" Crystal asked.

Jaylynn let out a cackle. "Are you kidding? I want four kinds. And buffalo wings. Hurry up and order before they close. This *is* a small town, you know."

Shayna laughed and shook her head. "They're staying open until two a.m. to feed the guard and law enforcement personnel."

Jaylynn went on. "Excellent. While you're at it, throw in an order of cheese bread, will you? And milk. I want a carton of milk. A really big one. In fact, I'll take chocolate milk if they have it."

"I'll buy," Dez said. "I don't care if it costs a hundred bucks."

Shayna laughed. "*Our* part will cost about a tenth of that. The rest is all Jay, baby!"

"Anything special for you, Dez?" Crystal asked.

"I'll just graze on Jay's leftovers."

Dez laughed with them, but before the others' giggles died down, she closed her eyes and once more fought the panicky feeling rising in her. She swung her legs off to the side of the bed and sprang up. "Crys, why don't you call in an order. I'll go get it." She reached for her wallet, which sat on the bedside table.

"Whoa, whoa, whoa, *chica*, everybody in town probably called in an order."

"Yeah," Shayna said. "They're all bellied up to the TV now watching the Convict Channel. Who has time to cook?"

Jaylynn let out a gleeful shriek. "What they should really be watching is Bostwick on *Extreme Makeover*. Now there was one *ugly* guy."

Shayna shook her head. "He was ugly through and through. There isn't a makeover in the world to fix that up. Blackheart Bostwick should be his name."

"Even Carson on *Queer Eye* couldn't improve him," Jaylynn said.

Shayna's voice took on a slangy sound. "He got *kind* hair. The *kind* that grow on a dog's butt!"

The three of them doubled over laughing hysterically. Dez smacked the wallet back on the bedside table, stalked into the bathroom, and shut the door. She leaned over the sink, turned on the faucet, ran cold water. *How can they be so jovial, so uncaring? My God, we could have died. Jaylynn could have . . .*

She wouldn't let herself think it. Cupping her hands under the flow, she let the cool water run, then splashed some on her face. When she reached to the right of the mirror for a hand towel, she caught sight of her face. With bags under her eyes and worry lines standing out everywhere, she looked positively haunted. *Well, at least I'm clean now.* She raised a hand and felt the top of her head where Bostwick had nailed her with her own gun. Her hair covered the throbbing lump. Four faint outlines of blue were starting to come up on her jawline. She touched her cheek and realized it looked like a knuckle pattern.

She thought if she could just beat the hell out of something—maybe punch a bag—she'd feel better. *I feel like I need to run or lift weights or do something physical.* She tried to roll her shoulders, but her left arm screamed in pain. She didn't even want to look at those bruises again. This made her smile grimly. There was no part of her that wasn't aching, and every moment that she was tense made her feel tighter and in more pain. If this kept up, she'd be crippled and curled up in a fetal position by morning. She shut off the water and opened the bathroom door.

Crystal was just hanging up the phone, and three sets of worried eyes turned to look over at Dez. "*Mi amiga,* I ordered. Thirty minutes, they say."

Dez tried to give a casual nod and glanced nervously at Jaylynn. Cheerfully, Jaylynn sat wrapped in blankets, her blond hair mussed and the white bandage on her forehead in stark contrast to the bruises starting to turn bluish purple on her cheek, lip, and temple.

Jaylynn reached out a hand, her face open and inquiring. "C'mere, sweetie." Like a man walking the plank, Dez moved slowly toward her partner. "Dez, honey, are you okay?"

There was not a word Dez could say without breaking down, so she just shook her head and kept her eyes glued on the floor. Lowering herself to the edge of the bed, she let out a giant breath. She didn't want to look at Shayna or Crystal, and she didn't want to have to explain a thing. Jaylynn pulled at her, and Dez let herself lean to the side into her lover's arms.

"Come here. You're exhausted," Jaylynn said in a soothing voice. Dez ended up with her head against Jaylynn's middle and her right shoulder wedged in the V of her legs. Her stocking feet hung off the end of the bed.

Shayna whacked Crystal with the back of her hand. "C'mon." She got up from the bed. "We're going to go pick up the goodies. We'll be back in a while."

Jaylynn protested that it was too early, but Crystal was already halfway out the door. "That's a good idea. And they don't have chocolate milk at the pizza place. Since we're early, we'll swing by the Gas-N-Go and get you some."

"Oh, you don't have to do that!" Jaylynn said.

"For you, girl?" Shayna said. "Anything! We'll be back in a while."

"Take my wallet," Dez called out in a tired voice.

"I know you're good for it," Crystal answered.

When the door closed behind the two women, Jaylynn ran her fingers through Dez's loose hair. Dez let out a sigh. The warm hand felt good—tingly and relaxing—as it made its way down to her neck and began massaging the tense muscles there. In a soft voice, Jaylynn said, "Were you scared?"

Dez nodded. "Badly."

"Me, too."

"Are you still scared?" Dez's voice was muffled.

"Totally freaked."

"You don't seem freaked."

"That's because I feel safe now."

"I wish I did."

Jaylynn patted her shoulder and leaned down. "I know. But it will pass. It always does, Dez. Just keep talking about it."

Then the tears came. They etched a silent path down to the blanket on which Dez's head rested. She wished she didn't see crying as a sign of weakness, but she did. In all that had happened over the last few years, she had discovered that it was impossible to hold back the tears forever, so she was glad to get it over with. Jaylynn held her, whispered soothing things, and stroked her hair.

"I felt like such a failure, Jay. I was sure I'd lost you."

"A failure? Why?"

"Oh, my God, when I saw you driving off—" She couldn't go on for a minute. "I nearly had a heart attack."

"I thought you'd take the shot."

"I was so torn. But I didn't know Crystal's gun. Never shot it before, so how could I predict what it would do? I couldn't risk hitting you instead of the tires."

"I thought as much. But it all worked out." There was a catch in her voice, and when Dez looked up, Jaylynn was crying, too. "I'm so sorry . . . so sorry."

"What?" Dez sat up, pulled herself up next to Jaylynn and adjusted pillows so she could encircle her tightly. "You did nothing wrong."

"That—that *asshole* should never have gotten hold of me down by the river! I was in another world. I didn't notice, didn't hear. It was my fault." Now the tears gushed out, and her body shook.

"Shhhh. It's okay." Dez soothed her, stroked her hair, and let her cry for several minutes. After the tears abated, she said, "It wasn't your fault. And you did all the right things, Jay. You left a trail of breadcrumbs." She laughed. "The forks in the road were a nice touch, too. But you gave me a path to follow, and you were resourceful all along the way—although I could have clobbered you for telling them we had a car at Lake Jeanette."

Jaylynn's grip tightened. "You about went apoplectic. I thought you were going to pop a vein, but it was all I could think

to do. I didn't want them to get away, and to be honest, I thought
Lake Jeanette was a *lot* further than it was. I was stunned that it
only took a few hours to get there. I was hoping to buy you guys
more time."

Dez kicked off her shoes and slid under the covers. She
gathered Jaylynn to her, and they lay on their sides tightly
wrapped in one another's arms. "I'm thankful for Crys and Shay.
I was out of my mind, Jay." Her voice dropped to almost a
whisper. "I think I might have totally blown it if it weren't for
them." The memory of the blood rushing through her head, of
the feral, animal-like helplessness, and of the tortured
desperation she had felt made her stomach cramp up.

Jaylynn didn't try to contradict her. After a moment, she
said, "All I could think was that if something happened to me,
you'd never forgive yourself." She started to cry again.

Dez raised a hand to Jaylynn's cheek and touched gently,
careful to avoid the bruised spots. "You're right. I wouldn't
have. I still feel responsible."

"But you're not the only one. I do, too, Dez!"

Drawing in a deep breath, Dez let the next words spill out
unexamined. "It's not our fault. We just sort of—collided with
Fate, or something like that. I don't think there was all that much
we could have done differently. As it worked out, we did
everything right. My only regret is that you and I missed one
another at the Explorer. Do you realize that we must have been
mere minutes apart?"

Jaylynn nodded. "I suppose it was better that it happened to
us than to those young girls from the WAO group."

"Good point."

"But Dez, he was so incredibly, totally, and awfully
disgusting." She shuddered. "Oh, I am going to have *such*
nightmares."

"I'll be here. I'll wake you and hold you."

"Me, too," Jaylynn said in a quiet voice. Then she let out a
giggle, causing Dez's head to bounce up and down twice. "I've
never been so thrilled in my life to be grabbed from behind."

"When? You mean up the hill from Lake Jeanette?"

"Yeah."

"Geez! There you were, floundering around on the path."
Dez wiped her face with her forearm and sat up. She resituated
herself at the head of the bed and leaned against the pillows next
to Jaylynn. "I figured if I didn't grab you, somebody else would.
How the hell many people were running around out there in the
woods anyway?"

"A passel, as my grandpa used to say. Two guards, two

convicts, Vanya, you and me and Crystal. And the entire Minnesota National Guard."

"Don't forget the FBI." Dez wiped her eyes on the sleeve of her t-shirt. "And the forest ranger. I liked Cabot a lot. Before we leave tomorrow, I hope I get a chance to talk to her."

"That'd be good. Since she works for the forest service, she'll have detailed maps of the trails, right?"

Dez stiffened. "You can't want to go out hiking!"

Jaylynn laughed, and she sounded so lighthearted that it brought a smile to Dez's face. "No, I've had more than enough hiking for one trip. Besides, I don't think I could get these sore feet back in those boots. It's just that I'd kind of like to gauge how far I actually walked and ran. I swear it had to be fifty miles."

"If you went fifty, then I went sixty. At least you got to be in a car some of the time."

"Precious little time."

They kept on talking about the details, sorting and rearranging the facts. Dez began to look at what had happened like it was a big, messy jigsaw puzzle for which various people held pieces. There were still some unexplained angles — parts of the puzzle that didn't make sense — but little by little, the pieces were falling into place.

Dez wasn't quite sure what happened, but in the process of discussing it all and trying to make sense of it, her tension slipped away. By the time their two noisy friends returned, each with a big armload of food and drinks, she thought she could make it through the rest of the night without crying.

THREE PIZZA BOXES, three half-empty two-liter pop bottles, and various wads of wrappings and napkins lay on the floor, the bedside table, and the foot of Jaylynn's bed. Tired, but happy, Jaylynn checked the bedside clock and saw that it was after two a.m. "These Buyck reporters sure must be working overtime. I bet their channel hasn't broadcast this late since the last blizzard!"

Crystal sat on the floor at the foot of the other bed watching the TV, which was tuned to the local channel. "It's getting sort of boring. Same ol' same ol' from these reporters."

"Well, hon," Shayna said, "why don't you go out there and give them an exclusive?"

"Not a chance," Crystal said vehemently. "It was hard enough getting out to the pizza place and back!"

Shayna lay on her stomach, head toward the foot of the bed. She reached over to tweak her partner's ear. "Chicken."

Crystal shrugged her off as Jaylynn giggled. She and Dez leaned against the headboard of their bed, and for the first time in hours, Jaylynn was completely comfortable: warm, relaxed, properly hydrated, and stuffed to the gills with pizza, chicken wings, and chocolate milk. "I'll bet we just ate five thousand calories."

Dez said, "You mean *you* just ate five thousand calories. The rest of us merely replenished ourselves like *normal* people."

"Yeah," Shayna said. "I keep expecting the creature from *Alien* to pop out of your stomach. Where could you possibly pack all that food?"

Crystal said, "Better question: how the heck can you sleep feeling that full?"

"It's a mystery," Dez said as she looked at her watch. "But that's it for me. Bedtime now."

Crystal rose. "Good idea. C'mon, *mi amada*." She tugged on her partner's arm, pulling her toward the connecting door. "Oh, *Dios mio*. If I don't miss my guess, I'm going to be too sore to walk tomorrow. Goodnight."

Once they cleared the doorway and closed the connecting door, Jaylynn looked into Dez's eyes. "Now wasn't that a little mean?"

Dez shrugged. "I didn't intend for it to be mean. They've been over here for hours, and I need time to wind down, to talk with you. Besides, the FBI is going to want to talk more in the morning. We need to get some rest." She swung a leg over Jaylynn and stepped across her, letting out a groan as she did so. "Crys is right. I've stiffened up big time." She stood between the two queen-size beds trying unsuccessfully to stretch.

Snuggling into the covers, Jaylynn said, "Oh, I know what you mean. I want to go brush my teeth. You want to carry me?"

Dez smiled. "Get up." Dez reached for her hand and helped her out of bed. "How's your knee?"

"Seriously sore." She took a step and winced.

"I'll get you more ice."

"Okay. That'll help. Even with the wrap, I can tell it'll be desk time for me for a week or two."

Dez went for an ice bag, and then got ready for bed. Jaylynn was already back under the covers when Dez came to join her. Jaylynn invited her to snuggle up and they lay there, silent, for a few moments.

"I feel like I've been in a bad dream, Dez, like I've sort of been in shock, and it's wearing off now."

"You did good. Just keep telling yourself—you were smart every step of the way."

"So were you." She pulled her partner close and buried her face into Dez's warm neck.

After a moment, Dez felt moisture. "Hey," she whispered. "Hey, you're crying."

"I can't help it," she said in a strangled voice. "I thought I was dead for sure."

"Oh, sweetie, everything's fine. I've got you, safe and sound." She tightened her grip and let her partner cry in her arms for a while. She knew how Jaylynn felt. Thinking back on the events of the last nineteen hours sent a chill through her, and she thought it was going to take quite some time to process it all. *Time for a trip back to see the counselor. Maybe for both of us.* Dez rubbed Jaylynn's back and shoulders, waiting until Jaylynn cried herself out, then tried to move things to more positive footing. "Tell me more about that Randall—at what point did you figure out he and Bostwick weren't on the same wavelength? I mean, back at the campsite he certainly seemed to be doing Bostwick's bidding."

Jaylynn shifted in Dez's arms and looked into her eyes. Dez purposely didn't wince, although as every hour went by, the bruises on her lover's face were becoming more apparent.

"Keith never wanted to escape from Kendall. Bostwick *took* him. He made the kid come."

"I guess that's the conclusion I've come to, too. And I've been thinking. There's one thing I haven't figured out. Bostwick shot the guy in Lot A and you guys roared out of the lot." Jaylynn nodded. "And he went a few miles down the road and stopped the car before going on. I followed the tracks and saw that."

"Yeah." Jaylynn shuddered and made a funny face. "He'd been drinking swamp water all night on the trail. Believe it or not, he had diarrhea." Dez snickered. Jaylynn grinned, too. "Thank God nature called several times so it slowed us down. He kept having to stop and go out in the woods."

"I eventually made it to that spot. What I want to know is who left seven .45 shells buried in a tidy mound of dirt under the car?"

"What?" Jaylynn got a quizzical look on her face. "I don't know what you're talking about. Let me see. Bostwick took the Russian's Walther and . . . oh, Dez, he gave *your* gun to Keith."

"That's what I thought. I struggled with Bostwick on the bluff above the lake. He had me pinned with a gun jammed into my neck. I thought the gun misfired, but then Crys and I realized there were no bullets."

Jaylynn's face went pale and her eyes wide. "You never told

me that part."

Dez shrugged. "Hadn't gotten around to it yet. Bostwick shot the Russian with my dad's .45, and Keith Randall had to be the one who emptied the remaining seven shells and left them in the road. I guess you were right about him, Jay. If he did do that, he saved my life as well as yours. If it weren't for that one small act of defiance against his captor, there'd have been three dead bodies instead of two."

"And this is supposed to be comforting?"

The alarm in Jaylynn's voice was so acute that Dez felt bad for bringing it up. "No, I guess not. It's just that it seems like we ought to stick up for that kid after all."

Jay's face became animated. "I agree. We could put a good word in for him, couldn't we?"

Dez nodded. "I believe we can. Maybe one decent thing could come of this after all."

"Mmm hmm. That would be nice." Jaylynn yawned. "I am so incredibly tired."

Dez reached over to the bedside lamp and clicked it off, then pulled Jaylynn close. She threaded her fingers through Jaylynn's hair and dropped off to sleep.

# Chapter
# Thirty-Seven

DEZ SAT IN the back seat of the Jeep feeling sleepy and content. Shayna drove down Highway 61 toward home while Crystal dozed in the passenger seat, her head resting against the side window. The late morning sun shone in Dez's side of the car, and the weak light filtering through the clouds was warm on her shoulder. She'd eaten a farm-style breakfast befitting a lumberjack, and so had everyone else, so nobody was particularly talkative.

Jaylynn lay cradled in her partner's lap, her face pressed into Dez's brand new jeans with one arm squeezed behind Dez's hips. She didn't look uncomfortable, but Dez thought it was amusing how tightly the sleeping woman could curl up. There had been little time in the last twelve hours that they hadn't been touching, and Jaylynn had spent the night wrapped securely in Dez's arms.

They'd only gotten about six hours of sleep, but Dez's mind wouldn't let her rest now. She kept marveling at all that had happened in the last day and a half. If she concentrated too much on it, she literally quaked inside.

In the front seat, Crystal jerked away from the window, shook her head, and let out a sputter. "Whoa. I was just having a dream we were running in the woods again." She ran her hands through her dark hair. "I could definitely live without dreaming *that.*"

Shayna reached over and patted Crystal's thigh and her partner let out a squeal. "Ooooh. A little sore, are we?"

"You are wicked, Shay—positively mean sometimes."

"Well, I'm sore, too."

"It was the squatting that did me in. At least you didn't have to squat in the dark and cold next to a dirty truck while crazy men shot at you."

Jaylynn sat up and yawned. "I guess I chose the easy path since I spent the last part of the evening facedown in the slime. Eeeeyuck! No squatting for me, though." She settled back against Dez's side.

Shayna looked in the rearview mirror. "How's your knee feeling?"

"Sore as hell. I'll be okay though."

"Shall we band together against our big bad butch partners and swear an oath never to go camping with them again?"

"No way," Dez said. "We'll just make sure next time we camp somewhere with cell phone service."

Jaylynn looked up at Dez. "Good idea. And you guys should look at the bright side. At least we got a good walk."

It took a few seconds for the groans and protests to die down, then Crystal let out a moan. "I don't know how I'm supposed to go on patrol tonight."

Dez said, "You're stuck, buddy."

"I know."

Dez kissed the top of Jaylynn's head. "Remind us, Jay, next time we go on a pastoral, relaxing vacation with you that we should all schedule some extra days for recovery."

Jaylynn grinned and smacked Dez's stomach with the flat of her hand. "Very funny."

Dez settled back and let out a sigh. Her body ached. Every limb, every muscle screamed a protest whenever she moved. She couldn't remember ever being so sore in all her life. *But it will pass*, she thought. *And we're all alive. It's amazing, but we made it through.* She looked to the front seat at the solid figure of her best friend, Crystal, then to Shayna, who navigated the Jeep with one hand casually gripping the steering wheel. She wondered how she would ever tell them how much they meant to her. Someday, somehow.

Jaylynn was warm in her arms, and she felt a surge of happiness that started at her chest and radiated throughout her body. It hurt to even shift in the seat, and Dez couldn't run right now if the world depended upon it. But that didn't concern her. She'd been able to run when it counted, and that was all that mattered.

She tightened her grip on Jaylynn, feeling a sense of possibility—of hope—and suddenly feeling so grateful for love and hope and joy that she could have cried. She smiled, forced back the tears, and relaxed. She didn't have to experience every feeling now or express all her thoughts. She had time. She hoped she had decades of time, but since she could never be sure, she leaned down and kissed the top of Jaylynn's head. "I love you," she whispered, and Jaylynn's answering squeeze was all she needed to feel, for the moment, entirely complete.

More Lori L. Lake titles from
and
*Quest Books*

# *Gun Shy*

While on patrol, Minnesota police officer Dez Reilly saves two women from a brutal attack. One of them, Jaylynn Savage, is immediately attracted to the taciturn cop—so much so that she joins the St. Paul Police Academy. As fate would have it, Dez is eventually assigned as Jaylynn's Field Training Officer. Having been burned in the past by getting romantically involved with another cop, Dez has a steadfast rule she has abided by for nine years: Cops are off limits. But as Jaylynn and Dez get to know one another, a strong friendship forms. Will Dez break her cardinal rule and take a chance on love with Jaylynn, or will she remain forever gun shy?

*Gun Shy* is an exciting glimpse into the day-to-day work world of police officers as Jaylynn learns the ins and outs of the job and Dez learns the ins and outs of her own heart.

Second Edition
ISBN: 1-930928-43-2

# *Under the Gun*

*Under the Gun* is the long-awaited sequel to the bestselling novel, *Gun Shy*, continuing the story of St. Paul Police Officers Dez Reilly and Jaylynn Savage. Picking up just a couple weeks after *Gun Shy* ended, the sequel finds the two officers adjusting to their relationship, but things start to go downhill when they get dispatched to a double homicide — Jaylynn's first murder scene. Dez is supportive and protective toward Jay, and things seem to be going all right until Dez's nemesis reports their personal relationship, and their commanding officer restricts them from riding together on patrol. This sets off a chain of events that result in Jaylynn getting wounded, Dez being suspended, and both of them having to face the possibility of life without the other. They face struggles — separately and together — that they must work through while truly feeling "under the gun."

ISBN: 1-930928-44-0
Available at booksellers everywhere.

Other Lori L. Lake titles
available from
Yellow Rose Books

## *Ricochet In Time*

Hatred is ugly and does bad things to good people, even in the land of "Minnesota Nice" where no one wants to believe discrimination exists. Danielle "Dani" Corbett knows firsthand what hatred can cost. After a vicious and intentional attack, Dani's girlfriend, Meg O'Donnell, is dead. Dani is left emotionally scarred, and her injuries prevent her from fleeing on her motorcycle. But as one door has closed for her, another opens when she is befriended by Grace Beaumont, a young woman who works as a physical therapist at the hospital. With Grace's friendship and the help of Grace's aunts, Estelline and Ruth, Dani gets through the ordeal of bringing Meg's killer to justice.

Filled with memorable characters, *Ricochet In Time* is the story of one lonely woman's fight for justice—and her struggle to resolve the troubles of her past and find a place in a world where she belongs.

ISBN: 1-930928-64-5
Available at booksellers everywhere.

# *Different Dress*

*Different Dress* is the story of three women on a cross-country musical road tour. Jaime Esperanza is a works production
and sound on the music tour. The headliner, Lacey Leigh Jaxon,
is a fast-living prima donna with intimacy problems. She's had a
brief relationship with Jaime, then dumped her for the new guy
(who lasted all of about two weeks). Lacey still comes back to
Jaime in between conquests, and Jaime hasn't yet gotten her
entirely out of her heart.

After Lacey Leigh steamrolls yet another opening act, a
folksinger from Minnesota named Kip Galvin, who wrote one of
Lacey's biggest songs, is brought on board for the summer tour.
Kip has true talent, she loves people and they respond, and she
has a pleasant stage presence. A friendship springs up between
Jaime and Kip — but what about Lacey Leigh?

It's a honky-tonk, bluesy, pop, country EXPLOSION of emotion as these three women duke it out. Who will win Jaime's
heart and soul?

ISBN: 1-932300-08-2
Available at booksellers everywhere.

Available from

# Regal Crest Enterprises, LLC

# *Stepping Out: Short Stories*

In these fourteen short stories, Lori L. Lake captures how change and loss influence the course of lives: a mother and daughter have an age-old fight; a frightened woman attempts to deal with an abusive lover; a father tries to understand his lesbian daughter's retreat from him; an athlete who misses her chance — or does she?

Lovingly crafted, the collection has been described as a series of mini-novels where themes of alienation and loss, particularly for characters who are gay or lesbian, are woven throughout. Lake is right on about the anguish and confusion of characters caught in the middle of circumstances, usually of someone else's making. Still, each character steps out with hope and determination.

In the words of Jean Stewart: "Beyond the mechanics of good storytelling, a sturdy vulnerability surfaces in every one of these short stories. Lori Lake must possess, simply as part of her inherent nature, a loving heart. It gleams out from these stories, even the sad ones, like a lamp in a lighthouse — maybe far away sometimes, maybe just a passing, slanting flash in the dark — but there to be seen all the same. It makes for a bittersweet journey."

ISBN: 1-932300-16-3
Available at booksellers everywhere February 5, 2004.

# About Lori L. Lake

Lori L. Lake was born in Portland, Oregon, and moved to Minnesota with her partner after graduating from Lewis & Clark College in 1983. She worked in government for almost two decades and resigned at the end of 2002 so she could devote full-time attention to writing, teaching, and reviewing. She teaches Queer Fiction writing courses at The Loft Literary Center, the largest independent writing community in the nation.

She is the author of five novels: *Ricochet in Time (2001)*, *Gun Shy (2001)*, *Under The Gun (2002)*, *Different Dress (2003)*, and *Have Gun We'll Travel (2005)*. A book of short stories titled *Stepping Out* was published in February 2004, and she has edited an anthology of stories called *The Milk of Human Kindness: Lesbian Authors Write about Mothers and Daughters (2004)*.

The novel *Gun Shy* won a Stonewall "Pride in the Arts" Literary Award for 2003, and in 2004, Lori's work won three Stonewall Awards: Fan Award for Favorite Author; Literary Entertainment Award for *Stepping Out: Short Stories;* and Favorite Short Story for "Afraid Of The Dark." In both 2002 and 2003, Lori was selected as the Twin Cities' "Favorite GLBT Author" by *Lavender Magazine*.

Lori loves to read, and she regularly writes book reviews for Midwest Book Review, The Independent Gay Writer, and JustAboutWrite.com. She is at work on her next two novels: a mainstream mystery and the fourth "Gun" book. You may write her at Lori@LoriLLake.com. Further information about her can be found at her website: http://www.LoriLLake.com.

Printed in the United States
33213LVS00003B/53

9 781932 300338